Measure's Measures

Also by Michael Boughn

Poetry

Iterations of the Diagonal (shuffaloff, 1995*)*

Dislocations in Crystal (Coach House Books, 1998)

22 Skidoo/SubTractions—Opus Minus One (Book Thug, 2009)

Cosmographia—A Post-Lucretian Faux Micro-Epic (Book Thug, 2010)

Nine Blue Moments for Robin (BlazeVox, 2012)

Great Canadian Poems for the Aged—Vol. 1, Illus. Ed. (Book Thug, 2013)

City—A Poem from the End of the World (Spuyten Duyvil, 2016)

Hermetic Divagations—After H.D. (Spuyten Duyvil, 2018)

Uncertain Remains (BlazeVox, 2022)

The Book of Uncertain—A Hyperbiographical User's Manual Volume 1 (Spuyten Duyvil, 2022)

Prose

Into the World of the Dead—Astonishing Adventures in the Underworld (Annick Press, 2006)

Business as Usual, A Novel (NeWest Press, 2011)

Measure's Measures—Poetry and Knowledge (Station Hill Press, 2023)

Editor

H.D.—A Bibliography 1905-1990 (University Press of Virginia, 1993)

The H.D. Book, by Robert Duncan, with Victor Coleman (University of California Press, 2011)

Resist Much, Obey Little—Inaugural Poems for the Resistance, with 18 others (Spuyten Duyvil, 2017)

Narthex and Other Stories by H.D. (Book Thug, 2011)

Dispatches from the Poetry Wars, with Kent Johnson (2016-2020, archived at the Contemporary Literature Collection, Simon Fraser University Library Special Collections)

Measure's Measures

Poetry & Knowledge

Michael Boughn

Introduction by Charles Stein

Station Hill Press
Barrytown, NY

Published by Station Hill Press, the publishing project of the Institute for Publishing Arts, Inc., 120 Station Hill Road, Barrytown, NY 12507, New York, a not-for-profit, tax-exempt organization [501(c)(3)].

Online catalogue: www.stationhill.org
e-mail: publishers@stationhill.org

Cover design by Susan Quasha

Library of Congress Cataloging-in-Publication Data
Names: Boughn, Michael, author. | Stein, Charles, writer of introduction.
Title: Measure's measure: poetry & knowledge / Michael Boughn; introduction by Charles Stein.
Identifiers: LCCN 2023011371 (print) | LCCN 2023011372 (ebook) | ISBN 9781581771954 (paperback) | ISBN 9781581771961 (epub)
Subjects: LCSH: American poetry—20th century—History and criticism. | Poets, American—20th century—Biography. | Poetics. | Allen, Donald, 1912-2004. | New American poetry, 1945-1960.
Classification: LCC PS324 .B695 2023 (print) | LCC PS324 (ebook) | DDC 811/.509—dc23/eng/20230718
LC record available at https://lccn.loc.gov/2023011371
LC ebook record available at https://lccn.loc.gov/2023011372

Land Acknowledgment
In the spirit of truth and equity, it is with gratitude and humility that we acknowledge that the Institute for Publishing Arts, Inc. and Station Hill Press reside on the sacred homelands of the Munsee and Muhheaconneok people, who are the original stewards of this land. Today, due to forced removal, the community resides in Northeast Wisconsin and is known as the Stockbridge-Munsee Community. We honor and pay respect to them, as well as to their ancestors and future generations, and we recognize their continuing presence in their homelands. We understand that our acknowledgment requires us to recognize our own place in and responsibilities toward addressing inequity, and that this ongoing and challenging work requires that we commit to real engagement with the Munsee and Mohican communities to build an inclusive and equitable space for all.

FOR

KENT JOHNSON

(1955-2022)

Contents

INTRODUCTION

Charles Stein

The Poetry of Initiatory Transmission

M*easures' Measures* collects essays by Michael Boughn concerned with the explicit poetics of an interrelated but individually distinct group of poets, most of whom came to prominence after Donald Allen published his anthology, *The New American Poetry*, with Grove Press in 1960. Boughn includes three poets and one philosopher that antedate the "Donald Allen" but are arguably that poetry's important predecessors and inspirers: Hilda Dolittle, Ezra Pound, and William Carlos Williams. The philosopher is Emerson. The Donald Allen poets treated are primarily Charles Olson, Robert Duncan, Jack Spicer, and Robin Blaser though with not inconsiderable glances at others.

The poetic practices and thematic attentions of these writers do constitute something like an "identity" for this group, whose work I want to characterize (following Boughn's ideas) as "the poetry of initiatory transmission." The poets not only mean to present the content of their poems but to transmit the conditions of awareness, imagination, and intelligence from which that practice of poetry and thought come to be.

Donald Allen organized his poets according to a series of categories: Black Mountain, Beat Generation, San Francisco Renaissance, New York School, etc. To what degree these categories are appropriate to the individual poets and to their associations with each other has been a matter of contention since the book's publication. (They were removed in later editions.) Appropriate or not, the categories have stuck. In any case, the group of poets of Boughn's primary interest cuts across them. Boughn exposes poetic connections among these writers and by so doing discriminates a field of activity within poetry generally. Each of them was committed to a practice of a poetry inescapably pertinent to how we take actual and imagined existence to be — take it in, take it up, or leave it out. This pertinence is transmitted to the reader, who is initiated into the world as the poem takes it. For Wallace Stevens the poem is "… the cry of its occasion /Part of the res itself and not about it," but by articulating the "occasions" of its concern, what a poem is "about" is an ineliminable aspect of its "cry." And the reader who in reading speaks the poet's words enters into the mystery that occasioned them.

The connections between Boughn's writers are something like Wittgenstein's "family resemblances." The poets are not primarily identified by categories that might include them, but belong to a network of interlocking pairs that might be diagrammed something like this:

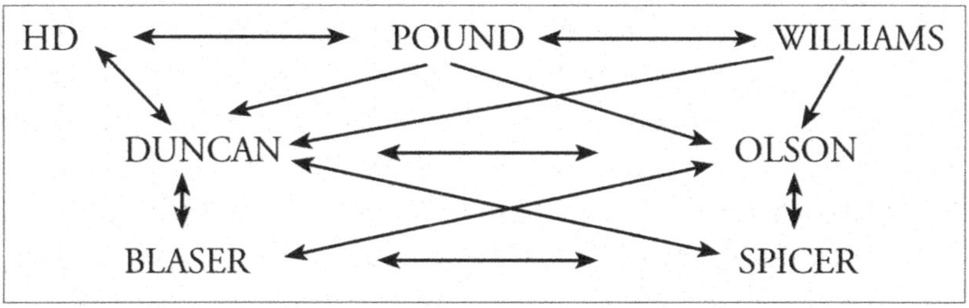

The title of Robert Kelly's early book, *Finding the Measure*, proposes a poetry that (in finding its measure indeed) projects how what counts as true or real comes to appear for the poet and for the reader, and how it can be realized in language. Such poetry in a sense implies Charles Olson's proclamation (in his essay, "Human Universe") that "reality is unfinished business." The work, by bringing concrete form to "What Is", deals indeed with that "unfinished business." But the measure *found* is not a measure *imposed.* It arises in the process of composition, initiating fresh possibilities with which a person might explore itself and the world—and "sets them into form." Concretely, the measure of the poem is the measure of its rhythms, the qualitative aura of its language, its way of carrying its content.

But Boughn also takes the measure of measure itself. To measure the measure is to accept the responsibility for the specific values of the poem's concern—both the values in the *poetics* practiced in the work and the values expressed by its content. The poet stands at the site where originary value configures itself and colors its world. But to make poems under this exigency challenges the traditional role of the poet and indeed the literary scholar as custodian of ontological categories ensconced in a world prior and subsequent to the poet's work—traditional generalities that presume a standard determination of reality and a measure of value which the poet disrupts at her peril. The poets in Boughn's book relish that peril. Measure and value become terms of attentiveness and acuteness of expression, not standards of moral, epistemological, or aesthetic certainty.

Michael Boughn's book, then, finds the measure for the work of a network of poets in the twentieth century for whom the participatory, inductive, indeed initiatic sense of poetry takes precedence over its "appreciation." There would be no essential distance between reader and writer. For both, the actualities and possibilities of poetry (and indeed the consequent actualities and possibilities of the world) are transformed. Poet and reader alike are "initiated" into forms of being emergent with the poetry.

Many of the essays in this book celebrate and affirm the vision of poetry of Charles Olson's essay, "Projective Verse" published as the first appendix in the Allen anthology. These appendices are statements on poetics by the poets in the book. Their presence highlights the editor's awareness that poets often develop a poetics as the condition for their own poetry. Some familiarity with their poetics may be helpful, and, as is the case with Olson and Robert Duncan, even essential, for participation in their work. One is not simply initiated into the sense of the poems, but into their take on the world and how poetry itself fits (or does not fit) into it. Boughn shows how Olson's essay was something of a battle cry to open the poetics of his own work, but which quickly proved relevant not only to other poets in the anthology, but to generations of poets to follow.

Boughn's reading of Olson develops throughout the book, is in fact a process. As Olson's general stance is to take the poet's physical body and its concrete situation in the earth's gravitational field as the context and condition for the work's coming to form, Boughn writes insightfully of Olson's later piece, "Proprioception", which focuses attention on that autonomic function as further extending the views presented in "Projective Verse."

Beyond the specific ideas about the work of the poets severally, Boughn focuses on poetics generally: how it may or may not correlate with intellect, imagination, and material existence as they are understood during their time. The pairings given above in the aggregate manifest a field that arguably plays a role in forming the appearance of our world. When a poetry is aligned with the multiplicity of its poetics, it becomes an inescapable factor in its time's ontological perspectives.

Olson's "Projective Verse" declares that verse in coming times (the piece was first published in 1950) must be "projected" from the concrete conditions under which it is composed. Olson understands that such an imperative is directly coincident with facts about America that held from its historical beginnings: its need to discover ways of living in the geography of the "New World" as well as its separation from the cultural determinants of European history. But Boughn recognizes that Olson's assumption of these differences must not be confused with "Manifest Destiny" or "American Exceptionalism." Olson's vision involves a cosmic context for the American westward march to the Pacific, but this is both the end point of a mass migration that began around 3500 BCE and the itinerary of a failed or abandoned vision, not an apology for continental expansion. Not everything undertaken under the myth of America can be reduced to U.S. propaganda and policy directives.

Early in *Measure's Measure* Boughn treats several poems of W.C. Williams to illustrate the major break with traditional prosody that comes to a grand fruition in the American poetry of the twentieth century. Olson's poetics responds to and extends that of Williams' and Pound's. It is picked up and becomes essential to Robert Duncan's and Robert Creeley's work. It demonstrates how Duncan's affirmation of the primacy of the poetic imagination develops in intimate correspondence with H.D.'s. Olson, Duncan, and Jack Spicer work their poetries that, though taking **concrete** personal experience as fundamental matter of the poems, nevertheless see the inexplicable source of the poetic form-bringing as decidedly other than the deliberate pre-formation by the individual ego.

Together with the late Kent Johnson, Boughn edited "Dispatches from the Poetry Wars," an online anarchic poetry quasjournal which took as its point of departure (with a confrontational if slightly ironical chip on its shoulder) the significantly heated controversies of the past century or so over issues of poetic practice and meaning, controversies that are by no means resolved today. One of Boughn's and Johnson's "poetry wars" that was no mere skirmish seems to have been (and continues to be) fought over the role that the "divine" or more generally the "sacred" or "the spiritual" might play in a poetry that abjures inherited poetic forms and traditional religious dogma. Boughn picks up on Olson's remark that the present age allows for a discourse based on "a secular that loses nothing of the divine." Olson's stance certainly has nothing to do with reinstating conventional, institutional religion. The "divine" for Olson is found within, not at all transcendent of, the material universe. Boughn sees Emerson as the source in American thinking of such a stance.

Boughn's treatment of Robert Duncan's relation to H.D. shows how the transmission and reception of a text are "erotic" matters, transmissions of poetic substance across affinity and affection—from writer to reader, and indeed from writer to writer. Through the conveyance of art experienced not as in an aesthetic detachment from life, and not merely biographically framed as an *aspect* of life, but where life and art so intrigue each other that only a determined conventional will to keep them apart can camouflage their identity.

Duncan's devotion to H.D.'s work was grounded in their shared sense of the primacy of the imagination. In H.D. the coinherence of imagination and existence allows her finest poetry to manifest both the psycho-poetic mood and the classical lyricism of her verse to project an aura that stands as the real. The ineffable speaks as the music of the poem, which is simultaneously the intimate and mythically concretized voice of the poet's persona; a mask worn so close that it articulates the face it disguises.

Clearly not all poetry is initiatory or projective. Projective verse cannot be merely decorative language ("common thought n'er so well expressed" (Pope)); it is not the public confessions of "the private soul at any public wall" (Olson); it is not an "objective correlative" (T.S. Eliot) for otherwise existent states (it is its own state rather than a representation of another one); it is not a performance of academically validated stylistic mastery. Rather, it articulates "a" if not "the" further being of the world; it transforms the quotidian according to the powers of the poet to do so and initiates the reader into the world of the poem by inviting or even inducing participation.

In "Projective Verse" Olson quotes a formulation of Robert Creeley's to the effect that "form is never more than an extension of content." Content as such extends itself in the act of composition by giving *its* form as the source of the form of the poem. A poetry that finds form thus must make itself open with all its powers to that which it attends. Form that is "informed" by actual existence must make itself open to it. It must become an open poetry, and consequently discover a mode of composition that is not determined in its form prior to the act of composition, which is in fact an act of discovery—simultaneously of content *and* of form.

Robert Lowell's famous wise crack that the poetry of his time (referring to the Allen anthology) was either "cooked or raw" was really *never* apt. But *today,* the raw is a significant array of alternative cuisines, and the cooked turns out to be a speciality only an etiolated cult of professors and antiquarians relish as dessert for an unacknowledgedly unappetizing supper on the real. Open form does not require that every poem must be, in Yeats's phrase, "All out of shape from toe to top," but that the poet attend to the precise form that the content of the poem might extend/project into verbal being because the world depends on it.

Measure's Measures

Measure's Measures

"The formula for the measure of heights may also be changed."
—Archimedes, "The Measure of the Circle"

We commonly speak of poetry and measure in the same breath, acknowledging an intimate and essential relationship between them. And breath's organization into rhythmic units is the key to thinking about how a poem is entangled with measure. Measure involves two terms, one a normative set of significations, the other, blank and silent. The measuring term, laid against this second term, translates it into a set of measurable units. It becomes comprehensible or usable. Its measure has been taken. We measure by referring one thing to something else, some arbitrary fixed unit or standard: an ancient, long-forgotten Anglo-Saxon girdle is the basis of a "yard," a bodily appendage is the basis of a "foot," a fixed rhythmic unit is the basis of "iambic pentameter." Measure, in one sense, is an act of translation, and, in another, the result of translating accurately and justly.

Poems intersect with measure where they involve the act of isolating and counting some feature of ordinary spoken language, setting the poemevent apart from it. Those features are breath events, rhythmic, phonemic patterns specific to any given utterance, as the utterance is specific to the rhythmic pattern of contractions of the intercostal muscles that found intelligibility in any given language. Poetry is the composition of those features into structures called prosody. Poetic measure has long been synonymous with what Samuel Johnson called "numbers," as in his dismissal of "unnatural thoughts and rugged numbers."

The normative set determines what is counted. In poetry, the normative set, or "constant," is usually formed by syllabic duration, number of syllables, stress pattern, or some combination of these linguistic features. Like a ruler held against a sheet of paper, or the calibrations on the lens of a telescope, this "constant" establishes a relational knowledge about the thing being measured, integrating it into a signifying set: the page is eight inches long, the star is 22 degrees above the horizon, each poetic line has five feet and five stresses.

But measure is never simple or singular. It amplifies. The one who measures always leaves some measure of themselves in their choice of measure. The criteria, the "constant," is a product of a particular imagination embedded in a particular set of relations at a situated moment. In one sense, every such act indicates a concern with precision and relation. In another, measure implicates certain historical obsessions, events, and developments—in one sense, the 18th century passion for strict order in poetry was implicated with the Restoration and the Enlightenment; in a different sense, the astrolabe was implicated with the conquest of America. In still another sense, those who do the measuring reveal fundamental concepts of their cosmology in how they chose to make their measures and, more importantly, what they chose to measure.

Some of the earliest known human artifacts, from 135,000 to 200,000 years old, are bones incised with notches which measure or delineate the full cycle of the moon, as if someone watched nightly, and tracked its waxing and waning, making sure that it took 29.5 nights to complete its full transformation. Alexander Marshack points out that "whatever the purpose of these objects, their occurrence throughout the Upper Paleolithic is a remarkable phenomenon—the earliest representation we have of a rhythmic arrangement with regular intervals, the beginning of the evolution that led to the ruler, the musical staff, the calendar, and the peristyle of the temple." Those marks, often in conjunction with incised images of creatures and plants, were a measure, playing some role in early relations of humans to their world.

So, what did those incised bones measure? To begin with, the cycle of the moon. With one of those bones in hand, the bearer could know precisely when the next new moon would occur. The moon's measure had been taken, and it now became a measure in turn. After ten such cycles, the geese or the bison would return. After nine cycles, the horse, whose image was sometimes inscribed within the notches' circuit, would bear its young. But the one who counts is also measured. The person who marked the bone watched the moon with great care. As Marshack reconstructs thousands of these objects, he reveals people with extensive knowledge embodied in story. Perhaps most importantly, they knew intimately a certain face of time; they lived and made their homes in time, apparently some kind of periodic or recurring time, though it may have been a face of time no one will ever know precisely again. So, what are they, these bone measures? Calendars? Star charts? Poems? Myths? Art? Spiritual texts? Whatever they were, they reveal an astonishing range of attention.

No one of those modes/moods of attention, those mindful relations suggested in the precise, careful etching of the notches, dominates or determines the others. They exist as part of a common eidos that touches what those in any given being-together share with one another. They measure that creative work of history and that eidos which is itself a measure, that is to say, a way of knowing. William Carlos Williams argued that "the only reality we can know is MEASURE." Poetic measure is not simply arbitrary, decorative procedure. It's crucial to poetry's vital knowing and information about the world we inhabit as it inhabits us.

In Alexander Pope's *An Essay on Man*, measure is complicit with certain perceptions regarding a specific concept of order:

> In Pride, in reas'ning pride our error lies;
> All quit their sphere and rush into the skies.
> Pride still is aiming at the blest abodes,
> Men would be angels, angels would be gods.
> Aspiring to be gods, if angels fell,
> Aspiring to be angels, men rebel:
> And who but wishes to invert the laws
> Of order, sins against th'Eternal Cause. (123-30)

This accentual syllabic verse is the one of the most rigorous forms English has produced: strict iambic pentameter, rhymed couplets, a coincidence of line and syntax. Significantly, the measure is based on factors of ten. Fives and twos: five stresses in every line; two syllables per stress; two lines per rhyme unit. It's called a heroic couplet. There are variations within the order. The last couplet includes two perturbations: the enjambment of the penultimate line and the anapestic penultimate foot. But the rupture introduced by these perturbations, clearly linked to the discussion of order, is immediately closed in the ultimate line and the ultimate foot, and the order of ten is effortlessly re-established in a gesture of astonishing, if understated, virtuosity.

In this verse, stresses are measured, syllables are measured, and rhymes are measured, all according to a standard measure, an abstract form known as the English heroic couplet, which is based, ultimately, on factors of ten. In that measuring, time is also measured since the poem is a time-factored event, a process, an unfolding. Aside from the syntactic and semantic temporal dimensions, the unfolding of meaning in time, the measure itself is a temporal dimension. One stress leads to the next in a predictable pattern and we follow through time until we reach the expected final stress, at which point we begin again.

Time presents us with many different faces: Slow time, the time a child knows waiting for Christmas, or a prisoner knows waiting for release. Hard time for the prisoner, and easy time if you can work it. Aging, time speeds up until the months fly by. The lover knows languorous time, ecstatic time, ruptured time. The scientist knows "real" Newtonian time. Let's throw in Bergsonian time, mythic time, sacred time, ludic time, profane time, wasted time, productive time. Some time repeats itself, looping back in dark, convulsive patterns that grip us in inevitability. Some time progresses, full of invention, surprise, promise, emptiness.

The time Pope's verse measures is notable for its regularity and periodicity, conditions that imply two others: reversibility and universality. Although subject to the occasional, controlled perturbation, nothing ultimately disturbs the underlying measure. The march of the measures establishes the regularity, the five within the twos, o - | o - | o - | o - | o -, and then the next set, ten over ten, perfection, the time of the metronome with one important difference: Metronomic time marches away into infinity, unbounded, the endless bursts of light from a quartz-based metronome. Rhyme measures out the time of this verse in closed periods. The march of the measures takes us to a limit where they turn back, begin again and proceed until they reach another limit marked by an identical sound. The sonal structure reverberates through the body enfleshing the time of the poem.

On a graph of two-dimensional phase space, it would form a circle as tracing the velocity and position of a pendulum or a mechanical metronome does. This is the circle's language, the language of the orbit, the clock face. It translates determinist and calculable trajectories of motion into time, holds motion to an absolute and regular rule which can and will be known within its ordered limits. It speaks the language of the factors of ten held to the rule of their perfect order. Ten over ten equals one. In the "Scholium" to the *Principia*, Newton has it as the dominion of One, describing the perfect order of the cosmos revealed in his numbers.

The eighteenth century is drenched in this time. Even Newton's anti-Trinitarian Christ is periodic, returning over and over in a pattern of corruption, restoration, and renewed corruption: an orbital Christ circling through eternity, periodically intersecting with time. Writing in 1779, Joshua Steele argued:

> In the time of the world, a natural day (night included) is a single cadence; the setting and rising of the Sun are the thesis and arsis; seasons and years are rhythmical clauses; the beginning and ending of this melody are out of our sight; but to human apprehension, the apparent are birth and death, and life is our part in the song.

Nature gives rise to the language of the poem's measure. Nature, the handmaiden of science, docile and obedient, willingly revealing her hidden orders to the inquiring (male) mind, measures the perfection of the poem which iterates and reiterates those orders. The poem copies nature, a mirror of nature's time, as the painting is a mirror of nature's space, three dimensional, absolute and real, extending evenly by virtue of its own nature; immovable space through which global masses roll, held to their perfect orbits by universal forces ticking off the moments of eternity in time.

But nature can equally become the mirror of the poem, just as the measure of the poem becomes the measure of the poet. Charles Gildon, in *The Complete Art of Poetry,* wrote in 1718: "… the Particles and Seeds of Light in the Primordial Chaos struggled in vain to exert their true Lustre, till Matter was by Art Divine brought into order, and the noble Poem of the Universe completed in Number and Figure by the Almighty Poet or Maker." The poem, rather than an imitation of Nature, is Nature's source and structure. Or rather, the poem and Nature are one. No mirror. One act, the act of Creation, of measured counting, shines through both.

This reversibility shatters the mirror. An eidos stands in its place, rich with the social imaginary significations it embodies. The poem's measure, a signifying act, is the measure of the world of which it is a part.

Almost two centuries later, in another poem about order and transgression, measure looks significantly different:

This Is Just to Say

I have eaten
the plums
that were in
the icebox

and which
you were probably
saving
for breakfast

Forgive me
they were delicious
so sweet
and so cold

By any standards of Pope's world, this collection of words would not qualify as a poem, much less a "metrically regular" poem. Dr. Johnson would have been seized with moral apoplexy at the mere suggestion. Yet Dr. Williams, in a 1950 interview with John W. Gerber, describes his poem as "metrically absolutely regular."

It couldn't seem more irregular. There is no regular syllabic structure. Lines vary from two to five syllables. Nor are the stresses predictably located within the lines. Clearly the lines are not isochronic: line six, for instance, has about twice the duration as line five. The same is true of lines 10 and 11. Less obvious durational differences exist between other lines. The poem also seems to eschew rhyme, unlike much of Williams' other work which is full of irregular forms of rhyme and off-rhyme. Only two obvious rhymes occur here: the rather weak link between "I" and "icebox" in the first stanza, and the stronger link between the two occurrences of "so" and "cold" which close the poem.

The poem seems to be a haphazard event, what Dr. Williams' critics call "prose broken into arbitrary lines." Yet it coheres remarkably. One reason for that, and probably the source of the regularity Williams referred to, is the one strong stress in each line. An order of one within the lines binds them together, signalling this as a distinct event. But it is not a dominion of One as it is in Pope's poem. The order does not reduce to one. One stress is measured out in each line and this one holds together a proliferation of syllables, an onslaught of "rugged numbers." The irregular proliferation of syllables prevents dominion, holding the order of one to a larger irregularity and complexity, an irreducible multiplicity of phrasal patterns which occupy the lines.

The 12 lines of the poem are occupied by seven distinct phrasal patterns or "rhythmic phonemes." Elsewhere they might be called feet, and Williams himself later refers to "variable feet" in his push to maintain a link between his radical measures, the revolution in measurement implicit in relativity theory, and the tradition of English poetry and prosody. Forget, for the moment, that the classical metrical categories were derived not from patterns of stress but from patterns of duration, and call line one a 3rd paeon, line two an iamb, line three an anapest, line four an amphibrach, and so on, grafting classical quantitative measures onto these rugged numbers. It won't matter because the measure will not signify. The vocabulary of the dominion of One will not explain this event, which refuses reduction. It apologizes for its rupture, allowing room for an order of one, but then delights in its violation.

There are no feet in this poem in a strict sense. Feet go, from the Sanskrit pad, as to pad, quietly in that case, or noisily, but always forward. Feet carry us forward through time and space, padding through the forest, marching to war, strolling down the boulevard. One in front of the other, the essential sequence of feet, the endless two within the five within the ten, the ten over the ten, validates their nomination within the dominion of One. They walk a line, round and round, or at right angles to the angle of incidence on out into infinity, depending on the force applied to them.

What Williams calls feet are not feet as we have come to know feet, though they resemble feet in their patterns, and may very well be called feet when the poet wants to make a point. But then both the classical categories of foot-based verse and these phrasal units ultimately derive from the same source—the rhythmic structure of the spoken language. These rhythmical phonemes found comprehension. The bursts of noise, of vibration, that shook, woke, calmed, possessed, agitated, and soothed us in the warm, wet, dark, long before we knew "one," tuned our souls to certain frequencies as they introduced us to the order of the world we were about to enter. This is what Williams means when he asserts that the constant of his measure is the idiom. Rather than abstracting the patterns from the language, organizing them into an absolute extrinsic ruling order which the living language must then be fit to, a dominion of One, Williams' poem derives its measures from the language as it proceeds, building a texture of sound that plays off the idiom's rhythmic vocabulary at the same time it proceeds in its articulation.

If each line is taken as a single phrasal unit, a measure (a variable foot if you will), then lines two, five, and 11 repeat, as do lines three and 12, and lines four, eight, and nine. Three repetitive patterns account for 66% of the lines in the poem. In addition, the unique phrases, one, six, seven, and 10, tend, through enjambment, to break apart and recombine in ways that echo the repeated patterns, further increasing the complexity of the metrical structure. But this repetition is fundamentally different than the repetition in Pope's poem. There, repetition works toward a uniformity and predictability of temporal experience, a regular order. Repetition is based on the fundamental identity and regularity of time and space. Any normal moment is characteristically the same as that which precedes it and that which follows it, and any variation quickly returns to the norm. This is the rule of that verse, the rule of the dominion of One.

Although equally involved with repetition, Williams' verse operates differently. Characteristically irregular, repetition creates a sense of time linked in unpredictable loops and accretive textures, an invaginated and curved time rooted in the perfectly ordinary. The syntax of dynamics still exists here, still echoes in the order of one, Williams' "absolute metrical regularity," but the time of the poem is no longer reversible. We can't turn around and march back along the unfolding syllables, the marching feet, without fundamentally disturbing their order. The irregularities cannot be extricated from the order. They are integral to it. The rupture can never be "corrected" or returned to a state of perfection, just as the devoured plums can never be restored to the Frigidaire. The concept of an absolute time and an absolute space, what Anton Reiser, whose *Albert Einstein: A*

Biographical Portrait Williams read, calls "the secret religion of physicists and philosophers till the critical year 1905," is gone forever.

Gone with it is any possibility of an absolute or "objective" measure of the order of Newton's "Absolute, True, and Mathematical Time." The measure becomes specific to the event relative to other events, to the speed of the events, to their momentum as they approach the speed of light. This is the era of the variable foot and the elastic inch, of curved space/time arching back on itself in great universal loops. Yet, within all the weirdness, a unitary order still lurks. Reiser quotes Max Planck as arguing: "But if time and space have been deprived of their absolute qualities, the absolute has not been disposed of finally, but has only been moved back a step to the measurement of four-dimensional multiplicity which results from the fact that space and time have been fused into one coherent continuum by means of the speed of light." The reciprocity in the heart of measure still speaks of a distance between us and our measure, an otherness to measure that validates knowing, a narrowing distance, but a distance nevertheless, a gap, the other side of which a rule holds, and hidden variables can explain whatever seems to evade us.

In one sense, the narrowing of the gap corresponds precisely to measure's approach to the idiom, as Williams has it. In Williams' case, as his own vocabulary indicates, the approach is relative to traditional English foot-based poetries he was fighting against. The order of one still establishes a difference between the poem and the language in our ear, signalling the event as other than ordinary, even while it attains to the realm of the ordinary. It asserts the possibility of measure at the same time it redefines it in terms of the ordinary at a time when democracy dominates political rhetoric and defines political probity.

That all changed in 1960 when Donald Allen brought the energies unleashed in the small press mimeo revolution of the 1950s together in the form of *The New American Poetry*. While the anthology gathered-writers with many different approaches to poetic composition, one text stood out as a clarion call to the changing of the prosodic guard—Charles Olson's essay "Projective Verse." Originally published as a pamphlet five years earlier, Olson's essay resonated loudly in an insurgent cultural moment, arguing for a revolutionary break with old abstract measures in a move toward flesh-based measure, grounded in body/breath/spirit/, or as he had it, ear and heart. This move opened poetic measure toward the embrace of an improvisational music that unfolds in the necessity of its further articulation. For Olson, this new relation to measure was the expression of a fundamental historical shift beyond the cultural structures of 500 years of modernity, a shift into the emerging unknown of history, a shift based on further opening the poem to the ordinary idiom of democracy's legacy.

What happens to measure when it approaches the idiom, or ordinary language, so closely that distinction begins to fail altogether, where even an order of one disintegrates into the chaotic multiplicity of unframed language? Jack Spicer, in the series "Love Poems" from the book *Language*, suggests such an order:

> Sable arrested a fine comb.
> It is not for the ears. Hearing
> Merely prevents progress. Take a step back and view the
> sentence.
> Sable arrested a fine comb. On the road to Big Sur (1945) the
> fuses blew every time we braked. Lights out, every kind of
> action. A deer
> Hit us once (1945) and walked sulkily into the bushes as we
> braked into silence.
> No big white, lightless automobiles for him. If he's hit, let them
> show him.
> Sable arrested a last stop ... I think it was in Watsonville
> (1945 sable arrested fine comb a)
> Past danger into the fog we
> Used the last fuse.

In much of Spicer's verse, as here, measure appears to collapse into syntax. Not even an irregular metric seems to rule. No order of one, no isochrony, not even recognizable patterns of phrasal repetition. The structure of the poem seems built on the sentence.

What are we to make of "Sable arrested a fine comb"? As far as syntax is concerned, this is a fine sentence. All the nouns and verbs are in the right places. Count them. It is a healthy sentence, even a handsome sentence. But just as it seems almost to make sense, it slips away. "Sable" is fine, presumably someone we will know more of later, though perhaps a strange name at that. Even "Sable arrested" is okay , though now the semantic dimension starts bifurcating in unusual directions, and we begin to get uneasy. Is Sable a cop? Is he or she French and in the act of stopping, a rather unusual direction for the sentence, but possible. But a fine comb? How do you arrest a fine comb?

We are brought up short by this ordinary sentence, faced with incoherence in its simplicity. The intense contrast between syntactic order and semantic chaos disorients, as the poem itself acknowledges, urging us to "Take a step back and view the / sentence." Normally we would be "in" the sentence at this point, as the sentence measured out the world in more or less predictable units and order. Unaware of how it structures the form of our relation to the world, we would be moving along the axis of combination headed toward a period and a sense of understanding. This sentence, for all its structural ordinariness however, repels us, and much like the deer which appears later in the poem, we find ourselves butting against it, trying to force sense from it: "No big white, lightless automobiles for him."

As it approaches the sentence, as the gap closes, measure suddenly fails altogether. Or at least measure as we have known it, measure as a term that translates difference into similarity. That mediational act which establishes what Michel Serres calls "the space of similarities" will not work in this spacetime (Watsonville 1945) of absolute dissimilarity ("If he's hit, let them show him"). Instead, the sentence expels the reader, leaving her outside looking at a wall. All the more frustrating, the word thing seems so badly to want to signify.

If it does eventually, as the poem itself slips into a measured language at the end, it is not as a revelation of truth, but precisely at the cost of truth. Order is achieved only through violence. "Past danger into the fog we / Used the last fuse," Spicer writes, invoking several traditional forms of poetic measure, including obvious lineation, enjambment, and rhyme, as he equates blindness with safety. Safety is order. Safety is the usages which assure us of "knowledge." Safety is the cocoon of language which insulates us, pretending to measure the unmeasurable, pretending to signify in the face of the terrible cloud of energy which incinerates signification (1945) along with human flesh, steel, and stones.

Absolute measure fails absolutely. No backup position is possible. No hidden variables, no secret rule rescues measure from its participation in and determination of the very parameters it seeks to know. The transparency of the Newtonian universe and its homogenous, isotropic space and time where cause and effect are clearly identifiable has given way to opacity, a universe that denies all access to "reality." This is a post-quantum mechanical universe, a universe where, as Ilya Prigogine argued, for any given system, "there is an irreducible multiplicity of representations, each connected with a determined set of operators." The mirror reveals, darkly, only the image of our selves peering into it.

The dark mirror, though, is only one possible representation of the nature of this fundamental multiplicity. In John Clarke's sonnet, "Negentropic Islands," the very multiplicity provides the basis for the restoration of measure, its reformulation or renewal:

> Suddenly I am speaking with several voices
> of legendary transport irreversibly upstream
> from the deficiencies of itinerate space-time,
> sufficiently hobbled by my new non-sequential
> paraxial encyclopedia proposition I can see
> Avalon right away, even without the optical
> an entire program takes shape, like Kokovoko
> in Melville's jacket pocket, ferro-electric
> cell stitching of limitropic niches entered
> by Planck-length porosities evaginated with
> little needles to poke Penelope's fingers,
> a bigger one for the Cyclops' eye in case
> you can't locate the Slinger on his eddy
> before another one drops dead, on arrival.

Although it reflects enough of the traditional sonnet form to be recognizable as such, this sonnet is not so much bound to a pre-existing order as it is in love with the possibilities of transgression and invention the order offers. It is improvisational.

One aspect of the traditional sonnet kept completely intact is the overall number of lines: 14. At the other extreme, a formal pattern of full end rhymes that would establish periodicity and predictability in the poem is nowhere to be found. The pentameter has given way to a range of syllables determined largely by a variable isochrony: the syllable count falls somewhere between 11 and 17 syllables per line. No repetitive stress pattern or patterns appear within those lines. Like Spicer's poem in that regard, the measure tends to collapse into syntax, though the lineation prevents total collapse, creating a limited range of strong stresses: three to six per line, with the majority of lines (11) having either four or five.

While the measure tends to collapse into syntax, the syntax is characterized by transgressions which disrupt the sentence's combinatory rush. What initially seem to be subordinate clauses moving toward completion of a larger syntactic order switch in mid-stream, becoming coordinate structures which turn against closure, creating a disorder which reopens the syntax turning the entire poem into one long complex sentence. "Sufficiently hobbled" in line four seems initially to modify the "I" in line one, but turns out to modify the new "I" in line five. Similarly, in line seven, "even without the optical" refers immediately to the appearance of Avalon, but then switches, referring to the formation of a program. This unstable, left-branching syntax works against the unpredictable but steady push of strong stresses downstream, as it were, away from the poem's originating moment.

Each of these elements measures a different time in the poem. The overall form itself, the sonnet, is a measure of permanence. The improvisatory lines and their variable stresses measure a stochastic uncertainty, Michel Serres's "erratic blinking of aleatory mutations." The basic drift toward syntactic closure is fundamentally entropic, while the unstable syntactic interruptions are negentropic. The poem as a whole is a complex entity demonstrating both "order" and "disorder," what Michel Serres, again, discussing organism, calls "a bouquet of times."

No one of these times dominates the poem. Neither order nor disorder prevail. In fact, they stand revealed simply as limits of measure, as faces of complexity, as arbitrary "stations" on a limitless scale. Real meanings exist, not as dominions, but as pockets, unconnected, stochastic, contradictory. Understanding is real. But it cannot encompass all signals at a specific time. Receiving the signal does not cause noise to cease to exist, anymore than noise negates the possibility of the signal. But no signal can encompass the noise or stand for all other signals.

The measure here delineates a world where the dominion of One fails utterly and along with it utter impenetrability, which, after all, closely resembles it. The shattered mirror lies scattered across a wild topos, each piece reflecting us (or not) in place, or a place we are composed in. Whatever relations dwell in the chasms between the pieces, they are other than one. As with the manifold vocality which opens "Negentropic Islands," this manifold commensurability bespeaks a fundamental shift from the entire ontological proposition (and its negation) to a teeming or swarming which never ceases in its turbulent flow to create more and more meanings. The mythic, the scientific, the ordinary, the extraordinary, the here, the elsewhere, the then and the now, all coexist in a "non-sequential, paraxial encyclopedia proposition" which measures out the poem as the poem measures the world of its originating energies.

William Carlos Williams proposed in *Paterson* that "the measure intervenes." Measure is relation. One incommensurable term is tamed or made to speak like another by means of an arbitrary code, a language of inches. A meaning is traced out on the body of the incomprehensible. In so far as the meaning is in terms we already know, univocality and dominion result. But measure potentially is also invention, improvisation, the revelation of unexpected significance. Measure is information, not only about us, but about the worlds we are part of, that compose us as we compose them, that we see in ourselves as we see ourselves in them. In that sense, the possibility of discovery always lurks in measure. The astonishing clarity and control of Pope's measure was a discovery, or part of a discovery, of a new cosmos, or at least a new face or facet of the cosmos. So too, the new measures in the twentieth century. Caught up in the great transformations taking place, those new measures have always been troubled by increasingly unsettled understandings of order and disorder. Some have even argued that "disorder" itself is the product of the new measures and that if only we could return to the old measure, "order" would be restored. But measure is not an issue of will. As Robert Creeley put it: "Measure, then, is my testament. What uses me is what I use and in that complex measure is the issue." As invention, measure is shaped in relation to forces beyond our control, forces that give rise to measure precisely as measure gives voice to them.

The New American Poetry Revisited—Yet Again

I have been teaching *The New American Poetry* for two years now, to young people who have never heard of *The New American Poetry*, much less of Charles Olson, Robert Duncan, or Frank O'Hara. For me and most of the poets I grew up with, *The New American Poetry* was a marvelous entrance into a new world—a bit like that moment in *The Wizard of Oz* where the world suddenly switches from black and white to colour. Part of that magic for me was contextual—having the incredible good fortune to stumble into Robin Blaser's course on Charles Olson in 1968 at Simon Fraser University, and to be introduced to the work by him. The anthology itself was magic in that it opened world after world and forever changed my understanding of what writing could do. So, opening a conversation about it in a room full of young people who have never heard of it is not only exciting, it is terrifically frustrating because every facet of it opens into such depths and complexities of knowledge, experience, and feeling, that anything I say immediately makes me realize how much I will never be able to say. The impossibility of teaching *The New American Poetry*, then, is always there, at the table, as the approach to the book begins.

One thing students do tend to get right away is how different it is as a book. Over the several years of their education in Literature , they have been subjected to numerous anthologies, usually of the Norton variety, but also including Norton wannabes like Pearson, Heath, Bedford, Prentice Hall and so on, Industrial Institutional Anthologies, and the students have the sprained wrists and aching eyes to prove it. What all these books share is so much mass they are nearly impossible to hold and read, really thin, translucent paper, small—very, very small—type, and a collection of writing that represents some committee's—actually several committees'—idea of something called the canon—an utterly arbitrary collection of writers determined by various professors' political preferences, debating skills, and level of competence. They also include a myriad of footnotes—in even smaller type—that often contain erroneous, misleading, or useless facts included to "help" the student by spoon-feeding them information.

Relatively small (450 pages), *The New American Poetry* is easily handled, easily read without a magnifying glass (11-point type), contains no footnotes (assuming, I suppose, that readers are capable of getting the information they need to read the poems on their own, and that it would be good for them to do that), and is assembled in groups of contemporary poets who form specific communities within the larger community the book proposes. All in all, a unique pleasure as an anthology. There have been plenty of critiques of its gender and racial shortcomings, but it seems from most of my students we are thankfully past those days when historical limits are judged by today's political limits.

To try and communicate some of the energy and excitement that *The New American Poetry* generated when we first encountered it, I show Ron Mann's *Poetry in Motion* early in the course. Although it was filmed some twenty years after the anthology was published, it includes several writers from the book—Adam, Creeley, Ginsberg, Baraka, McClure, Snyder—as well as other poets—some younger, some contemporary—who picked up and developed the various possibilities opened by the anthology. For students it is almost always an eye-opener to witness the performative dimension of the work—which Mann's film emphasizes—since they have mostly only encountered poetry in very small type on thin, translucent pages, disfigured by multiple footnotes (see above). It is also useful to see the fruitful legacy of the anthology as it played out in poetries as diverse as The Four Horseman, Jayne Cortez, Ted Milton, and Ntozake Shange.

I start with Olson's "The Kingfishers" and "Projective Verse," because—well, Olson opens the book and he was for me, and many others, one of the book's determining figures. He remains immense in my recollections of the shockwaves *The New American Poetry* sent through the intellectual and artistic worlds in the 60s. I have come to see the way he brings readers to the limit of their ability to read, and challenges them to go further, a challenge most students are desperately in need of. The fact that he remains an object of often hostile attention indicates, I think, his continuing importance, even in the midst of various attempts to dismiss him or turn him into some kind of imperialist bogeyman.

Those two texts are among the most difficult in the book, and the students' initial response is always dumbfounded silence. They have few, if any, tools to help them get into the thinking of those pieces, so the first job is to help them articulate questions that will lead into the work. What is projective verse for instance? The essay has been—and still is—read by many as determining a specific set of rules for composing poems—a "construction technology" as one recent critic of Olson put it (demonstrating a contemporary trend to foul literary gestures with technological metaphors), a set of rules or procedures necessary to produce a specific kind of verse. If you give this metaphor authority, the essay will read as prescriptive. It becomes "imperial," for instance, imposing its techniques—in effect, colonizing if you stick with the metaphor—those who yield to it, or are overcome by its prodigious energies. Or it becomes what someone else called "verse technology," something to be operated like a tow motor or a high speed punch press (both of which I have operated and can testify are nothing like composing a poem). As if you could switch it on, feed it some material, and out comes verse that can be identified as "projective."

But if it is not prescriptive, what is it? It does start out proclaiming "the HEAD, by way of the EAR, to the SYLLABLE / the HEART, by way of the BREATH, to the LINE," as if this was a formula for producing something. Even at the time I first read it, however, it seemed clear to me—a very young poet with a couple of adolescent poems under my belt—that I was not meant to take this as a rule, but as a provocation. Olson was breaking every rule in the book, I thought. That was the essay's beauty. So how could he possibly want me to take his rule-breaking as a rule? I can't say now why I thought that. Looking back, I am tempted to see the essay's energies already at work, kicking me into a new register of vision.

Years later, Jack Clarke, who worked closely with Olson, would explain his own poetics to me in terms of Blake's four-fold vision, which he also connected to medieval exegesis with its four levels—literal, allegorical, moral, and anagogical—each level increasing in complexity. Taking

Olson's essay literally, even then, seemed to me far too simple-minded, even if I didn't yet have the vocabulary that would yield the idea of Blake's "single vision." At the root of my discomfort was a kind of skepticism: I didn't believe it possible that someone of Olson's stature and brilliance wanted to tell me how to write, much less wanted me to write like he did.

It is a curious essay, "Projective Verse," and deeply provocative even now. It's curious because while proposing itself as a piece on poetics/prosody, it slips into a philosophical discussion on the nature of being and knowing, ontology and epistemology as the philosophers have it, entangling it with poetry. Stan Persky, in a recent conversation, suggested to me that the first step in teaching poetry is to explain to students how poetry is a "linguistic mode of knowledge," comparable to narrative or mathematics. A mode of knowledge, or, say, thinking, is like what I just called a register. It assumes that our experience of knowing something is not singular (as the word "know" might lead you to believe), but multiple, diverse, and dynamic. The kind of writing that Descartes put in motion—analytic skepticism—does yield a particular mode of knowledge, but it is not the limit of knowing or thinking. Mathematics yields a different knowledge of order and structure, one completely beyond my capacities but that I occasionally have brushed up against in awe. Narrative knowledge is grounded in specific senses of time and their repercussions. Poetry is (among other things) knowledge as multiple, layered simultaneity, the experience of meaning in multiple registers at the same time, an experience of gnosis.

Olson's essay not only discusses poetry but approaches it in its tumultuous energies, its rhythmic vigour, and its complexity of thinking. As an example, it is not concerned to limit or constrain our way of writing, but to open them into a recognition of our new circumstance (post-modernity) and the new modes of being/knowing it has bequeathed us. It is a critique, then, among other things, of the reality put in place by the developments of Descartes' fabled division of the world into subjects and objects. For Olson, the "body" is the site—or just is—those new modalities of being/knowing. But because "body" in the Cartesian, which is to say modern, imagination, is immediately set against and divided from "mind," or "soul," or even "neuronal activity," Olson's first job was to find a further way to think what we are beyond those divisions, a task he took on in *Proprioception*, but that permeated his work even as early as "Projective Verse"—and the poem is part of that.

In fact, we are the poem, in that the poem and the proprioceptive self—as he articulates and enacts it in *Proprioception*—correspond in modality. The turn to the breath and the ear is not meant to curb or control our enthusiasm, but to haul us back from textbook rules and fined-honed sensibilities and locate us in our physical/mental/imaginative selves before they are assaulted by the Cartesian disfigurement. This is not just about writing, or rather, it proposes to extend writing's meaning, the sense of the act, into the anagogical. This is what Olson did, and wrote—when he swept us away.

Young people tend to be swept away as they move from their families into the extended world. They may be swept away by cults, by passion, or simply by the habits of generations locked into consumption cycles. Those swept up in Olson's extraordinary intelligence and force of soul, in his rhythms and the brilliance of his vision and language, were legion. And like any legion, myriad and diverse. Part of Olson's insight was that the days of the "private self," the self-contained, expressive individual invented by modernity and necessary to its culture, were pretty much over, if they had ever actually existed. He lived in a world of relation—literally of correspondence—and that fueled his intelligence—his *heartmind* as Robin Blaser called it. Some of the legions were part of those circles of correspondence, actively engaged in conversation with Olson in many different ways. Others, not so much. All of them are pejoratively referred to in the criticism as "disciples," a fitting word choice that reflects the critics' anti-clerical, 18th century world view as it is tied up with the rear-guard defense of bourgeois individualism.

Self/no self, individual/group—it's a curious problem, intricately woven through the question of how we are to be here now, which, for Olson, was the knowledge the poem bears—or can bear, if it is opened to its potential. Olson's epic, *The Maximus Poems,* was the locus where he attempted to do that. To say that *The Maximus Poems* was an eye-opener ain't the half of it. It was breathtaking in its scope, its daring address to the tradition it broke into, and to the poets who had shaped 20th century poetry—its rhythmic imagination, and its sustained excitement of discovery. This last element—discovery and all that implies—was central and determining from the beginning of this Odyssean journey. Olson begins in a local, particular, ordinary Gloucester, and sets sail in a box. The joy of the poems was traveling with him. Some readers were overwhelmed by that and gave themselves over to sad imitations. Some saw that happening and recoiled in horror, muttering curses at the disciples and imitators, and condemning Olson as an "imperialist," as if his purpose was to colonize and control other writers. Others found a way to another mode that yielded neither to abjection nor rejection, but to con-versation, that turning together that is the mainspring of mind at work.

For many years Jack Clarke had a poster on his dining room wall, a photo of a young boy and an elephant. They sit in a field on stools side-by-side, facing away from the camera, the massive bulk of the elephant to the right. The little boy wears a fancy shirt with puffed sleeves and a loud print, the kind of shirt someone in a circus might wear, suggesting a working relationship between the two. The photograph focuses on the small boy's right arm which extends less than a quarter of the way around the elephant's huge, lower body in a tender gesture of companionship. This, Clarke would explain, was the image of his relation to Olson.

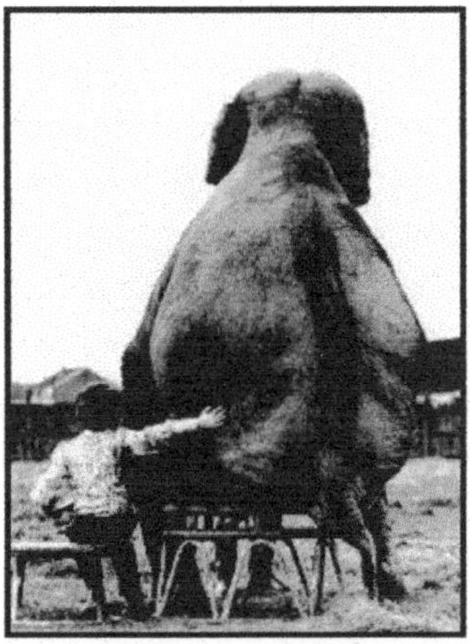

A lot could be said about what Clarke saw there. It falls outside our usual categories of relations between such disproportionate sizes and power. They tend toward emblematic binaries like "dominant/subordinate," "powerful/weak," "leader/follower," or "priest/disciple." All of these binary arrangements assume power to be exclusionary and static, a zero-sum game in which it resides either here or there. The complexity of relation in Jack's poster has to do with the way it puts knowledge and love into play as dynamically reordering power into a proceeding correspondence, a furthering of the elements whose particularities are not lost, even as relation refigures them. The key word in this new relation is love. If there was one lesson I had to single out from all that I learned from Robin Blaser, it would be the understanding that love is thinking/knowing. This is what Robin meant when he wrote of the heartmind, which is consonant with Olson's proprioceptive self.

In any case, *The Maximus Poems* were a continual provocation for many reasons, not the least of which was their refusal to fall into a set pattern, their real, active commitment to the open, especially with the publication of *Maximus IV V VI,* an extraordinary book that introduced a new world. More so than Pound or Williams, more even than Zukofsky, Olson reconfigured the epic into a constant push into the unknown, an actual exploration, a laying bare of the poet's unfolding further. That commitment took Olson into an unwavering encounter with the world's showing forth—*apophainesthai* as he has it (from Henry Corbin) in "Maximus at the Harbor."

Marvels and wonders abound in the epic journey Olson records in *The Maximus Poems,* notwithstanding a common accusation that it is "imperialist" because of some inherent quality of the genre, and specifically in the case of Olson, related to the imperial ambitions of the United States. At one point, it's true, epic occupied the pinnacle of an imagined hierarchy of literary genres, and in that sense lorded its power over the literary world. And with Virgil, it did become a tool for mythologizing the Imperial State. But that was Virgil's trip, not Olson's, and not some inherent necessity of the form. Ovid turned it into a celebration of Eros and transformation. Lucretius turned it into a mental journey deep into the heart of the thought of the cosmos. Alice Notley turned it toward a mythology—the imaged thinking—of the inner world of the human as configured in regimes of hierarchical, gendered power. As a genre, epic is open to all that, and more, depending on how the form is approached and how the conventions are deployed.

Olson was never a fan of Virgil or his epic. Driving back as far as he could go, he looked to Sumer and Hesiod for his inspirations. Homer was the limit, he argued, of an earlier energy that was free of the constraints of institutionalized Literature and its worship of the individual and his personal creations. From Homer to Melville, he notoriously claimed, nothing interesting really happened with writing. Having made his powerful rhetorical point, of course, he immediately turned to Shakespeare for prosody, and to Dante and Blake for vision. But what drove him to the epic was the possibility of protracted discovery, not the power of a hierarchical form, the epic as opening rather than closure.

If a genre is a set of conventions and expectations, then the art of the epic lies in composing those conventions into revelations of our circumstance and engaging expectations with surprise. Traditionally, the epic ends with homecoming—but how that convention is deployed is always significant. *Maximus* leaves us in a box upon the sea, a sense of home which is at the heart of Olson's understanding of postmodernity, and antithetical to imperial. A student wrote to me after the course was finished and told me that for her, "Projective Verse" was the first time she had understood the identity of "form" and "content," that a poem is form/content emerging in the same way light is wave/particle. Olson would be pleased I think, in that this is the beating heartmind of his thinkingwriting.

And in that sense, Olson should have pride of place in an anthology of diverse poetries, even though it no doubt annoyed Frank O'Hara, whose "Personism" manifesto later hilariously parodies "Projective Verse," among other things. If *The New American Poetry* is Olson's loud, demanding energies, it is no less O'Hara's dry wit and surgical humour: "As for measure and other technical apparatuses, that's just common sense: if you are going to buy a pair of pants you want them tight enough so everyone will want to go to bed with you." Mind you, a lot happened between 1950—when "Projective Verse" was first published—and 1959, when O'Hara wrote "Personism" for Donald Allen. The literary/artistic field O'Hara entered when he graduated from Harvard was already reshaped by multiple energies, including those unleashed in response to Olson's essay.

"Projective," in that sense, was just a word that was put into play at a moment already roiling with diverse energies chomping at the bit of a genteel poetry, that, if nothing else, ruled the roost of mainstream publication. It is a kind of nonsense word that stands for making up your own rules as you proceed. The fact that O'Hara got nearly as many pages as Olson in the anthology (35 vs. 30) makes the younger poet as much an exemplar of the new poetry as Olson, even though their poetries are utterly different. As linguistic modes of thought, to return to Persky's proposal, both operate in the same register that locates us in a box upon the sea, or in front of a newsstand in Manhattan the day Billie Holiday died. In both cases, what's at stake is the world—not a world informed by either elsewhere or nowhere, but this world and its form, the forms it breeds out of its own tireless bringing forth, some of which we call "ordinary," some of which we call "sacred," both of which come together in Olson and O'Hara in a tremendous (to tremble) astonishment. To think that you can fix that generative flux into in a single configuration of particularities and specificities, that that specific knowledge exhausts the ranges of our knowing relations as we engage the flux of particularities and the endless revelations of specificities, is rather sad given the sumptuousness of what is denied, which is always more. More Gloucester. More Billie Holiday. More of this ineluctable and intractable event we find ourselves thrown into.

This is a long, devious way from where I started, typical of the course conversations take in relation to this book. And it still doesn't begin to cover the depths of thinking *The New American Poetry* brings to the table. The impossibility of fully opening those depths to the blank faces around the seminar room can be overwhelming, or it can become part of a move toward unleashing a ruckus in the room. At least if you're lucky. That's what makes teaching it, thinking about it, different than any other anthology. For the young people coming to it cold, in complete innocence, not just of the book, but of poetry itself beyond some meagre exposure to the Romantics and Eliot, it can be like running into a wall face-first. But if you can get them to address the wall as something they bring to their reading, and then show them how to begin to take it apart, it will begin to yield the book's astonishments and clarities, introducing the students to a new modality of thinking and knowing. Some more than others, of course. But it seems to me that you probably couldn't ask for more than that from a book.

Major and Minor Bullshit in the New (Olde) Literary Discourse

Given the pressure to achieve success amid the grotesqueries of today's neo-liberal culture market, it probably should come as no surprise to find those old staid measures of literary excellence, major and minor, resurfacing. This, after all, is a time when the President of something called The Poetry Foundation can publicly declare the mind is a marketplace, and not be tarred and feathered and run out of town on a rail by raging poets. On the contrary, they line up in front of him with their hands out. It is a bit surprising, though, to find them popping up and circulating in the writing of poets who claim some historical relation to those poetries which sprang up in the 50s and 60s, precisely as alternatives to the elegant formal constructions then dominating the academic imagination of poetry's limits.

That time percolated, boiled over, with astonishing creativity and bold gestures, whatever its limits and historical determinations—a time of immense potentialities that arose out of combat with the formal perfections and traditional concerns of the ruling verse culture anchored in University English Departments. Chief among the targets of literary propriety was the notion of "the literary" itself and all the tight-ass little distinctions used to buttress it against the threats of "inferior" and "minor" poetry. That included concepts of "literary excellence," for instance, and the categories that were mobilized to determine it. It also included those old saws, "major" and "minor."

Yet here they are once again popping up in the most surprising places. A recent addition to Facebook, for instance, calling itself "Tendencies: Poetics and Practice," advertises itself as "a series of talks by major poets."

The title itself is interesting in the way it gives pride of place to something called "poetics" and relegates poetry to a vague generalization called "practice." At least I assume that's where the poetry is hiding. They never say. "Poetics," it seems, is the new desirable commodity in the intellectual marketplace of the English Department of the Spirit, as Jack Spicer called it. Recently we were treated to news of a gathering called "Rethinking Poetics." Once again, no mention of poetry, which seems to have gained a reputation as being soft on spirit or something of that order. Soft, anyway. Not theoretical enough where theory (which is what they mean by "poetics") provides a hard, material measure that can produce practice—maybe even praxis—as well as occasions to have many conferences.

Practice/praxis, rather than poetry, comes up once again in the description of the series of talks by the major poets who will explore "the relationship between contemporary poetic manifesto, practice, queer theory, and pedagogy." This rhetoric seems to want to appeal in some oblique way to the technological: manifestos, practice, theory, pedagogy, all this is part of the commensurable, the technical. Poetry, which is none of that, once again gets hidden behind the rubric of this thing called "practice," a verbal gesture that links the mess of concepts here to some distant Marxist, New Left discourse about "theory" and "practice" (or "praxis" for the hard core), and so announces itself as suitably "political" in currently acceptable terms.

The fact that only "major" poets can address these tendencies is telling. Presumably "minor" poets, because of the minorness of their practice, could not possibly be as profound as poets whose practice is deemed "major." Or perhaps only major poets have the technical skills to adequately address the technical complexities of "practice." If nothing else, the addition of "major" in this context introduces the specter (the specter haunting practice?) of aesthetics into the measure of the value of poetry. You can't throw around categories like major and minor without some implicit method of aesthetic qualification that allows "impartial" (Kant called it "disinterested") judgments of art.

In the case of "Tendencies… ," the rhetoric is actually minor bullshit. Their major poets are really their friends, and, although the thoughtlessness of the rhetoric is annoying, it doesn't seem to be much more than uncritical slogan mongering, another leftover New Left practice from the 60s and 70s. In other examples of the renewal of this aesthetic rhetoric, the bullshit becomes more major as in last year's dismissal of the work of Robert Creeley and Edward Dorn by Aram Saroyan for the Poetry Foundation. Saroyan, whose avant-garde credentials are impeccable, seems to have been possessed by the ghost of Richard Tillinghast who, in 1983 in the *Nation*, loudly (maybe a bit hysterically) announced that "Creeley is not a major poet."

Saroyan begins by noting the deaths of all the poets he held dear as a youth in the 60s—Charles Olson, Robert Duncan, Robert Creeley, Edward Dorn. He then announces that since they are dead, we can see "the shape of their careers," as he calls it. Seeing the shape of their careers, Saroyan is enlightened and is finally able to acknowledge certain obvious facts; to wit, while Olson and Duncan are "major American poets," Creeley and Dorn are not.

"Career" is another word like "practice" that seems to be spreading like a cancer through the current discourses about poetry. We are to assume that all poets have careers, which implies progress through remunerative work (teaching) toward a climax identified as success (or not)—and then, presumably, retirement. A career. Curiously, critics deploy this concept of "career" to, as they say, "denaturalize" the choices writers make in the course of their writing lives. What that means is anything a poet thinks she is doing just because she is a poet is really an illusion because what she really is doing is having a career. Career, it turns out, is in fact a natural and inevitable category, unlike the other ones, presumably because it is sociological and therefore true. Writers are then necessarily engaged in making choices and undertaking activities that favourably position them, in relation to success in the literary marketplace, in the same way businesspeople position themselves for financial success in the economic marketplace.

Many writers have such careers, no doubt Saroyan among them. Robert Creeley and Edward Dorn did not.

A lot of words might be used to describe the poet's relationship to poetry: calling, vocation, work, or even mission come to mind. These words emphasize a different relationship to the process than career, a relationship grounded not in an externally-validated measure of success, but one that arises out of an inner necessity, an attempt to recover what Hegel invoked as an original relationship to art when he pointed out that "art no longer provides for the satisfaction of those spiritual and intellectual needs that earlier peoples and times found in art and in art alone." Definitely not a career. He lamented the loss of art's power to originate and shape the meaning of whole cultures, an interest that drove Charles Olson's attention to the Mayans.

Olson also moved from a sense of art tied up with something called originality. This originality does not have to do either with novelty, a market-driven characteristic meant to appeal to desire's perpetual disappointment, or metaphysics. Rather, it locates art in some imaginary 0° of creative engagement, a creative engagement that is formative. Whereas Hegel grieved over a loss, Olson celebrated a possibility arising out of the ruins. Art as career has to do with the imaginary boundaries of a common world limited to metaphorical extensions of relations determined by business. Hegel—and after him, Heidegger, Arendt, Warburg, Agamben, Nancy, Cavell, and any other number of thinkers, including Creeley and Dorn—mourns for art actually obliterated by a world grounded in such thinking. For them, what we call art begins precisely at the point where this literary business ends, where it is destroyed.

It began there for Creeley as well as for Olson, as the ten volumes of their correspondence testify. Creeley had no interest in a literary life as defined by the culture when he was looking for a way forward with his work. "The light moves, so to speak," he wrote in "Why Bother?", "and those who see it have secured an 'originality' quite beyond that qualified by terms of personality or intent.... One can be famous in many magazines, but not in those given to the definition of what a poem right now, can be." What a poem right now, can be, concerned him, and what a poem right now, can be, measures the world—this common and fractured world of our tenuous experience. "What uses me is what I use and in that complex measure is the issue."

Creeley was never after more than that. He was delighted by the occasional prize, more so than, say, Olson or Dorn would have been, but he never aspired to some notion of literary excellence that constitutes the fundamental value of a culture of professional Literature, a culture of men and women of good taste. He never compromised his understanding of what writing right now, can be to make it more acceptable to the arbiters of literary excellence. He saw himself as part of a group of international writers who had moved writing into a new zone, and he felt that recognition was due for that work, including the Nobel Prize.

Saroyan dates Creeley's descent into the world of "minor" poetry with the publication of *Pieces* in 1969. Creeley's third large collection (his fourth Scribner's poetry book), *Pieces* is the occasion where he set about destroying Literature fully for the first time. Saroyan represents the writing as "very short notations arranged down the pages with a kind of blithe insouciance, as if to say, I'm a poet and therefore this is poetry." But in fact Creeley's approach to the line in *Pieces* was no different than in his previous books, and some of the "pieces" in the book, such as "The Finger," are as substantial, if not more so, than anything he had yet written. What differed was Creeley's active attack on the distinction between what was suitable for the work and what wasn't, and how that material was to be handled.

In *Pieces*, Creeley decisively moved for the first time beyond the limiting idea of "literary material," what Tillinghast called "the large human issues that are traditionally associated with major poetry," and Saroyan, drawing on Henry James (of all people), identifies as "felt life." *Pieces* was revolutionary because it included a range of language—quotations, impressions, poems, prose, correspondence, dreams—texts that swarm, constituting the tissue of whatever that elusive thing is we call the real, pushing writing toward what a poem right now, can be. Dedicated to Louis Zukofsky and driven by a radical Emersonian commitment to the common, the music of Creeley's writing is exquisitely composed out of the ordinary sounds that make up our lives, lives that are far fuller of small issues (pieces) than of large ones, or that are unable to distinguish between them.

The destruction of art was central to what Olson and Creeley "were pissing at," as Olson put it in a September 7, 1951, letter to Creeley. Dorn came at the problem from a different angle, but with a similar spirit. Dorn's mature work, from *Gunslinger* on, located itself in relation to the possibilities of satire as an expression of his deep commitment against all forms of moralism, especially as they manifested themselves in the idiocies of American cultural and political life. He had no interest whatsoever in either "large human issues" or "the felt life," which themselves were just moralistic standards of literary excellence hearkening back to the Fugitives and their frantic defense of Christian culture. But then, neither had Rimbaud nor Artaud. Nor for that matter, Pope nor Dryden.

As Saroyan attempted to slip in "the felt life" as an a priori condition of literary excellence in relation to Creeley, he attempted to slip in the "musical complexity and felicity of the Elizabethans" as the a priori condition in judging Dorn. The obvious absurdity here is that if anyone could lay claim to the musicality of the Elizabethans, it was Creeley, although he always approached that music through what he had learned from Zukofsky and Miles Davis, and always with a sense of playfulness and humour. Dorn was closer to Pope than to John Clare. What's even more absurd is that in the process, Saroyan slips in a little Nancy Reagan just-say-no-to-drugs moralism as a way of "explaining" why Dorn "lost his music."

Dorn also sought the destruction of art. "You see," he told Barry Alpert in an interview, "I don't want the poem to be susceptible or dependent on textual considerations which are external to it." He was speaking of *Gunslinger*, and specifically of the appearance of Heidegger in the poem. This is the same Heidegger who, in conversation with Hegel, proposed that art as "truth telling" had been replaced by art as "aesthetic experience," and that in order to recover art as truth, art as aesthetic experience had to be destroyed. "I think the function of the poet in present-day America," Dorn told Stephen Fredman, "... would be to stay as far as possible from all permanent relations to power.... [W]ho cares about the National Book Award or the Pulitzer Prize? Those are not by anyone's reckoning important, one way or another." Saroyan suggests this leads to a "hipster's cutting, sarcastic instrument, often so elliptical as to be incomprehensible." This is another way of noting that Dorn's heretical embrace of satire was always antithetical to the given modes of versification, and so will always be alien to men of good taste. Saroyan writes from within the magisterial palaces of aesthetics, while Dorn was never more than a high plains drifter.

This is not meant as a defense of Creeley and Dorn against the major bullshit of the new aestheticians. Their work stands for itself, and will continue to be a source of energy and ideas for other writers looking for ways to rethink the possibilities of poetry outside the boundaries of literary power. What is of interest is the way that old forms of hierarchical power, armed with moralistic aesthetic categories, have remounted their patrols at the boundaries of Literature, and the way those categories casually slip into the vocabularies of people who should know better. The openings that Olson, Creeley, Duncan, Dorn and so many others fought for, have nothing to do with Literature and everything to do with reclaiming the world and reclaiming poetry as a unique mode of linguistic knowing. Creeley especially has suffered from the criticism that his work never engaged the political issues of his day, but there is nothing more political in our circumstance than to reclaim the world from the cultural banalities, political moralisms, and aesthetic idiocies that expunge experience in some universal lock-down of the imagination. Major and minor have nothing to do with it. It has everything to do with the "obligation to the divine," as Dorn called it: "The obligation would be self-evident. It's divining like science is divining."

Robert Creeley's Anger

Why, then the world and all that's in't is nothing,
The covering sky is nothing, Bohemia nothing,
My wife is nothing, nor nothing have these nothings,
If this be nothing.
—Leontes, *The Winter's Tale* I. ii. 293-6

Robert Creeley's intense, often unrestrained anger, especially as a young man, is the stuff of literary legend. Stories abounded in Buffalo in the 1980s when I lived there, much of that time spent as Creeley's amanuensis at the State University of New York at Buffalo. One of my favourite stories, which I think I heard from Betty Cohen, although I can't recall for sure if it was she, and will never know if she, if it was she, had scrambled it or even made it up, related how some straight up academic at a faculty reception for a writer insisted on dissing John Coltrane to Creeley while grazing at the ubiquitous cheese platter, wine glass in hand. After becoming increasingly frustrated and angry trying to reason with the man, Creeley, in a rage, picked up a knife and chased him around the table trying to stab him until cooler heads intervened and disarmed the poet. Another story involved Creeley and Amiri Baraka drinking at the bar at the Central Park Grill. At that time, the windshield wiper factory still operated in the Tri-Main building next door to the bar, and a group of workers on their break, as was their habit, came in for a liquid lunch. Standing next to Creeley, one of them muttered, "Who let the nigger in?" or words to that effect. Creeley immediately smashed his beer bottle against the bar, put the jagged end against the man's throat, and instructed him to apologize to Baraka. Which the man did—expeditiously.

Neither of these events may have taken place as narrated here, in this world, if at all. In the manner of urban legends or myth, the stories circulate with a life of their own and "facts" have very little to do with the truths of their narrative force and form. The fact that they circulate is the only fact required, given the almost mythic quality the young Creeley's anger assumed both in the world and in his work. That anger came up recently in a review of Robert Creeley's *Selected Letters* by Robert Archambeau. Archambeau focuses on the poet's angry dismissal of other poets and writers—"spewing bile" he calls it at one point—using about four of the six pages of the review to detail what he calls Creeley's "combative and intolerant" behaviour. Archambeau does nod to other narratives in the letters, especially the story of "a network of the isolated few reaching out and supporting one another," but Creeley's anger and his alleged vindictiveness in relation to other poets is the main show. Creeley comes out looking violently competitive, someone who, no matter what his remarkable successes, remained arrogant, whiny, ungrateful, and endlessly jealous.

Archambeau frames his portrait of Creeley in the context of the "poetry wars" that exploded with the 1960 publication of *The New American Poetry* and continued through the 90s to the new millennium. Contrary to Archambeau's assertion, however, the wars have never ended, as his review amply demonstrates, although they have morphed into different formations and modes of engagement. Creeley, as Archambeau notes in the title of his review, was a warrior in the post-1960 campaigns and his anger needs to be viewed in the context of that moment and its attendant hostilities and power struggles. It was a time when the levers of power—the magazines, the teaching positions, the prize committees—were all in the hands of a conservative cabal suckled at the teat of T.S. Eliot's cultural and literary criticism. One dimension of Creeley's anger was a response to the systematic exclusion of poetries that didn't fit the Eliot mold. What Archambeau doesn't acknowledge—or perhaps simply doesn't understand—is that poetry mattered then in ways that have since been lost in the fog of "creative writing" that has enveloped the literary world. Creeley's passion registered that.

Eliot's legacy was mired in a reactionary response to the historical developments of modernity as its contradictions gave rise to a world of commercialized value and the effervescence of popular culture. His solution—condemn the changes, become a high Anglican, and fight a rear-guard action in defense of Christian Culture—shaped his equally reactionary attitude toward poetry. While Pound, H.D., and especially Williams sought ways forward, understanding poetry as a particular mode of knowledge that could reveal new perspectives and relations to the changing cosmos, Eliot holed up in the church, condemning "strange gods," defending "Christian Culture," and turning his poetry into a kind of linguistic censer. At the heart of the difference was the understanding of prosody. For Eliot, the ghost of a meter was the sign and form of stabilized value, the antithesis of Williams' variable foot which located the imagination in the constant act of attention to the unfolding world and its political conflicts.

It was no accident, then, that many of the poets of *The New American Poetry*, notably Duncan, Olson, Dorn, and Ginsberg, among others, were deeply involved in various ways in the anti-war resistance of the 60s and 70s. Their poetry was part of what was called the Movement; it roused crowds; it was read to others on the street, in cafes, living rooms, and auditoriums, both reflecting and instigating resistance. Even Creeley, who agonized over not being able to write explicitly political poetry, was active in the resistance. Meeting him for coffee with Robin Blaser in Montreal in 1969, I was naively shocked to witness his near self-flagellation over his inability to write political poems. He was genuinely upset, while Blaser patiently and comfortingly reassured him that the mere form of his poetry was deeply political. I understood that to mean that the specific attention it required reoriented the reader outside the War Machine and its daily habit. And that was/is deeply political. Poetry is understood as a mode of thinking, and prosody is its soul. Olson's essay, "Projective Verse," had the tremendous force it did, not only because it lifted the darkness and opened composition to the limitlessness of the imagination, but because it treated prosody and thinking/being as one. Poetry mattered.

It still does, but not in the public sphere Archambeau is part of where it has been displaced by the Commercial Poetry Product and its doppelganger, the self-branded avant-garde Text, both of which abandon poetry as a mode of thought and turn it into a commodity to be used in pursuit of art booty—prizes, grants, academic positions, invitations to the White House. Poetry mattered because, as Olson and Creeley hammered away at in their correspondence, it measures the world. It is not a pretty little thing made out of seven types of some established trope and shaped into well-wrought, ironic objects to be displayed in some prestigious journal with "Review" in its title. Writing to Olson in 1950, early in their correspondence, Creeley said: "I get so sick of mags like PR, with piece after piece trying to finish themselves off, to fit an arbitrary form, never growing from the nerves of the man, always /—like the 4 Quartets—/ adjusting / themselves." The question here is not so much about organic as about dynamic, where Emerson takes it, into energy. The stake is the world, one that is "finished off", or one that encounters you as you encounter it open-ing to the formations open-ing to encounter.

This is not the world that Archambeau cites. A sucker for sociology (and its stealth cosmology), he invokes Pierre Bourdieu to reduce Creeley's poetry to a "career choice," proposing Creeley's anger as a manifestation of the "social aging of art:" " … a process in which one group—generally marginal, young, or both—seeks to discredit those who practice the art differently." This identifies Creeley's anger as competitive resentment. There was a reason that Charles Olson stated that "sociology is shit," and this, along with other arguments that attribute Creeley's anger to, for example, the "feminization of masculine space," is an excellent example of it.

A lot has been written about Robert Creeley's poetic stance, to which his anger is integral if not foundational. Perhaps most famously, he is known, after Charles Olson's dedication of the first Maximus volume, as the Figure of Outward. Years ago, I puzzled over that because I could not imagine a more inwardly dedicated poetry than Creeley's. Olson sails out into the universe in a box, but every twist and torsion in Creeley's writing forces the inner toward a further detail, articulation, or intensity. I eventually puzzled it out. Outward isn't a function of the "content," but its arrangement in words as they emerge in Creeley's attentive composing. The outward, then, as the outward-ing of that inner intensity. And at a level that transports the words and events to an extreme register that sometimes manifests in rage and violence. Donald Wellman describes him as "an epistemological poet always reaching with the finger of his mind to the edge of thought: 'Birds sing still at the edges of hearing.'" The appropriateness of epistemology to Creeley's prosody may seem counter-intuitive, given his militant presence-ing and apparent simplicity, but in so far as it describes informing relation, it is crucial. Precisely the relation of knowing determines the movement of Creeley's language. He is an epistemological poet to Olson's ontological poet.

Will Montgomery locates his stance in refusal: "Refusal becomes, sieved through Creeley's formal choices, a refusal of communicative plenitude. Ellipsis, compression, syntactical uncertainty, and the insistent breaking of the line make hesitancy and un-decidability integral to the overall effect of the poetry." The refusal goes beyond communicative plenitude to the existential, the stuff of the poem's knowing and Creeley's being-in-the-world. "There is no giving," Creeley wrote. "The mind / beside the act of any dispossession is // lecherous. There is no more giving in / when there is no more sin." Refusal is implicated in a post-sin state of desire that is giving/not giving in—the tension of uncertain presence, although whether the end of sin is more than a hopeless wish remains unstated, continuing to hang over the irresolution, the refusal, of the end.

In any case, it is a state of rigorous, singular encounter/attention/engagement. Creeley disdained the measured, on-the-other-hand, self-reflexive pretense to objectivity that Archambeau idolizes in his description of an unnamed scholar's criticism of a paper Archambeau read at some conference: "C had taken a step back and seen not only the irksome text in front of him, but seen himself looking at it." Did he also see himself seeing himself looking at it? See himself seeing himself seeing himself? At what point does the "divided self" stop dividing in the interest of fictional disinterest and just get on with it? The notion that somehow Creeley would or could "stand outside himself," as Archambeau fantasizes, looking "not at those he despised, but at himself looking at them," betrays a breathtaking ignorance of Robert Creeley's work and of the fundamental stance that oriented it, while remaining blissfully blind to Archambeau's own hidden moralisms, as if "detachment" was actually a state of superior intellectual achievement rather than a disguise for a hidden system of arbitrary valuations and power relations.

John Clarke, in his masque, *Blake*, the 7th book of *A Curriculum of the Soul*, situates a certain world of poetic relation in the early 70s in a mythic Bolinas where poets enact the dynamics of the then current poetry world as figures from Blake's poetic cosmos. A fourfold text, it negates sociology in its complexity, resonant with meanings that expound/expand Blake's thought while making apparent (apparencing) the forces and forms that drive the dynamic we call here. They are the forms of the poetic imagination intersecting our lives, informing them, determining relation. In a wild narrative that includes portraits of Tom Clark, Bobbie Louise Hawkins, Kenneth Rexroth, Don Allen, Charles Olson, Ted Berrigan, Joanne Kyger, and John Thorpe among others, Clarke tellingly locates Creeley as Ulro, a character wracked by guilt and a sense of sin that alienates him from the world. In Blake's mythology, Ulro is the embodiment of single vision, the loss of divine vision in a state of spiritual opacity. It is the monological spirit of modernity as theorized by Descartes, Newton, and Locke, grounded on an unshakable alienation between subject and object, inward and outward, self and world.

The sexual dimension of Ulro (lechery, Creeley has it, unhealthy, sexual indulgence) is figured in the promiscuity between Ulro and Oothoon, who are discovered by Ulro's wife, Beulah, dancing naked, "displaying their giant limbs to all the winds of heaven." Beulah, for Blake, was the image of prodigality, the sexual union of opposites, the overcoming of compulsive binaries. Blake drew Ulro as a man and a woman tied together back-to-back. He embodied an unstable relation or condition, a violation of marriage, that old, gendered trope of the iconic union of masculine and feminine in a potential plenitude. "No spirit," Ulro proclaims in Blake, "but the receptacle, the container, or cabinet of the spirit, where in it lies, for the signature stands in the essence and is as the lute that lies still …." All his life, Robert Creeley held that any easy proposition of meaning was implicated in the death of the world, and in so doing, he kept the world, sphinx-like, in front of him, utterly, persistently, tantalizingly all that is the case, but that must be said and resaid without ever being able to say it, since as soon as it was said, he hated it. Love was the impossible solution.

As a spiritual discipline—Creeley would hate that designation—or, say, an active epistem/ontology, such a stance/poetics relies on a state of constant tension which is impossible to maintain and so leads to the despair of isolation from the immediacy necessary to the tension: "All night the sound had / come back again, / and again falls / this quiet, persistent rain. // What am I to myself / that must be remembered, / insisted upon / so often? Is it // that never the ease, / even the hardness, / of rain falling / will have for me // something other than this, / something not so insistent—/ am I to be locked in this / final uneasiness." Built into this line of inquiry is the unspoken issue neuroscientists refer to as "the hard problem," i.e. what is consciousness? If once it was a divine spark, and later an epiphenomenon of neuronal activity, Creeley's perennial uneasiness, his unanswered question, addresses it only as "nothing further."

The seeming solution so often for Creeley is love, not as a resolution or transformation, not as the accomplishment of plenitude beyond the face of the world's stony reticence, but as company in hopeless resignation: "Love, if you love me, / lie next to me. / Be for me, like rain, / the getting out // of the tiredness, the fatuousness, the semi- / lust of intentional indifference. / Be wet / with a decent happiness." To lay next to him, as he pleads for her to do, only yields mutual isolation, side-by-side, company, but conditional at that (if you love me), and of a sad order of use (Be for me) that finally yields only further despair.

For Creeley, poetry was a moral force in a world given to degraded language, mindless war, endless spectacles, and spiritual gluttony. As he wrote to Olson in 1950: "My impotence. To either shake off or get beyond the sense of this current biz. It revolts me, turns my stomach, sickens altogether. I hate the whole of it, despise, loathe & feel contempt for every damn one who deals in it. The nation: fucking idiotic lying/: perverts. Perverts in the head/rotten, filth, hate, hate, hate. Voices: oily, & shrewd, know, exact, how to lie attractively to each and every one. Against that, just that, we put a handful of sounds/one feeling, two, a complex: love." The morality, however, does not lie in some proposed solution, but in the act of world preservation, of engaging and revealing an integrity whose multiple intensities continually resist reduction to any final articulation. A morality of refusal.

But the nothing-further becomes just-nothing when the inevitable dispersal of the intensity leaves only a hole where the world was. One of the most angry, violent, painful moments in Creeley's early poetry occurs in "The Hole." The poem begins peacefully, in the silent moment of the inception of the poem and the thought of filling it. It then moves to anxiety about spilling, to a story of complete release recalling swimming naked and peeing into the lake, then, from urine to feces, to the injunction, "Wipe / yourself, into / the tight / ass paper is pushed." The shock of transition is painful. It is as if the pleasure of the previous moment of release couldn't be allowed to persist without a brutal, penetrating correction. The implicit violence of the "is pushed" in relation to the hole is amplified when it leads to the memory of Fatty Arbuckle raping a girl with a Coke bottle. From there, the poet fingers his own ass, forces anal sex on a partner who screams in pain, and notes his family's and a teacher's sexually-charged anatomical details. A kind of phantasmagoria of anal/genital pleasure, pain, and violence that locates composition in its shadows (the filling of the hole), the poem ends with a claim for pleasure it immediately negates: "Everywhere / there is pleasure, / deep, / with hands / and feet. // I want / to, now I / can't wait any / longer. Talk // to me, fill / emptiness with / you, empty / hole." The "wanting" may yearn for the pleasure of release, of orgasm even, but the "can't wait any longer" realizes nothing, merely expresses frustration. Only some hopeless attempt to fill the emptiness of the absent world with talk (or poetry) remains, a world of endlessly deferred articulations, a hole of meaning which is by this point a kind of cosmological arsehole. In "Anger" he has it as "an open/ hole of horror, of // nothing as if not / enough there is / nothing. A pit—...."

Creeley's anger dwelled and bred in this pit. It was no ordinary anger that comes and goes over a slight or an insult. It ran deep in the poet's life. He related it to the loss of his left eye at two years old, compounded by the circumstances of its removal when he was five, and the death of his father when he was four years old. The eye, although wounded, wasn't removed until after his father's death. The excision was arranged secretly by his mother who told him nothing of it. At five years old, months after his father's death, she delivered him to the hospital where unbeknownst to him, a surgical team waited. She left him there, where, confused, he was taken away by staff. When he awoke, his eye was gone. The missing father, and the missing eye, become part of an anger that finds its object in another absence, the absence of meaning, a missing world. A profound loss, it takes on the near heroic energies of a stance, an epistem/ontology. In his autobiography, Creeley notes that the tracks of the ambulance that took his father away into silent absence, a hole, marked for the child "the end of that previous time entirely."

While deeply implicated in Creeley's anger, the events can't explain its continuing role in his life. Other people forgive, forget, go into therapy, move on. But as "The Hole" demonstrates, anger was a defining aspect of Creeley's cosmology. The empty hole at the end of the poem ties together mouth, asshole, vagina, and world in a multi-valanced image of sexual aggression, emptiness, and the violent attempt to fill it. Creeley sometimes connected that vision of the senselessness of the real to his singular eye. He was fond of pointing out how both he and Robert Duncan, who had a famously wandering eye, literally saw the world differently than most people. One eye will not yield three dimensions, much less four or more.

Anger was also a method, a discipline of (momentary) rupture. The commonplace of anger, as Creeley put it to Tom Clark, violently breached the containment of self, that, on its own, it could never get beyond. Creeley told Clark the story of a schizophrenic child kept in a cage by her mother during violent episodes. The caged child at one point acquires a knife, lashes out through the cage with it and stabs her captor/ caregiver: "And you think," Creeley says, "is that the imagination—is that the providence necessary within the commonplace? That having anger is the only system that can quote 'deal with' the commonplace of anger?" The often-quoted poem, "Anger," begins with the commonplace, a house full of family settling in for the night, "The children / sleep, the dog fed, / the house around them / is open, descriptive." "Descriptive" is a funny word, seemingly locating the house now as some set piece whose description pre-exists it.

When truck lights suddenly illuminate it—"lights bright there, // glaring, the sudden / roar of its motor, all / familiar impact // as it passed / so close"—its descriptiveness is called to attention. Not surprisingly, "He / hated it." The cage of the self suddenly lit up around him. The rage that follows both satisfies and frustrates, both is a hole and fills a hole, until the speaker becomes dissociated from himself, and pronouns proliferate in a strange transcendence into the open and the empty: "Then / as the shouting / grows and grows / louder and louder // with spaces / of the same open / silence, the darkness, // in and out, him- / self between them, / stands empty ...." The deep urge to find a home, a familiar place, with another, a wife, a love, complete, as if meaning were a fulfillment of relation, a prodigality of union that is beyond union, drives "Anger." But meaning, and even sense which is its ground, dancing beyond the face of the moment, yields to a completion, a description, that is the death not just of sense, but of life itself. Anger is the knife that lashes out through the bars. Pitched high enough, it is a beyond the self, a face of the infinite, the open. Until the anger releases, and the bars return.

Like Leontes' anger in *The Winter's Tale*, the rage that arises from his inability to know unequivocally that Hermione has been true and that his son is truly his son, Creeley's anger continually circulates around his belief in the impossibility of certainty which defines knowledge. Nothing can convince Leontes. All criteria fail his insistence on certainty. As a result, his wife and son both die and his daughter is lost to him. The world is annihilated by his refusal to simply acknowledge it. Stanley Cavell calls it "a portrait of the skeptic at the moment of the world's withdrawal from his grasp," and argues that it is "not an ignorance but an ignoring, not an opposable doubt, but an unappeasable denial, a willful uncertainty that constitutes an annihilation." Creeley's anger, like Leontes' rage, is both the response to—and the practice of—a radical skepticism. "The Shakespearian portrait," Cavell says, "lets us see that the skeptic wants the annihilation that he is punished by, that it is his way of asserting the humanness of knowledge, since skepticism's negation of the human, its denial of satisfaction in the human (here in human conditions of knowing) is an essential feature of the human, as it were, its birthright."

Although the anger calmed in his later years, the radical skepticism of his literally monological vision remained militantly determining. In his last essay on age and Whitman, Creeley criticized Whitman's 1859 poem, "You tides with ceaseless swell" for its lines, "You tides with ceaseless swell! you power that does this work! / You unseen force, centripetal, centrifugal, through space's spread." Whitman recapitulated the rhythmic vision that had informed his poetry since the 1855 edition of *Leaves of Grass* with its merge and merge and ceaseless merge. Creeley will have none of it. "The sea," he says, "can't be put to such a simplifying reference—it's too real." The monologic vision manifests in two annihilating judgments. It assumes that Whitman's is a "simplifying reference," as if there could be no question that such a phenomenon might actually manifest in the sea, an integrally entangled force of creation, not unlike Charles Olson's sense of "migration." Not a reference at all, but a profound recognition. And it assumes a particular definition of "real" that is limited to the world of Creeley's skepticism. "Too real" for Creeley always means nothing-further.

None of this is to say that he wasn't astonishingly kind and generous in every way imaginable. Such contradictions were at the heart of his intensities. Rachel Blau DuPlessis tells of how, when she was a young mother, Creeley came to her aid at a conference when, on stage, her two-year old child threatened to fatally disrupt the event. While Ginsberg heckled from the audience, Creeley suddenly appeared on stage beside her to help manage the gear-and-child-laden retreat with some dignity, and to stay with her in the playground outside, keeping her and her child company while the conference concluded. That attention and sensitivity to the intractable human dilemmas of others, and his willingness to give whatever he had to help in whatever situation, was a constant determination of his person. After he came into the possession of institutional largesse in the form of a funded chair at Buffalo, he spread it far and wide, freely, liberally, a veritable Johnny Appleseed of funding, with no attempt to use it as a form of power or control. He bestowed without question resources on young poets and scholars to help fund their emerging energies. He kept money flowing to perennially destitute poets with no means of support beyond their poetry. There is no telling how many poets Creeley supplied with necessary sustenance over the years.

That generosity extended to an openness, curiosity, and an infectious sense of humour he shared freely with everyone. He was the very image of Emerson's poet, common, democratic, generous, and essential to the measure of the times. He was never the hideously clichéd "Old Sage of Buffalo" that Archambeau proposes. In fact, if Archambeau had said that to Creeley's face, he might have gotten popped in the snoot—at least in the old days. Creeley did not suffer fools lightly, and poetry mattered to him in ways that the current generation of "creative writers" like Archambeau cannot begin to understand. Poetry was his life, not his living. It was not a means to an end, whether that end was some meagre appointment or some equally meagre prize. It did matter to him that his accomplishments were recognized. The idea, however, that, like the current manufacturers of Commercial Poetry Products, he "jockey[ed] around for fame and position" is laughable. His anger continued well after his recognition and success because he continued to care about poetry, and because his militant, existential cosmology never wavered and continued to inform his judgments of what poetry should and could do. He may have mellowed, but he didn't change. I'll say it again—poetry mattered to him. Really mattered. And although Archambeau claims that the poetry wars ended and that Creeley's anger was a lingering "resentment" that outlived its occasion, in fact, Archambeau's review is proof that the poetry wars are very much alive and well, and the enemies of Creeley's poetry are still at the wheel, even if they are more "detached" now, less forthright.

In the late 80s and early 90s, Creeley's anger turned toward a group of poets who had studied with Charles Olson and had formed the Institute of Further Studies to continue the work they started with him. On Olson's death, they initiated the *Curriculum of the Soul* project, based on Olson's poem of the same name. Jack Clarke assigned 28 topics from Olson's poem which together would constitute the curriculum, a kind of epic as Al Glover describes it. Creeley initially agreed to take on the topic of "God," then switched to "one's own mind," although he delayed it for almost 20 years before finally withdrawing. Meanwhile, in 1991, Tom Clark published his biography of Charles Olson and sparked a vigorous debate over his ultimate representation of the poet. Creeley supported Clark's vision of an Olson deeply-flawed by narcissism, sexism, and bullying. Jack Clarke, Harvey Brown, Al Glover, and Ralph Maud, found reason to criticize the biography for incorrect facts and uncharitable and sensational caricatures of complex issues (the *Library Journal* reviewer wrote that it "reveals that Olson grappled with homosexual impulses, took hallucinogens and dominated those around him, seeking periodic release from inner demons in frenzied floods of images"). Ralph Maud spent much of the rest of his life detailing word by word every inaccuracy (and they are legion) in Clark's book, although Clark simply ignored him and reissued the biography in 2000 with all factual errors intact.

For Creeley, the issue was complicated. Poetry was part of it, but it also had to do with both how Olson, his friend, would be perceived going forward, and how Creeley would be perceived in relation to him. Olson was a powerful, oracular poet and his writing of the world, its details, its history, its persistent, mysterious otherness, attracted various kinds of attention, including a kind of abjection before "the master." In some way, that tied in to Creeley's own anxiety about the perception of his relation to Olson. In the introduction to the second edition of Clark's biography, Creeley refers to Richard Elman's description of him as Minimus to Olson's Maximus, and insists—correctly, but clearly with some anxiety—that "our 'life in print' had been remarkably shared." They were, he insists, equals, and the Institute of Further Studies and its Curriculum became, for Creeley, an abandonment of that equality in some kind of worshipful relation.

It wasn't (that's another story, as they say), but it was easy enough to make it look like that and it served his purpose to do so in order to better locate himself as not that. When he describes Olson in the introduction (ignoring the lurid aspects of Clark's narrative) he only addresses the early Olson with his central concern for "historical geography," the Olson of the correspondence of the 1950s. Creeley ignores the late Olson, the reader of Henry Corbin and Avicenna, the Olson of Dante and the rose of the world, the Olson of "A Curriculum of the Soul" and "Poem 143—the Festival Aspect." One looks in vain at Creeley's writing about Olson for reference to "the end of the World Tree," or "Out of the light of Heaven…the flower / grows down, the air / of Heaven," or "the left hand is the calyx of the Flower / can cup all things within itself" and so on. For him, Olson was never oracular, prophetic, or even just spiritual, but was an ordinary fucked up guy, not unlike Creeley himself, who was solely attentive to "[a] tracking of the earth in time." That may be, but Olson was increasingly concerned with the eruptions of eternity into that time.

The poem and the world of the poem was also at stake. Creeley's militant commitment to refuse plenitude, to address a world of no-further, never faltered. Olson's poetry increasingly opened into the otherness of the world. His reading of *Avicenna and the Visionary Recital* influenced not only his writing, but arguably led to the ta'wil he performed at Berkeley in 1965. Creeley points out that Olson "moved the art to an exceptional capacity for thinking itself," so that "poetry had no longer a simple literary or cultural practice." But he needed for his own purposes to keep it located in some monological frame. To grant authority to the students of some further Olson was to undermine in his mind the integrity of his own stand. And worse, to become identified with it.

I encountered (rather than witnessed, which I also did) Creeley's anger the year before his death when in a phone call our conversation turned to Clark's biography. After some back and forth, with, to me, uncharacteristic but increasing intensity, even anger, he demanded that I declare myself in support of it. It was, after all, as he stated in his introduction, the story: "The story matters, all of it—and what Tom Clark gathered here, in a way he acknowledges and I respect, is as much of it as I or anyone else seems to know." I demurred, pointing out that its documented errors were legion, that the story Charles Boer told in *Charles Olson in Connecticut* was of a different man, and that Jack Clarke, in his reviews of the biography, seemed to know, if not more, then at the very least, other dimensions of Olson's person that qualified or contradicted Clark's narrative in significant ways. But Bob was having none of it. His anger became palpable over the phone as he pushed me one last time to sign on, and when I told him that I couldn't do that in good faith, he told me that I would no longer be hearing from him. I was stunned, but knowing of the volatility of his relations, and that other friends he had cut off were later reembraced, I expected the time would come when we would move beyond this difficulty. Unfortunately, he died the following year. We never spoke again.

Robin Blaser's Exody and Some Mechanics of Splendour

"All research on the labyrinth ought properly to begin with the dance."
—Karl Kerenyi

The last part of my title is lifted from Robin Blaser's "Image-Nation 21 (territory", where it refers to the person of the poet chanting, as that poem has it, in the windy cables of bridges. That personalization of "mechanic", with its Hart Cranian overtones, stands in relation to both thinkers whose work I want to address here, Ralph Waldo Emerson and Robin Blaser. It also extends beyond that into the notion of a field of knowledge that has to do with the study of motion, as well as the ways in which that motion becomes a kind of routine operation, something ordinary, mechanical. Overall that hovers an image out of America's cultural past: an old car, say a '46 Hudson or a '52 Ford, with the hood up and some guys bent over the motor, endlessly tinkering with the contraption, to make it go, but equally for the sheer pleasure of the tinkering. In this case, that contraption is of a certain brilliance and the tinkering speaks to a habit of relation, where habit, like Thoreau's habitation, is a place we build in the world to dwell in, to inhabit. Again, this is a habit of motion which, in the most recent of the "Image-Nations" in print, Blaser calls exody.

In 1838 Emerson addressed the tiny class of six graduates of Harvard Divinity School. In the "Divinity School Address" he sketched out in the form of advice to the students the reasons for his own conversion from the pulpit. He proposed what he sometimes calls the sacred as evident in a specific relation to language, to the word or Logos, a relationship, he argued, that had been lost by the church. This relation is twofold: language arises from experience and is full of the specifics of a life, and because of this, is prophetic and cosmogonic. It names the world truly, where we understand, I think, the word truly as an accuracy bearing what Giorgio Agamben calls "the mark of the Sphinx," an honouring of the enigma that is the barrier between those two terms that stand so centrally in the troubled imagination of language, signified and signifier.

In *Stanzas*, Agamben's Sphinx addresses the troubled thinking of language crucified on the cross of presence and absence, identity and difference. In the one case, we are left with an absolute intelligibility whose immeasurable brutality we have witnessed all too frequently. In the other, we are left isolated and alone, unable to know anything of the world:

> The ainos (story, fable) of the ainigma is not only obscurity, but a more original mode of speaking. Like the labyrinth, like the Gorgon, and like the Sphinx that utters it, the enigma belongs to the sphere of the apotropaic, that is, to a protective power that repels the uncanny by attracting it and assuming it within itself. The dancing path of the labyrinth, which leads into the heart of that which is held at a distance, is the model of this relation to the uncanny that is expressed in the enigma.... [U]nder the sign of the Sphinx must be placed every theory of the symbol that, refusing the model of Oedipus, focusses its attention above all on the barrier between signifier and signified that constitutes the original problem of signification.

He goes on to call this, following Aristotle on the symbol, "a connection of impossibles, not a relation of manifestations."

For Emerson, this sense of the word as a site of connected impossibles, impossible connections, has partly to do with his recognition of the endless conflict between knowledge and knowing. The "Divinity School Address" registers a moment when the forms of knowledge (call them Christianity, or Unitarianism, or Hegelian Idealism) are no longer adequate to the act of knowing, or worse, negate it, when knowing, your knowing and my knowing, is discredited by the perfection of knowledge that proposes to have completed it, as if it weren't something we did every day. Within that perfection, what Robert Creeley in his introduction to *The Holy Forest* calls "skillfully accomplished enclosure," Emerson found a skepticism that separates us from the act of knowing which is always, as he has it elsewhere, drawing a new circle that constitutes our further self. "Men have come to speak of the revelation as somewhat long ago given and done," Emerson writes, "as if God were dead," where what he here calls God dwells and means precisely in a connection of impossibles: "The child amidst his baubles is learning the action of light, motion, gravity, muscular force; and in the game of human life, love, fear, justice, appetite, man, and God, interact."

If we seem to hear in the rumbling of this cleavage between knowing and doubting the distant echo of some ancient quarrel about poetry and philosophy, this rumour seems borne out all the more given the response to Emerson's talk. As Robert Richardson reports in his biography of Emerson, the Harvard Unitarian elite, led by Andrews Norton, launched a vociferous public attack on him in the press, accusing him of "vagueness, inconsistency, impiety, nonsense, infidelity, blasphemy, and 'foulest atheism'". It was thirty years before he was again invited to speak at Harvard.

Emerson then set about inventing something we could call "a new thinking", a new wording of the world, one that dwelled in the imagination of a healing of that wound. This thinking constantly tinkers with incommensurability, a mechanics of splendour where we understand that brilliance to lurk in each of these words, waiting to found a world, where finding, as Stanley Cavell has it, is founding and what we have to find is right under our noses.

Two ways forward present themselves here, both of which lead to Robin Blaser's work and what it has given us. One way heads off through the common world Emerson reclaimed for philosophy, a reclamation aimed to challenge both traditional philosophy's highfalutin disdain of it and Jacksonian democracy's opportunistic degradation of it (a degradation we hear daily in the clamour for the purity of some "outside" of politics that will finally fix the problems of democracy). This common is the central topic of the *Essays* which open "There is one mind common to all individual men." Common as shared, common as ordinary, as commonplace, it dwells in communicable, in communion, in community, rendered available to all.

The other way heads off through abandonment and transition as the essential features of our condition. "This one fact the world hates," Emerson famously says, "that the soul becomes." This becoming which forever destroys the "past" even as it preserves it, is the face of eternity in time. It undoes all attempts to hold time to a set use, even as it cuts us loose with no home to give us succor. One of these paths has to do with what kind of words we choose, the other with how we get from one word to the next, and what we think to do with them. Together they propose a constitution, a habitation adequate to the possibilities of this place and, Emerson believed, the people we are, which is the people we might be.

Last night I got into an argument at the pub with a poet of Blaser's generation but not of his inclination as writer. It was an old argument, tiresome, really. What is the relationship of form and act? My interlocutor described the different poetries at stake in terms of the old Levi-Straussian distinction between "raw" and "cooked" poetry, as if it was an issue of finish. And in a way it is, though not quite, I think, the way he intended. When Emerson in "Experience" reminds us of the evanescence and lubricity of that which we would clutch, he speaks, among other things, to the idea of such a finish, both the texture of the surface, its finish, and the mode of limitation that determines its final form—how it finishes. Writing either addresses it or doesn't. Emerson addressed it in every word, hence the extraordinary experience of reading his language that repels even as it provides continual flashes of profound insight, a surface that denies our desire to clutch or hold, which Emerson calls "the most unhandsome part of our condition," even as it provides a sense of elusive coherence. The Harvard elite called it mistiness. I would call it a surface finish which refuses finish, or refuses to finish.

"Image-Nation 24 ('oh, pshaw'," brings us into the American world of just such a proposition. It works and reworks the facts of that life in a long meditation on the forming and informing of the poet's being and on the god-lore, as he puts it, in all of its manifestations, that everywhere accompanied and interacted with it. The poem delivers us to a world of astonishing details, details in which the common and the marvelous are indistinguishable, in which they, it, constitutes the simple matter of life, of any life. The "drat!" which opens the poem and resonates throughout the body of its words, draws us into a labyrinth of thinking and sounds, of sounded thinking, the splendour of which, like the lingering democratized god in drat, is all too often lost to monotony.

In *The Bow and the Lyre*, Octavio Paz, another transplanted denizen of America, invokes André Breton to get at the strangeness of this common world: "Breton has said: la véritable existence est ailleurs. That elsewhere is here, always here and in this moment." Emerson envisioned just such an elsewhere-here which activates the common world, charges it with difference, dissolving and dispersing the Authority which otherwise would condemn the world to monotony. In his America, which is the America we encounter in the words of Blaser's poem, "a new yet unapproachable America" as Emerson has it in "Experience," democracy is exactly the "drat" of Blaser's memory and imagination, the intricate implication of that thinking the other into our daily exclamations, these very ordinary noises, and especially the frustration of this one. Octavio Paz, again, another American whose thinking is so much a part of this marvelous tinkering, goes on to write: "Real life opposes neither the quotidian nor the heroic life: it is the perception of the spark of otherness in each one of our acts, not excluding the most trivial. These states are often massed together under a name I consider inexact: the spiritual experience."

Lingering here in the democracy of these words, of Blaser's words, which is now a kind of bridge, or let's say, bridging, as in the bridging that has woven itself in and out of attention here in relation to sundry cleavages and gaps. Whatever the shores such a bridging brings together (not the least of which are the shores of the phonemes which are the constitution of this sense), Hart Crane reminds us of the marvel of the flight, the bridging, itself:

> Through the bound cable strands, the arching path
> Upward, veering with light, the flight of strings,–
> Taut miles of shuttling moonlight syncopate
> The whispered rush, telepathy of wires.
> Up the index of night, granite and steel–
> Transparent meshes – fleckless the gleaming staves–
> Sibylline voices flicker, waveringly stream
> As though a god were issue of the strings ....

This coming together of flight and song, and their issue in that last suggestive "As though ..." brings us then squarely into Blaser's exody, that moment in "Image-Nation 24" that both closes and opens, and delivers us to "Image-Nation 25," which is also called exody, and throughout which the eyes of the image of the wandering Jew follow us, "into corners—to the end of the boxcar parlour—even into the brilliance of reading under the library table." We are caught in the gaze that Jew—and those others, out of Egypt and heading home—until we find ourselves already there, in the movement itself. "The coming only is sacred,"

Emerson says, locating something called the new as that on which we found (find) our selves , where that is understood as common, ordinary, and the self is always further.

If that exody resonates with the sound of feet shuffling in ancient dust, we can also hear in it a stitching together of songs, an echo of the art of the rhapsode, which returns to that intersection of form and act where I'm caught in the words: movement, abandonment, new and the filiating kinetic of the entanglement of mind, language, world. Especially that turn in Blaser's work, which makes itself felt in the rushing of the breath through these endless lines, in the opening up of the syntax of this common speech into the distances of the high plains of the common heart. Ovid comes to mind, as he often did for Blaser, and the transformations of his carmen perpetuum, or the "quick darting breath" in Blaser's own early poem "Herons", where "...the snake / changes its skin out of honesty." In any case, it's not simply singing as celebration, though that's here too, but singing as knowing, where all these issues are glimpsed, or overheard, in the rising of the human voice out of the depths of a life and into the brilliant air where we follow it.

The H.D. Book

"Today I will allow myself whatever projects of what might come of this mining (You've to dog and come to see what I mean / where I, in that poem, almost wanted to point to that word "come"; because there is something about real thought that is as autonomous as ejaculation; and has the further mystery of the orgasmic if it have spirit)."

—Robert Duncan to Norman Holmes Pearson, July 2, 1960

The H.D. Book is one of the great lost texts of American poetry. In 1959, when he began writing the book, Robert Duncan was already an accomplished and well-known poet, connected with the Berkeley renaissance, the San Francisco renaissance, as well as Black Mountain College and the Beat poets. He had published a number of important works including *Heavenly City, Earthly City, Medieval Scenes, Fragments of a Disordered Devotion, Caesar's Gate, The Venice Poem,* and *Letters,* and was about to appear in Donald Allen's anthology, *The New American Poetry.* His mature work, however, was yet to come. *The H.D. Book* would be the alembic in which it was gestated.

Composed between 1959 to 1964, *The H.D. Book* appeared in little magazines from 1966 to 1985. It was never published as a completed book, however, in Duncan's lifetime. Perhaps *lost* overstates the case, since it was never forgotten, but for some 40 years, the only access to the text was photocopied assemblages of the various little magazine publications treasured and passed from hand to hand by Duncan's loyal readers. A complete, edited version of the book remained elusive, the stuff of endless complaint and speculation.

Duncan began writing *The H.D. Book* when H.D.'s friend and literary executor, Norman Holmes Pearson, asked him for a short homage for H.D. on her birthday in 1960. Duncan had long admired H.D.'s work. As he tells the story in the opening chapter of *The H.D. Book*, her poem "Heat," read to him by a high school English teacher, was his first experience with the magic of poetry, an experience that led him into his lifelong devotion to the art. What began as a simple homage, quickly turned into an epic meditation and exploration of what Duncan felt were neglected dimensions of the history of modernism, as well as the hidden springs that fed its roots and the work of the poets and writers he took as masters: H.D., Ezra Pound, D.H. Lawrence, William Carlos Williams, Edith Sitwell, among others.

Duncan's early work on *The H.D. Book* coincided with his correspondence with H.D. which lasted for about two years (not including an early letter from 1950), from July 1959 until her death in September 1961. Much of the thinking that echoed in the letters Duncan and H.D. exchanged took formal shape in *The H.D. Book*. Talk of myth and Hermetic philosophy mixed with and informed their talk of other poets. Both shared a history of connection to esoteric, repressed spiritual practices, what Wouter Hanegraaff calls "rejected knowledge." H.D. had been raised in the Moravian Church of Count Zinzendorf and during the 1920s had traveled in circles that engaged with magic and spiritualism. Duncan had grown up in a family with a history of relation to Theosophy and spiritualism. This common experience bound them.

More importantly, both had turned away from such practices, although not the knowledge. H.D. wrote to Duncan how Yeats and his wife, Georgie, had invited her to Oxford—presumably to participate in a Rosicrucian ritual—but "something held me back." Duncan interpreted this as "the disinterest of a growing thing for possibilities outside its law, its real," and proposed that Yeats (unlike H.D.) seemed not to have known "the numinous woodland and shoreland, the events of god outside the ritual." Duncan, an inveterate anarchist, maintained his commitment to an inner law, often, if not always, opposed by an outer law, a demand by society to conform to its practices, even when they were the rituals of obscure cults. What Duncan and H.D. learned from their youthful experience was not a set of beliefs or practices dictated by churches or cults, but a deep sense of the possibility of other modes of knowing the world. These modes of thinking, grounded in the freedom of the imagination, were fed by lost or excluded material, material deemed silly or superstitious or heretical by a society whose forms of life dictated a totalitarian "normality" based on scientific materialism. For both poets, the matrix for poetry was in the spaces between those given forms where life escaped dogma. They shared a commitment not to the *this* or the *not this*, not to the *self* or the *other*, but to the fissure from which such forms arise into the conditioned contingencies of the given.

These recognitions held important political implications for Duncan, whose anarchism arose out of an Emersonian commitment to a further self, a self whose moral perfectionism led Duncan toward the recovery of what had been lost or forgotten, as part of his commitment to the fullness of the world—what he called, "What Is." His sense of the world's uncontainable wildness was linked to his resistance to the suffocating culture of bourgeois conformity he knew from his youth in Bakersfield, California. His pacifism—which went hand in hand with his anarchism—grew out of that, as did his attention to what was not known, or not allowed to be known, rejected or forbidden knowledge, modes of being subject to repression and erasure, among other things, say, the obscured sign of his homosexuality in the official constellations of the culture. The hidden from sight. The occult.

If there is a master word that haunts the thinking in *The H.D. Book*, it is, in just this sense, *occult*. In a letter to James Broughton in Notebook 5 at Berkeley, Duncan wrote how he wanted to compose "a poetry with the meaning entirely occult, that is—with the meaning is containd not as a jewel is containd in a box but as the inside of a box is containd in a box." In, call it *Bakersfield*, modernity had realized itself in a social world of drastically constricted possibility. "The agreement of reasonable men was to quarantine the fever of thought," he wrote. The collective imagination of its own "virtue" gave that world permission to impose a strict sense of the "normal" (not to be confused with the "ordinary") on the community. Part of that normality is the acceptance of a given world without depth, what has been called a *disenchanted world*, referring to the Enlightenment's legacy of equating the "real" with the material and the commensurable, a world restricted to measurable quantities.

"Occult" is a loaded word in such a culture. The restricted vision that dominates the idea of knowledge in such a world gives rise to counter impulses that result in illicit or scandalous traditions of cults with elaborate theologies and ritual practices. Hanegraaff calls the language associated with these traditions "tainted terminology" along with "magic" and "superstition." Illicit theologies and ritual practices are identified as "the Occult" and deemed ridiculous superstitions. But beyond the organized ritual cults lay all that is outside the limits of the "normal;" worlds of hidden fact, hidden history, hidden mind, hidden body, as if all of us live on the edge of an occult reality that is really quite ordinary.

Duncan's reading of Freud located Freud's unconscious as just such an occult reality, a site of mysterious energy and impulse that shapes our daily lives while remaining below the threshold of consciousness. Much of that energy is libidinal, and for Duncan, tied to the traditional knowledge of Eros rooted in ancient human experience and banned and repressed by Judeo-Christian doctrine. Another central issue is the patriarchal dismissal of the authority of both actual women and that range of human experience traditionally identified as the "feminine". Occulted beneath layers of patriarchal authority, one result of that diminishment was the repression of the knowledge of the leading role women writers played in the invention of modernism. At a time when anthologies and university reading lists contained almost entirely male authors, Duncan argued for the centrality of women in those ranks. He was a pioneer in singling out and tracking down the work of Edith Sitwell, Mary Butts, Djuna Barnes, Dorothy Richardson, Mina Loy, and Laura Riding and arguing for their importance as the hidden authors of modernism.

H.D. was the main focus of this revelation. At the time Duncan began writing *The H.D. Book* in 1960, H.D. had been dismissed from the ranks of serious poets by the official arbiters of literary taste and had largely disappeared from public recognition. Until the 1950s her reputation had rested, however incorrectly and fragilely, on her ongoing identification as the quintessential "Imagist," a hangover from her work of 35 years earlier. Then Randall Jarrell and Dudley Fitts publicly dismissed H.D.'s *Tribute to the Angels* (1945) and *Flowering of the Rod* (1946), characterizing her visionary poetry, as Duncan notes several times in *The H.D. Book*, as "silly." Following that, Karl Shapiro and Richard Wilbur dropped H.D. completely from the 1955 edition of Louis Untermeyer's influential anthology, *Modern American and Modern British Poetry*, thus banishing even her Imagist poems from the halls of academically acceptable poetry. She became lost, occulted to the official world of poetry, her work out of print, her memory kept alive by a few dedicated readers.

The H.D. Book, in one sense, was an effort to undo that injustice, that occultation. Duncan humorously imagines himself several times as a knight coming to rescue H.D.'s honour with her scarf tied on his arm. In the process of unpacking the hidden assumptions and judgments that led to Jarrell's condemnation of H.D. as "silly," Duncan found himself increasingly caught up in the revelation of further lost or hidden dimensions in the history of modernism. Duncan's recovery of an occulted H.D. began specifically with a poem, "Heat," which, like the scent of the *madeleine* in Proust's novel, opened into a cosmos, as if it were a seed, and that cosmos, that world, was hidden within it. In his revisions to Chapter 1, Duncan eventually added an epigraph from A. E. Waite's book on the Rosicrucians:

> As regards the Lost Word, it is explained that the sun at autumn has lost its power and Nature is rendered mute, but the star of day at the spring tide resumes its vital force, and this is the recovery of the Word, when Nature with all her voices, speaks and sings, even as the Sons of God shouted for joy in the perfect morning of the cosmos.

Both Waite and Duncan are playing the idea of Morning against the notion of Enlightenment. In "Ideas of the Meaning of Form," Duncan writes: "The crisis of the Enlightenment was the crisis Keats saw recapitulated in Coleridge's collapse from the inspiration of 'The Ancient Mariner' and 'Cristobel' to the psychic despair, the rationalist obsession, of later years."

This invocation of the "lost word" marked Duncan's entrance into a world of hidden things—lost words—coming to light, the light of a recovered Word, a perfect morning: the hidden memory of Miss Keough's classroom, the hidden (esoteric) writing presented by the teacher to the few students worthy of it, the hidden intensities of feeling brought to mind by the poem, the hidden worlds of thought behind the stultifying bourgeois superficialities of Bakersfield, and the hidden meaning of "image" behind it all. "The poem had a message, hidden to me then," Duncan wrote, "that I felt but could not translate, an unconscious alliance that made for something more than a sensual response.... More than sensation then, more than impression, gave force to the image. It was not only a vivid representation of sensory data but an evocation of depth." The depth of the world was hidden, brought out by Duncan's meditation on "image" and "imagism." "There is a crucial difference between the doctrine of the Image where Poetry itself is taken to be a primary ground of experience and meaning in life, and the image which is taken as a fashion in the literary world." This thinking then led him to a tradition that goes back to Renaissance and Medieval Hermeticism, the Troubadours and the *trobar clus*, Hellenistic Neo-Platonism, Gnosticism, and Arabic angelology, in which Images (and the Imagination which is their ground) mediate between another world and this, open this world to hidden powers.

Occult histories, occult teachings, occult memories, occult mind, occult inheritances, occult language, and above all, occult meanings—Robert Duncan unfolded them all in *The H.D. Book* in a proliferating, symphonic performance of, as he puts it in a letter to Norman Holmes Pearson, thinking as orgasm, thinking as an explosive release linked to Eros, rather than the traditional notion of a disciplined exposition, Logos, with footnotes and citations. The importance of *hiddenness* itself unfolded along with them, orchestrated into a weave of shadow and light—in corners and at the far edges of the mind, where a certain kind of light or enlightenment cannot, or at least will not, reach, playing itself out in shadows dancing. What is hidden is constantly brought into the light of the language of the poet, a frail light, finite, playing over the face of what is hidden, bringing it to attention. That is, after all, the poet's craft—to bring what is hidden to our attention while honouring its hiddenness.

At the heart of this concern with the occult was Duncan's quest for, as he puts it, a poetics. Duncan pushed his sense of "a poetic" far beyond a concern with literary criticism and literary theory. The Oxford English Dictionary has "poetics," as "the branch of knowledge that deals with the techniques of poetry." This notion of knowledge and technique is closer to Duncan's intent, but even here knowledge must be understood in the fullness of its etymon, *gna*, the *gna* at the heart of gnosis and knowing which has to do with the apprehension of that which is beyond the Logos, what the Logos necessarily excludes, leaves hidden. Technique follows from that. Allen Ginsberg's mantra (via Chogyam Trungpa)—"first thought best thought"—resonates here. Duncan was uninterested in Ginsberg's temporal focus—he worked, reworked, and then revised his reworkings, some might say obsessively, always pushing toward a more finely honed articulation. But the *first* remained shining through all that.

For Duncan, it was more specifically a question of opening to the occult dwelling in the first, of responding to what is hidden in every moment, in order to reveal the plenum of the world, both the visible and the invisible. If Ginsberg found that in the spontaneous, the unedited, Duncan found it in the immersion of mind in the process of creative release—thinking as orgasm.

In this sense, knowledge and technique are wed to vision as it extends beyond the visible, the materially commensurable to, say, the visionary. Duncan's sense of a *poetics* was rooted in the recognition that what is seen is always already informed, full of form that determines what is seen and how it is seen, even though the forms may remain hidden. His proposal had to do with the claim that arose from the Enlightenment's argument with the *ancien régime*, that the knowable is limited to the commensurable, and that the incommensurable is what came to be called "superstition." Only in the late 18th century did "superstition" move from a sense of idolatrous religious practice to a sense of any "irrational" belief (including religion). This grounding of knowledge in the material and rational was part of a vision of the cosmos as matter in motion bound by laws, a vision that went on to determine the culture of the West in modernity. Duncan's quest for a poetics was a quest to extend his vision beyond those limits to include all that such a culture excludes or hides from itself, as well as what those selves who were formed in such a culture are blind to.

In Book One of *The H.D. Book*, Duncan pursued this opening through its multiple implications, sketching out the great themes that run through the book by tracing them in H.D.'s work: hidden or lost traditions of thinking about Eros, hidden or lost modes of organizing time and space, hidden or lost modes of self or person, hidden or lost understandings of the source and nature of form, and finally the profound sense of exile that is the lot of the poet who undertakes to recognize and recover these lost things. Duncan was led on in these inquiries by his ongoing argument that the dismissal and occultation of H.D. arose from the unexamined belief, in fact the delusion, that the terms of Realism, as an aesthetic doctrine grounded in and grounding the culture of modernity, were "real," where "real" marks a reduced and utterly measurable world.

Duncan argued for an expanded sense of the "real": "The crux for the poet is to make real what is only real in a heightened sense. Call it his personal feeling, or the communal reality, it exists only in its dance, only to its dancers." Again and again, Duncan comes back to Randall Jarrell's dismissal of H.D.'s great visionary poems of World War II, written in London during the Blitz. In what came to be known as her war trilogy, H.D. presented the violence of the war as rooted not in politics or economics, but in a cosmic spiritual conflict. The forces of light and darkness, life and death, battled it out over London in H.D.'s poem resembling the powers described in ancient Gnostic gospels. Gods played out eternal struggles. Angels came and went bearing messages of hope. Old narratives of death and resurrection reasserted themselves in mundane events. And through it all, the poet asserted the experienced reality of the vision, identifying herself with the prophet John of the *Book of Revelations*, and his simple declaration: "I, John, testify." Randall Jarrell dismissed this testimony as "silly," by which he meant frivolous and unworthy of serious consideration. Duncan located that word in its etymological roots and used that to reveal the shallowness of Jarrell's philosophical/cultural grounding. Jarrell became, in that sense, along with his cohort, representative of modernity's arrogant superficiality, its insistence that only the visible, not the visionary, is *real*, and its subsequent "desecration of the psyche in the definition of reality set by the Protestant ethic …."

In Book One of *The H.D. Book*, these themes are explicated in the form of digressive essays which identify what Duncan calls "the stars and their potential patterns," a metaphor he develops in Book Two, through which hidden forms emerge in the sky, constellations of the mind, forms that bind Tiamat, the dragon of chaos. At the heart of it stand H.D., Pound, and Williams, that configuration of poets, that constellation of stars, who led Duncan into the permissions of poetry. Around them circulate the lights of others—Freud, Joyce, Arnaut, Blavatsky, Lawrence, Yeats, Dante, Frazer, Stein, Mead, Harrison, Nietzsche, Browning, Avicenna, Malraux, Plutarch, Plato, Iamblichus, Corbin, Apuleius … the circle expands in its complexities as Duncan tracks the relationships that defined the emergence of this possibility of poetry not to "describe" the world, but to ground it in "the dissolving of the boundaries of time," to rouse the form and content of the world "as the ritual devotee seeks to arouse the content and form of the god."

In Book Two Duncan left the essay behind and moved to a new form—and the idea of form is central here—the daybook. The daybook reintroduced time as an element of form, locating thinking in its temporal fragility—its finitude—even as it subverted the temporal by repeatedly returning to the same issues from different angles. This repetition, which some have criticized as if it were a question of bad "style," was an expression of Duncan's growing sense of the open-ended nature of his undertaking as his quest for a poetics began to absorb the lessons of his first essays into what he called the *Opus*. To return again and again was his method. With each return, new facets of meaning stand revealed, new depths of thought get plumbed. His understanding of "palimpsest" is at the heart of this. In the opening of Chapter 7 which is dated with multiple dates (October 8, 1964 and March 20, 1961) in his last revision, he wrote:

> I seek now in working upon the later draft of the book not to correct the original but to live again in its form and content, leaving in successive layers record of reformations and digressions as they come to me. The form realized then is not to be a design immediately striking, like those housing developments and landscapings that rise where disorderly areas of a city have been cleared away, but it may be like an old city—Freud's picture of Rome upon Rome—in which in the earliest remains, in the diary of March 10th to March 15th, March 20th to March 29th, then May 25th of 1961: later additions may appear, anachronistically like the Gaudi restorations in the gothic cathedral of Palma or the Casa Guell's art-nouveau romanticism in the midst of old buildings, where we are aware of periods of creative activity and conservative inertia.

These accretions are revelatory. Each passage opens the work to the further emergence of still hidden form and content. No singular "meaning" exists to be recovered, only the potentiality for further meaning to be encountered. Meaning is not a sum to be arrived at, but an ongoing engagement unfolding in the poet's language. As Emerson, anticipating Duncan by some 125 years, pointed out in the address to the Harvard Divinity School that got him banned from speaking at the university for 30 years, "Men have come to speak of the revelation as somewhat long ago given and done," going on to argue that like the "refulgent spring" (which is of the mind as the mind is of the world) with which he opens the essay, only a continually renewed opening to the "moral sentiment," a commitment to knowing rather than knowledge, can keep the revelation alive and full of meaning.

Book Two became an enactment of the dynamics discussed in Book One, or more accurately, the discussions of Book One, the essays, were converted into the form of their contents, form that goes on to continually recast and renew the contents, or perhaps to resituate the contents as emerging form. In his essay "Towards an Open Universe," he proposes that "[w]e do not make things meaningful, but in our making we work towards an awareness of meaning; poetry reveals itself to us as we obey the orders that appear in the work." Duncan's analysis of Roheim's Freudian study of the ritual practices of the Arunda in Book One, became an opening into an actual ritual invocation of the forms and powers hidden within Duncan's thinking of H.D., forms and powers that daily and momently erupted into the poet's consciousness, emerged from his language.

Dream became increasingly important as a channel for the emergence of hidden information, unconscious content, occult meaning, roiling to the surface of thought, as in the Sally Rand episode that runs through Chapter 8. Emerging from sleep, Duncan jotted down the remnants of a dream of which he remembered only an image—caressing H.D.'s naked back—and the words, SALLY RAND, words that left him feeling uneasy, even repulsed. Sally Rand, the name of an infamous fan dancer, initially seemed to offer Duncan nothing. But working and reworking the material, the words began to yield. What they yielded was a field of thinking in which each moment bloomed with a new significance, a new form erupting from the language that had unknowingly contained it. It is a masterful performance of the very ritual engagement Duncan had written about in Book One.

When Duncan began *The H.D. Book*, much of the literary history that he recovered had been suppressed or ignored by the institutional Literature police. His concern, especially with the work of the women who were so central to the invention of modernism, was unprecedented. Edith Sitwell, Laura Riding, Djuna Barnes, Mary Butts, and Dorothy Richardson, had all largely disappeared from any common awareness, ignored by the almost entirely male cohort of professors who collected anthologies and wrote literary histories, patrolling the boundaries of Literature. That history was part of the occult content he sought to bring to light. And while his discussions of the work of Pound and Williams, of Yeats and Eliot and Lawrence, are a significant contribution to the criticism of modernism, his focus was not on the literary, but again on those aspects of the work and its context that were considered out of bounds by the strict moralisms of the New Criticism.

The H.D. Book is fundamentally neither a work of literary criticism nor literary history. Nor is it, as some have proposed, an attempt to articulate a literary theory. In fact, the book is deeply anti-literary in just about every way possible. In the same vein, although it delves into the thinking of various esoteric cults including Theosophy, Hermeticism, Rosicrucianism, Neo-Platonism, Gnosticism, and psychoanalysis, it is neither a Theosophical nor a Hermetic nor a psychoanalytic text. Duncan's concern throughout was to create a space, an opening, into which the hidden, the occult, could emerge. Long before the wave of post-War European philosophical thinkers entered the awareness of North American academics, Duncan was already exploring the significant moves they were to make to reopen the world to the multiple realities foreclosed by modernity's singular Real. The indeterminacy of meaning, readerly texts, the diversity and multiplicity of the truths of the world, the fluid boundaries of "time" and "space," the fictional subject, all these openings into those dimensions rendered occult by the disciplinary institutions of modernity, were the playgrounds of his thinking.

His goal was straightforward—to achieve a poetics. For Duncan, the idea that poetry could arise from a theory—be it a theory of linguistic production, a theory of economic production, or a theory of psychic production—was not only ridiculous, it profoundly damaged the spirit of poetry. Poetry for Duncan was always inextricably implicated with *What Is*, his designation of the world's uncontainable plenitude. And that plenum was fully determined, at any given moment, only with the admission of what was outlawed, repressed, excluded, ignored—what was hidden. This is the occult reality that defines the unfolding engagement of *The H.D. Book*. No theory can approach that. Instead, a poet, a maker, must find/forge a methodology that allows *What Is* to emerge, to find forms. Just as there is no singular Truth that can be theorized, there is no singular methodology. Each poet must find their own way into that process. It is a spiritual ordeal.

As he pursued this quest through the writing of *The H.D. Book*, Duncan published *The Opening of the Field* (1960) and began to compose what many feel are his mature works—*Roots and Branches* (1964) and *Bending the Bow* (1968). Out of impatience with the distractions of the competitiveness and careerism that took over "the poetry scene" in the 1970s, Duncan vowed not to publish for 15 years, even as he continued to work on his final masterpieces. In 1984 he finally published *Groundwork–Before the War*, but died before its companion volume, *Groundwork–In the Dark* made it into print in 1987. All of this work springs from the remarkable quest for a poetics recorded in *The H.D. Book*. "The poet and the reader," Duncan wrote, "who if he is intent in reading becomes a new poet of the poem, come to write or to read in order to participate through the work in a consciousness that moves freely in time and space and can entertain reality upon reality." *The H.D. Book* is a unique record of such a journey.

H.D., Robert Duncan, and the Question of the Occult

It has become acceptable, even essential, in the last several decades, to speak of an occult tradition that contributed significantly to the development of modernism. Such a thinking of tradition invokes a particular world, not unlike what Eliot invoked in "Tradition and the Individual Talent"—a world, at the very least, of authoritative texts whose influence arises out of a handing down from one writer to another. Others—you could say—consume this influence, learn it, absorb it, mentally ingest it, reproducing and altering the information at the same time, and often using it as the basis not only of writing, but of whole sets of institutionalized practices.

Demetres Tryphonopoulos has usefully and thoroughly summed up this occult tradition. In a series of "begets," Tryphonopoulos moves from the religio-magical cults of antiquity to the Greek—Oriental synthesis of late Hellenism, through Orphism to Pythagorianism, Gnosticism, Neo-Platonism, Catharism, Cabalism, Hermeticism, Alchemy, Rosicrucianism, Freemasonry, Mesmerism, Swedenborgianism, Spiritualism, and Theosophy, linking them eventually to the work of Yeats, Pound, H.D., Eliot and others. He is careful to point out how heterodox and fluid the transmissions are. Even so, the sense of continuity, or of a "movement" as he calls it in the title to his essay, is overwhelming.

But an unspoken question haunts this catalog of myriad names. Where does this perennial interest come from? What maintains the steady transmission of these texts? Some have attributed its longevity to a disenchantment with modernity's secularism, but the tradition predates modernity, as Tryphonopoulos' list testifies. Is it possible to consider this question outside the bounds set out by the idea of the "occult tradition" itself? Something here resonates with a moment within the correspondence between Robert Duncan and H.D., a knot of meaning in which Duncan establishes the ground of their bond in a mutual relation to the occult that is outside the sense of continuity or tradition. In fact, Duncan's very sense of the authenticity of their bond lies in an aversion to it. On October 27, 1960, H.D. wrote to Duncan how Yeats and his wife had invited her to Oxford to participate in an occult ritual, but something held her back. Writing back to H.D. on October 31, Duncan notes his own "holding back" from the Hermetic Brotherhood of his adoptive parents: "... what I wanted to write was the rightness of what held you back, that prepared you, instinct for life or of life." Later, in The H.D. Book, he sums it up this way: "... I am unbaptized, uninitiated, ungraduated, unanalyzed. I had in mind that my worship belonged to no church, that my mysteries belonged to no cult, that my learning belonged to no institution, that my imagination of my self belonged to no philosophic system. My thought must be without sanction." And I wonder what he meant when he wrote that the holding back is an "instinct for life or of life?"

The question of belief is important in considering these questions. Almost universally, the critics and scholars who in the last 25 years have turned the occult into a major determining dimension of modernism, invariably refer to a "belief," or the "adoption of a belief." Even someone as sympathetic as Tryphonopoulos refers to "theories and practices" in defining the occult, to a "hidden gnosis" understood as a body of knowledge, and to a "heterodox mixture of a relatively small set of doctrines" which imply a relation of something called "belief." Leon Surette, in his book on the birth of modernism, defines the occult as metaphysical speculation "about the nature of ultimate reality and our relation to it" and states that the "touchstone" for distinguishing the occult from other traditions is "a belief that throughout human history certain individuals have had intimate contact with the divine ...." He goes on to write of the display of "occult beliefs," in Yeats' and Mead's work, and eventually to the proposal of the "ubiquitous occult belief that true wisdom belongs to the remote past when man was close to his divine origin." Devin Johnston takes it a step further by referring, in relation to Robert Duncan, to "using dictation as a dramatic staging." Helen Sword refers to H.D.'s early visionary experiences as "figments of her imagination" and says of

H.D.'s Second World War communications with the dead that "she believed" them to be from dead R.A.F. pilots.

There are many points where you could argue with these various characterizations of the occult, but for me, the most important issue is not in those details but in the definition of the relation to them as one of belief. Unacknowledged in these discussions is the fact that this language implicitly carries with it a specific cosmology that is at odds with the phenomena it proposes to explain.

Philosophy has a long and complex engagement with the idea of belief, one that tends to merge at a certain point with a psychological engagement. The discourse tends to focus on the difference between belief and knowledge and the distinction between true and false beliefs. Philosophy traces this discussion back to the rationalism of Socrates, who attempted in his dialogs to bring his interlocutor to the recognition of certain false beliefs which obscured his relation to the truth. To believe in something is to regard it, rightly or wrongly, as true.

But the meaning of the word "believe" in English has shifted radically in the past, and especially with the full onset of modernity in the 16th century. Previous to that moment it was related to love and meant literally to hold dear where lief meant beloved, precious, agreeable. To believe in God in that context was not to assert that God existed against the claims of skeptics. It was to declare your love for God, or as Wilfred Smith argued in *Belief and History*, to pledge yourself to God.

> The affirmation "I believe in God" used to mean: "Given the reality of God as a fact of the universe, I hereby pledge to him my heart and soul. I committedly opt to live in loyalty to Him. I offer my life to be judged by Him, trusting His mercy." Today the statement may be taken by some as meaning: "Given the uncertainty as to whether there be a God or not, as a fact of modern life, I announce that my opinion is 'yes'. I judge God to be existent."

The transformation of the word came with the growth of the authority of science over the determination of what is and is not true, the shifting sense of what constitutes knowledge. As knowledge became identified with the commensurable, with certitude and factuality, belief became more and more identified with the realm of fantasy and even delusion. Materialism, empiricism, and scientific positivism render knowledge as a function of measure. This is premised on the idea that there is an objective which is distinctly other than the subjective and that the subject can realistically measure the object. Smith points to the entry for belief in the Random House dictionary: defined as a conviction or opinion, the example is "the belief that the word is flat." No one, Smith points out, can reasonably be described as "believing the world is round." So "belief" becomes a marker for not-knowledge.

What does it mean, then, to say that H.D. and Duncan "believed in the occult?" Well, first of all, it means that they could just as reasonably—probably more reasonably—not have believed in the occult. In fact, although these critics are careful not to judge this belief as true or false, reasonable or delusional, the associated sense of delusion always hovers around the word. Secondly, it means there is "an occult" to believe in (or not believe in), a thing, a body of tenets or propositions, secret knowledge, even as Johnston has it, a set of gestures, that are recorded in a collection of texts. Above all, it imposes on our perception, our thought of this relationship, a deep structural sense of an "objective world" within which an "observing subject" operates. Within this world, to say that you believe in something is to simultaneously say that you don't know it, that you can't prove it.

This is not the world that Duncan and H.D. shared. On the contrary, it is the world they shared an aversion to, to use an Emersonian term, and the recognition of that aversion is the basis of the relationship. Emerson is apropos here because he was the first American thinker to move beyond the frame that these terms erect in the mind and propose a New World, as it were, a new thinking of and with the world. Emerson's aversion is raised in relation to the idea of something he calls conformity, and although much of that great essay "Self-Reliance" locates conformity in relation to a world of manners and morality, it becomes clear as it progresses that the stake is much larger. "The civilized man," he wrote, in "Self-Reliance,"

> has built a coach, but has lost the use of his feet. He is supported on crutches, but lacks so much support of the muscle. He has got a fine Geneva watch, but he has lost the skill to tell the hour by the sun. A Greenwich nautical almanac he has, and so being sure of the information when he wants it, the man in the street does not know a star in the sky. The solstice he does not observe; the equinox he

> knows as little; and the whole bright calendar of the year is without a dial in his mind.

Or you could say our modes of being necessarily carry with them restrictions that limit, or define, the world we find ourselves in, that we conform to. What is then lost to vision constitutes something that could be called the occult. In any case, it is hidden from the vision of those who conform to the world as defined by coaches, clocks, and almanacs.

Let's turn the tables here for a moment and locate the structures of belief as part of a particular visionary relation to the world in which much of it is lost to our sight, our vision. Henry Corbin, the great scholar of Islamic philosophy and the visionary imagination, put it this way: "We are discovering that the I and the World, the modes of being of the personal subject and the regions of being which it explores, are not two things which get juxtaposed, but presences within each other, an interpresence, an indissoluble correlation, and a structure." Emerson gives it a slightly different twist:

Thoughtless people contradict as readily the statement of perceptions as of opinions, or rather much more readily; for they do not distinguish between perception and notion. They fancy that I choose to see this or that thing. But perception is not whimsical, but fatal.... For my perception of it is as much a fact as the sun.

When Duncan appealed to H.D.'s aversion to attending Yeats' seance, and compared it to his own holding back from his family's Theosophical beliefs, he was suggesting not so much an epistemological bond as an ontological one. He and H.D., he was saying, are in another world, a region of being that is immediate and actual. It is a world of correspondences in which various modes of being—physical, spiritual, celestial—correspond to each other, in which sense circulates in unprecedented and unanticipated forms. It is not a question of belief or textual transmission. It is a question of seeing beyond the Given. In *The Voyage and the Messenger*, Corbin proposes it as a "mode of being," as if the way we know is a register of the way we are.

> ... your mode of understanding reveals your mode of being, and ... the significance revealed in your manner of understanding is dependent on your mode of being. This provides a very clear distinction between, on the one hand, a type of philosophical thinking which

> proceeds indifferently from any sort of contingent object, subjecting it to logical operations; and on the other hand, a subtle growth of transparence, linked to something unique, and whose rigor consists of this very uniqueness.

The very idea of the occult for us carries with it the permanent sense of scandal. There is no escaping it, and in fact, the scandal is often a large part of its attraction for some people. Partly for that reason Duncan, in a chapter called "Occult Matters" in *The H.D. Book*, affectionately but critically looks at the very tradition lately discovered by the critics. But almost as if in response to the misapprehensions woven through that occult tradition, he expands and transforms the range of the occult to address all that is esoteric, all that is hidden from us but shapes our lives, like dark matter or dark energy affects the gravitational field of the universe and everything in it. In Book 1 Duncan writes about occult knowledges of Eros, time, space, self, form and exile, all the fundamental aspects of our lives, as if to open the idea of the occult beyond the scandalous to include the ordinary, in so far as our ordinary lives are haunted by these matters that we are unaware of, that we fail to see.

Esoteric is of more use here than occult in thinking of what bound H.D. and Duncan. Commenting on Suhrawardi, the 12th century Iranian philosopher, Corbin wrote, "there is the fundamental contrast of the opposition between batin (esoteric) and zahir (exoteric). The esoteric, the hidden, manifests itself while yet remaining veiled as part of the exoteric—that is to say, within that which is apparent to everyone from the first." Like the occult, the esoteric is hidden, but it is not the stasis of a tradition or a body of knowledge. The esoteric exists in relation to a process of revelation and vision that is not predetermined in some dogma or belief or set of texts, but is always available in some new form to those who are open to it.

In *The Sword Went Out to Sea*, one of three texts she referred to as her Commedia (books that Duncan sadly never had the chance to read), H.D. enacts a process that is remarkably similar to what Henry Corbin, in discussing the visionary recovery of the esoteric in *Avicenna and the Visionary Recital*, identifies as a ta'wil, an unveiling through a spiritual hermeneutic or exegesis.

> Ta'wil usually forms with tanzil a pair of terms and notions that are at once complementary and contrasting. Tanzil properly designates

> positive religion, the letter of the Revelation dictated to the Prophet by the Angel. It is to cause the descent of the Revelation from the higher world. Ta'wil is, etymologically and inversely, to cause to return, to lead back, to restore to one's origin and to the place where one comes home, consequently to return to the true and original meaning of a text.

This is the process H.D. performed in much of her prose, a process that is often confused with a fictional form called the roman á clef. It is a recitation that leads through the writing and rewriting of certain significant events to reveal their deep, spiritual significance, to return them or open them to their origin.

In *The Sword Went Out to Sea*, H.D. wrote: "What is accomplished will be in the writing, but the writing does not matter." H.D.'s exegesis reveals layers of correspondences between elemental forms, the esoteric dimensions of meaning that resonated within certain events that informed her life. The well-known table-tapping episode that is the basis of the material for much of *Sword*, is really irrelevant except as another moment of the eruption of this form, the "truth of the Spirit's revelation to itself." "It was," Delia Alton says, "... a superimposition of the past on the eternal. Out of the legend, the history, the myth of all religions, the white-robed, perfect image had stepped, clad in contemporary garments, to greet me."

H.D., through the persona of Delia Alton, discounts the occult dimension of these events: "... contacting entities from outside," she says, conjecturing on the cause of the delirium that gripped her after the war, "must take it out of one. Provided there are entities from outside. We know so little, nothing at all really, about these things." This is hardly the voice of someone who "believed in the occult." She made this assertion several times during the narrative, as if to answer the critics before they could chirp up with their predictable accusations of silliness or imaginary figments. If it is the staking out of a kind of agnosticism in relation to the immense dark areas of our experience that others identify as the occult, it is not purely negative in its implications. It also affirms the profound evasiveness of the world. It is an implicit commitment to remain open to what is outside, what others tune out; exclude from perception because it doesn't fit into categories of authorized knowledge or made to conform to current modes of official measure.

Call them eruptions of wild sense, where sense is understood, after Jean-Luc Nancy, as the condition that breeds meaning. The imagination does not create them. It is the organ that gives them form. It is not a question of believing or not believing. The question is what do they mean, these images the imagination throws up, informing the world. When Duncan wrote of what prepared "you for, or of life," the life in question, I would argue, is one that is full of this wild sense that often is ignored or invisible. To be prepared "for, or of life," is to meet its mystery with the same embrace you meet its familiarity, to unbind your eyes, as Emerson says. The holding back Duncan noted is a rejection of what Emerson calls "communities of opinion," that make us false in each particular so that our every word chagrins us.

"My life is for itself," Emerson wrote, "and not for a spectacle. I much prefer that it should be of a lower strain, so it be genuine and equal, than that it should be glittering and unsteady." The instinct for, or of life comes into the picture precisely here. There was in fact a relatively broad fascination with alchemical, Hermetic and Theosophical texts among certain circles in the early 20th century (as there was in the 11th, the 15th and the 19th). It was a fascination that led to grand gestures, organizational bureaucracies, ritual performances, even careers. But all this fascination with the texts, with public displays of belief, with ritual magic, and internecine battles between competing organizations were part of what Emerson located as spectacle. As phenomena, such displays were of another order than the bond that Duncan shared with H.D. That was grounded in the living experience of the esoteric reality that informs our lives, the further reality "within that which is apparent to everyone from the first," the ground that gives rise to the perennial interest in the texts. It was lived experience, a life that was open to what Duncan called *What Is.*

H.D.'s Recitals

Although H.D. has been recognised primarily for the invention of imagism and her contributions to the creation of modernist poetries, she was also a serious and prolific prose writer. Like her contemporaries, James Joyce, Virginia Woolf, Gertrude Stein, Dorothy Richardson, Mary Butts, and Djuna Barnes, H.D. saw herself as working to break with the traditional forms of realism, and to reshape fiction toward some active recognition of the terms of life as she encountered them. She published four novels and several novellas and short stories during her life. Judged commercially unviable, several more novels including the three post-war novels she called her "Commedia" remained unpublished until recently.

The novella "Narthex" and the short stories "Ear-Ring," and "Pontikinisi (Mouse Island)" were published during a period of intellectual ferment and introspection for H.D. "Narthex" came out in 1928, two years after her novel *Palimpsest*, written during the early years of her relationship with filmmaker Kenneth McPherson. "Ear-ring" and "Pontikinisi (Mouse Island)" were published in 1932 and 1936, during the years of her analyses with Mary Chadwick, Hans Sachs, and Sigmund Freud. In the same period, she published other prose works including T*he Usual Star*, *Nights*, *Mira-Mare and Kora and Ka*, and *The Hedgehog*, a children's story written for her daughter.

In her early 40s, she was revisiting and rethinking the events of the first half of her life, especially the three remarkable experiences that occurred on her first trip to Greece. After being abandoned by her lover and nearly dying in the flu epidemic of 1918, H.D. was rescued by a young admirer who became her lifelong partner, Winnifred Ellerman (Bryher). After nursing H.D. back to health, Bryher, the daughter of an English shipping magnate, took her and her newborn daughter, Perdita, on a cruise to Greece and Egypt. During the course of the trip, H.D. had three visionary experiences which she wrote and rewrote in a number of different texts over the rest of her life: on the way through the Greek Islands, she encountered a guide, in the form of a fellow passenger, who showed her a vision of dolphins; later, on the same trip while in Corfu, she saw a series of images on the hotel wall; and then witnessed a series of visionary dance scenes with Bryher. These events became central to her thinking of herself as she visited and revisited them, as well as the unfolding configurations of significant relations that followed them. They held an occult meaning that she attempted to reveal through textual exploration in both poetry and prose.

H.D.'s prose has a very specific feel to it. It can almost be claustrophobic at times, especially during this period of her writing, caught up in a mode that rarely concerns itself with descriptions of either a natural or a social world. Like Virginia Woolf in *The Waves* and Gertrude Stein in *Three Lives*, H.D. attempted to recreate an experience of mind at work in language. Like Woolf and Stein, she approached mind in language through a static dynamic (or dynamic stasis) and in forms of repetition which reinforce that, which is to say, nothing much seems to happen though it doesn't happen with a great deal of energy. The sense of a slowly transforming sentence unwinds toward a revelation of deeper meaning, but little in the way of, say, "character development," a key element in the traditional realist novel. In so far as there are events, they are mental. But whereas both Woolf and Stein (and Joyce and Faulkner) locate in their writing a social world not unfamiliar to the novel as literary form (even as they transform their vision of it), H.D. never quite does. With Woolf, you get glimpses of an English world full of the faded grandeur of a disappearing Empire. With Stein, you get glimpses of a young American black girl's physical and social location at the turn of the century. But rarely does H.D. give you even that much, partly because to do so would be to enter the world of the novel.

The novel (and the short story as a development of that form) as a form is tied historically to a mode of perception or understanding that itself reflects a mode of being contracted or restricted within the thought of a singular material world. It has been a laboratory for theorizing the Lockean individual and its relation to Comtean "society" within the parameters of a world of matter in motion. Much of the 19th century was spent grieving that as a terrific loss while revelling in the new forms of self, space, and time it brought into play. By the 20th century, the grief gave way to an exploration of the new freedom and an explosion of new forms. But Joyce, Stein, Woolf, and Faulkner, for all their radical deformations and inventions, never step out of that cosmology. In some ways, those writers' freedom with conventions signalled the end of (the authority of) those conventions, their imminent transformation into something completely different. In other ways though, it endorsed the limits of those forms. *The Waves, Ulysses, Three Lives*, and *The Sound and the Fury*, all push the idea of individuality into contortions of linguistic enactments of mind, but they don't abandon the cosmology in which that individual is crucial to its order and the limit of its knowledge. Different senses of psychology, one of the central "human sciences" that theorizes the dynamics of the individual self, dominate the various attempts to present that self in language. And psyche's defining twin, its perpetual dancing partner, is always something called "society," which is understood as an existential limit determined by the various tyrannizing opinions and hierarchies of relation that make up a world of individuals.

For H.D., the Persons who filled her life were akin to Images. Her relation to the Image as bearer of meaning was determining for much of her life. She first gained recognition as a poet when her early poems were published in 1913 in *Poetry Chicago* under the name, "H.D., Imagiste." Following that she became identified with the movement called Imagism, and her poetry came to define the quintessential imagist poem, even though she quickly moved beyond the limitations of that early work. As with Paul Robson in "Red Roses for Bronze," individuals became powers in the cosmic drama of her life, active images of nodes of sense, unfolding players in a cosmos full of meaning. In some sense, the writing takes place outside time, or rather, in terms of H.D.'s own experience, introduces the Image to time, while simultaneously introducing time to the Image. H.D., even in her most "realist" prose, was never concerned to represent the social dimension of experience. Instead, she came back to certain events, certain moments, an array of selves that she circled around, or in on, as if with each pass she got closer to the meaning that they embodied. These are not "social" lives, "social" selves, or "social" situations. They are hierophantic powers.

H.D. used prose to loosen the stasis of the Image, while maintaining its hierophantic intensity, to move the sense of time away from modernity's relentless historical progression toward a sacred drama, a kind of mystery play. Her relation to D. H. Lawrence provided an early occasion for this writing. She wrote and rewrote various aspects of her life that she associated with the Lawrence Event, producing what she identified as a number of rough drafts, including manuscripts she marked for destruction but which ended up being published as *Paint It Today, HERminone*, and *Asphodel*. *Bid Me to Live* was the final draft of this protracted work, a novel of extraordinary density and complexity missing in the drafts.

In the intensifications that arose out of this new push, the world was (re)constituted as textual deferral in the continual reading and rereading of the events and persons that defined the parameters of her life. Events, in other words, were located as a Text with an esoteric, inner meaning that was accessible through exegesis. But reading was inextricably tied up with writing, and so the repeated recitations yearn after a closer and closer relation to the image extension of the moment—exegesis as a return to meaning:

> She must say something. The only thing that vied, in clarity, with debit and credit, and the idea of numbers ruled on paper, was a flight of silver, that was yet a violin that, with all its exaggerated and emotionally timed rise and fall, swept over their heads, out to the bluer aether. With it, as she watched it, were those sharply defined impressions of columns, cut against blue, against violet, against deep violet, against purple, as the sun sank beyond Lycabettos. Lycabettos rose like a ship about to set sail, Hymettus rested like a ship in harbour. Only the Acropolis remained static, itself a harbour, an island above a city, a city set on a hill, an idea that, in all its eternal and remote dimension, still cut patterns in the race mind, the human consciousness, now murky with din and battle, as that violin's rhythm and sway, cut pattern across fumes of countless cigarettes, the dreary reiteration of a thousand diplomats. She must hold on a little longer.

In this moment from "Ear-ring," as the recital proceeds to intensify, Archie Rowe, for example, becomes far more than a mere boorish bourgeois socialite. As the columns of debit and credit of his imagination are resolved into the columns of the Acropolis, he is revealed as voice of the social itself, the debit and credit dimension of the world that demands attention, "murky with din and battle," even as the music of the writer's song reaches after some other "columns" and the eternal patterns they cut in the mind.

Madelon, in the same story, is equally more than an artist on a trip to Greece with her friend. She is the embodiment of an ancient desire for what lies beyond, just as the Russian woman is more than she seems:

> Madelon looked at the girl frankly, but now saw her as something, again, different. But what she saw her as she could not yet say. Was the Russian woman doomed, by some law deeper than the social law of gossips and of diplomats? Were rigorous laws functioning here, laws far older than the Norman Conqueror, the authentic county inheritance of the head of the British school, at work here? Was there some vein of mystery, some occult knowledge that they all shared? Was mid-west right to ignore Salamis, except as a stepping-stone to oil wells, and was little Allie (upstairs sleeping) protected and fore-warned, when some authorised academic snob purloined her pen knife from her? Could they, even today, dig too deep? Was it wise to penetrate below a surface that the British school so carefully kept in its place, that an opera-bouffe royal family had the wit and courage to ignore, that Archie Rowe, with a mother from Achaea, went to Oxford expensively to forget?

Even the diamonds become more than diamonds as the recital reaches its "climax" and they become a doorway into a new "layer," a new dimension:

> Don't look at the diamond. Eleanor is shuffling her feet and I'll have to wait till Rowe, tediously, takes leave before, upstairs, I can burst into this new layer, this new discovery, before I can tell Edd, or E.E., as I have learned to call her, how she can paint pictures like that. This is the new music. Everything seems unrelated yet diametrically related, as you slant one facet of a diamond into another set of values.

H.D.'s "fiction" is often referred to as *roman à clef*, "a novel that represents real people," *The Bedford Glossary of Critical and Literary Terms* says, "in the guise of novelistic characters bearing fictional names." You can read H.D.'s work in these terms. The characters who circulate through these stories began as "real people." She does return to the same persons in her writing, often under the same names, as well as to the same events. They have been identified many times: Gareth, Raymonde, Katherine, Daniel and so on, translate into Bryher, H.D., Frances Gregg, Kenneth McPherson, Ezra Pound, Cecil Gray, Richard Aldington, Robert McAlmon, the people who constituted the meaningful relations of her life. "Narthex," "Ear-Ring," and "Pontikinisi (Mouse Island)" involve the usual suspects and, in "Pontikinisi (Mouse Island)," a familiar event, sometimes referred to as "the stranger on the boat" story. But in another sense the definition of *roman à clef* begs the question since the terms it uses are all obscure or contested—"represent," "real," "fictional," and "character," far from having clear meanings, are the sites where high modernist fiction waged its struggle with realism, H.D. no less than Joyce or Woolf.

Beyond that, the idea of the *roman à clef* itself is usually connected to some sense of caricature or satire, some social commentary or critique that makes the "representation" of "real people" significant beyond mere gossip about who was sleeping with whom (although that is invariably of some interest)—Huxley's *Point Counter Point*, for example, or closer to (H.D.'s) home, John Cournos' *Miranda Masters*, in which H.D. is presented in a less than flattering light. But that is not what H.D. did in her fictions. There is no sense of caricature or satire. Nor is there the necessary fascination with what we call the "social" which is a prerequisite for that. On the contrary, H.D. seems interested in undoing the ground of such a possibility by turning language toward an original intensity that was commensurate to her experience of a world bursting with sense, thriving with forms, beyond the social, with an inner truth that shines through the things of the world—the world as "Pear Tree," one of her most well-known Imagist poems, or, as in the story "Ear-Ring," diamond:

> ... she wanted something, unrelated to time, related to infinity, to communicate with something unrelated to time, related to infinity.... You related time-out-of-time, to time-in-time and you get snatches of each, in bits of jagged-off triangles... .It was the sharp edge of a cut-off triangle that must be the one facet of that diamond. That must be each facet of a diamond that was a new way of thinking.

This deep concern fuels her transformation of imagism into narrative. This turning of language is the defining element in H.D.'s perpetual, metamorphosing quest in both her poetry and "fiction" and has nothing to do with the impulse behind *roman-à-clef.*

This process was not unique to H.D. One of the closest descriptions of it is given by Henry Corbin in his discussion of the recitals of Avicenna and other Arab visionaries. The process, "ta'wil," operates within a very specific sense of the world: "Ta'wil" as Corbin writes in Avicenna and the Visionary Recital:

> ... usually forms with tanzil a pair of terms and notions that are at once complementary and contrasting. Tanzil properly designates positive religion, the letter of the Revelation dictated to the Prophet by the Angel. It is to cause the descent of the Revelation from the higher world. Ta'wil is, etymologically and inversely, to cause to return, to lead back, to restore to one's origin and to the place where one comes home, consequently to return to the true and original meaning of a text.

The point here is the sense of a depth and dimensionality to the world that yields to exegesis. Call it esoteric compared to the world we live in during the rush and clamour of a day—the literal world that seems to end at a singular explanation, and yet contains within it access to further meanings waiting to be unlocked. In such a world, each person who radiates in your life bears further meaning in the folds of their selves. In "Narthex," Raymonde, Daniel, and Gareth, all characters in other fictions, other recitations, are embodiments of powers struggling to become legible, a "hieroglyph language" she calls it. Recognizing they are part of that language, Raymonde comes to see them in a new light, so to speak, accomplished through the recitation, a new state of being.

Growing up in Pennsylvania in the Moravian Church, H.D. early on had the example of Count Zinzendorf, the 18th century leader of the Church, to guide her sense of this "hieroglyph language." Zinzendorf, who took over leadership of the Unitas Fratrum (the original name of the Moravian Church) in 1723, initiated a cult of the Wound within the church, a radical feminizing and sexualizing of Christ's body that captivated H.D. Although the church later rejected Zinzendorf's vision and expunged much of the record of his work including many of the hymns he wrote, H.D. saw in this moment an eruption of the knowledge of the perennial cult of love that reappeared in pagan mystery religions, Dante's love cult, erotic troubadour mysticism, the Cathars, and the cult of the Madonna. The Moravian Love Feast, as their service was called, could be added to this list, in name if not in action.

Zinzendorf also developed the notion of "the Church within the Church," the formation of an inner circle of initiates and devotees who would maintain the original (esoteric) mission of Christianity in the face of its corruption by a profane world. In an essay on her own work, "H.D. by Delia Alton," H.D. specifically mentions Zinzendorf's plan and relates it to a further lost, or inner, history that her work engages:

> Zinzendorf had re-established a branch of the dispersed or "lost" Church of Bohemia. This Church, to my mind, shows marked traces of the still earlier dis-established or "lost" Church of Provence, the Church of Love that we touch on, in *By Avon River*. The fascinating subject of the Hidden Church, the Church within the Church is touched on in "The Secret," the section of *The Gift* that reveals the child's affinity and actual connection with the old Jednota of Bohemia, or the Unitas Fratrum as re-established by Zinzendorf, across the frontier in Saxony.

This sense of an inner and outer reality to "life," an exoteric and esoteric dimension, is not concerned with the "social" other than as a text from which to initiate a movement beyond it. In "Narthex," H.D. writes:

> A word, a foot-step or a sea-wind fluttered banner ... waft of fresh scent, heliotrope in boxes, everything changed everything ... wisteria pulled off a wall in passing, stuck in an under-mannered tourist's coat flap ... the eyes of Miss Smithers from Newcastle-on-Tyne, Daniel who sat unmoved, yet fully sensed it. Raymonde had only to say "Veronese," "balcony" and she knew he saw what she saw. Hierograph ... beating in the air, dot and tick and tick and dot of super-sensuous language ... the fluttering of the streamers of the a-symmetrical symmetry of the lion banner, the tilt of a summer sun-shade, the fluttering of a pigeon ... everything means something, a candle on a candlestick, a bird pecking at a brioche ... heaven is getting things (thoughts, sensation) across in some subtle way, too subtle to grasp with intellectual comprehension ... this hieroglyph language she and Daniel had between them.

In this writing where "heaven is getting things across," everything has meaning, meaning that unfolds in the "characters/real people" of the writing, whichever dimension you address them in, all ciphers of something else, some further meaning that is explicated by being written and rewritten: "... the ... ta'wil ... is not an allegorical exegesis," Corbin wrote in *Creative Imagination in the Sufism of Ibn 'Arabi*, "but a transfiguration of the literal texts, referring not to abstract truths, but to Persons." H.D. was never interested in the historical dimension of the novel nor its conventions the way Joyce or Woolf or Faulkner were, even though, like them, she attacked the formal conventions as a way of freeing the energy of the (evolving) form toward her own ends. Her writing has nothing to do with the traditional concerns of the novel (or short story). These persons are not characters nor is this Newton's (or Einstein's) space/time. The space of this writing remains the soul, and the time is the time of Time itself. The social is a (largely opaque) abode within it.

"Narthex," "Ear-Ring," and "Pontikinisi (Mouse Island)" are visionary recitals in that they are the passage of the soul from one level of experience to another, one level of reality to another, where a further sense of meaning reveals itself—where vision expands, grows into new astonishing spaces. They are full of that sense, but it is never completed, never contained, never finally deciphered. Beyond it, for those who are interested, are hints of even larger, more intricate spaces, which they adjoin. In a description of another collection of her stories, H.D. wrote: "... they are individually separate, dedicatory Chapels or Chapters .... They are Chapter-houses, adjoining some vast Cathedral." Her work opens into this Cathedral, an opening that remains unique to her writing among all her contemporaries.

How Long Is Long Enough?

"If you tell me a novel or a film is long, I know you mean long for a novel or long for a film, and that their actual respective lengths are likely to be of different orders of magnitude, and I also know that you are not referring to the number of pages or the length of the reel of film, although these might be indicative of what you are measuring, which is the relative duration of the time required for the reception of either (with this in mind I measure the *Cantos* as about 116 metres long, compared with *Tjanting* at only 38 metres.)"

—Peter Middleton, "The Longing of the Long Poem"

When I was asked to participate in a discussion of The Long Poem, I must admit my initial response was to decline based on a long-held, deep distrust of the conjunction of those two words, "long" and "poem," a strong feeling they are, to put it straight, nonsense. I don't believe there is such a thing as the Long Poem. And since I don't believe in it, my thinking went, I ought not to talk about it. But the sudden, unexpected opportunity also got me thinking about it again, and in the process of thinking I became less certain of everything. That's the problem with thinking. It had to do with the various unresolved senses of "long," churning away in what seemed to claim clarity, even a kind of unity. If there are not just one, but two anthologies of Canadian Long Poems, at least some people must know what they are. But the questions lingered: Is a poem a long poem, as many have asked before me, just because it's—long? And if that's the case, then how long is long enough to be a long poem? Or is a poem a long poem because it can lay claim to some common generic feature—beyond indeterminate length—some, say, structure or convention? Or, as Smaro Kambourelli has argued, to an "evolved form," a specific, restless resistance to generic definition?

There is, I should add, a third use of "long," one that is not specific to the question of form, but that seeks to include all forms that are thought to be ... lengthy. In that case, "long poem" is a very general descriptor, an empty container that includes epics, as well as the "verse novel, verse narrative, lyric sequence, lyric series, and collage/montage," to quote a rather dubious Wikipedia entry that begins "The long poem is a literary genre including all poetry of considerable length." Whoever wrote that was clearly unfamiliar with the definition of genre which necessarily is defined by some common feature, usually a convention or set of conventions. They also rather shamelessly embrace tautology as if it were meaningful. And although it is related to the first sense of "long" above, there is a subtle difference in that the earlier sense seeks to define a commonality of length rather than just turning "long" into what Humpty Dumpty called a *portmanteau word*. In other words, is there such a beast as the Long Poem, or are there just a bunch of lengthy poems?

Both Michael Ondaatje and Sharon Thesen, the editors of the Canadian anthologies, allude to the problem in their introductions. Ondaatje talks about a "form or a 'size' or 'structure'," leaving the determination hanging. Thesen says (in the preface to the second edition), "Definitions of the long poem, whether genre-based or argued within a range of poetic practice, have entered such a borderless place that to justify selections based on definitions is pointless." But neither addresses the apparently unresolvable ambiguity as a possible problem.And perhaps it isn't.

Perhaps something else is at stake. Comments in the introductions to both anthologies suggest they were part of a particular political moment, in the world of writing and publishing, and at least to some degree, were interventions designed to make sure certain writers and certain concerns with writing were heard in a world of official literary powers often hostile to them. Ondaatje is explicit, claiming that the long poem was "ignored by anthologists, schools, and the general reading public," and that his anthology was meant to rectify that ignorance. Twelve years on, Thesen is less clear about the political situation, but claims to continue "Ondaatje's work," as well as to record her own pleasure in reading, which, although diverse, has always centrally included work consonant with the poetics of what is commonly called, for better or worse, the "New American Poetry," after Donald Allen's anthology of the same name.

In 1979, when the first *Long Poem Anthology* appeared, the poetry wars were raging in both Canada and the U.S. In Canada, they mostly circulated around nationalist issues. Should Canadian poets take their lead from certain Americans, or forge their own national voice, independent of… well, certain Americans? The question of what the authentic Canadian voice was dependent on didn't seem to extend much beyond that particular rejection and the embrace of northern landscapes, although some poets tenaciously clung to a conservative UK tradition, even as many of the most interesting and adventurous poets in the UK turned to the new American poetics, while Americans and Canadians of the projectivist bent embraced certain Brits, including Basil Bunting, David Jones, Eric Mottram, Tom Raworth, Bob Cobbing, Jeff Nuttal and many others.The conservative turn in Canada—a turn which saw in certain academic circles, for instance, Edward Thomas valued over William Carlos Williams as exemplary of modernism—was crucial in the development of what came to be called Canlit, although Sharon Thesen argued with me that "projectivist" poetics "… was the influence that best characterized what came to be canonical Canadian poetry for a few decades (bringing Canadian poetry out of British modernism)." This seems true if you are looking at Canadian poetry from the West Coast, where writers like Fred Wah and George Bowering gained a national authority and Robin Blaser's presence was mostly embraced. If you are looking at it from Ontario, however, where Robin Matthews led the charge against the U.S. Imperialist/Black Mountain invasion, only Victor Coleman and bpNichol stood up to defend the new poetics and they were marginalized at the time.In the United States, the poetry wars took place over the question of form. The "new" poets began by rejecting the hold the New Criticism had on the literary imagination, especially as it was fostered by the institutional disciplinary tools of the University English Department. The opposition to the new poetics was—not to put too fine a point on it—mobilized to save Western-Civ-As-We-Know-It from barbarian anarchy, a fight in the tradition of T.S. Eliot's war on strange gods and the rearguard defense of "Christian culture" by the Fugitives. The projectivists articulated it as an embrace of open, as opposed to closed, form. This distinction still circulates.

Interestingly, the antagonist in both wars was the same group of writers, referred to loosely as the Black Mountain School, with special focus on its putative "leader," Charles Olson, not to mention others in his cohort such as Robert Creeley and Robert Duncan. The primary struggle in the wars had to do with control of publication. Jed Rasula's *American Poetry Wax Museum* remains the best account of those conflicts. The enemy of the established literary powers in both countries was the range of radical poetics put forward in Donald Allen's *New American Poetry*, with Olson's essay, "Projective Verse," the primary target, because of its wide influence. As Leon Surette pointed out in a review of the first *Long Poem Anthology*, every "poem in the volume, derives from the large population of American and Canadian poets associated one way or another with Black Mountain. Black Mountain is, of course Charles Olson; and Charles Olson is *The Maximus Poems*."Ondaatje might have titled his anthology *The Anthology of (lengthy) Canadian Black Mountain Poetry*, and it would have meant as much as—if not more than—the *Long Poem Anthology*. As a political maneuver, sticking with "long poem" gained more exposure for a range of poetry which was denied access to university journals and reviews and mainstream literary publications. And that fact makes the term "long poem," to a certain extent, a subterfuge. It is not something to spend a lot of time arguing about when the real issue is poetics, not length.

But that is not the end of the political implications of the Long Poem as it proliferated in the 70s and 80s and beyond. Poets wrote lengthy poems in the 19th century, but no one, to the best of my knowledge, addressed them as part of a corporate entity known as the Long Poem. They were thought of generically as epics, narrative poems, historical poems or what have you. Only recently have they been identified as Long Poems. That development occurred after Charles Olson's death in 1970, when a new academic industry arose breeding journals, articles, books, anthologies, conferences and various critical apparatuses to publish its manifestations, argue about its nature, and bolster the careers of academics. And this is where my own unease becomes more acute. If "long poem" was for Ondaatje and Thesen a way of furthering the exposure of New American projectivist poetics, in the hands of Olson's burgeoning critics, after his death, it paradoxically became a way to reject Olson's contribution, especially as it related to his work with the epic.The vanguard of this rejection arose partly out of the new academic feminist criticism located within the same university classrooms that had housed the New Criticism for so many years, as well as in the pages of "avant-garde" journals such as *L=A=N=G=U=A=G=E* where intellectual concoctions of Marxist and linguistic theories were turned on Olson and the epic. Frequently, the two tendencies crossed paths. Marjorie Perloff, for instance, out of what she calls her "original animosity," attacked "Olson's sexism, evident in so much of the poetry and criticism," although eventually she settled her rejection of his *work* on his treatment of women in his *classroom*. She went on to play a crucial role in attacking Olson's reputation in the Academy while promoting the careers of various poets in the so-called "Language" group. Those poets (Ron Silliman, Charles Bernstein, Barrett Watten, etc.), whose New Left/quasi-Marxist political stances included a critical rejection of the epic form as it had been developed by Olson, identified it with various nasty political habits including patriarchy, totalizing thought, megalomania, and even imperialism itself. The epic was sidelined "through any number of encoded restraining orders and forms of administrative detention that reflect the larger bureaucratic nets we are trapped in," as Ammiel Alcalay has written of Olson's work.

It is not that this tendency was responsible for the rise of the long poem and the proliferation of the discourses about it/them. But it did play a significant role. Barrett Watten, in an interview with Manuel Brito, is quite explicit that the Language school "reacted almost violently against the bardic tradition," which is code for Olson's epic as well as the work of Robert Duncan, Robert Kelly, Gerrit Lansing and others. Replacing myth, which is at the heart of Olson's thinking, with what Watten calls "the material signifier," the "Language poets" moved poetry from visionary to sociological/analytical, emphasizing "dialectical materialism" even as Marxism began its inexorable, historic collapse into the catastrophes of the USSR, Albania, China, North Korea, and Cambodia. The various conventional elements of the epic—the hero, martial engagements, feats of prowess and virtue, trips to the underworld, etc.—were identified with "toxic masculinity." There were notable exceptions such as Alice Notley's brilliant *The Descent of Alette*. But the epic's traditional position atop a hierarchy of genres, not to mention the uses it had been put to in poems like the *Aeneid* or the *Song of Roland*, contributed to accusations of imperial bias. And to dare to propose to write a Republic became seen as arrogant and totalizing.

At the same time, Olson's impulse to get past the "lyrical interference of the individual as ego" was widely embraced, both as a resistance to modern individualism and to the lingering domination of the New Criticism with its focus on the lyric poem. The problem was how to proceed in the spirit of the new American poetics launched by Olson without falling into what was seen as his sexist, imperialist, totalizing form. And the answer, I am suggesting, for many writers at the time was to embrace something called the Long Poem. Since the essence of the new American poetics is summed up in the phrase "open form," "long" could then lead into just about anything.And I am not suggesting there is anything wrong with that. To be *sui generis* is thought by many to be an admirable state, although often implicit in it are lingering notions of authenticity and originality that remain questionable in the current intellectual climate. And poets, given their propensity for a kind of spiritual orneriness, are not above inventing a genre when the mood strikes them. Spicer's and Blaser's "serial poem" for instance. Although it is now sometimes subsumed under the aegis of the Long Poem, the serial poem remains a strong, widespread specific genre in and of itself.

And genre, as the title of Smaro Kambourelli's book, *On the Edge of Genre*, makes clear, is the issue here, if only because "long" stands in the place where we are used to encountering generic descriptors—epic poem, lyric poem, narrative poem, serial poem. You stick "long" in there and that's what people hear. But what genre gives us that long doesn't is design, and what design gives us is a measure of meaning. There are obviously many different ways of looking at genre. The academic arguments are fierce and seemingly complex, although mostly they seem to fall out along that old divide between realists and nominalists that has been with us at least since Aristotle. Are the boundaries or edges we ascribe to genres real, or are they just names that artificially (or artfully) mark off a range of practices? Rachel Blau DuPlessis, in her analysis of the long poem, brings in Derrida and his famous essay on the law of genre to try and subvert that distinction, but I think the last place we want to go to think about genre is to the French (as much as I respect Derrida's thought) whose history with genre is completely different than our own, say, "new world," or "democratic," relation.

The French have a long history of struggling with the idea of the absolute hierarchy of discrete genres, a kind of image of their old, lingering class system. They tend to think of genre much as they think of, say, nationality. Derrida's subversion of genre is specific to that struggle. Here, the word "Canadian" does not signify in the same way the word "French" does in France. It can be no less poisonous, but it is a different poison. Even when Derrida is subverting the meaning of genre, arguing that "a text would not belong to any genre. Every text participates in one or several genres ..." he is operating with the understanding that there is such a thing as one or several of them and that texts belong to them. Of course, he goes on to argue that every genre also contains its Other, as they say in the theory biz, arguing for contamination as opposed to purity.

We, on the other hand, are far looser in our thinking of genre as we are in engaging our mongrel sense of nationality. Rather than resisting genre, I embrace it. Not genre as some pure form, however, even one contaminated by its Other. Rather than Derrida, I go to Ridley Scott or Joel and Ethan Coen for my sense of genre, neither as discrete nor contaminated but as possibility, potential, kind of like the playground in the park up the street from my house. Scott and the Coens have different approaches to genre, but where they overlap is in their sense of genre as an opening into play. Each of their films begins with the thought of a genre, and then plays with its conventions and expectations turning them to their own uses. The imaginal playground is full of structures—bars, ladders, slides, swings, tunnels, boxes of sand—that are an open invitation. There are no rules about how to engage them, and kids will always find new ways, even though there are limits as to what the structures will allow.

My joy with genre arises mostly in relation to that invitation to play, and in the process, to make something interestingly entangled in time. Stanley Cavell, in his study of the genre of the "remarriage comedy" (a genre he discovered), says this about it: "... later members can "add" something to the genre because there is no such thing as "all its features." ... [M]embers of a genre share the inheritance of certain conditions, procedures and subjects and goals of composition, and that in primary art each member of such a genre represents a study of these conditions, something I think of as the responsibility of an inheritance." In a somewhat similar vein, Giorgio Agamben, in a little book called *Nymphs*, explores his teacher Aby Warburg's sense of *image* as an indeterminate form entangled in time. What some people call "style" is a record of that entanglement. Writing about the 26 images of nymphs on the 46th plate of Warburg's *Atlas*, Agamben asks, which is the original nymph? And his answer is none. "The nymph," he writes, "is an indiscernible blend of originariness and repetition, of form and matter." The images, he goes on, "are made of time—they are crystals of historical memory, crystals which are 'phantasmatized' … and round which time writes its choreography."

We can say something like this about genres, that they are phantasmatized forms around which time writes its choreography, and in that sense are always both discreet and contaminated at the same time. I can't think of a better way to describe my own relation to the epic genre as I wrote *Cosmographia—A post-Lucretian faux micro-epic*. If poetry, as Stan Persky proposed to me, is a mode of thought, genres are specific inflections of that mode. That is, genres are modes of thinking through specific issues and ranges of meaning, specific conditions, that poetry has concerned itself with for a very long time. They are playgrounds for writing.

Crucial to this thinking is the understanding that conventions are not simply decorative but meaningful. When Olson turned to the epic, it was because he wanted to write the world, not the self (which is not to say the self doesn't come into it). That included history, in so far as history (that Angel) is where the world's depths are revealed. For Olson, the conventions of the epic, say, it's vocabulary of forms, or what Cavell calls features, opened into time's choreography. Take the hero, for example, and look at what happened to that thought in the work of the Coens or Scott. We are introduced variously to Jeffrey Lebowski or Thelma and Louise in inflections of "hero" that utterly resituate us in relation to the accident of being in the world.

I can cite any number of women who have brilliantly used the same formal possibilities to rethink the world—Alice Notley's *The Descent of Alette*, for instance, or Sharon Doubiago's *Hard Country*. In *Cosmographia*, the possibility arose out of an outburst from an originating moment in the exclamation, "Razzamatootie," shouted by drummer Dannie Richmond in Charles Mingus's tune, "Eat that Chicken," which I first heard in my friend Stuart Wilson's bedroom in 1962. It was the beginning of the world, and when it came back many years later, Razzamatootie unexpectedly split into Razz and Tootie, who became the kaleidoscopic heroes of the poem. Homer might not recognize them as such, but such is time's choreography that we are called on as poets to testify to the complexities of *now* even as we honour those of *then*. As I write this, now in a coffee shop in the barren outskirts of Mississauga waiting for my daughter's hockey game to begin, I am listening on my iPod to Aki Takase play "In a sentimental mood," knowing that Duke Ellington couldn't in his moment have imagined this astonishing take on his music but would love it if he were here to listen to it now. Such is Olson's *Maximus*, a bold opening into the thinking of his time.

That word, "open," keeps cropping up and requires some thought. Openness is perhaps the most consistent defining quality of long poems, especially in so far as it is understood as the beating heart of process, the quality Ondaatje identifies with the long poem. Olson's pervasive and persistent commitment to Whitehead's philosophy is certainly active here, but he was just one (loud) voice among many arguing for this stance—hence, Allen's anthology, which itself was just one crystallization of these concerns, one phantasmatized choreography of time's particular emerging energies. Process was, as they say, in the air. As Oliver Cusimano puts it an essay on Agamben, "As the text is an accident of a practice, therefore *not* designed, *not* meant, there is no way to predict what it might be."

This, however, is not to be confused with any particular form, even with the idea of emergent form. Openness occurs not in the resistance to genre, the mixing of genres, or even the destruction of genre, but in the relation to each and every word—or even each and every phoneme. Form and content—the yin and yang, the wave and particle of meaning's accident—are never limited by any particular thought of their possibility.

In one sense, *Cosmographia* would seem to be the antithesis of open form. It began as a plan suggested to me by Ezra Pound as I flew over his grave on the island of San Giorgio Maggiore headed toward the Venice airport. I happened to be reading Flann O'Brien's *The Third Policeman* at the time, and the rest, as they say, is history. Or poetry. It's *Cosmographia* in any case. I knew it had to be 12 books since it was a micro-epic, and I proceeded over the next few days to write down all the titles for the books and the individual cantos, allowing two notebook pages for each poem, shaping them into a distorted kind of arc informed by incoming information from Homer, Lucretius, Ovid, Dante, Blake, Pound, and Olson, not to mention Ogden Nash and Charles Mingus—among others. I thought I had it under control till the cows got in. They snuck into the poem through a platitude in Canto 2—something about bygone eras chanting Helen's name till the cows come home. They then proceeded to wander through the book belching, chewing cud, farting, stampeding, and eventually turning into the Suitors in Book 12. They would constantly surprise, delight, and occasionally annoy me with their antics, insisting that the poem was as much theirs as it was mine, that every phoneme was a barn door they might wander through when I least expected it. I did not resist genre. I embraced it, and the cows were fine with that since it was one more home for them to get back to.

They were sent as a lesson about *open*. To be open has nothing to do with plans, however elaborate, with generic boundaries, or even, as some have suggested with endings, as if not having an ending is the same as open. The open occurs in every word or it doesn't occur at all. Which brings me back to "long." Just as no plan, no structure, no genre can rule out the open, so any attempt to close the barn door on "long" will finally fail because the open is not a choice—it is the very nature of our condition, the terrifying and delightful non-ground we think we don't stand on. Poets will write lengthy poems for many different reasons, using many different techniques, tools, and devices, but as soon as you attempt to lock them up in The Long Poem Corral, watch out. Sure as shootin', one of them will go loco, kick down the gate, and the next thing you know they will be all over hell's half acre, snorting, stampeding, grazing, emitting large quantities of methane, and generally raising a ruckus guaranteed to leave the corral in a shambles. For myself, I am content to leave it there—to let the cows have their way, to leave lengthy poems to their own devices, and to leave the Long Poem to the metaphysicians.

The Interstices of Poetry Wars

for Jack Spicer

"Poetry lives in the interstices, not in the structures."
—Robert Duncan

We inherit the somewhat contentious phrase, poetry war, from intellectual conflicts that arose in the wake of the publication of *The New American Poetry* in 1960. When the new, post-war, postmodern energies that Donald Allen brought together in his anthology ran into the wall of a conservative, formalist Establishment, a poetry war broke out on multiple fronts, giving rise to, among other things, an underground poetry culture of resistance, resourcefulness, and Emersonian self-reliance within living networks of mutual support. Arguably, the war itself began in the aborted duel between Ezra Pound and Lascelles Abercrombie in 1912 (figuratively speaking), and continued through the travails of the Objectivists before erupting into the self-proclaimed poetry wars of the 60s and early 70s.

More recently, the term applies to the now notorious event that occurred nearly 40 years ago in San Francisco, during the screening of a film on Louis Zukofsky, when Duncan got into a confrontation with Barrett Watten. Patrick Dunagan reminds me that other fronts in the poetry war were also active at that moment and points to Duncan's conflict with Denise Levertov, and the now near mythic events at Naropa immortalized in Tom Clark's *Poetry Wars*. Robert Duncan was very much a part of these conflicts and was central to the San Francisco event. And while some people, I know, have expressed ennui and irritation at the continued attention to the confrontation between him and Watten, which they apparently consider too old or lacking substance to be of interest, I think it remains central to an understanding of our situation and the situation of poetry today.

It began in 1978 when, after the screening of a film on Louis Zukofsky, Robert Duncan walked on stage during a presentation by Barrett Watten and took the microphone from him, symbolically asserting the continued precedence of the New American Poetry over what he saw as the re-emergence of the New Criticism's formalism in the work of what came to be known as *Language Poetry*. This brand came to stand for a diverse range of poetries responding to what is called the "linguistic turn" of the 70s and 80s, many of which did not share the same commitments to the formalism central to this discussion, and hence is meaningless in one sense. Nevertheless, the name became part of a marketing campaign by critics like Marjorie Perloff and linked to the identity of several poets, propelling them into university faculty positions and the center of critical attention. Duncan had spent much of his artistic life battling one dominant, institutionalized formalism, and having won, he was in no mood to see it rise again from the ashes in the form of neo-Marxist materialism.

The war erupted into the open six years later, when David Levi Strauss wrote an introduction to a screening of the Zukofsky film along with a film on Duncan. After detailing the history of the films, Levi Strauss related a story of the confrontation between Duncan and Watten in 1978 that outraged Watten's cohort who, led by Ron Silliman, responded in kind. The barrage of letters to *Poetry Flash,* a Bay Area poetry news tabloid, that followed, became the top poetry news story of 1978. *Poetry Flash* upped the stakes by inviting a contribution from linguistics' professor George Lakoff, whose writing provided a theoretical support for Language poetry. That provoked poet Tom Clark, who responded with a piece called "Stalin as Linguist," which, to say the least, further inflamed the debate.

At that moment the poetic energy unleashed by the *New American Poetry* split into a self-declared avant-garde who ran with the oppositional energy of the NAP, but grounded it on sociology and philosophical materialism; and an unorganized NAP remnant circulating around the poetics of Duncan/Olson/Creeley/Ginsberg grounded in *Kali* energy, the incommensurable *creativedevouring* plenitude of the world, and poetry's articulating entanglement with its morphogenesis and its potential for transformative gnosis. I am using gnosis here in a non-specialized sense of knowledge that exceeds the bounds of "reason," which Charles Olson, going to the roots, significantly located in the work of the ear (knowledge as *gna*) rather than the eye (knowledge as *vid*).

At the very beginning of his essay "Man's Fulfillment in Order and Strife," written 10 years before the incident at the Zukofsky film screening, Duncan stated: "I find myself a prejudiced member of a very small community of belief in strife with other poets about what the poem is." It was a moment in the poetry wars when the established, university-based poets of the New Critical movement, dismissed and shut out the poets of the NAP. Duncan was a self-admitted combatant in the poetry war that followed. The stake, as he articulated it, was a determination of what the poem is, and what the poem is, he goes on, is a *World Order*, as it is also *of* an order of *all* poetries. The poetry war, the strife as he calls it, develops because of "incompatible ideas of what *world* and *order* are."

In a late clean-up operation, the forces levelling the world through the cultural economy of general equivalence and universal commodification—what I call The Doom Program—successfully reoccupied poetry's upper social orders in the U.S. and integrated them into its institutional structure. The difference between *worlds* and *orders* here circulates around this occupation of poetry which integrated it into economies of use. Let me be clear. The war is not about this kind of poetry or that kind of poetry, and certainly not about anyone who ever got a teaching gig or won some prize money because someone recognized their terrific work. The war is about resistance to the displacement of *becoming-with(in)-poetry* by *being-over-poetry*, a change that quantifies it, turns it into a product that, if it meets certain understood standards and regulations, can be exchanged for a variety of rewards. Nor is it about *us vs. them.* This occupation of poetry touches us all, entangles us all. It is a struggle each of us must confront in our own lives as poets.

Duncan saw it coming early on and understood the challenge it presented to his sense of poetry's work. You could even argue that he occupied the center of a moment of mythic origin, a moment of conflict between orders that gives rise to an origin, a new ordering or relation of orderings. Duncan sensed the significance of the moment that night in San Francisco and came prepared. As David Bromige related in an interview, "... Robert appeared in his full, Romantic poet regalia, the Spanish cape, the Spanish hat.... It was for effect. But it was also the effect on him too. He had his manna when he was in that garb. He could fight off evil magic." Duncan walks on stage to fight evil magic, takes the mic from the yielding hands of a stunned Barrett Watten, and sets in motion—or materializes—a conflict that continues to play itself out 40 years later.

But of course, that wasn't the first time, although every time is also always the first time. It's a wave in a pattern that echoes in time. It marks a moment in recent literary history, even as it reveals within its folds, layer on layer of homologous events, a morphological nest, a palimpsest, a form of event that resonates out of Nothing to reveal itself in Ovid's erotic, metamorphic challenge to Virgil's structural empire of words, or the challenge implicit in the Pearl Poet's rugged alliterations to the colonizing iambic pentameter from the South. Not to mention the poetry wars between the Provençal and the Dolce Stil Novo poets, and the entrenched Latin verse they wrote against. Or Whitman's barbaric yawp aimed in part at the genteel poets of Cambridge, Massachusetts. Or Emily Dickinson's rhythmically broken psalms, directed at the chorus of sanctimonious voices pouring from the church down the street. You may be squeamish about the word *war*, but the conflict is undeniable and universal. It is the energy of renewal.

At the time of our mythic origin conflict in 1978, the issue was declared (by Duncan) to be *fun* vs *tedium*: "I just want to get some sense of fun in this," he says of his interruption. But that fun rests on an entire world order that rejects formalism and the quantification of poetry, whatever name it goes by. Watten proposed to split Zukofsky "down the middle," separating considerations of the poem from his life and reading the work as a *thing*, arguing that Zukofsky's "structuring devices" were mathematical and that he, Watten, was attempting to get the words to interact with themselves. "Structuring devices" is Watten's name for his materialist displacement of myth which arguably was the secret agenda of his presentation. Echoing New Criticism's dismissal of biography in the pursuit of a quantified text, he asks Duncan, "How are words your life?" to which Duncan responds, "what we are reading *is* life, not math—it has something to *say*." And he proceeds to call to attention the swarms of meaning that circulate in Zukofsky's poems, dancing through them, drawing out the allusive, elusive worlds they weave from sound and mind. He offered this as an alternative to Watten's analysis of phonemic progression and graphed curves. In that sense, the issue was not about personalities, not about Duncan and Watten. Or it was only Duncan and Watten in so far as they were the bearers of worlds and orders that were and are incompatible.

As Stan Persky once told me, poetry is a unique linguistic mode of knowledge, a mode that dwells, as Duncan says, in the interstices. The knowledge that poetry bears, the thinking that it opens, its transformative gnosis, ruptures the given separations, activating *bodymind,* opening it into disOrders of meaning within and beyond the habitual orders that hold us in the clutches of the Doom Program's isolating structured categories. Writing of Hölderlin, Jean-Luc Nancy locates the exactitude of the poem's calculation in "touching" of the transmitting body, so that the voice of the poem "is not phonation alone: it is the transmitting body, the body open to the outside as the transmitter of its 'inside,' which is only given in the transmission.... The point of contact, the touching-of-the-opposite, is the opportune exactitude of the calculation that delivers sense or that delivers up to sense, by suspending the uninterrupted course of sense." William Carlos Williams puts it somewhat differently to the same end: "for everything / and nothing / are synonymous / when // energy *in vacuo* / has the power / of confusion // which only to / have done nothing / can make / perfect."

Confuse, suspend, to have done nothing, render inoperative—you could call it, as is popular in some circles who like scientific sounding words, *defamiliarization*, but only if defamiliarization is understood as *the shaking of the Sistrum*, that magical act Plutarch describes in *Isis and Osiris*: "The sistrum also makes it clear that all things in existence need to be shaken, or rattled about, and never to cease from motion but, as it were, to be waked up and agitated when they grow drowsy and torpid." It's what George Quasha calls poetry's "healing principle." One minute you are walking into a lecture hall with 300 other students. The next you are swept up into the *mysterium* of the *tremendum* by the glaze of rainwater on a red wheelbarrow beside the white chickens.

The poetry wars exist and are important. They force us to pay attention, to think of the struggle to keep alive and active the knowledge of the interstitial space of poetry's dwelling within the poet. The poetry war at this moment involves a fight for a space for an un-commodified relationship with its transformational gnosis. Duncan was clear and unequivocal—the poetry war begins within the poet and the stake is the world. It is projective, to use the word of his friend: "In the struggle to undo all the particular claims to order in Poetry, the critical battles, the movements that ruled for a period, setting up laws and definitions to establish what is in order and what is out of order, and then are replaced by other movements … —these battles carry into the public field the inner battles of the individual poet's soul."

For Duncan, the heart of the war involved keeping at work "contending forces and convictions," so as to not lose sight of the world's divine mongrel excess, its prodigious antagonisms, contra-dictions, and differences, to avoid, as Emerson said, binding your "eyes with one or another handkerchief, and attach[ing] [yourself] to some one of these communities of opinion," as most men do. "This conformity," he goes on, "makes them not false in a few particulars, authors of a few lies, but false in all particulars."

According to Duncan, keeping the war alive is the poet's calling, the very essence of the poet's vision. But if the poet projects the poetry war as the manifestation of her understanding of her responsibility to what Duncan calls What Is, a further fold lurks in the plies—the commitment to discord and disorder within the work itself as crucial to the poet's responsibility to keep language true to the emergent world, to remain open to the myriad vibrations at the foundation of morphogenesis. Only that way can you meet the poem halfway, allow it its freedom to introduce you to what you hadn't anticipated, hadn't known about, permit it to lead you through the transformative gnosis which occurs in relation to the exact calculation's suspension of the uninterrupted course of sense and the *in-voca-tion* of the *tremendum*.

Duncan is quite clear—the poetry war is archetypal and projective. And it's important because in a profound existential sense, poetry matters. Poetry war, discord, disorder, general pain-in-the-assness, preserve and activate potential resistance to the epochal tidal pull toward the reduction of all value into some specific weight of imaginary metal in its myriad forms, Moloch's final victory. Poetry war agitates the knowledge of what a poem does beyond some mechanical measure having to do with curing social ills or doing away with injustice, as if those issues could only be addressed in one way, on one plane, from one direction. There can be no justice without beauty, any more than there can be no beauty without justice. And that work takes place on many different planes.

While occasionally under certain conditions, poetry can have a specific material effect, as it did in the U.S. in the 60s, or the USSR and Eastern Europe in the 70s and 80s, mostly we have no idea what it does or where it does it. We can say, definitively, that its presence alone makes the world different. And better. Try to imagine a world without the *Bhagavad Gita*, *Popol Vuh*, *The Book of Psalms*, *Enuma Elish*, or the *Kalevala*, without the *Iliad*, *Beowulf*, *The Pearl*, the *Sundiata Epic*, *The Canterbury Tales*, without Dante's *Commedia*, without Rumi, without Shakespeare's or Wyatt's or Sidney's sonnets, without Donne ....

At a recent meeting of a group of young writers, mostly former students, someone raised the age-old complaint, "why do we bother? no one reads poetry." To which, as everyone else nodded in jaded agreement, a new member of the group demurred—everybody has a favourite poem, he said. And he's right. Poetry occupies our worlds in ways we forget about or don't recognize, lingering in corners of the mind maintaining unperceived channels of sense. Poetry wars are crucial to keeping in mind that point of contact where the opportune exactitude of the calculation occurs in the suspension of the uninterrupted course of sense, shaking the sistrum, reminding us of our further responsibility.

Beyond "Projective Verse"— The Poetics of *Proprioception*

Over the years, Charles Olson's thinking about the nature of the poem and the work that goes into it changed, as you would expect from someone with his deep commitment to *process.* "Projective Verse" (1950), while ground-breaking in the distance it took poetics beyond Pound and Williams, failed to live up to Olson's developing sense of the postmodern reality that the poem, as the bearer of news, must be adequate in its composition. Two issues, in particular, concerned him: First, how to move beyond modernity's increasingly sterile, materialist secularism—which limits knowledge of the human to sociology and psychology—without losing secularism's advance, its overturning of hierarchical, authoritarian control systems, and its opening into promiscuous democracies of sense. And in addition, how to move beyond the thinking of form as an extension of content, which, while it broke the back of prescriptive formalism, still was caught in a dangerous dualism and a temporal precedent. *Formcontent* emerges out of the contest of forces activating the field. It's a move that rethinks the central proposals of "Projective Verse," with an eye (and an ear) toward their further evagination. Bumping up the stakes is the thought that what's to be won or lost is the world itself. It's not a question of literature which will always bring writing into some market where it will have to answer to another demand beyond the necessity of its specific sense. In *Proprioception* (1968), the chapbook he assembled from several different pieces, he addresses both issues when he writes a pre-Deleuzian body-without-organs, a body with no inside, which evades any concept of form/content while radiating immanence.

At stake is what Olson calls an American "secularization which … loses nothing of the divine …." Echoing with Whitehead's "urgent requisite" for a secular theory of god, Olson moves beyond it by displacing "god" with what he calls "the divine," a quality (an adjective without a noun) rather than a thing, an extraordinary value implicit in the ordinary stuff of the world. While proprioception may seem a strange title for such an undertaking, it picks up from "Projective Verse"'s defining concern with the body (eye / brain // ear/ breath) as the source of the poem and then reimagines the postmodern body itself as a way into the poetics. Proprioception is a word more likely found in texts on kinesthetics than poetry: "the unconscious perception of movement and spatial orientation arising from stimuli within the body itself." The crucial word in the definition, *body*, sits there, seeming to refer to something so familiar that we don't even question its meaning. But it's not familiar, not this *body*. The imagination of the modern body is structured around a proliferation of binary oppositions that begins with *inside* and *outside*. Its invention was part of the Renaissance, and occurred when Vesalius cut open the outside of a body to reveal its *contents*, the object-organs that filled the inner space, and mapped them in his anatomical texts. That *inside-and-outside* is reiterated in distinctions like mind and body, spirit and flesh, as well as qualities such as ideal and sensual. Call it the old Cartesian one-two. Olson, for whom this distinction recalls the binary division between form and content, sets out to write a postmodern body that can be the source of a new poetics that escapes the pull of form-and-content. Olson's challenge to those limits begins with a redefinition of *body* as a cosmos of unplumbable dimensions, not some lump of stuff imagined beyond, or even in conflict with, another energy level called, say, "mind," or in another context, "idea." And certainly not some vulgar Marxist notion of "meat" as in "meat before mind" as some have proposed.

This elusive sense of the *(±)body* is tied up with Olson's understanding of "secularization." As Charles Taylor minutely detailed in *A Secular Age*, the emergence of the secular world out of the body of the Medieval sacred world was a long and intricate struggle of one small ordering intervention elbowing another out of its way over hundreds of years. One of the most significant and defining results of the transformation was the elimination of mind from the world. Relocating it solely within the precincts of the "human" set up, the classic conflict with "body" which is now located in the distinction between subject and object (and the whole mess of distinctions that flow from that and circulate around it). In the process the world loses what we might call sense. It is the loss of all sense other than some projection of the human.

Secularization begins as a reclamation of the authority that humans once handed over to an imagination of a *beyond the world* that lent the world sense. Olson's notion of a secularization that loses nothing of the divine begins with the recognition of a duplicity to both terms. Secular, not as a world divorced from the spiritual, a world of matter without sense, a world from which the last vestiges of mind have been stripped other than as they are contained in some idea of the "human." What Olson wants to hold on to has to do with maintaining the ordinariness of a world without some further reference. In a letter to Robert Creeley written on November 28, 1951, he identifies the job he and Creeley are, as he puts it, "pissing at," as "to force the particular to yield dimension." Olson's sense of what he calls in *Proprioception* "the divine," is not concerned with personalities or some appeal to a "thing beyond," but with what he calls the *world's* "depth" or "dimension," which arises out of the complexity of the ply on ply of an implicated, invaginated surface.

The distinction between secular and divine originally determined two different modes of business—business with the church or business with the "world." Later, secularism comes to strip the world bare. Then it is implicated in the ongoing argument between science and religion, and, in other guises, materialism and idealism, all that scholastic bickering. Both sides ground themselves on a diminishment of the ordinary, either to dismiss it or to leave it barren. For all Olson's resistance to Emerson, Emerson sets about to heal this wound, from the 1838 "Divinity School Address" forward. Both men are moved to reclaim the ordinary from its reduced status in relation to something imagined as higher or more profound. "In this refulgent summer," Emerson begins "The Divinity School Address," "it has been a luxury to draw the breath of life." In Olson's body the depth, or sense of the world, like Emerson's luxurious breath, is nowhere other than here. *Proprioception* targets the body/mind duality not, as some have suggested, as an attempt to elevate the [modern] body *within* the duality, but in order to move beyond it, to move further.

The *(±)body* Olson begins with (which he puts in quotes to indicate that this "body" is not to be confused with that old body of Christian,

Marxist, or even Darwinian determinations), generates the sense of the world's depth or dimension. This depth has to do with the divine Olson wants secularism to preserve, to lose nothing of. The first two words of *Proprioception* after the head "Physiology" are "the surface," which is what we do have, sometimes disastrously, as if we can't get beyond Ahab's pasteboard mask. But Olson's surface immediately opens into a cavity. It is not, as with Ahab, the wall of a prison, something to be punched through. Not an "interior," either, however, but a folding and refolding, an invagination and evagination, a complexity of overlaid surface leading to an opening up, an extension of the single surface of the Moebius strip in folded and unfolded complexities. An interior would involve an exterior and these would inevitably lead back to a container, and something contained. Olson will have none of that.

This is not, then, a problem of something called "ideology," (the imposition of forms of life on a "subject"), but a problem of something called "thinking," which is an address to how we are here. Olson is after something like *bodythinking*, where that thinking takes place at the edge of being, the body's being, an edge which is everywhere, the infolded surface with its openings and "organs" (which are organ-izations of the surface) and moving tissues. The problem with various materialisms and idealisms is that they think they know what matter (and ideas) is. Emerson sends them all off to Oregon, circa 1838, to get in touch with the world as yet untouched by their categories of experience. Melville might have dropped them off with Pip in the center of a boundless sea to the same effect. Olson unleashes a prose on them that utterly confuses the distinction. No inner, no outer, no conscious, no unconscious—no inhabitation—but the mystery of an identity (unconscious, archetypes, projection, soul, movement) that arises out of the body's cavities, foldings, frictions. The stuff of creation in action, this refulgent summer. *Proprioception* addresses the question, 'how do you imagine that?', and especially, 'how do you realize it in writing without falling into the habitual reinforced by old modes of writing?'

Logography, which follows *Proprioception,* proposes that each word, like the *(±)body*, is infolded with movements of meaning far previous to their phonetic transcriptions. The body of language, then, is the word. To let the world in is to unleash these movements of meaning by freeing words from a grammar which locks them into relations called ideas that overwhelm the sounding of each word event. If that's taken as ground here, then one of the crucial things we fail to know from within our given limits is the complex identity of sounds, as we fail to know the complex identity of the *(±)body*. The *(±)body* radiates sense—not because it contains something else (mind, idea, soul, spirit)—but precisely because of the movement of its infolded surfaces and cavities. It is sense in motion.

Poems are things made of words, or to get even closer, *things of words* where *thing* resonates with its ancient Germanic sense of *assembly*, *gathering*. Invisible words instigate invisible worlds of unforeseen entrapments and licentious engagements. The infolded meanings that circulate through words also call out to other words. Rhyme proliferates leading one word on after another, the ear exulting in the music of "Uruk, Erech, Orchoe, Warka" that has resonated now for thousands of years. It's a deep satisfaction arising out of the words calling each to the others, and in the calling, the chatter of meanings and near meanings and the blunt refusal to mean at all in the joy of sounding.

An argument with the Given always animates the range of possible choices. Things in William Carlos Williams' proposal—*no ideas but in things*—are at war with a poetry of abstract ideas, neat and bloodless, perfectly arranged with seven types of ambiguity, and no possibility of surprise beyond elegance. But the *image* that then moves in to replace them as the anchor of *things* itself, eventually becomes a grave of poetry, pretty and pat and ever ready to sit there speaking politely of the poet's feelings, analogically and metaphorically destroying the specificities of the world.

For Williams (and Pound and H.D.) the *image* (as Robert Duncan pointed out in *The H.D. Book*) is hierophantic, and in that sense, does not *contain* ideas, but is kind of transmitter/transmission. What it transmits is tied to Olson's sense of the secularization that loses nothing of the divine. (Henry Corbin, in his discussion of Ibn 'Arabi, has image as the "form and condition of theophanies," where the *phanic* then becomes the showing, the locus where something breaks through to show itself.) For Olson, document in one sense displaces image (document as the body of "history"?). But by pushing toward the word, he draws the document back into a language of sense breaking out of a world of sense.

All this talk of sense, however, has skirted around an obvious omission—the bleeding of sense into senses, or of senses into sense—back and forth, sense and sensual, warp and woof, the weaving of the world.

To talk of the sense of the world is to invoke its sensuousness, its *hereness* to the body. Olson implicitly suggests this in his postscript to the first two sections of the book where he proposes landscape as bringing the land into the eye's view—the singular, specific measure which yields dimension. If it is a question of knowing, that knowing is determined in the sweep of the eye which returns to body's limit as ground of a new discourse—going back (or in) to get out (or further). Logography—word writing, Olson calls it—knowing and seeing being so close for us, the whole vocabulary of knowing circulates around the visible and the obscured.

In Olson's postscript to *Proprioception* and *Logography*, the immediately visible matters—what you can comprehend in a single view, a sweep of the eye. Here sense is borne precisely in the sensuous. If words are the bearers of sense well before they are manipulated into combinations of meaning which some idea controls, then the landscape itself becomes a kind of word and a kind of body. This cosmos arises in an instantaneous knowing that is not relational, not based on a proliferation of connections, but on the instantaneous presentation of a world. Always this sense of different knowings, of knowing differences, but knowing them here, as they array themselves around us, hard against the fact of what can be seen in one glance. Beyond that lie only stabilities of relation determined in abstraction. Here, the body of words, that identity or integrity, figures as an index of lost or obscured distinctions that are known instantly.

This question of specificity haunts every word of *Proprioception*. To make the particular yield dimension. One negation of that is the idea of progress. Olson's move to a historical discourse focuses on the word "hinge." Hinged civilizations are suspended outside the machine of progress, each unique and precise in its specificities. They unfold, or open, rather than progress. Olson's notion of hinges reclaims the past for a new sense of history—history freed from that abstraction which removes it from us and makes it the mechanical object of some panoptical subject. "Hinge," to hang—suspend, to waver, to be in suspense. What's at stake is to get, as he puts it, outside or backward of the modern lock on the past as *leading to*, where not only is the specific discounted and lost in the relentless march toward reason and justice, but the full complexity of history itself is lost. Olson's hinges open history to the creative, the suspense of creation. The moments he defines are complexes of specific relations, specificities of time, unique.

In the same way, he goes after abstract notions of "society," which he has as the body of our common relations, each one specific. Olson's sense of "society"—that strangely inhuman 18th century invention—or say its sense of coherence—is as a factor of our humanity. Society is precisely the product of the ascendency of the secular. It was what was left to us when the divine was removed as the informing force of our relations. But stripped of its sense—no longer informed by any organizing force—it becomes the expression of "chance." Even the historically-determined "society" of Marxist imagination consists of persons reduced to and arbitrarily distributed among universalized abstractions called "classes" which in turn determine forms of mind. In one sense, chance is a name for the open, the creative. But here, Olson uses it to indicate an evasion. If society is the name of the distribution of people, who is where and why may seem a ridiculous interrogation, but that is part of the problem—the abandonment of a sense of order (as opposed to organization)—and a consequent rejection of our being in common.

Class, in this sense, is simply a given, at best a distraction, at worst, a self-imposed prison. As with Emerson, the only condition and limit that matters for Olson is the self, and society is a function of that, not a determinant, the body of the common relation of our selves. It is neither to be rejected nor acquiesced to, but entered into with the full power of our realized selves. At a time when much of the discourse concerning society among those around Olson consisted of a rejection of bourgeois forms of life as if they were the total and essential definition of "society," Olson moved to reclaim it as the sphere of our common lives determined in the specificities of each person's world-in-relation where "world" is the particular limit each and every self/body brings to the being in common.

This relation is not about, say, "contracts," any more than it is about "classes," which themselves are a kind of empty form waiting to be filled. Contractual thinking implies a world of separate, distinct, self-sufficient entities, say, individuals. Class is the antithesis of that, the man or woman defined by a generalization. In both cases, society is emptied of the sense of the necessary being in common of specific persons.

Behind all these elements is Olson's implicit drive toward the recovery of the sense of the world. Sense is not what we experience as meaning unless it is *almost-meaning*, meaning that dances just in and out of the range of vision without ever settling. This is Emerson's method in the first and second series of *Essays*, his "form," a form F. O. Matthiessen and his predecessors criticize as "mistiness." It seems *misty* because it evades settling into recognizable patterns of development. It avoids the universalizing that would clarify sense into meaning without remainder. His unit of composition is the sentence. Olson calls upon this form in *Proprioception* as well, to keep the field open. Hence the focus in "Grammar—a book."

Locke's sense of language, developed by Emerson and Thoreau, leans on the noun and the verb—Emerson's sense of language as fossil poetry. Olson moves away from noun and verb to adverb and pronoun and article (as adjective)—the invisible words that order—form the relations—of noun and verb. Adjective not as descriptor but as locator. Why, who, the, that, those, which, like, a—words that introduce space, distance, relation. He begins with the word "why," although the layout of words on the page makes it difficult to determine a beginning or an ending, or a precise relation between the various sections spread across the page. Still, the word in the upper most left-hand corner of the page—where most English readers would begin— is "why." Beneath that is "how." Then, in a three-sided box, set at an angle against the rest of the type on the page, is an analysis of the word "quantum," which picks up again in another distinguishing box on the facing page. The concern with *quantum* moves toward quantity and one of its synonyms is *corpus* which returns the thinking to the range of the body. "Quantum," Olson asserts, "is the neuter case of a pronoun, not an adjective." This moves into the heart of one of the main lines of his thinking in his grammar book—e.g., to recover sense as implicit, infolded, rather than internal, which inevitably invokes an external.

Again, sense is not meaning, which is identifiable if not quantifiable. The sense of the world is the potential of its being written and the concern for writing at the centre of *Proprioception* is for articulation of a mode of writing that is adequate to such a world. Jean-Luc Nancy has it: "There is sense only on the [flowering] surface of sense. Never fruit to be harvested...." The connection to quantum opens into the discrete multiplicity of the world that is always more than, or beyond, the sum of the multiple parts.

Olson pushes this sense of quantity even further to bring to light the sense of the invisible words that constitute an actual sense of language before the constitution of an idea—or meaning—in a sentence before signification. Beginning with quantum, he raises the issue of measure within the discreteness of the world—"the character of a thing by which number or measure is applicable to it"—this is a quantum and it is also quantity. As with body, the issue here is the specific and determinable order (say, form) of each specific thing, so that sense arises out of it, not as an imposition or a reference, but as an explication of its specific *thisness*, its haecceity. Quantum, then, as Olson has it, not as an adjective, but as the neuter case of a pronoun, specific and implicit within the body of the word.

The attempt to recover a sense of language (language sense) as it once worked to locate another kind of relation to the world, in fact locates another kind of world, a world whose sense resonates from within each specificity. If there are implications for writing, there are no less implications for how we think the world and/or how it thinks us. His point is there can be no new writing without a new world, or at least a new sense of the world—or world of sense. It's not a question of literature which will always bring writing into some market where it will have to answer to another demand beyond the necessity of its specific energy. The literary brings form into play as something to be mastered and managed in the quest for proficiency. It fosters a measure that determines "excellence" so that the prize, the promotion, the authority, can be awarded on an "objective" basis—or at least with a rationale. The projective moves into a realm outside that set of considerations pushing writing toward the mere recognition at every moment of what must be said, the unmanageable tumultuous sense of the moment.

Proprioception embodies that moment. Neither an exposition nor an analysis, it is a complex Event, a happening of language that identifies the sense of the real in its multiple explications of body, word, syntax, history. In *Proprioception*, Olson presents us with the new world in a way "Projective Verse" was unable to because there, form *was* an extension of content, and the projective was still a kind of dream or memory of what was to come. Just as there are no *contents* of the body, no *interior*, there is no content in *Proprioception* to extend a form from. There is one surface, one stream of sense weaving itself in and out of infolded and unfolded complexities of flesh, language, event. Call it the secular which loses nothing of the divine. Or call it projective, the flowering edge of sense itself, erupting in unpredictable and unmanageable arrangements of the real.

Picking Up the Injuns—Poetics as Transformation

I HAVE BEEN THINKING ABOUT POETICS LATELY, mostly provoked by the editorial work on Robert Duncan's *The H.D. Book*, and the question of what Duncan was up to as he wrote it. What kind of book is it? Some people have proposed that *The H.D. Book* is Duncan's attempt at literary theory; others that it is literary history. Editing the book, however, it became clear that although Duncan's work involves both—certainly the history more so than the theory—it is primarily concerned neither with history nor theory. Its primary impulse is a quest for a poetics. This, in any case, is what Duncan calls it. Quest, from the same Latin root as question and query, is a search. And for Duncan, the history of the quest in Medieval writing, especially the Arthurian cycles, turns it into a romance; a romance he enacts in the 700+ pages of the book with fidelity and imagination.

This idea of a quest has something to do with the imagination of the transformative ground of poetry. At a time when people can go to university to get a PhD in "Poetics," the idea of a quest suggests that poetics results not so much from reading and studying, as it does from a spiritual ordeal, like a quest for the San Graal. For Duncan, this orientation (in Henry Corbin's sense of turning towards an inner rising sun, an inner Orient) took him *through* a particular literary history, the history of the forgetting of women at the inception of modernism, that extraordinary period of radical exploration and innovation in the arts that went on from about 1905 to 1925. It impelled him *through* the rediscovery and reclamation of other hidden histories and hidden minds. That was the first stage of his quest. The second, which occupies Book 2 of *The H.D. Book*, involved following that knowledge into an event, committing himself to the transformations that arose out of the passage through that occulted knowledge. The third stage was *Roots and Branches* and *Bending the Bow*, and the work that followed as he realized the transformation in his poetry.

Charles Olson's sense of a poetics shares a similar commitment to an actual transformation, the kind of transformation that took place in the Alchemist's crucible. I read Olson's little book, *Proprioception*, as an attempt to defend and develop what he calls an American secularization that loses nothing of the divine. His joining of two words that normally would be mutually exclusive is telling. We operate in a frame of mind where "secularization" and "divine" cannot coexist in the same space. In fact, the growth of secularization in the West is measured precisely in terms of the recession of the divine, what's been called the disenchantment of the world. But here Olson brazenly links them and does so in relation to his thinking about what we call "the body."

Secular and divine, as they operate in the imagination of modernity, are what William Blake called "opposites." Rather than just opposing ideas, for Blake they are part of the structure of a visionary state humans find themselves living within and moving through. What we think of as the secular, Blake identified with the visionary state of Generation, or twofold vision. It is the imagination of a barren world without depth, stripped of life and mind and left to the meager measurements of Newton's calipers. Blake sometimes pictured Generation as a man and woman tied together back-to-back. To bring them into another relation where they yield to, say, an embrace or love, is to open the imagination to another dimension, the threefold. For Blake, Beulah was an erotically charged vision of a complex living world, beyond the opposition of secular and divine. Olson imagined it in *Proprioception* as a new body, which is to say a new mode of being in the world that could lead into a furtherness, say, the fourfold.

Al Glover suggested to me that the different modes of the fourfold as they appear in the work of Olson, Blake, Medieval theories of exegesis, and Jack Clarke are perhaps fundamentally incommensurable with each other. I hear what he's saying about the danger of forcing specific modes of thinking into equivalencies. And no doubt there are incommensurable elements, but for Jack Clarke, I think, at least my sense of Jack, the isomorphism of Blake's four-fold vision and the traditional Medieval four-level exegesis, for example, (or the Buddhist Kayas—sometimes three, sometimes four) testify to a deep common rhythm where the fourfold and the anagogical resonate with a similar experience of extended dimension and depth. Whitman's wave, maybe. In any case, each of these modes of thinking about perception and knowledge are similarly grounded in the understanding of a movement toward a deeper and richer experience of the world, one that is lost to us in the various materialisms and positivisms of modernity.

Olson's imagination of "body," which he puts in quotes to distinguish it from our usual sense of body, is a single surface which, through invagination and evagination, folding and unfolding, creates out of itself a complexity of organs and cavities. What we think of, and have thought of, as the contents of a vessel—consciousness, the unconscious, self, soul, mind—arise in Olson's sense of body out of the movement and frictions of this complex surface—integral to it. It is a *bodymind*, in the same way the world is *seculardivine*. This move is crucial to Olson's quest for a poetics that escaped the trap of traditional notions of form and content (and their opposites), what Whitehead called "the bifurcation of nature" into mind and matter. Form and content, in that context, become part of a cosmology that is based on a world of mutually exclusive opposites.

Some people have suggested that this argument is a "mystification" of something called a "natural body" and ignores contemporary theories of the "socially-constructed body" and of the self as a so-called "subject position," erected by something called "society" in those bodily construction projects. Michel Foucault was one of the early sources for this thinking of discursive bodies. What he left us was a brilliant critique of modernity and the Cartesian subject. As a critique though, it is in relation *to* that order, a site of demolition as it has been called, not beyond it. Even the structure of the argument which sets up something called essentialism as the mutually exclusive opposite of something called constructivism locates it within a Cartesian structure. The notion of the self as a "subject position," socially imposed on a body still has them in a dualistic discourse anchored firmly in relation to that old humanism that begins with the distinction between self and society. Olson does give us a critique—in *Mayan Letters* he calls it "Original stupidity." But the thrust of his thinking is toward a way out of that treacherous mental trap toward something further. It is a poet's thinking, a poet's technique—a quest for a poetics which involves a profound transformation, what he calls a "new stance."

In *Proprioception*, Olson addressed something he calls "society," going so far as to give us a theory of society, though it is hardly recognizable as sociological. His interest here, as always in his quest for a poetics, was focussed on specificity and away from generalizations. As he wrote to Robert Creeley, what they were "pissing at" in their intense correspondence was how to make the object yield dimension. This was where he located the *seculardivine*. Anything that robbed the object of its specificity countered that process. And, crucially, the self was no more than any other object—merely another singular, irreducible force in a field of forces. This was a post-Cartesian move toward the possibility of a *bodymindself* beyond the limits of modernity's disciplines and resistances. For Olson, that meant going back to figure out how to go further.

Or this, in any case, is how he put it in the letters to Creeley that were published as *Mayan Letters*. *Mayan Letters* has been described as ethnology and cited as evidence of Olson as ethnologist. I would respectfully suggest that's ridiculous. Charles Olson was never anything other than a poet. Ethnology, as one of those Enlightenment inventions like sociology (which Olson identified in his *Bibliography on America for Ed Dorn* as "a lot of shit"), is deeply rooted in modernity's addiction to binaries (its foundational gesture being the creation of an Other suitable for study, i.e. a subject of Power), and to some lingering notion of objectivity (and, of course, subjectivity) that is crucial to its sense of itself as a "science," though a "social" science as they say.

Olson never had any interest in those terms or the disciplines that authorized them, especially the idea of "science" as a rigorous method of investigating an "objective" world (although he was sympathetic to a Whiteheadian visionary science). "How can I pick up these injuns," he asks Creeley, most unscientifically, and then later, by way of further explanation, "for their nouns, undone, are my nouns." His complex interest in the Mayans began here, not with a sense of objective distance or study—the imposition of power—but with a sense of identification and the desire for transformation. The Mayans were not other to him; they were a mysterious possibility of his American self, a further unfolding.

This identification was a sign of his quest for a poetics that would reorient his self, reconstitute it. Olson always thought of our condition as the outer limit of a box that got put together sometime around 1200 BCE. To imagine the *postmodern* (as he famously put it), Olson turned to the archaic, both modes of being outside the box. If Sumer was the high-water mark of human civilization and the back wall of the box, it rested on the foundation of Pleistocene humans, our evolutionary sweet spot, as Olson drove further back seeking an imagination of being in the world that could give rise to a new poetic energy.

The Mayans were another instance of that, one that offered him a literal entrance through a hands-on encounter with the actual material remains of their culture, an American culture at that, which, following his work with Melville, who constituted the front wall of that same box, became an important condition (Olson's sense of *America* always included the whole place, pole to pole). *Mayan Letters* are remarkable not for some ethnographic description of a cultural other, but for their record of a poet's struggle "to pick up the injuns":

> I have been in the field, away from people, working around stones in the sun, putting my hands into the dust and fragments and pieces of those Mayans who used to live here down and along this road.... The big thing ... is the solidity of the sense of their lives one can get right here in the fields and on the hill which rises quite steeply from the shore.

From having his hands deep in the Yucatan earth digging up pieces of the Mayans, Olson dives into a critique of Pound and Williams, the Scylla and Charybdis of his imagination of the condition of poetry he inherited.

He locates the failures of Pound and Williams in their inability to grasp the substantive change in history and their failure to realign their methods in relation to the new materials. Pound's ego, while turning time into space, lost all emotional diversity. Williams, while opening his poem to emotion, gave up space to the limits of Patterson. Olson ties both problems to what he calls the question of nomination and then turns to his reading of Mayan glyphs as an alternative because "they were hot for the world they lived in & hot to get it down by way of a language which is loaded to the gills of the FIRST GLYPH with that kind of imagination which the kerekters have a way of calling creative."

> ... What continues to hold me, is, the tremendous levy on all objects as they present themselves to human sense, in this glyph-world. And the proportion, the distribution of weight given same parts of all,

> seem, exceptionally, distributed & accurate ... And the weights of same, each to the other, is, immaculate (as well as, full).

Olson articulates a sense of language beyond the representational (and non-representational, its opposite). Each "word" cum "glyph," each nomination as he encounters it in the glyph-world embodies the fullness of the experience of, the disposition of, the world in language. It is an experience of specificity, of language not as limit or restriction, but as the stuff of creation. It is a move toward what he calls in *Proprioception* the *secular that loses nothing of the divine*, a language that incarnates the ineffable in the specific materials of the world.

What I am calling the *bodymindself* entered Olson's thinking here at a crucial juncture. "I ought to get off to you about the *flesh* here," he wrote to Creeley during a rant about North America's obsession with "improvement." "BUT the way the bulk of them (the 'unimproved') wear their flesh ... the flesh is worn as a daily thing, like the sun, is—& only in this sense—a common, carried as the other things are, for use." He went on, "The result ... is, that the individual peering out from that flesh is precisely himself, is a curious wandering animal." If Olson's language here still struggled against the tendency to describe the experience in terms of an inner and outer, the thrust of his thinking was toward an experience of the whole fleshy somatic self as he encountered it and absorbed it among the descendants of the Mayans:

> jeesus, when you are rocked, by the roads, against any of them—kids, women, men—it's so very gentle, so granted, the feel, of touch—none of that pull, away, which, in the States caused me, for so many years, the deepest sort of questions about my own structure, the complex of my own organism, I felt so very much this admission these people now give me.

This admission, as he called it, is a moment of transubstantiation, an alchemical transformation of the whole self into a new being, one that is like the Mayan as he was able to recover that—and through that recovery discover the ground of his poetics, freed from what he saw as the failures of Pound and Williams, especially in relation to history:

> The capacity for (1) the observation & (2) the invention has no more to do with brick or no wheels or metal or stone than you or i are different from, sd peoples: we are like. Therefore, there is no 'history.'

I am back to where I started, then, with the proposition that poetics is not a theory, it's not thought or rethought—it is a condition of being that the poet wins through struggle. Duncan's quest for that new condition led him into what was hidden all around us, what he called the occult—hidden histories, hidden mind, hidden processes—as a way to open the hidden dimensions of the world into his careful music. Olson's quest led him back as a way further out into possibilities—necessities, really—of the world to come. There is no better place to end this then than deep in Maximus:

> No Greek will be able
> to discriminate my body.
>   An American
> is a complex of occasions,
> themselves a geometry
> of spatial nature.
>   I have this sense,
> that I am one
> with my skin
>   Plus this—plus this:
> that forever the geography
> which leans in
> on me I compell
> backwards I compell Gloucester
> to yield, to
> change
>   Polis
> is this

—"Maximus to Gloucester, Letter 27 [withheld]"

Poetics' Bodies—
Some Poetry Wars, 1913-1990

When Donald Allen's anthology, *The New American Poetry*, hit the bookstores in 1960, it became the source and focus of an unprecedented wave of excited argument about poetry across North America, not to mention England and parts of Europe. That moment has been visited and revisited numerous times. Its historic intervention is often noted and celebrated, but it has also been minutely examined for its errors and exclusions as much as its accomplishments, notably the predominance of white males in its selection of poets. Whatever criticisms hindsight has granted, however, no amount of revisioning can lessen the fact of the enthusiasm that met its publication. And although the excitement was equally over the rhetorical explosion of Allen Ginsberg and the brilliant understatement of Frank O'Hara, Charles Olson stood at the centre of it, a fact that was not of his making, but for which he was to be subject of increasingly shrill criticism in the years that followed.

Apart from the new poetry, the major contribution Allen made was to include in his anthology a section on poetics, the principles of the making of the poem. It was unprecedented in the aesthetic climate of the 1950s, and, as a number of people have pointed out, distinguished Allen's anthology from its competitor, *The Poets of England and America.* "Statements on Poetics" mostly consisted of fragments culled from journals, notebook entries, previous magazine publications, excerpts from poems, etc. Allen led off the poetics section with Olson's essay, "Projective Verse," which had been first published as a chapbook in 1955 by then LeRoi Jones' (later Amiri Baraka) Totem Press. In the year that followed, the essay generated a significant buzz, significant enough that Frank O'Hara, when pushed by Allen to write his own statement of poetics, would see fit to lampoon it in "Personism," typically wry, humorous, and sassy. Still, Olson's essay seemed to strike many people the way Emerson describes genius in the opening of "Self-Reliance," as the recognition of their "own rejected thoughts." Its brilliance resonated loudly, both in its recovery of the body as the source of poetry, and in its extension of that thinking into a radical proposition about the fundamental shift in the nature of "the Real" that such poetry engages.

As O'Hara's "Personism" indicated, resistance to the essay, or at least to the enthusiasm that it provoked, was almost as quick to develop as the enthusiasm itself, and while initially focussed on Olson, quickly found its target in those who were caught up for many different reasons in the enthusiasm. The reasons for the resistance are as manifold as the reasons for the enthusiasm. Some people did not recognize themselves in Olson's energetic prose and claimed to find it dogmatic and bullying. Others, committed to the conservative poetics of the New Criticism, found it meaningless and anarchic, and perhaps a little threatening. Still, others felt the enthusiasm was indicative of a kind of servile adoration and that Olson fostered that, or at least thrived on it.

The word "Olsonite," which was originally adopted as a positive if ironic identity by poets in the Tish group in Vancouver (simultaneously identifying it with toilet seats), gradually became part of a pejorative vocabulary that included "cult," "disciple," "guru," "devotee," "follower," "true believer," and other terms that were current in 60s and 70s as negative descriptors of various religious and fringe political sects run by powerful, authoritative individuals who exploited weaker followers. It came to embody an anxiety about the loss of "autonomy" in the face of manipulative power, as if no other network of authority and relation was possible, as if "individualism" was both natural and innately admirable, a situation which arose among many artists and intellectuals in reaction to the consumerist conformism that defined USAmerican culture. The anthropologist Victor Turner called it "the clichés associated with status incumbency and role playing."

The resistance to Olson grew during the 60s, 70s, and into the 80s, when certain events in Buffalo sealed his diminution and eventual "falling out of favor" as Susan Howe put it in a 2011 interview. The public attacks on him and his work were often articulated in terms of continuing accusations of his cult-like status as a "High Priest," as well as the increasing authority of a sociological critique that dismissed him and his magnum opus, the epic *Maximus Poems*, as manifestations of patriarchal oppression and control. The poem, and indeed the whole project of writing an epic that he had taken up from Ezra Pound and William Carlos Williams, was represented as a "totalizing" attempt to control the world through language in the interests of patriarchy. But while this was the public face of the assault on Olson's diminishing reputation and influence, arguably the deeper issue was poetics.

Olson's determining statement on poetics, "Projective Verse," had fired the imaginations of countless people through its insistence on returning poetry to the reality of the *bodymind*, liberating it from the intricate aesthetic rules of the schoolmen poets and opening it to the emergence of unprecedented knowledge. His insistence on head, heart, ear, and breath was a thinking of the poem as emerging out of the body's deep, ancient, rhythmic complexities. Poetics, as Olson understood it, was a quest, a spiritual ordeal that led to a transformative gnosis that opened the poet to certain energies informing the world, that Olson made evident in the dynamic irregularities and energetic push of his prose. This difference in thinking poetics played a crucial role in establishing his authority, and later in dismissing it.

The word "poetics" has been around for a while, though its meaning changes. Aristotle's *Poetics* was primarily a set of genre definitions (tragedy, epic, comedy), desired effects (fear, pity, wonder), their result (catharsis), and the rules and methods necessary to create them. Milton refers to poetics as the "laws of a true Epic poem." Purely technical in the sense of addressing poetry (and drama) as governed by laws external to and formative of its composition, poetics became identified (and discussed) as prosody and aesthetics in later thinking. The only question facing the poet is whether or not he or she knows the rules and is able to master them well.

The very definition of poetics has been a site of contest and a major source of poetry wars since at least 1913, if not 1897, when Wordsworth and Coleridge published *Lyrical Ballads*. They didn't call it poetics. Mostly they wrote about diction, content, and prosody as the sites of their technical adventure and its radical democratic implications. Writing about an old leech gatherer in composed language that approached the common speech of ordinary people, while staying other than that, was a critical move in recognizing the cosmological earthquake then taking place and its reordering of the *discriminations* of meaning. By 1913, Wordsworth's breakthrough had been mostly reabsorbed into a verse regime characterized by sentiment, nostalgia, and iterative forms.

Declaring war on that literary formation, Ezra Pound and H.D. invented *Imagism* and returned poetics to a front line of the battle over poetry's particular value. The crisis of representation that had been building for a hundred years raged in Europe and North America. It left no ground for the Real and no external, transcendent zone of rules. The quality of the poem became determined by the poet's imaginative relation to form (Williams), or the attempt to reiterate and revivify a relation to the rules (Eliot). For the first time, poetics was identified not with rules, but with what might be called a mode of being, the poet's existential implication in the world. And that mode of being was increasingly identified with the fundamental transformations of history, the emergence of new forms of life, new "bodies," in a newly emerging world. Poets became what Pound called "antennae."

Hilda Doolittle, a friend of Pound's at the University of Pennsylvania, had relocated to London in 1911 at his urging. Together with Richard Aldington and a number of his acquaintances, she spent time at the British Museum Reading Room, translating and reworking Greek poems while using their particular energies and forms to inform her own. She was 27 years old and about to change the course of literary history. Three of her poems had appeared in the January 1914 issue of an influential new magazine in the U.S., *Poetry Chicago*. Of the three—"Priapus," "Epigram," and "Hermes of the Ways"—the first two were her reworked translations of poems from the *Greek Anthology* and were signed "H.D." The third was "original" and was signed "H.D. *Imagiste*." And so her name—or, even better, her initials—were identified with the new poetry.

H.D.'s work became, at least momentarily and somewhat ironically, exemplary modernist poetry by embodying the restrained form of ancient Greek verse charged with an energy that Robert Duncan called *hierophantic*, an opening of the poem up to further forces beyond or within—in relation to, in any case—the immediate occasion. This "archaic-innovation" disrupted perceptual automatism and opened the poem's field to powers and energies from "outside." She was informed by intensities of being (in other times referred to as "angels" or "gods") that she made known in unprecedented language events, transforming an imagination of that spare classical Greek beauty into the ultimate form of modernity: simple, common, intense, what Charles Olson called "a secularization that loses nothing of the divine."

Ezra Pound, who organized or produced most of the promotional activities that launched the imagist group as an international phenomenon, had targets in mind for his often-inflammatory pronouncements on poetics. The Georgians, poets associated with an annual anthology of the same name, considered themselves representatives of the "modern" development of poetry, but were still heavily under the influence of Tennyson and the lingering forms of late Romanticism. For Pound, their romantic spirit and often antique "poetic" diction and constructions ("We are thine, O Love, being in thee and made of thee …") were the height—or depth—of genteel banality. In his drive to clearly distinguish between the new sound and look of *his* "modern" and the sentimentalized Romanticism of the Georgian's "modern," Pound wrote a series of manifestoes/essays on the nature of Imagism that introduced poetics into the argument in an unprecedented way.

"Poetics" at that time were determined by sets of rules such as George Saintsbury's *Historical Manual of English Prosody*. The English Saintsbury, having written a definitive, three volume work on the history of English prosody, a word that took the place of "poetics" in pre-twentieth century discourses on the techniques of poetry, decided to produce a book that summarized the rules of verse. It became the authoritative text on poetic technique. As late as 2007, critics still acknowledged the importance of Saintsbury's work because "until fairly recently [it] dominated much prosodic thinking." As Ammiel Alcalay pointed out to me, "if a student wants to actually learn something about the classical/traditional ear, that's where i send them. also, i would say that saint's prosodic ear/sense would align much more with what's familiar to us than the bad eliot imitation new critical official verse line."

That said, Saintsbury did propose prosody as a genteel collection of historical rules governing the writing of genteel poetry for a genteel class of male writers. The manual implicitly located the poet as a man of good taste and accomplishment who had mastered the rules of verse. Those rules were based on mastering set rhythmic forms. "[L]ines," Saintsbury wrote, "possess a definite rhythm based on what is called double and triple time; that these integers (the lines) are made up of corresponding or proportionate fractions to which it has been usual to give the name 'feet' …." It was a vision of specifically English poetry, and, Saintsbury argued, the order of the form reinforced English culture, aka, Civilization-as-we-know-it. Meredith Martin identifies his sense of prosody as an aspect of what she calls his *desperation* "to preserve not only the classics as a discipline but his understanding of the classical English gentleman, with an education that set him apart from others."

For the Georgian poets, Sainsbury's prosodics offered the perfect justification of their own poetic processes, including a stage of "conception." A purely mental response to external stimuli, conception, the idea of the poem precedes any involvement with language: "the inspiration of some imaginative experience completely establishes itself in the poet's mind, as an affair of clear imagery, vivid importance, and delightful excitement: also, as a focus of varied and perhaps only just suggested associations and allusions; but above all as a single inclusive harmony, however complex, of all that it contains." Myron Simon goes on to point out that "[v]erbal art has no place in it…. As soon as the poet is perfectly aware of his own experience—of all that can be seen and felt in it—then, as far as he is concerned, expression is complete …. But if a poem is to come of this, what happened in the poet's mind must somehow be made to happen in other minds: the image and its meaning must be conveyed to us…. So now begins the stage of technique." This poet represents what Ahab in *Moby-Dick* called *the perfect man*, an embodiment of the ideal features of the human (English male version) determined in the matrix of modernism: a self-contained, autonomous, self-aware individual in control of complex information which he is able to convey to others because of his mastery of certain techniques.

Ezra Pound's *Imagiste* was a whole other kettle of fish. "A few don'ts by an *Imagiste*," first published with H.D.'s poems in *Poetry Chicago* in 1914, proposed not just a new kind of poetry, but implied a new kind of person who created that poetry. It was not just a question of replacing one set of rules with another, although Pound certainly did something like that with his various injunctions regarding composition. More importantly, he challenged the prescriptive manual by implying an identity rather than an instrumentality between the poet and her poetics. Pound presented the poetics of Imagism as more than the mechanics of the poem, and the poet as more than the master of technique. If the *poeisis* in "poetics" has to do with the making of the poem, it no less has to do with the stance of the poet, the making of the maker. The poet is an *imagiste*, a *bodymind* in process rather than a mind mastering and implementing the idea of formal means toward an aesthetic experience.

Pound thought that poetry was capable of initiating states of consciousness that escaped the banal mental traps and automatism of early twentieth century consumer society. If the traps were forms of life determined by the secular grind of a world depleted of all value beyond the dollar, Pound's *imagiste* was extraordinary in so far as she was the embodiment of "an intellectual and emotional complex in an instant of time," an eruption of *value/meaning* into the wasteland of contemporary life. She could compose words into rhythmic forms that delivered that complex (rather than represented it). She could think through cadence; her music was in her body rather than in abstracted forms. She could see/tell "the truth"— "its force will lie in its truth, its interpretative power (of course, poetic force does always rest there)." Her intensity of being was identical to the intensity of her words. And the stake was the body: "Let us consider the body," Pound wrote in "Psychology and the Troubadours," "as pure mechanism. Our kinship to the ox we have constantly thrust upon us; but beneath this is our kinship to the vital universe, to the tree, and the living rock ...." He went on to contrast the consciousness of poets whose minds "are like soap bubbles" to those whose "thoughts are in them as the thought of the tree is in the seed, or in the grass, or the grain, or the blossom." Pound would call this thinking *pagan*, in contrast to the *humanism* that historically overwhelmed it.

Although T. S. Eliot supported Pound's campaign to replace a faded Romanticism with an intense modernism, his own sense of image as what he called "objective correlative" had a different cast to it, a different meaning. Eliot's objective correlative centred, as he put it, on creating a "set of objects, a situation, a chain of events which shall be the formula of that *particular* emotion; such that when the external facts, which must terminate in sensory experience, are given, the emotion is immediately evoked." It relied on the governing schema that defined modernity, dividing the world between an active subject and the object it acts on. In Eliot's formulation of that relation, the writer creates an image of the object(ive) which creates a subjective (emotional) response. It is a closed economy, Descartes' *cogito* in relation to the alienated world of its making.

H.D.'s image was "hierophantic," a form of information about other registers of the world without and within the particular incident of its invocation. To achieve the knowledge that is the poem, the poet transforms herself even as the knowledge transforms the poem. A knot of knowing and transforming. Its intensity had nothing to do with intentionally arousing emotions and everything to do with creating a language event that resonated in multiple dimensions. Poetics was not some technical system for organizing language into a specific form called "a poem," but a matter of orientation toward and within "an intellectual and emotional complex in an instant of time."

H.D.'s poetics were rooted in a thinking of what Pound calls "freedom," liberation from the bounds of a secular, wholly material world (the object of Eliot's objective correlative) shackled to the space/time dichotomy of Newtonian physics. "It is the presentation of such a 'complex' instantaneously," Pound says in his manifesto, "which gives that sense of sudden liberation; that sense of freedom from time limits and space limits; that sense of sudden growth, which we experience in the presence of the greatest works of art." This experience constituted a new knowledge that was an old knowledge, a transforming knowledge, just as H.D.'s poems constituted an experience at once radically old and radically new. Although the argument was not yet articulated, the lines were being drawn, and they had to do with the thinking of "the body" and its relationship to the rhythmic knowledge of the poem.

The excitement generated by Imagism led to the inevitable iterations based on copying forms. Form forged out of the dynamism of the transfigured body, the transformative gnosis, became a shell filled with banalities in the shape of pictures and too many words. Pound called it Amygism, dismissing Amy Lowell's "Imagism" as the work of a "democratic beer-garden." His alternative, Vorticism, while renewing his sense of Imagism's relation to energetic form, also drew on Allen Upward's proposition in *The New World* that the nature of the Real needed to be rethought. Upward rejected the dualist notion of energy and matter (and subject and object) as separate ontological categories, and imagined instead what he called the "whirl-swirl" of creation, the network of infinite relations of interpenetrating and interdependent forces. Process, as Whitehead and quantum mechanics would later have it, became the fundamental reality, and the poem was the event of that "whirl-swirl," a vortex.

Eliot's poetry, with its regulating ghosts haunting the arras, its contemporary ironies, and its deep nostalgia for the imagined order of the past (preferably white, straight male, and Christian) dominated poetry for many years. The image, rather than being what Robert Duncan called the "nexus of an experience," became a rhetorical figure useful for "expression." Eliot's poetry and criticism found its perfect audience in a group of scholarly poets at Vanderbilt University in Nashville Tennessee. Committed to the reactionary plantation culture of the ante-bellum Southern U.S. as a counter force to the alienating pressures of urbanism and industrialism, first the Fugitives, and then their offspring, the Agrarians, dominated the production and criticism of poetry from the late 20s through the 50s. Their texts (*Understanding Poetry, The Well-Wrought Urn*, "The Intentional Fallacy," etc.) delineated the poem as a self-contained, self-referential aesthetic object without reference to the poet, the poet's specific political world, and especially without an uncontrolled process. Its perfections were exemplary of the cultural achievements of the world lost to Sherman's marauders and carpetbagger predations, and resonated with Eliot's sense of Christian culture.

The codification of this Methodist critical address and its necessary object, what came to be called The New Criticism, found a welcoming home in University English Departments hungry for a legitimizing "science" of literary study that moved beyond notions of appreciation and edification. The theorists and practitioners of the New Criticism—John Crowe Ransom, Cleanth Brooks, René Welleck, Robert Penn Warren, W.K. Wimsatt, Monroe Beardsley, etc.—used their authority to establish and edit prestigious journals including *The Kenyon Review*, *The Southern Review*, and *The Sewanee Review*, which then became the gateway to literary recognition, establishing both the value of Literature and the site of its presentation while promoting poetry that adhered to a poetics grounded in the differentiation of form and content and the achievement of formal aesthetic "excellence." Literary excellence, rather than transformative gnosis, became poetry's motive.

Meanwhile, Pound's poetics found adherents in two young poets who resisted the Methodist takeover of the Poetry Plantation: one was

Olson and the other, six years senior to him, was Louis Zukofsky. Zukofsky was on it first. He first wrote to Pound in 1927 and visited him in Rapallo in 1933. Olson, who worked for the Roosevelt Administration during World War II, didn't come to Pound until after the war when he visited him at St. Elizabeth's. Both poets came to Pound for poetics, but each found a different range of thinking at stake. Louis Zukofsky came for the discipline of Pound's sounded knowledge, the dynamic balance of what Pound called *melopoeia*, *logopoeia*, and *phanopoeia*. Born an outsider in a Yiddish speaking household of Jewish immigrants, Zukofsky's ear was astonishing in the range of its precise discriminations which played as subtly on the intellect as on the ear. His continuous intellectual struggle with Marxism provided a shifting ground of unresolvable political tension engaged with the thinking of justice.

Olson, also from a family of immigrants, though a generation removed, was born into a New England still full of the thought of the American Revolution and its potential to unleash a new world. For Olson that "American dream" was real. He was an immigrant's kid who was able to get an education at the finest schools in USAmerica. That experience was central to his thinking, from his high school commencement on Emerson's "The American Scholar," to his pre-war Melville studies at Wesleyan and Harvard and its fruit, *Call Me Ismael,* to his writing of the *Maximus Poems*. America was both a radical potential, a projective possibility, and a catastrophic failure. Determined to write an American epic, he went to Pound to find a way to bring history into the poem as part of an active conversation rather than a range of reference, a sublated presence rather than a past. Like Zukofsky, he constructed a poetics on Pound's three-fold discrimination, but he took Pound's sense of sound and pushed it toward what he called action, and later, projective.

Zukofsky's and Olson's difference is probably most evident there. In keeping with his musical thinking, Zukofsky approached the poem as structure. His poetics had to do as much with his sense of Bach as it did with Pound. The statement on "objectivism" he published in 1930 is characterized by a language of charged stasis. He calls it "rested totality" which he relates to "apprehension satisfied completely." These are aesthetic terms that he links to his idea of *sincerity*. Although he doesn't make the connection explicit, Pound's observation that the Chinese character for sincerity was "pictorially the sun's lance coming to rest on the precise spot verbally" surely resonates here. These minor units of sincerity, Zukofsky proposed, could be arranged and resolved into a "structure" of one apprehended unit, art form as an object. In that sense, Zukofsky was intent on locating himself in a specific tradition of artists whose work achieved a recognizable level of aesthetic complexity and intensity modulated in the case of poetry, as he said, from lower-level speech to upper-level music.

Olson's vocabulary, on the other hand, focussed on the active and dynamic as opposed to the structural. "Projective Verse" is divided into two sections. The first addresses the poem's relation to the body, and the second expounds the philosophical implications of this relation to Olson's thinking of postmodernity. Olson zeroed in on Pound's understanding of poetics as transformational gnosis, and returned it to the "body" as poetry's source. Heart, breath, head, and ear are the ground of the poem. His poetics with its emphasis on the poem as a kinetic event, what he calls "projective," couldn't be more different from Zukofsky's rested totality. If Zukofsky's poetics demanded an intense intellectual/sonal construction, Olson's demanded a dynamic "body" to project the energy of the event. It was not modernity's body with its necessary divisions, exclusions, repressions, and hierarchies. He rethought its orders in terms of a single invaginated and evaginated, folded and unfolded, complexity of surface beyond modernity's compulsive dualisms.

Olson's poetics were explicitly entangled with his philosophical/historical thinking of the postmodern. Part of his projective thinking of the world beyond the inherited structures of authority that im-press us as they order the minutia of our lives, poetry was a mode of knowledge that opened the world to unanticipated form and meaning, just as polis, he said, was compelling the world backward to open space for new form and meaning. Olson's push removes poetics from literary discourse which it reveals as a limitation of modernity, part of a mental world in which something called the "self" inhabits a "body" and works a "mind" to measure the "objective" world for its use, say, as objective correlative. The self is autonomous, rational, and subject to meaningful affect. The same self expresses those structures of minute authorities as identity and turns the poem into a revelation of self, what Olson called "the private-soul-at-any-public-wall."

The pressure from the weight of the inherited world forces itself on the poem and the poet and can only be countered through transformative gnosis entangled with the unfolding energies of history, or, say, creation, or reality and the poet's pushback, her compelling of the world back. In "Projective Verse" Olson calls that counter force *stance*, which is to say relational refiguration of the dynamic forms of creation, the emerging of the world. Another name for it is *further* in Emerson' sense of the self as always further. Olson's poetics, in other words, were cosmological rather than aesthetic. This figured in another crucial difference between him and Zukofsky—the relation to the literary.

If Zukofsky felt some resentment for being ignored by the literary establishment, for Olson, the literary was always just another disciplinary apparatus of the modern cosmology, a stricture on the imagination. Its structures of reward and punishment impose limits on the artist. The idea of "literary excellence," for instance, while seeming "natural," rewards an effort recognizable within certain approved bounds as "art." The prizes, the grants, the positions are inducements to stay within the limits, or, if you must go outside, to do it tastefully and in a manner that does not fundamentally challenge the order of authorities. Olson's sense of poetry existed outside those structures, since its goal was not prizes or acknowledgement but knowledge, knowledge of the world beyond the operative categories of constraint administered and enforced by the university.

The differences between Zukofsky and Olson never led to war. It was more a mild skirmish. Zukofsky dismissed Olson's epic poem, finding only a few "lyrical bits" of interest. He complained that "Projective Verse" was a derivative of his own poetics as articulated in "Sincerity and Objectification," and that Olson's "objectism" was a direct theft of his own proposal in 1931 that "A poem. A poem as object.... Perfect rest." As Olson's fame and influence grew, Zukofsky expressed distaste for what he considered Olson's "didacticism" and he joined certain circles in criticizing Olson for his so-called "disciples," finding the excitement Olson generated to be unbecoming and hucksterish.

For his part, Olson invited Zukofsky to teach at Black Mountain College, which Zukofsky couldn't afford to do, but otherwise had little to say about him. In the Berkeley event, Olson at one point challenged Zukofsky's authority: "The Ides of March, yeah, where it turns out Catullus, who was a wealthy cat, even if his grandfather still spoke Irish—Er—that—and that ain't unusual, right?—I mean, like, have we got an instance of Catullus? Did Louis Zukofsky's translation become

President? (LAUGHTER.)" His dismissal of "objectivism" in "Projective Verse" spoke silent volumes about his assessment of Zukofsky's 'perfect rest.' But although the two poets never engaged in hostilities over their differences, those differences lingered and later found expression in another poetry war.

Olson's greatest performance of contempt for Literature and demonstration of his commitment to a further, unclassified knowledge was his "reading" at the Berkeley Poetry Conference in 1965, a four-hour marathon dismissal of the institution's forms and expectations and an uncontained spiritual revelation, a ta'wil in the Avicennan tradition. His success can be measured by the howls of protest it provoked and its continuing mischaracterization as a "drunken rant," and "an absolute travesty." His biographer refers to it as "swaggering" and "confused," and brings in an apparently distraught Robert Creeley, a kind of Greek chorus clutching its pearls, to ask, "Is *this* the Charles Olson we all know and love?" as if Olson had been possessed or had revealed his sexual attraction to mops. And in one sense, the answer was, no. This was an Olson Creeley didn't know, or didn't want to acknowledge, an Olson venturing outside the preserve of Literature, challenging his peers to follow him into the uncharted territory of a Nation of nothing but poetry.

They weren't, for the most part, interested. There were reputations still to be made and bolstered. Prizes to win. Lifetime achievement awards to receive. Worse, although Olson had located himself outside the recognizable and defining authorities of modernity, all his actions and relations were measured against the norms of bourgeois modernity, refiguring them as failures. It was a major counterattack on a poetics based on a move beyond modernity's relational forms of authority and the enactment of the projective as transformative gnosis, as post-modern flesh in action, an activity that by its nature is common since the individual has lost its quiddity.

This fact of the common, or communal, as the ground of poetry and scholarship was explicit in Olson's notion of polis. Following Jean-Luc Nancy, polis is what "*happens to us*—question, waiting, even imperative—*in the wake of* society," what appears to us as "neither a work to be produced, nor a lost communion, but rather as space itself, and the spacing of the experience of the outside, of the outside-of-self." One of the ways Olson's poetics as enacted in the Berkeley reading are antithetical to the literary (in both senses) is in their insistence that such a discharge of energies arises from the circulation and generation of those energies within just such a space as Nancy identifies, and that that process is the act in which what we call community, our *being-in-common*, reveals itself to itself. But recast in the light of modernity's "norm," such a dynamic signifies *failed individualism* and is caricatured in terms of power inequities and abuses and defined in mostly religious terms mobilized in the Enlightenment to attack the old regime: acolyte, disciple, devotee, follower, believer, on the one side, and high priest, guru, etc. on the other.

Olson's "polis" was not limited to a critique of USAmerican consumer culture and imperial politics, or to some limited, materialist historical geography of Gloucester. It was a plan of action, a fractal process that resonated on multiple levels but always began as local. The idea of a being-together of scholar/poets working in some new, active sense of *relation* was realized most notably in the *Magazine of Further Studies*, a publication of the Institute of Further Studies, a group of Olson's students, scholars, and poets dedicated to a projective engagement with the thinking that emerged in relation with Olson. Unique in its concept of the *space of the magazine*, the *Magazine of Further Studies* ran to six issues between 1965 and 1969. Writers in the loose network of relations Olson was a significant part of contributed poems, reviews, essays, and *sui generis* material, often in conversation with each other within and across issues, enacting relational energetics and undoing any sense of *separate minds*. The poetics of the "body" extended into this common body of thinking where *further* was an opening into an autonomous zone of new thinking emerging in the process of relational exchange and provocation.

A culture of dynamic tensions, polis is present in the mutual push-back of finitudes in active relation that unleashes what's always more than the appearance of the relations. Describing his relationship with Olson, Michael Anania wrote about quarreling: "There was, more than anything in Charles, a sense of common purpose among poets. In that first year we quarreled and haggled over gestures that initially at least seem too sweeping too broad. He would listen—"I hear you—," he would say, leaning toward you—then move you back, not to evidence or argument, but consequence." The principle of selection for admission to the conversation had less to do with extraneous factors, say, gender, than it did with the ability to push back, to be an active participant in a rough and tumble conversation. Olson didn't want observers hanging around the polis when there was work to be done. Like the call and response dynamic of jazz, the dynamic of polis as *being-in-common* required active engagement and constant exposure.

It was confusing for those entangled in a writing culture based on individual achievement and reward, ideas of autonomy and originality, and a separate, regulated zone called Literature, in which one can accumulate prestige and power. While they could recognize Olson's polis as a possible physical geography, as specifically, say, Gloucester, Massachusetts, with a documented history, they couldn't follow him in his late journeys into modes of entangled reception of the sense that in-formed that geography and history. They especially couldn't see the ways Olson developed and nurtured that sense of polis as active relation in actual circumstances. From their perspective, Olson's actual on-the-ground polis as local practice was only comprehensible as the abandonment of "individual autonomy" and was defined in pejorative terms of relation reduced to power inequities rather than relational dynamic and exchange. The vocabulary establishes the targeted practice as tainted, as *not-Literary*, as a violation of the integrity and sanctity of the individual, even as the loss of sanity, as going ga-ga, as Robert Creeley put it, and therefore, to be held in contempt.

The real problem was even deeper and had to do with cosmology. Recognizing that meaning had to be rethought in the context of a world that had lost its orientation to the onslaught of modernity's culture of general equivalence, Olson argued in *Proprioception* for a "secularization that loses nothing of the divine," pushing to overwhelm that binary division between secular and divine with a sense of a further unmapped plenitude. Like Emerson, who gave up the pulpit for the lectern and the sermon for the lecture, Olson worked through his poetry to find a new, postmodern stance that moved beyond both the religiosity that turned the world over to some other authority, and the secularism of modernity that left the world dead and at the mercy of insatiable human hunger. Like Whitehead's "god function," Olson's secularization that loses nothing of the divine is a radical gesture of conservation, neither and both at the same time, a difficult move beyond compulsive dualisms into a world without previous articulation. To find some articulation in his search among stones, Olson turned to sources as diverse as Jung, Henry Corbin, Maria Sabina, and Hesiod. Shamanism, myth, Avicennan angelology all circulate through Olson's orders of thinking, extend the world, opening it beyond the closures of modernity. That is what he meant by postmodern.

Olson and his poetics were the focus of immense attention in the 1960s. One story of the poetry wars of the 60s and 70s pits the "outlaw" poets of *The New American Poetry* led by Olson against the "establishment" poets of *The New Poets of England and America* and the New Critics. Robert Lowell distinguished the different poetries as "raw" and "cooked," indicating the issue as finesse or décor, but ignoring the question of the *meaning*, of form and form's relation to poetics. Olson never led anything, but his thinking on form and movement and body, a new *body*, caused a lot of excitement that generated a lot of poetry and a lot of thinking. It was projective and many people found it moved them to some further dynamic of relation at work. Criticism of Olson came both from a conservative poetry establishment and from academia, states which frequently overlapped. If his poetry was sloppy and careless, his criticism/scholarship was even worse, lacking all standards of thoroughness and rigour. At Buffalo, after his death, a dismissive attitude toward his work and his, say, relational networks, continued to grow among poets and academics.

At the same time a far more destructive war on Olson's poetics was beginning to brew in unexpected quarters. Open hostilities began in earnest almost as soon as Olson's body was in the ground. In 1973, Marjorie Perloff published an essay in *ELH* called "Charles Olson and the "Inferior Predecessors": "Projective Verse" Revisited." She attacked Olson's poetics as derivative, accused William Carlos Williams of advancing Olson's poetics only because it promoted his own ideas, and accused Olson of both plagiarism and hypocrisy. Over the years, "Projective Verse" was dismissed as just another manifesto, as a phallocentric diatribe, and as the delusion of presence, among other things. In 1996, Charles Bernstein, then the Gray Chair Fellow at the State University of New York at Buffalo and founding member of the English Department's Poetics Program, published a parody of Olson's essay called "Introjective Verse." He began by mocking Olson's use of open parentheses, a typographical innovation Olson used to indicate the projective kinetic outwards. Bernstein turned them inward, and while the device was meant to undo the authority of

Olson's stance, it ended up revealing the difference between Olson's poetics and Bernstein's as grounded in different relations to the body, and especially to Olson's sense of the *seculardivine* postmodern body.

In an adroit display of textual manipulation that continually undercuts the text's propositions as a demonstration, presumably, of some indeterminate poststructuralist alternative to Olson's postmodern dynamics, Bernstein winds up arguing, in debt to Zukofsky's "perfect rest," for stasis: "The introjective poet staggers from the failings of her own boasts to that syntaxophony where language digs in, where sound echoes, where utterances concatenate, where, inevitably, all acts stall." That "stall," echoing with Zukofsky's stasis, is the essence of an alternative poetics, though the word "poetics" once again comes under the stress of a torsion that shifts its meaning away from any relation to "body" or transformational gnosis, toward "structure" or, where the Poetics Program located it, "theory." In any case, he divorces poetry from any effective energetic outcome: "I take it that INTROJECTIVE VERSE teaches nothing, that that verse will never do what the poet intends either by the tones of her voice or theater of her breath." Like all parody, the destructive aggression of "Introjective Verse" toward the original is masked by a veneer of laughter.

After Olson's death, the gradual institutionalization of the poets and theories promoted by *L=A=N=G=U=A=G=E*, a magazine edited by Bernstein and Bruce Andrews which ran between 1978 and 1981, undermined Olson's poetics while claiming to be its heirs. Although the group that came together in the magazine was diverse, many of the poets shared a lingering Marxist materialism, an interest in the theories of the Frankfurt School, and a commitment to formalist theories of poetry. For those like Robert Creeley who were critical of what they caricatured as the "worship" of Olson by "acolytes," and who dismissed readings of Olson's spiritual adventures, so-called Language poetry offered a materialist, secular option. In 1990, Bernstein, through Creeley's active intervention, replaced Creeley as the Gray Chair of Poetry at SUNY Buffalo. Buffalo, once the site of Olson's teaching, and later a centre of Olson studies and home to an active part of his legacy in the form of The Charles Olson Memorial Lectures, became a battleground in the poetry war over the nature of Olson's work and the legacy of his poetics.

Between 1988 and 1990, a series of events took place in Buffalo that effectively displaced Olson as a significant figure in the development of a visionary, projective postmodern poetics, and replaced him with the portrait of a disreputable, male chauvinist, alcoholic poet of historical geography whose main contribution to poetics was developing a certain use of documents and scholarship in the poem. During this period, Robert Creeley, who had held the Gray Chair in Poetry for many years, was quietly looking for a replacement. He was also pushing to get Susan Howe, who was desperately in need of a job, hired by the English Department. Bernstein and Howe had both been to Buffalo numerous times to give talks and readings sponsored by Creeley.

In April 1988, the Gray Chair and the English Department at SUNY Buffalo held a conference called "Radical Poetries/Critical Address." Marjorie Perloff, a major academic advocate of Charles Bernstein and "Language" poetry, was invited to give the Keynote Address for the conference, and also, according to John Clarke's correspondence, to respond to the panel on Charles Olson made up of Clarke and Don Byrd. Clarke, a poet, Blakean scholar, musician, and professor who considered himself Olson's "student" was central to the Institute of Further Studies. Byrd was a professor at SUNY Albany, a poet, and author of a respected book on the *Maximus Poems.*

Before the panel occurred, a switch was made, and Susan Howe was given the respondent's job. Having been given the papers before the panel, Howe proceeded to ignore them both and to excoriate Olson as an unreconstructed sexist, a monster whose poem enacts violent brutality against a generic "her." Rhetorically, Howe's polemic located her as "balanced" between two unresolvable relations to Olson. One was the recognition of his genius and her debt to that. The other was horrified outrage at what she presented as his violent, paratactic manipulation of images and language, and his blatant misogyny. The emotional weight of the address was focussed heavily on the outrage over Olson's alleged sexism.

Howe infused an appeal to sociology with Calvinist moral outrage as a way of reducing Olson, whose size, she admitted, she hated ("I get tired of hearing that Charles Olson was six foot seven."). She began by citing Olson's use of the words "cunt" and "tit" in two poems, but without any attempt to explain why, other than their mere presence, they were evidence of sexism according to Howe. She went on to quote a passage from Olson's poem, "Tyrian Business." The passage which begins, "or one *so* far back she craves to be scalped, / and dragged over the ground" is part of an address to dance. The section that precedes this is the well-known "how to dance / sitting down" passage, which connected Olson's sense of the grace of movement with a mode of being. The following section quoted by Howe is a critical description of the dancer Martha Graham and what Olson saw as the brutality of her movements, in contrast to the grace of the previous section. Ignoring the context, Howe presented it as an example of the brutality of Olson's "masculine imaginary," as if it were a fantasy of his desire rather than his negative critique of Graham's choreography.

Perhaps just as important as her misrepresentation of Olson, was her dismissal of the work of Clarke and Byrd, which, by implication, extended to the whole world of Olson scholarship. Implying there was no dialog between "sons" and "daughters," Howe absolved herself of responding to the men's work because it was "patronymic discourse" unworthy of address. In doing so she announced her allegiance to the critics of Olson's poetics and to the academic culture of sociology. Her attack garnered praise in the English Department, and shortly after, she was offered first a Visiting Professorship and then a permanent position in the English Department at SUNY Buffalo where she participated in the formation of the Poetics Program. "I am glad to hear things with Jack get more open," Creeley wrote to her on March 24, 1989. "It was such a sad impasse."

The reaction against Olson and his legacy continued to develop at SUNY Buffalo. For 10 years, the university had been home to the Charles Olson Memorial Lectures. Initiated in 1980 by Robert Creeley (in conjunction with John Clarke) at Clarke's urging, they were intended to honour Olson by providing an opportunity to engage and further his thinking. The inaugural lecture was by Robert Duncan. Michael McClure, Ed Sanders, Joel Oppenheimer, Diane di Prima, Philip Whalen, Tom Clark, Robin Blaser, and Allen Ginsberg followed. The choice of speaker was negotiated between Creeley and Clarke. The initial lectures by Duncan, McClure, Sanders, and di Prima seriously engaged with Olson and his legacy. Later, however, Creeley began to use the lectures to fund certain cash-strapped poets, regardless of their relation to Olson. While admirable in terms of its generosity to the needy, Creeley's choices undermined the intellectual reputation of the lectures. In 1985, he offered them to Philip Whalen. Whalen protested that he knew nothing about Olson, but Creeley assured him that didn't matter. All he had to do was talk for three hours. The same situation recurred in 1988 with Allen Ginsberg who had nothing to say about Olson, and used the lectures to repeat his well-worn "first thought best thought" presentation. The reputation of the lectures disintegrated, and along with it, Olson's reputation. Duncan McNaughton's performance in 1988 was the nail in the coffin.

Creeley was away in Finland during what witnesses agree was the disaster of the 10th Annual Charles Olson Memorial Lecture. Olson's diminishing reputation in the SUNY Buffalo English Department sank further. Once back in Buffalo, Creeley cancelled the lectures. Whether this was the result of a specific performance or had been decided previously was never made clear. Later, Jack Clarke wrote to Tom Clark of that moment: " … next thing was the Olson Memorial by 'that minister of Berkeley' (RC), which Bob cancelled— and the whole issue is over the "spiritual" (the Curriculum as you know is of the Soul)— … Creeley & I have always 'parted company' on this issue, but it wasn't openly stated because there was no occasion— till now); now, finally, this "groundswell of resentment and possessiveness" (RC) has become the occasion, the occasion of the public exposure of different "frames" (Bob's word) of Olson by people who knew him at different "times" in his life. And any "special view" of Olson might be called possessive of him, but I think what has "spooked" Bob (his word) is this what he regards as religious contexting of Olson."

The elimination of the lectures eliminated one last remnant of Olson's influence in Buffalo, and in fact, of Olson's importance as a radical thinker worth listening to. The final blow to Olson's reputation was the 1991 publication of Tom Clark's biography of Olson, *The Allegory of a Poet's Life*. Its portrait of a narcissistic, bullying drunk perfectly fleshed out the image of Olson as a patriarchal, sexist monster, and became fodder for reviewers who used it to dismiss Olson's work as a fraud. The book caused an explosion of argument and counterargument over its value, with Creeley leading the defense and Ralph Maud, a somewhat obsessive Olson scholar (but what scholar isn't a little obsessive?) minutely detailing every error in the book—which Clark ignored when he published a second edition.

In 1990, Charles Bernstein, through Creeley's agency, was appointed The Gray Chair Fellow, over the objection of other senior poets in the Buffalo English Department who felt the Chair should represent other modes of poetry. The same year, Susan Howe was appointed to a fulltime professorship. They then founded, along with Robert Creeley, Dennis Tedlock, and Raymond Federman, the Poetics Program at SUNY Buffalo, formalizing the end of Olson's influence, replacing him in the obligatory story of poetic origin with Louis Zukofsky as the mediator between them and Pound. Poetics, as their program states, is "the sum of the theoretical languages that define and inform the term *poesis* as construction and making." The spiritual ordeal involving gnosis and transformation was replaced by "theory." The knowledge that Olson sought was abandoned to the ontological narcissism of "construction." Official poetics in the United States were then determined either to be the technique of creative writing classes or the theory of the UB Poetics Program which you could get a PhD in. Olson's radical rupture had been capped and buried. In a 2011 interview, Susan Howe publicly regretted the loss of the older poet's work. "Olson has currently fallen out of favor and it's too bad," she said. "I remember the thrill of first encountering the *Maximus Poems IV V VI* in The Cape Golliard Press, 1968 edition." The ground was cleared for the neo-liberal grotesqueries of the 90s to spread through every corner of the world of poetry.

Poeisis, Poetics, and Morality

It is probably impossible to separate poetry, and art, generally, from questions of morality, no matter how hard you try. And people have tried, for a very long time. When Oscar Wilde, at the end of the 19th century, famously stated "there is no such thing as moral or immoral books. Books are well written or badly written," he staked out a post-Pater aesthetic territory that attempted to redefine the parameters of most of the thinking about the question that preceded him. It's one of three possible relations that Tzvetan Todorov argues have held true over 2000 years of arguments: 1) poetry should be in the service of moral principles that exist beyond it; 2) poetry, art, should define morality, since beauty is the highest form of human activity; and 3) poetry and morality are autonomous from one another, and never the twain, etc. Wilde weighed in after a very long time of art and morality being wed in a restrictive bond, with art cinctured by moral codes. Starting with Plato's expulsion of the poets from the city, and continuing pretty much until the late 19th century, that first relation dominated thinking in the West. Wilde makes the case that the two categories—Art/Beauty and Morality/the Good—are mutually exclusive. But Todorov goes on to argue that even though they are autonomous, Beauty and the Good are connected by three inescapable links—the immoral but necessary cruelty of the artist, the beauty poetry contributes to the world, and the increase of intelligibility it adds. Even at its most disconnected, art, it seems, is still connected to a moral discourse.

Poetry always speaks from the world, or just *speaks the world* (not to be confused with The World), formed in its originating energies, even as it resonates with its source in eternity. Drenched in the sense of the world, poetry utters the wild logos of our condition here, at the end of some time we know, that is also the beginning of some time we don't yet know, or only have an inkling of. And in that speaking, that *ordering/uttering* of the tumult of the world, poetry necessarily touches on realities that are subject to moral judgment, though your understanding of what that means will depend on how you think morality, or in philosophy's lingo, the Good, which flows from your imagination of the world. Wilde's words invoke the frightening spectre of a world in which extraneous moral codes determine what art can and can't do, regardless of the world it finds itself in and that speaks through it, a thought that is antithetical to modernity's sense of art's mission. And the agents of those codes, the censors, are never far away, animated by some frenzied idea of enforced obedience. I am old enough to remember when every film in North America had to be approved by an official Censorship Board, when D.H. Lawrence and James Joyce were banned, and when all married couples on TV slept in twin beds.

But censorship is never old news. In so far as there is always a Party of Return, the thinking of *further* will always meet resistance, and censorship is one of the main tools for attempting to hold time back, subject to a purified imagination of an untroubled past of real, recoverable value. In 2021 in the United States, a record number of attempts were made to censor books in libraries, mostly by right-wing religious groups opposed, for instance, to immoral (realistic) representations of sexuality, or historical narratives that acknowledge the centrality of slavery to the development of USAmerican culture. But the political/religious right is not alone in this outbreak of censoriousness. A whole new totalitarian movement haunts the post-Wall left, dedicated to imposing a moralistic view of gender, race, and sexuality in the determination of acceptable art and language. Should you disagree with—or even question—their position, you will likely find yourself blackballed in some hellish social media madness for not toeing the ideological line.

But questions about morality and art are never simple, never limited to black and white, and as with many issues, much of the complexity (and confusion) arises from differing definitions of the same word, in this case what's meant by "morality." In the most general sense, it is the knowledge of the difference between right and wrong, the acknowledgement and acceptance of The Good. But depending on how you understand "knowledge," not mention "right" and "wrong," the sense can shift radically. In the Judeo-Christian tradition, moral law is literally writ in stone, an immutable code bestowed on humans directly from God. Emerson challenged that idea of morality. He recognized the loss of a foundational ground on which to establish it. "Gladly we would anchor, but the anchorage is quicksand," he wrote, as science, technology, and business rapidly ate away at the authority of religion and the spiritual knowledge that founded moral knowledge in the 19th century. Emerson proposed instead that morality is relational and arises in the necessity, the necessary struggle, to make ourselves intelligible to those we are addressed to, and in that sense to be committed to a further, better self. Stanley Cavell calls this moral perfectionism, where the perfection is not an achievement but a commitment to a process.

In Mark Twain's *Huckleberry Finn,* Huck is the embodiment of Emerson's self-reliance. He faces a dilemma that arises from the moralist code written in stone, as well as various legal statutes, that states categorically, *Thou shalt not steal.* According to the law of the United States, since Huck's friend, accomplice, and occasional saviour, Jim, is an escaped slave, he literally "belongs" to Miss Polly. The code holds Huck morally obligated to return her stolen property, and since he is struggling to be a moral person, that's what he decides to do. But when he starts to think about it, when he looks in Jim's face and recalls the times Jim has helped him, and saved him, and comforted him, Huck sees a friend, and that friendship is implicated in a moral sense of loyalty, love, and the recognition of a certain debt. Which will prevail? A code that demands Huck return his friend to a condition of slavery without consideration of the people and their actual relationship? Or Huck's knowledge of Jim and his obligation to his friend, his commitment to a world of actual relation? Morality for Emerson is a deep experience of right and wrong that arises out of a relation between people. *Moralism* is not morality. It is founded on a code, an immutable set of laws etched in stone, utterly divorced from any human interaction. Grounded in a deep structural binarism, it divides the world into mutually exclusive categories, beginning with good and evil.

Think of it as a Compulsive Paralytic Binary Syndrome (CPBS). Because morality necessarily involves considerations of The Good, it also invokes The Bad, and then, if you are not careful, you will find yourself propelled into a perpetual state of terminal Binary-ism where the world divides endlessly into opposites—good/bad, moral/immoral, masculine/feminine—that proliferate, fractal-like, into every aspect of your thinking of the world—white/black, strong/weak, male/female, mind/heart, reason/imagination, feeling/thinking—each component an exclusive purity. William Blake pictured it as a man and woman tied together back-to-back—a marriage of perpetual isolations, of impossible (sexual) union. He called it a state of Generation.

Emerson confronted it in his reckoning as a minister with the emptiness of church rituals, and especially the ritual of The Last Supper, where people mouthed Christian words in church but made no place for them in their workaday lives. It was form bereft of content. Once you separate the ritual act from the content of the act, in the most sacred of gestures, the world becomes emptied, unoriginal, a place in which the thinking of *truth* loses orientation along with a point of origin that guarantees the honesty and virtue of the acts that arise from it or out of it. When general equivalence determines the World, exchange value overwhelms all other modes of value, especially thinking connected to spiritual values that mediate between the human and the divine. Degraded, those values—virtue, honesty, valor, integrity—eventually lose meaning. Morality, the moral life, becomes an empty form, much like the ritual of The Last Supper that motivated Emerson's exit from a religious vocation.

Authentic is a word relevant to this thinking, though it is currently out of favour, even slightly scandalous, in sociological circles, especially in so far as it is associated with the troubled thinking of *subject* or *self.* That address, following Theodor Adorno's *The Jargon of Authenticity*, defines *authentic* as the idea that an autonomous subject is in accord with its innermost, "true feelings." Since in those circles subjective autonomy is seen as an ideological construct, authenticity, according to the Adorno view, is nothing more than a delusion, an ideological manipulation, designed to facilitate the operation of a free market economy.

But what if, instead of thinking "self" as an abstract *subject* deluded by ideology, you think of it as a relational *worlded* authoritative finitude with the potential to make grow, to create, to author and authorize. This is close to Emerson's sense of authenticity, out of the Greek root, *authentes,* self-doer. In that mode of thinking, authenticity is not about the identity of an abstraction called a "subject" with another abstraction called its "inner feelings." Authenticity is not about identity at all. On the contrary, it is about difference, the commitment to a further self. It is a measure of the self's ability to authorize its own address to the furtherness of the world — as Emerson (and Cavell) would say, to make itself intelligible. Then the authenticity of a poem has to do not with the nature of some subject's "voice," but with the struggle manifested within the language to make the world's furtherness intelligible. Arguably, to do that is a moral gesture.

As Todorov pointed out, however, morality is sneaky and given half a chance, it will find a way to insinuate itself in some form even into otherwise seemingly anti-moralist stances. Art gets its comeuppance in a lot of different ways, even in discourses that claim to reject moralism. Judging work morally objectionable, and banning or burning it, is only the most obvious mode of attack. Moralism also sneaks in through assumptions about value that seem "natural." Take the opposition between "virtuous sentiment" and the "virtue of intellectual imagination," two mutually opposed modes of "poetics" recently proposed as part of a critique of the "moralism" of popular poetry that positions itself in line with social justice issues and identity politics. The distinction between these mutually exclusive modes of composition is apparently just technical with no moral judgment involved. But ironically, as part of a larger argument against "moral poetry," it ends up making its own moral judgment. In this anti-moralist aesthetic, "virtuous sentiment" is moralist in its outlook, which produces inferior poetry, while (the virtue of) "intellectual imagination," free of morality, is paradoxically moral in its amoral stance which produces superior poetry. The conclusion is one *ought* to write poetry of imaginative intellect.

The options here are old and narrow, notwithstanding the updated vocabulary and clever word play. Something called "virtue" plays a role in both categories, though somewhat sneakily. *Virtuous* is an adjective, *virtue* a noun, and as the grammatical function shifts in the opposition, so does meaning. In days of yore, virtue meant something different than it does now. In the 13th century, virtue was the quality of a first-class Knight and had to do with strength, even manliness, which makes sense given that the Indo-European root of the word, *wi-ro, means "man." By the end of the 14th century, however, what constituted "moral qualities" had begun to shift as the last remnants of Feudalism and courtly culture faded away, and the new market order replaced them with its own values. First, religious values replaced courtly values, and virtuousness came to signify the possession of excellent moral qualities as defined by religious authorities, especially chastity. And in so far as chastity became more and more a state imposed on females, you could say it became "feminized." Its focus was on controlling women's sexuality, including the notorious belts. There were never chastity belts for men. Even today, while someone might speak of a virtuous woman, it's unlikely they would describe a man that way. Chastity is a tool of the patriarchy to control female sexuality.

For the Euro American radical intelligentsia who embraced intoxication and sexuality in the 19th century as a tonic for the hypocrisy and self-righteousness of bourgeois culture, "virtue" was a sign of duplicity and shallowness as they witnessed "upstanding" citizens claim to be virtuous by day, while indulging in drunkenness and lechery, and killing the occasional streetwalker, at night. Robert Louis Stevenson nailed it in *Dr. Jekyll and Mr. Hyde.* That sense of duplicity remains, while the issue has shifted. Whereas 75 years ago it had to do with sexual purity and abstinence from intoxicants, these days it more often refers to political positions involving identity, race and gender, i.e., what is called "virtue signalling," a negative label for a self-righteous social media behaviour, which, it seems to me, is the sense that informs the negativity of the phrase, "virtuous sentiment." On the other hand, and this is definitely an on-the-one-hand-and-on-the-other-hand moment, as a noun in the phrase, *the virtue of imaginative intellect,* it signifies something very different, harkening back to the original sense of valour, something noble, even… manly.

Once the binary division is established (the virtuous sentiment vs. the virtue of intellect), moral value (good vs. bad) immediately slips in to locate one half of the division as The Good. It introduces a valuation of two opposed modes of human knowledge, say "sentiment" and "intellect" (or to use an old literary recognition, heart and head, or even behind that, feminine and masculine), finding one wanting in relation to the other, at least as far as poetics are concerned, and poetics are a big deal these days, arguably bigger even than poetry. Partly that's because *poetics* sounds kind of scientific, which is good if you want to be taken seriously by people who like measurable, scientific sounding stuff. It's the *ics* at the end. ICS. It's hard and precise, like mathematics, semiotics, axiomatics, probiotics, or athletics. You know something is there when you hear that. It's serious.

The focus on what's called poetics is relatively recent. It started around 1960 with Donald Allen's anthology, *The New American Poetry*. Given the oppositional nature of his anthology, Allen knew he was in for some critical turbulence, that the Authorized Poetic Authorities would dismiss the poetry in his anthology as unworthy of serious attention because of its rejection of preconceived form and traditional conventions, and its embrace of improvisational techniques congruent with a shift in world view. In an era when the Poetry Professoriate made its living analyzing how many kinds of ambiguity it could discern in a lyric poem, when the metaphor for poetic excellence was a "well-wrought urn," and poets were expected to fit their "content" into some "form" that pre-existed it as proof of their expertise, the poetry Allen gathered was labelled "uncooked" at best, and at worst mere prose broken into lines—unworthy of serious consideration as poetry, in any case.

Allen sought to head off some of that noise by including a section by poets on their modes of composition. In a final section of his anthology called "Statements on Poetics," Allen located the poetry in relation to serious thinking that arose from and with the poetry about the nature of composition. It was meant as a support for the poetry. Most of the contributions are short excerpts from poets' journals, or previously written statements where they thought through and articulated the process of their work. The one exception was Charles Olson's "Projective Verse," a major statement about poetic composition and cosmology that became a rallying point in the poetry wars that followed.

First published in *Poetry New York* in October 1950, and then as a pamphlet by Amiri Baraka's (LeRoi Jones) Totem Press in 1959, "Projective Verse" fused Olson's thinking about poetry, philosophy, cosmology, mathematics, geometry and history into a wild exploration of our postmodern condition and poetry's entanglement in it. He begins by displacing the "human" from the centre of the poem's attention, to allow in the world and prepare the ground for his emerging vision of the absolute immanence of the divine in the specificities of the mundane "secular" world. His notion of the "projective" energy of the poem resonated with the same spirit that animated the improvisational work of contemporary jazz musicians. In an intellectual arena dominated by intricate analyses of formal elements, Olson's essay dropped like a bomb—a stink bomb, maybe, but a bomb, nevertheless.

While Olson posed his open field poetics against the poetics of what he called "closed verse," he did so to clarify poetry's response to the profound historical changes we are caught up in. He did not locate it in a moral framework of right versus wrong, nor in a linguistic crisis of referential versus non-referential, but in an historical framework of temporal process (*nowpast*). And in a necessary cosmology. He did not attempt to make a moral judgment, because he had no theory to measure truth against, no wrong to his right, only a stance which he enacted in his work because of his recognition of the profound difference of our historical moment from what preceded it. All the work he had put into getting to the place where he could write the *projective* had gone into an actual spiritual ordeal and transformation, rather than the development of a theory.

Olson's trip to Yucatan in 1950 was central to the struggle as he sought a deep relation to meaning, specific to the actual space of "America," and outside the box of European modernity. Look, he said, this is where we are now. This is how Time is moving, this is the turbulence we are all swept along in, this is what it means to our relations. What forces are in play? What can poetry do to measure that? In this cosmological process, poets need to transform, to become the transforming voice of that transformation, that process of emergence. Olson's friend and companion, Robert Duncan, underwent a similar process of spiritual ordeal in quest for a "poetics," though in his case the ordeal involved undertaking the epic work that became *The H.D. Book*. For both poets, achieving a "poetics" involved an actual struggle, and a change, a transformation that led to a new stance or mode of being. Poetry flowed from that. Poetics, from that perspective, is not a "theory" but a transformative struggle alive in every word.

Following Allen's introduction of poetics as support for poetry, it soon became an independent focus of energy and attention. Poetics really came into its own in the mid-70s, with the ascendence in the U.S. of what's called generally *Language Poetry*. As has often been pointed out, Language Poetry was an ambiguous descriptor covering many different writers and modes of writing. But some things they arguably shared, among them a rejection of "representationalism," a sociological critique of the traditional lyric "I," and an attention to the thickness of language.

Not unlike Richard Nixon's contemporaneous suspension of the gold standard in 1971, the theorizers of Language poetry sought to divorce language from a referential ground that anchored it. Quickly colonizing a literary territory called *avant-garde,* Language Poetry thrived by taking up Olson's practice of poetry based on scholarship, while substituting Adorno and Saussure for Homer and Melville, and sociology for mythology. They found theoretical support in the European intellectual address to language and developed a theory of poetic signification they buttressed with reference to contemporary post-structuralist and linguistic critics such as George Lakoff.

In so far as poetics became more and more closely identified with theory, which can be studied and learned in classrooms, it opened itself to bursts of moralist judgment. Theory operates within a world of competing ideas that explain phenomena, and based on that explanation proposes further practice: one *ought* to write poetry of imaginative intellect rather than poetry of virtuous sentiment. Unlike a spiritual ordeal that yields a stance in-formed by knowledge, theory yields an idea that competes with other ideas. The rejection of theories of the autonomous subject in control of representational language (meaning as the identity of word and object) gives rise to theories of a socially constructed self informed by ideology and of language as self-referential (meaning solely as a result of difference within the system). Hence the "virtue of imaginative intellect." Ignore for a minute the way "virtue" in this formation not so subtly signals entrance to a moral zone. It's implied that *imaginative intellect* is free of "self" contamination (as in self-expression and sentiment) where self is understood as created and manipulated by ideology and expressed in feelings. It is an exclusionary category.

By joining imagination and intellect, two pure, abstracted modes of mind, it implicitly rules out the impure "not-mind" of Western thinking: emotion, also known as *heart,* and in a "degraded" form, as *sentiment(ality)*, or, in Adorno-speak, *true feelings*, which are seen as ideologically conditioned modes of a socially constructed self tradionally conncted to femininity. It proposes a correct way of composing poetry, one that is free of the unconscious domination of ideology's formation and manipulation of desire. Then, given the categorical imperative to write poetry of imaginative intellect, the value of the individual poem is lost to an abstraction that automatically excludes as unfit any work that does not belong to the category. The specific judgment of the work of this poem or that poem is lost to moralist generalities such as "virtuous sentiment," a degraded mode of writing implicitly identified with the "feminine" (heart, feeling, sentiment). I doubt that the author of this critical binary had any such sexist point in mind, but such is the power of the Compulsory Paralytic Binary Syndrome to sweep us into moralist lockdowns.

The issue is *poeisis*, or the relation to *poeisis*, the event of the making of the poem. Poeisis, from whence our word "poetry," etymologically "to make," names the process of the emergence of form/meaning. The question is, as a poet, what is your relation to that process? In a way, when it comes to poetry (which, given its name, has a special relation to poeisis), the difference between poeisis and poetics echoes Aristotle's distinction between *poeisis* and *praxis* but reversed. For Aristotle, if poeisis is "to make," its goal is oriented toward something beyond itself—a pot, a ship, a painting—unlike praxis which for Aristotle is action undertaken strictly for itself, for the value implicit in it—returning money you found, helping someone who fell get up. But the world has changed a bit, and poetry in early 21st century North America no longer bears the cultural value it did for Aristotle. Given the minor status of poetry in our culture of general equivalence defined by spectacle, it's fair to say poeisis, the making of the poem, is an act, generally speaking, undertaken for its own sake.

Some poets, it's true, find ways to use poetry for personal advancement: a limited kind of fame, prize money, status positions, departmental promotions, even, occasionally—if they are lucky—sex. But for every one of those Players, a thousand other poets write neither for gold nor glory, but simply because they must, even in the currently degraded world of poetry competitions and low-level prizes. They write because they know on some level poetry matters. Poetry calls them into its orders of language and attention. Some do it spontaneously and sporadically out of a deep impulse. Others do it studiously and regularly, responding to the centuries of poetry that preceded them. Some write from deep feelings of anger over injustice or the ever-astonishing joy of love. Some write out of intellectual excitement. Some write in a scholarly frenzy. Some write for fun. Some are possessed. Some do it badly. Some do it exquisitely. Some bore you. Some excite you. Some teach you. The difference has to do with the nature of their *poetearmind*, the way the poet's sounding of the poem thinks. That's poetry—*thinkingsounding*.

The issue, then, is not this theory or that theory, this poetics or that poetics, virtuous sentiment or the virtue of imaginative intellect. Poetics has a goal in mind. Its relation to poeisis is disciplinary, the production of a specific mode of composition. That can produce interesting poetry given the *poetearmind* of the writer, a necessity even for imaginative intellectuals. It also produces a lot of dreck given the rarity of the *poetearmind.* The kinds of composition I am thinking of here engage poeisis as an ordeal, an action, a struggle to achieve unprecedented truths in language events, say even, authentic language events, specific events that have no goal beyond their own transformative articulation.

I read somewhere that I have now forgotten that poeisis, to make, was first an action that transforms and continues the world. That makes sense to me. Morality enters in so far as the maker, through a spiritual ordeal, comes in touch with actual energies that she transforms or translates into language. It is not a question of technical production. Nor is it a question of linguistic theory. It is not even a question of creation in some romantic sense. Poetry gives voice to thought reconciled with matter, time, spirit, locating *person* in their actual world. The poet's soul is tuned to frequencies most people are unaware of, and her job is to transform those energies into language that remains true to them. This is where morality haunts poetry. Because there is no greater good than the virtue of truth.

What Is Soul and Why Might It Need a Curriculum? Charles Olson's "A Curriculum of the Soul" for Skeptics

It is pretty much impossible to talk about a curriculum of the soul without first addressing the troubled word, "soul," and what might be meant by that today. Alternately the word raises hackles and causes eye to glaze over, trailing behind, as it does, lingering notions of immortality, spiritual substance, the transcendental, and memories of endless scholastic bickering. Still, we can't seem to shake it, either. Even if we are satisfied to reduce it to, say, an epiphenomenon of neuronal activity, or a society of subsystems, or a socially constructed subject position, it is difficult to explain how it gets a sense of humour, not to mention a sense of dread or awe. Or how it can love. And be loved. Wittgenstein addresses this in *Philosophical Investigations* when he writes: 'I believe that he is not an automaton", just like that, so far makes no sense. My attitude towards him is an attitude towards a soul. I am not of the *opinion* that he has a soul."

I doubt that even the most hardened, unapologetic materialist constructivist treats his, her, or their friends as epiphenomena of neuronal activity or even socially constructed subject positions. It is hard even to imagine how you would do that outside of some genocidal madness where all those souls were reduced to disposable objects, mere subject positions in a world of matter in motion: Jew, for instance, or faggot, or Kulak, or commie. Stripped of a sense of meaningful, creative force in a deterministic world, the self loses *all* sense, even specific political sense. How, after all, does a subject position know what *justice* is, much less feel the necessity to fight and sacrifice for it? That is in fact the absence of soul—not just its death, but its obliteration, its utter and complete loss. To imagine a moral imperative of any sort relies on some sense of the human beyond the merely material. Soul, in that sense at least, lingers on in our relations, in our struggle to define a moral stance for these times, if not in our discourse.

Or some of our discourses. In others, it remains front and centre. You would expect to find it in the writing of Henry Corbin, for instance, one of Olson's favourites thinkers, whose studies of Islamic thought are rich with discussions of the soul and its work. Even there, though, it is not quite as straight forward as you might anticipate since Corbin often locates his thinking in a phenomenology of the imagination rather than some doctrine of spiritual substance. In fact, when you start looking into the word, you find it popping up in the most surprising places. Gilles Deleuze, for instance, the philosopher of *desiring machines* in a delirious world, has a chapter in his book on Leibniz, called "The Folds in the Soul." "A soul," he writes, "always includes what it apprehends from *its* point of view, in other words, inflection. *Inflection is an ideal condition or a virtuality that currently exists only in the soul that envelops it.* Thus the soul is that which has folds and is full of folds." Deleuze wrests the word out its theological determinations and relocates it in his idea of human virtuality, which is another way of addressing our circumstance as creative rather than determined. Ian Hacking, another contemporary philosopher of a different order, also comes back to the thought of the soul. In his examination of the uses and misuses of the idea of multiple personality and theories of so-called repressed memory, he proposes that "[m]emory as narrative and the sciences of memory are branches of the same stem, the secularization of the soul."

Hacking points to the source of our problem with what he calls secularization, itself a troubled word with multiple interpretations. Our historical sense of the soul has been intimately connected to our thinking of the sacred and the transcendental. In the most general sense, the soul was seen as the animating and vital principle in humans, attributed faculties of thought, action, and emotion and often conceived as an immaterial entity with a sacred, even immortal, destiny. Arguments then ensued about the rational soul, the vegetative soul, the nature of the substance of the soul, the soul's affinities with matter and so on *ad inifinitum.* Secularism destroys the context in which such thinking can make sense.

There are a couple of ways you can look at secularism. One is as an historical process in which the authority of religion is displaced by scientific materialism. This is the story that science and philosophy tell, a story of progress from superstition to enlightenment, from belief to reason. In *A Secular Age*, Charles Taylor examines the details of this process, carefully going through all the minute changes that took place over the centuries as the world was completely redefined by new institutions. At the center of those changes, Taylor argues, was the determination that mind belonged solely to the human, leaving the world as the passive object of our often-rapacious attentions. A secular world in this sense is one liberated by reason from the shackles of ignorance, a world in which politics, culture, and knowledge—among other things—are wrested away from the authority of the idea of God and turned over to human beings. It is also what has been called a disenchanted world.

In that light, the secular can also be seen as a visionary state, a perceptual modality. This is how William Blake locates it. He calls it Generation, or two-fold vision, the second state in an array of visionary possibility that extends to the four-fold. Sometimes he imagines it as a man and a woman tied together back-to-back, but famously he also pictured it as Newton sitting on a rock in a barren world measuring a geometric form with callipers. Each state—Ulro, Generation, Beulah, and Jerusalem are among the names he associates with them—exists eternally, and humans wander from one to another. Secularism, in this sense, is an absence, a limitation or a truncation of possibility, a constriction. What is constricted is the ability to see the fullness of the world beyond the dichotomies that a certain frame of mind casts it in.

In either case, the context within which the thought of the soul makes sense is denied and common ways of thinking "soul" collapse, leaving us in a shambles. Much as we might like to agree on a coherent world of value and meaning in which the thought of the soul makes collective sense, such coherence is lost in the shattered authority that has yielded the clamour of countless competing voices articulating incommensurable visions of the world. But even though it is improbable that we can agree on an adequate designation of "soul" for our time and circumstance, we can't quite rid ourselves of the thought of it either. Pascal famously proposed in that "man infinitely transcends man." If this proposal leaves Descartes in the dust, it does so by reminding us we can never actually contain ourselves in our ingenious definitions, that something further always remains. Maybe that's why soul won't go away.

My first serious encounter with the eschatological complexities of soul was in my friend Stuart Wilson's bedroom in 1962. He had just assembled his first stereo and we were listening to the new Charles Mingus septet album, *Mingus Ah Um*. The first cut was a Mingus composition called "Better Git Hit in Your Soul." Later, for those of us of a certain age, there was what came to be known as soul music. Aretha Franklin, Otis Redding, Little Richard, Ray Charles were the apostles of soul, the explicators of the great Dance. But for me it was always Mingus who was there first, laying it out so clearly and unequivocally. When he said you better get hit in your soul, you knew he meant it—and he was just the guy to show you how to do it, too. There was no way not to get hit in your soul when he unleashed his music, no way to quibble over definitions and logical fine points. There you were, *body-and-soul* as another song goes, and that was that. Soul as an experience, then, an event, a *being here*. Ray Charles said, "Soul is like electricity, like a spirit, a drive, a power," and he wasn't just whistling Dixie.

If our sense of soul is confused, or left orphaned in the shambles of our condition, it is not limited by it. When Olson wrote his curriculum, which is actually "of" and not "for" the soul, he was after something further, something beyond that shambles, though the shambles figured large in his thinking of where we are coming from. By making the preposition "of," Olson emphasized the roots of "curriculum" in a literal course or track, and ultimately in the act of running. This curriculum is about process, about moving on, but where we are to move to can only be determined in the act itself, in the encounter with the elements at the edge of the world. Such a thinking of soul locates it not as a thing, but as a specific dimension of experience, a resonance, a mode or relation, what Emerson means when he points out that "[t]his one fact the world hates; that the soul *becomes*."

For Olson such a mode or resonance arises from the infolded surfaces of a "body" in motion in the world giving rise to a sense of specific moving depths, one of which he called soul: "the soul then," he wrote, "is equally 'physical'," throwing quotes around physical to let us know it is not other than soul itself. In *Proprioception* he relates that "body" and its depths to what he calls an American "secularization which … loses nothing of the divine," something, he said, that we don't want to lose, as if it had been hard won and was fragile. Olson links this thought to his reading of Whitehead, suggesting that "seeing process in reality redeems all idealism fr theocracy or mobocracy, whether it is rational or superstitious …." For Olson, the sense of secularization he invokes comes up somewhere between the two possibilities. If it is a visionary state, it is one in which the authorities and hierarchies of the traditional notion of the *sacred*, as well as of the Rational, are overturned by the new energies of something called democracy, in so far as we understand, as Jean-Luc Nancy has proposed, that democracy has "available to it no identifiable authority proceeding from a place or impetus other than those of a desire—of a will, an awaiting, a thought—where what is expressed and recognized is a true possibility of being *all together, all and each among all.*" I love this thinking of Nancy's. *The Truth of Democracy* carries the thinking of democracy beyond some meagre sense of the political into "thinking that 'democracy' *is spirit* before being political and social form, institution, or regime."

In this sense both Nancy's "democracy" and Olson's "secularization that loses nothing of the divine" are modes of what Blake calls the threefold, a being in the world past its division into mutually exclusive opposites, call it *being apart*, whether they are body/soul, form/content, or secular/divine. This world, say, a *new world*, is related to the quest Emerson outlines in the "Phi Beta Kappa Address," the turning away from the "sublime and beautiful" toward "the near, the low, the common," another radical expression of the spirit of democracy. "That which had been negligently trodden under foot by those who were harnessing and provisioning themselves for a long journey into far countries," Emerson wrote, "is suddenly found to be richer than all foreign parts." What is trodden under foot is the ordinary, but what an ordinary it is. Like Charles Mingus, Aretha Franklin, Otis Redding, and Ray Charles, who brought the sacred over into the ordinary world, brought gospel and blues together into a marriage, a new music, a secularized divine, Olson was not about anything after or other, other than here as here is always further, always calling us on. Call this "soul" the instance of sense itself, the *here I am* as it resonates to the beat of the world. "The soul is a magnificent Angel. / And the thought of its thought," wrote Olson in "Maximus at the Harbour," is the rage / of Ocean : apophainesthai".

Olson picked up this Greek word—*apophainesthai, that which shows forth*—from Henry Corbin. It comes up in Corbin's discussion of the way a mode of understanding expresses a mode of being, so that "it goes without saying that this *mode of being*, Paradise, can be realized, can exist 'in a true sense,' only in a person who precisely *is* this Paradise." This showing forth, like Deleuze's virtuality, is a revelation of the deeply creative core of our *being here*. As Olson locates it in the poem, there is no division, no dialectic—the world/soul shows forth for the soul/world showing forth. The showing forth everywhere is a being here, a getting hit that cannot be denied, utterly strange and utterly dear at the same time.

Finding ourselves suddenly showing forth, suddenly being here, where *here* is a shambles of markets and blood (shambles, ultimately out of old English *scomul,* a table for vending, eventually meat, a butcher shop) in which all the old landmarks have been leveled or replaced with identical Walmarts or Starbucks, or are unrecognizable under a thick coat of crude oil bleeding from a pierced and wounded earth, a curriculum might be of some use. The curriculum Olson arrives at in his "poem" is arrayed with what seems at first glimpse to be wild abandon over two pages in *The Magazine of Further Studies* #5. Interestingly, soul, which is one of the points of attention, never made it to the topics Jack Clarke assigned, almost as if it was unnecessary or redundant, since that is in fact the outcome of the whole event.

The piece begins in the middle of the second page with the underlined "heading," "A Plan for a Curriculum of the Soul." The topics Clarke picked for the curriculum project start under that with "the Mushroom" being number one, then spin down the page and around to the right, up the first page, and then left, back to the top of the second page where they finish with "Sensation and Attention | [training in exhaustion & | completion." But you can also start, if not begin, at the upper left hand corner where English speakers would ordinarily begin to read a page with the proposition, "how to live as a | single natural being | the dogmatic nature of | (order of) | experience," almost as if we were meant to understand that as another opening into the event. Beyond that, the language explodes across the pages, deployed around a notably empty centre.

It is after all a *curriculum*, which comes from the Latin *currere* "to run, move quickly" and is a cognate of *current*; hence, a running course, a track which, although it has a starting line and a finishing line has no

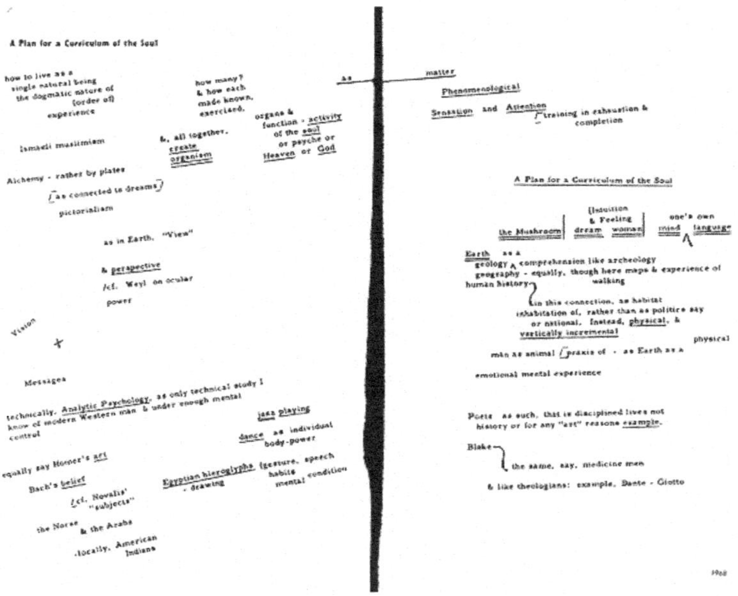

beginning and no end. Yet even in the midst of that wheeling clamour with its central void, an unstable syntax appears and disappears like a will o' the wisp, dancing in and out of the whirling configuration. If there is a "soul" to it, an identifiable *being here* or *showing forth*, it is centered on a sense of dynamism, the lay out surely and the sense of the track, but also the drift of the thought dancing with the words in the vortex of energy that sweeps them around the page.

Over and over, Olson comes back to movement and force—jazz, dance, Mushroom, organism—and the dynamics of invention and vision—perspective, Blake, Bach's belief, Dante—scattering them along the course of the curriculum, a course that finally has no beginning, no end. This is not a curriculum that can be understood in terms of history, as if it could be outmoded or dated, replaced with subjects having to do with the internet or social networking (let's call it 'fashion'), as if they were more relevant to our current condition and need. It is a curriculum that is focussed on energizing the soul, provoking it into action in relation to the beginning-less origin that is our constant condition, opening our eyes to where we always already are.

It is a re-orientation. Henry Corbin locates the Orient not as a place in the physical world, as Jack Clarke once reminded me, but as a direction in the imagination, a place of morning light, not unlike Thoreau's rising sun which is but a morning star. A course of study, a reorientation, might, then, offer a sense of direction for renewing the *how* of our being here, which returns me to Olson's "body." Given the possibility of a depth that gives rise to a relation that yields a "world" where no world is given, Olson's curriculum constitutes a course of world formation or re-formation in process where the process is the *being here*. Call it an epic, a journey whose vehicle and whose goal (say, "home") are never more nor less than a box upon the sea.

Olson, Empire, and the Thinking of America

"Spurning the clouds written with curses, stamps the stony law to dust, loosing the eternal horses from the dens of night, crying: *Empire is no more! and now the lion and wolf shall cease.*"
—William Blake, "A Song of Liberty"

"Do you think that men who have enjoyed the blessing of liberty will calmly see it snatched away?"
—Toussaint L'Ouverture

"You have no power over my body, neither can you do me any harm ..."
—Anne Hutchinson to John Winthrop and the General Court of the Massachusetts Bay Colony, 1637

"This country is without hope. Even its garbage is clean ...."
—Jean Baudrillard, *America*

US America's reputation—a quaint word in relation to a long history of violence, conquest, and exploitation—beyond its own shores has been in tatters, at best, in much of the world for a very long time. At "best," because tatters at least retain some mark of the imagination of a time of distinguishing first energies that promised a new world. At worst, with no tatters to recollect that original thought, America is simply a force of destruction, cruel and violent, obliterating everything unique and dear in the world, everything of value. It relentlessly degrades the human world into a homogenized, universal *culture-market* made up of billions of *consumers*, indistinguishable except for their market profiles. It transforms the physical world into a never-ending river of commodities to feed that market, while virtually enslaving whole populations to produce them. Jean Baudrillard's observation after his cross-country U.S. jaunt sums it up: "[America] is a world completely rotten with wealth, power, senility, indifference, puritanism and mental hygiene, poverty and waste, technological futility and aimless violence ...." While the rest of the world finds this obvious, inhabitants of the United States seem almost aggressively oblivious to it. They continue to repeat the mantra that America is *the best* and *the greatest*, that the world should pull up its socks and get on board the modern-democratic-hygienic express because lots of goodies are to be had, including its best-selling products, *democracy* and *liberty*. And so they drive into the sunset, one hand on the steering wheel, the other on a Big Gulp, ignorant of the fact that they are the shimmering embodiment of an esoteric doctrine known as *exceptionalism*.

It's all tied up with the thinking of *America*, a word with many different registers of meaning beyond the name of the United States. The U.S. is a juridical/political entity occupying part of the northern half of the western hemisphere. Geographically, America is that whole western hemisphere, north, central, and south, pole to pole. One of the habits of USAmericans that annoys the other half billion inhabitants of the hemisphere is their assumption that *America* belongs to them, dismissing the rest of us.

But *America* means more than geography. It is an idea, and like all ideas, has a history, though it tends to get lost in the political uses to which the name is put at any given moment. And the history is entangled with other ideas and events. The idea of American exceptionalism was active by the time of the Revolution, central to the commitment of U.S. leaders to spread Republican democracy around the world. It has been the focus of academic debates over the meaning of America since about the time Charles Olson published *Call Me Ishmael*, his first address to America, in 1947. Shortly after that, the premier issue of *American Quarterly*, published by the University of Minnesota, hit academic library shelves across the U.S. Both events were part of a moment in which the active thinking of *America*, as well as America's thinking, opened into a range of attention and authority it had never been granted. The founding of The American Studies Association followed from *American Quarterly*, which then became its voice. The initial issues of the magazine reflected a strangely naïve intellectual patriotism, probably because the university was still mostly the preserve of privileged white men, and they thought of America as … well, theirs—which it was. Describing his essay as "another chapter in the history of American patriotism," Merle Curti, in that first issue, proposed to make a "contribution to a larger study of the images that peoples in other parts of the world have held of the United States." It was, he said, to be a scholarly contribution toward persuading the world of America's exceptional status as the avatar of modernity.

The American Studies Association changed over the years, along with the university that nurtured it and the object of its study. In the 1960s, with millions of people in the streets fighting for civil rights, the promised but still undelivered equality, and the end of the war against Vietnam, the thinking of *America* shifted to a decidedly more critical mode. Universities began the transformation from finishing school for future leaders and managers of the nation, to job training centres for the middle class. At the same time their dominant moral focus shifted from anxiety about preserving Christian culture toward an attention to social justice. The curtain of modernity's consensus was pulled back, exposing the "white man" operating the levers of illusion. Authority (which is always problematic in America) fragmented and American Studies became a centre for theoretically engaging the *exceptionalism* that justified an America of deceit, oppression, aggression, greed, and exploitation.

Olson's book was part of this conversation. Developed from his master's thesis at Wesleyan in the 30s (and his salvaging of Melville's dispersed library), and fine-tuned during his coursework with F.O. Matthiessen in the American Civilization program at Harvard, *Call Me Ishmael* entered the growing world of Melville scholarship and the American Studies context it was part of, loudly announcing its difference. Rather than the smooth, seamless rational coherence of sanctioned scholarship, *Call Me Ishmael* unfolds into ir/regulation, dis/continuity, in/coherence. Olson's thinking forays beyond the forms and usages of academic scholarship, radically reassessing Melville, his novel, and the America it addressed. Just as *Moby-Dick* announced the end of the rule of the "empire of forms," *Call Me Ishmael* assaulted the authority of a scholarship divorced from the blood and tears of an actual world, what he called in his "Letter to Melville," an "abomination" and "false & dirty." Rather than symbol and allegory, Olson disclosed the economics of the whaling industry as

Melville's narrative measure of American expansionism. Whale oil, he argued, was the black gold of its day, and whaling the economic engine of the emerging American economy and its drive for world hegemony. Ahab's maniacal assault on the white whale mirrored America's drive to consume the world, a drive founded, he proposed, on cannibalism.

Most people track American exceptionalism to John Winthrop's 1630 sermon, "A Model of Christian Charity," written on the Arabella just offshore from the new world. Winthrop appropriated the biblical reference to describe the new colony as a "city on a hill," a shining beacon to the rest of the world. That part comes at the end. Most of the rest of the document justifies social and economic inequities as God's will, and establishes rules about money. It lays out the nuts and bolts of managing the new colony, from how to mediate disputes over ownership to the proper controls on lending and borrowing. While the authorizing ground of the document remained the Puritan covenant with God, the rules governing the order of the community were made up, based on perceived and projected needs of the group in a strange new land. It established the order of the new society with a *text*. Winthrop did not appeal to either family or utopia, the traditional models for community. "What is displaced," Sacvan Berkovitch points out, "is both visionary (a medieval utopia) and actual (familial, communal, and geographical origins). What comes into place is broadly modern: a community written into existence by contract and consent, through a declaration of principles and rules that bend tradition to legitimate a venture in colonial enterprise." Establishing the founding order as textual mattered. Although it would have horrified Winthrop to think so, this gesture projected modernity beyond theory into an actual world without foundation, and opened it to the antinomian implications of liberty.

America was unique in that regard. Even Baudrillard admits it: "America is the original version of modernity. We are the dubbed or subtitled version." That may or may not be exceptional, but it was the first time anyone had established the order of a political body outside the authority of tradition or the transcendental. Upping the ante in 1776, the further act of founding proceeded to incorporate the intellectual pyrotechnics of the Enlightenment in its textual ground. A nation based on philosophy as it was being written by mortal men. It was barely imaginable, a cosmological earthquake. People got excited:

> A vision from afar!
> Sound! sound! my loud war-trumpets, and alarm my Thirteen
> [Angels!
> Ah, vision from afar! Ah, rebel form that rent the ancient
> Heavens! Eternal Viper self-renew'd, rolling in clouds,
> I see thee in thick clouds and darkness on America's shore

William Blake's "Song of Liberty" addressed the thirteen rebellious colonies as "Angels." In the collective imagination of that moment, America opened into an unprecedented range of relational possibilities and prodigalities that, as Blake said, rent the ancient heavens, leveling hierarchies, further democratizing the authority decentered in the Reformation.

Baudrillard goes on, "I cannot help but feel [America] has about it something of the dawning of the universe." The dawning of the universe is serious business. He doesn't specify what it looks like, but it doesn't matter because the dawning itself is the point, just as the textuality is the point in Winthrop's founding sermon. That figurative first light connects to an old American thinking about newness, beginning, discovery, illumination, about an opening beyond the imposed cruelties of the known, in the discovery of a new world. Baudrillard's response registers the perennial American sense of liberty from the drag of history—which is both its doom and its promise. If the founding texts result in a couple centuries of bad faith, they also crucially preserve the possibility of re-writing the Real.

Charles Olson's artistic engagement with America begins with the proposition, "I take SPACE to be the central fact to man born in America," the opening sentence in his first book. Arguably that engagement never ends. He came by his interest honestly. America was an unprecedented opportunity for Europe's poor in the 19th and early 20th centuries. It offered them land, independence, and the right to participate in the redistributed sovereignty of the Republic, none of which were available to them in Europe. But it also promised the liberty not to participate if they didn't want to. After a couple of thousand years under the thumb of one monarch or another, with one bunch of Cossacks or another riding through their hovel, it sounded pretty good, even if there were no guarantees. To the young Olson, growing up in the heart of the old, revolutionary United States surrounded by its monuments and battlefields, America looked like a promise realized. The son and grandson of a working-class immigrant family, he lived the promise, attending some of the finest schools in America and realizing what his family could never have achieved in the static class bound structures of Europe.

At Worcester Classical High School, Olson was exposed to the wild outburst of American writing from the mid-19th century. It balanced his classical education and added depth to a sense of a particular America of value. Emerson, Hawthorne, Thoreau, Fuller, Dickinson, Whitman, and Melville challenged the authority of the empire of literary forms (and the thinking that is tied up in it), opening new paths for writing and thinking in the same American space that Olson shared with them. Emerson was the heart and mind behind it. Olson chose his essay, "The American Scholar," as the subject of his commencement address at Wesleyan. Emerson's call to arms arose out of anxiety about the timidity of American art and scholarship in rising to its unique occasion and producing something new from within its own specificity. The fact he thought it possible testifies to the emergence of some new spirit, one he identified with "the near, the low, the common." At the same time, he proposed that American specificity as transitive, not thinkers, but thinking, which he in fact did. His condemnation of "Genius" that "leaves the temple to haunt the senate or the market" and his passionate, demonstrative love of the process of thinking, its surprising activity, rather than its accumulation and possession, left a deep mark on Olson.

Olson's landmark essay, "Projective Verse," folds Emerson's "Man Thinking" into what Olson calls the "projective," which entails not only a mode of writing, or even, as Olson states, a stance, but a whole new propositional real in which such a stance can find traction. Emerson recognized the unfolding (American) real in the loss of bedrock truth or law, say its textuality. Mood displaces knowledge, or at the very least, casts it in its tone, leaving knowledge with no truths to grasp. "Gladly we would anchor," he wrote, "but the anchorage is quicksand." It won't just not hold you; it will swallow you.

Baudrillard notes the other side of the modern: "America ducks the question of origins; it cultivates no origin or mythical authenticity; it has no past and no founding truth. Having known no primitive accumulation of time, it lives in a perpetual present." That lack of accumulated time leaves serious conversation in America a difficult event. Without history, or at the least some common representation of the past besides cartoonish "myths" of shared turkeys, felled cherry trees, and perennial victories, there is no given common ground from which people can begin to address each other and their situation. On the other hand, these same conditions entangle and shape Emerson's moral perfectionism, his prescient tropological morality with no foundation in law. Contradictions multiply without any hope of rectification. Contra-diction, against the word which is the hope of rectification. The idiocy of liberty.

Emerson leverages that "Self-Reliance" into an uncompromised (groundless) but easy engagement with the emergent world, "the nonchalance of boys who are sure of a dinner," he calls it. Olson finds confirmation of that new cosmology in Whitehead's process philosophy. He works out one of its implications is his critique of inherited prosodic modes (what used to be called the "laws of verse"), as the enactment of nostalgia for a non-existent ground. Prosody is cosmology, the rhythm and rhyming of knowing. And the freedom to shape prosodic form outside the given, to make something new, something that equals the real itself, becomes entangled with the thinking of liberty.

Liberty is an uneasy thought these days, largely because of the duplicity that surrounds it. After nearly 350 years of slavery and its aftermath in Jim Crow, segregation, institutional lynching, and programmatic lethal violence by police, the word rings hollow. When the U.S. waves the flag of "liberty," while laying waste to anything that gets in the way of its expansion, liberty becomes a joke, the punchline in a story about how to distract a sucker while you lift his wallet and leave him stranded. It's an old American tradition that goes back to John Winthrop, again, and his "Little Speech" in 1645. Responding to a failed attempt to challenge his power to manipulate elections, he contracted liberty into two opposite possibilities, predictably a good kind and a bad kind. Outside the law, he said, liberty involved acting like an animal: it was "common to man with beasts and other creatures. By this, man, as he stands in relation to man simply, hath liberty to do what he lists." A certain terror lurked in the shadow of that "lists," one where animals and humans listed to do unspeakable things with each other in the tenebrous reaches of the wilderness. Winthrop called it *natural* liberty, gobsmacking "Nature" and exposing it to all manner of assault. The good kind of liberty, logically consistent with his gender theology, offered an early taste of later Orwellian developments. You were to use your liberty, Winthrop said, to freely give up your liberty, like a good wife freely gives over her liberty to her husband when she marries. He called this patriarchal travesty *civil* liberty.

Anne Hutchinson was decidedly not a good wife in Winthrop's terms. She was an antinomian. She held that salvation was through grace, not works, and that the Christian was therefore not bound by moral law, which freed her from the (patriarchal) authority of the colony's religious "leaders" cum tyrants. More importantly, because of that, she refused to stand down when ordered to do so by Winthrop and the General Court. She was not only a bad wife, she was also disobedient. Her lawlessness extended from the theological to the domestic in a defiant assertion of her liberty from the authority of the patriarchal Court. In a show trial that could have been a model for Stalin's judicial monstrosities, Hutchinson was condemned as a heretic and an instrument of the devil, and, along with her family and followers, expelled from the Bay colony. They were later killed in an Indian attack on Long Island. In a journal entry dated September 1643, Winthrop coolly described the massacre of Hutchinson and her family and blamed it on them for having "cast off ordinances and churches."

Winthrop was surely thinking of his old antinomian enemy when he distinguished between lawless (animal) and lawful (human) liberty. Susan Howe has proposed that antinomianism, lawless liberty or liberty from the law, is an elemental American mode of thinking and writing. She locates its beginning with two exemplary women: Hutchinson and Mary Rowlandson. In Hutchinson's case, the lawlessness is obvious. The intellectual repercussions flow out of her arcane theology into issues of the liberty of conscience and freedom from mental law. Her antinomian belief in a covenant of grace was in many ways less threatening than her refusal to recognize patriarchal law on any level, her open defiance of Winthrop and the General Court.

Rowlandson represents a different face of lawlessness. Captured by Indians during King Philip's War and held in captivity for 11 months before being ransomed, Rowlandson wrote about it in a strangely conflicted narrative. Howe proposes that Rowlandson went through a kind of reverse conversion that lurks in her text beneath the socially required rectitude of her surface narrative. She "excavates and subverts her own rhetoric," Howe points out. In Howe's reading, Rowlandson's captivity exposed her to the world beyond the pale and she tasted the openness of the wild as she relished the taste of raw horse flesh. She was set on "a forced march away from Western rationalism, deep and deeper into Limitlessness, where all illusion of volition, all individual identity may be transformed—assimilated." This image embodies Winthrop's nightmare of natural liberty.

Not actually antinomian in the religious sense that Hutchinson was, Rowlandson's narrative still resonates with the potential freedom opened in the entangled encounter with American space. Even the implicit duplicity of its form, a captivity narrative containing a secret conversion narrative, speaks to the lawlessness just past the frontier. Antinomianism and liberty, although not the same, both question the law and stand disobedient before Winthrop's Court and his "civil liberty." Antinomianism involves opposing the *nomos* which is grounded in custom and usage. Liberty, out of the Latin *liber*, refers to the absence of restraints and is connected through liberalis to a sense of generosity. Liberty is perhaps more open in the prodigality of its possible dispositions than antinomianism, which it provides ground for. While Howe persuasively locates Emily Dickinson's work as antinomian (although not in the root, religious sense), it can't be separated from the discourse of liberty. Liberty, Emerson said, is "the doctrine of poets." They both fed into what Howe calls "the primordial struggle of North American literary expression."

In that expansive sense, antinomianism and liberty are two aspects of the thinking of writing as they affect the determination of the next word, how the forming of language is engaged, whether left to a habit that evades thinking or a rule that tries to abolish death, or embraced as an articulating entanglement with the finitude of an imperfect emerging. Howe points to the radical textual formations of Dickinson's fascicles, and argues that the ongoing (male) editorial regularizing of her wild, eccentric forms indicates the war in American culture on antinomianism, especially on female writers. But Emerson is still everywhere in Dickinson's thinking, from his proposal for an American art and writing that "announces what no man foretold" to his call for writers to "upheave nature." (One is breathless watching Miss Emily hide behind a cracked door, listening to Emerson talk with her brother, unable to come into his physical presence.) Dickinson's challenge to the authority of thought and form answers that call. So do Whitman's invention of a new line and his challenge to the laws of Christian moralism. And Thoreau's (and

Emerson's) invention of a new form of writing thinking, formerly known as "philosophy." If liberty masks U.S. hegemonic violence with a razzle dazzle phantasm, it is no less this thinking of freedom among words—among many other things. Its nature is extravagant and prodigal in its im-perfections.

What Howe calls "the erasure of antinomianism in our culture" is related to what others refer to as "Empire," at least as it metaphorically entails the eradication of difference and the elimination of resistance to its totalizing power. It came on hard and fast in USAmerica, lurking in Winthrop's rhetoric as much as in the land grabs and outbreaks of violence against the indigenous peoples. Francis Jennings argues each of the English colonies was a mini-Empire, and they all quickly embraced genocide against their new neighbours, playing one tribe against another, as they began their relentless invasion across the continent. In 1638, under the command of Captain John Mason, English colonists allied with Narragansett warriors bypassed a military engagement with Pequod warriors with whom they had provoked hostilities, and instead attacked the Pequod village at Mystic, where they massacred over four hundred undefended and unarmed children, women, and elderly. They then beat a retreat from the enraged Pequod warriors who had been waiting to fight them elsewhere, until they were resupplied with arms and men and turned and destroyed the Pequods. They wrapped up this initial exercise in genocide by systematically tracking down survivors, executing captured males, and either killing the females, giving them as gifts to allied native tribes, or selling them as slaves in the West Indies. The United States emerged from the blood and enslavement of the Pequods, while arguably America was lost.

Melville, so crucial to Olson's thinking, tended to identify his boats with *America* and to load their names with significance. The Confidence Man's steamer is "Fidèle," *faithful*, but also *believer*, a poke at the gullible, self-deceived Americans living merrily in the midst of an unacknowledged horror. *Pequod*, the name of Ahab's ship in *Moby-Dick,* is even more pointed, identifying that floating, catastrophic America with its founding genocide, as if America was lost before it was ever found. Olson confronted the loss early in the poetry: "About seven years | and you can carry cinders | in your hand for what || America was worth," he stated in *Captain Christopher Levett (of York),* written in early 1958.

It was a complicated loss, tied up with Olson's complex sense of the destructive energies unleased by the failure, as Emerson had it, to actually discover America. Slavery figures in it. Although slavery was not the defining institution in New England that it was in the South, Olson does address it in "Letter 14," in story of John Hawkins, a slave trader, and the way in which his "business" was part of the failure of America. Christopher Levett, on the other hand embodies a particular relation to the world, the stance Olson also writes about in relation to John Smith, and Hawkins' father, William, who "made friends / among the natives, Sierra Leone / or Brazil // And had such honor / in the new places ...." Smith, another early European explorer, was significant for Olson because he "was doing it for one of the very first times. It's a different thing, to feel a coast, an ancient thing this Smith had, what men had to have before Pytheas." This timeless mode of encounter or entanglement with the wild/world (which Olson translates into his sense of the *postmodern*, groundless and projective) is also initial, not as time-factored, but as always further.

In "The Kingfishers," his meditation on change and renewal, Olson identified it with the ancient Mayans, one of the first people in America, who, Olson says, because of that, were "hot to get it down the way it was." That "hot to get it down the way it was" points to the same attention Olson found in Pleistocene humans as they invented the human in the shadow of the retreating glaciers: "A new world took form," Carl Sauer, Olson's favourite geographer, wrote, "developing the physical geography that we know. The period was one of maximum opportunity for progressive and adventurous man." That relation remains a potentiality, waiting to be activated. For Olson, two factors figure in the loss of that *ontological adventure* for the Maya, and presumably ourselves: the slippage of attention, a kind of epistemological failure or laziness, and "that other conqueror we more naturally recognize / he so resembles ourselves," Conquest is one name for it, Ahab's mad drive to kill the whale, a compulsion Melville connected to the fear of death and modernity's controlling subject.

Olson ran smack into it during his war time work at the Office of War Information. Whatever lingering sense he might have nursed about the moral purpose, as Ken Warren has it, of the United States as a force for world historic change, ended in his recognition of the decidedly immoral political machinations and maneuvering for post-war expansion and world dominance that gripped the state apparatus from the front lines to the upper echelons of the U.S. government. It was a deeply transitional moment for Olson in which his belief in the transformative power of American democracy, a belief grounded in the fight against fascism which saw him justify certain political choices he later rejected, come crashing down. It wasn't abstract. He was in the thick of it, making calls as the ground shifted under his feet. His plan to reenergize the practice of democracy in the U.S. ran headfirst into the new Praetorian Guard of Coca-Cola marketers imported from Madison Avenue to sell the war and prepare the ground for post-war American expansion into the ruins. Olson tried to carry on but he was censored into silence. Rather than write ad copy to sell American hegemony, he resigned:

> (o Statue
> o Republic, o
> Tell-A-Vison, the best
> is soap. The true troubadours
> are CBS. Melopoeia
> is for Coke by Cokes out of
>
> Pause

Soon after, he severed his ties to the Democratic Party which had been grooming him for leadership. At Berkeley, he referred to this moment of renunciation as his "only advantage:" "And in fact, the only advantage I have is that I didn't [run the country], so I can stand here among men who have done what I couldn't do, can't do."

It not only marked the end of Olson's political career, it marked the end of any lingering illusions about the value of the U.S. as moral agent of change. It marked the beginning of his resistance to U.S. violence in all its forms, from international economic and political conquest to cultural homogenization and commodification, to the continuing war with antinomianism, to its aggressive national narcissism and ignorance of anything other than its meagre fantasy of its own "exceptional" self. In recent years, Olson has been accused, among other things, of complicity with something called Empire, and specifically American Empire, a notion that circulates widely, although often without much attention to questions about "Empire's" composition, or even its existence. Mostly these days, "Empire" functions as a metaphor for evil, rather than as a descriptor of an actual organization of power. The threat of the Imperial Death Star replaces discriminations of sovereignty in discussions of the role of the U.S. in the world.

Once the metaphorical fog gets cleared, questions surrounding sovereignty and Empire are multiple and complex, and related to the United States, seem to come down to two possibilities: there is an American Empire, but it differs from historical Empires because it developed out of a new form of sovereignty; or, however brutal the push for U.S. hegemony may be, there is no American "Empire" because, as Walter Scheidel argues, "[i]n the most fundamental terms, the capitalist world system is not conducive to archaic flavors of territorial conquest, and it is hard to conceive of any realistic scenario that would make long-term violations of this principle appear both desirable and feasible." This is not to deny the fact of U.S. hegemony, its military interventions, its control of international monetary policy, and its self-interested manipulations of trade. But it does clarify how metaphorical distortions obscure rather than illuminate actual dynamics.

Complexities aside, the analyses point to sovereignty and law as determining issues in understanding American power. They are relevant as well in understanding Olson's relation to America. A specific unprecedented form of sovereignty developed in British North America. It differed from the forms of sovereignty that other European colonial powers imported to the new world, mostly because the various European colonizers came with different intent and encountered different worlds.

In Mexico, the Spanish found a world they knew well. The enormous, complex, oppressive Aztec imperial bureaucracy with crowns, priest castes, nobility, warriors, and slaves, was much like home. Sovereignty was centralized and hierarchical. The Spanish, who were there for the loot and not settlement, took over by replacing the ruling class. In 1521 Pedro de Alvarado allowed a large group of Aztecs (mostly nobles) to gather for a religious ceremony at the Main Temple of Tenochtitlan. While they were in the midst of their worship, the Spanish massacred them. Once the seats of power were vacated, the Spanish moved in and started running the place. One of the first orders of business, learned from the Christian destruction of pagan religions in Medieval Europe, was razing Tenochtitlan and building Mexico on its ruins. The natives were subjugated and used for labour.

For all its own horrors, British North America differed. English colonizers did not import monarchical sovereignty. Instead, they invented a new form based on their particular (though not exceptional) American experience. While Spain transferred its transcendent, monarchical sovereignty to Mexico, in British North America, as Michael Hardt and Antonio Negri point out in their book, *Empire*, republican sovereignty developed in relation to the settlement of a new kind of space. Sovereignty was reorganized as a "universal republic, a network of powers and counter-powers structured in a boundless and inclusive architecture." While the "imperial" nature of this sovereignty is a subject of contention, its revolutionary structure isn't. As Hardt and Negri argue, "Against the tired transcendentalism of modern sovereignty, presented either in Hobbesian or Rousseauian form, the American constituents thought that only the republic can give order to democracy, or really that the order of the multitude must be born not from the transfer of the title of power and right, but from an arrangement interior to the multitude, from a democratic interaction of powers linked together in networks."

Hardt's and Negri's new form of power is *made* rather than *bestowed* from above. Grounded in text, it established the common, the ordinary as the metric of the Real. De Crevecoeur described this state (of being) in *Letters from an American Farmer*. Travelling through the New York countryside, he observed there was no " ... hostile castle, and haughty mansion, contrasted with the clay-built hut and miserable cabin, where cattle and men help to keep each other warm, and dwell in meanness, smoke, and indigence. A pleasing uniformity of decent competence appears throughout our habitations." He goes on to condemn both the horror of slavery and the savagery of the frontier, so he was no dewy-eyed *Americainiste*. But he recognized something new when he saw it.

The founders of America, at least the ones who wrote about it, had no problem with Empire. In fact, only in the last century has Empire taken on the associations with evil currently identified with it. For those early Americans, the Roman Empire, with its republican structure, stood at the pinnacle of civilized accomplishment. Besides providing artistic and architectural inspiration, it became the basis of their program for using republican democracy as a control apparatus. Whether this meets the requirements to be classified as Empire is less interesting than the new reality it introduced to power. Rhizomic, to invoke Deleuze, rather than vertically rooted, it operates through networks. It "is constructed on the model of rearticulating and open space and reinventing incessantly diverse and singular relations in networks across unbounded terrain," as Hardt and Negri observe. The experience of "liberty" (which everywhere infused the European air in those days, informing new thinking about self, authority, nature, economics, government, knowledge, time, space, and God) is at the heart of it. Sovereignty, Hardt and Negri point out, is "affirmed, different from the European one: liberty is made sovereign, and sovereignty is defined as radically democratic within an open and continuous process of expansion." This new phenomenological space is "free of forms of centralization and hierarchy typical of Europe" and European colonial ventures such as Mexico. It *opens* into a new potential experience of *spacetime.*

The question of space and time and self—what they are, what their relation is, how are we to think of them past the now defunct Cartesian schema—are central to Olson's thinking in everything he wrote. While they are Given within any specific epistemological framework, they are always propositional. From Pliny to Copernicus to Newton to Einstein and Bohr, the proposition changes with the epistemology. Mythic time, circular time, empty time, shopping time, bent time, all appear in the shifting focus of mental lenses' concentration. *Spacetime isare* opening, foraying, furthering past any settlement of the moment. Olson's SPACE as he engaged it in the beginning of the Melville book registered a new opening. This opening rends, shattering the integrity of feudal time with its hierarchy of sacred days and the divine wheel of their turning. It spreads out, opening as/into liberty. Connected to the hegemonic narrative of the American "frontier," it implicates liberty in the removal of the indigenous populations not just from sight, but from memory. Hence what Melville in 1855 in *The Confidence Man* called the metaphysics of Indian hating in a chapter wryly titled "Containing the Metaphysics of Indian Hating, according to the views of one evidently not so prepossessed as Rousseau in favour of savages." Melville identified that hypocrisy as a poison in the heart of the United States, then in the midst of the so-called Indian Wars, the final genocidal wave that eliminated the aboriginal populations from American space. There can be no frontier if people live on the other side of it.

But the frontier was only one fact of the *opening* as millennial event. Contradictions erupt in irreconcilable openings beyond that. In Mexico, the native population provided slave labour for the extraction of wealth and so continued to provide value to their conquerors. In the U.S., native populations obstructed expansion and so were erased from the U.S. national cultural memory other than as figurative elements in adventure narratives or moral allegories of Rousseauian primitivism. The moral corruption of the removal of Native Americans from their land marked the birth of the U.S. in genocidal violence. But the opening of the liberty of this new space was/is multitudinous and ontologically contradictory. While the *otherness* of the natives was encountered as an obstacle and eliminated, the *otherness* of the *spacetime* beyond the "frontier" became part of an unprecedented, determining experience of the Real. Octavio Paz locates it as a contesting otherness beyond the range of psycho/sociology, that *wild* that Mary Rowlandson *discovered-herself-in-and-in-herself*, the dark matter of the world that abides within the common. Paz, in *The Labyrinth of Solitude*, has it as the *other side* of reality and links it to poetry's *openness*: "[A]lthough tied to a specific soil and a specific history, poetry has always been open, in each and every one of its manifestations, to a transhistorical beyond. I do not mean religious beyond: I am speaking of the perception of the *other side* of reality." The complexity of any moment and its irrepressible prodigality of meaning and sense are not a matter of historical narrative (a chain of causes leading to), nor are they reducible to a moral consistency. They are part of the experience of an otherness that fills without ever quite fulfilling while opening into the transhistorical and transnational.

The hegemonic drive of the U.S. across North America continued occupying space and expanding its networks. But *otherness* is entangled in the emergence of this new mode of sovereignty. Liberty's sovereignty is extravagant, not allegorical. The potential spills out infiltrating minds with potential form. Olson's SPACE is one fact of it. Large, he says, and without mercy. That SPACE and the colonizing, genocidal space of Manifest Destiny both emerge in liberty's opening. But whereas Manifest Destiny concluded at the edge of the continent, Olson's projective opened into the wild that is excluded from the United States, that "natural liberty" that resists any foreclosure of form in the name of law.

Olson's attention always focussed on the big picture and what it revealed about the otherness of our circumstance. His sense of the violent historical conflicts between peoples was contextualized within his thinking of migration as the constant fact of the human: "Migration in fact (which is probably / as constant in history as any one thing: migration," which, he goes on, "always leads to a new center." He is careful to keep its feet on the ground, specifying it as "the pursuit by animals, plants & men of a suitable / ... environment." On this scale, movement problematizes moral judgment since the forces involved are inhuman. Humans merely move with and within the inevitable and perennial process of the world. Olson took one of his leads here from Brooks Adams' proposal that two great migrations (or, as Adams called them, Expansions) defined Indo-European history. Driven by revolutions in metallurgy, radical new technologies, one extended from 3500 BCE to 284 CE (during which time assorted empires rose and fell to the delight of later historians), and the other from about 1000 to 1897 and after, which included the invasion, conquest and settlement of the Americas by Europeans and the birth of several actual Empires.

In "Bibliography on America for Ed Dorn," Olson contrasted this view of the orders of time, which he called millennial, to what he here called "history," another word that takes on multiple meanings in his thinking depending on his focus. Here humanism defines "history" both in scale and content. It gives coherence to the (made-up) story of the human. The millennial opens into movements on a scale that renders the human insignificant. Migration is constant. Flows of peoples up out of Asia and across what became Europe; flows of "three huge drives from the Polar North down on to the three legs of the future;" flows across the Bering ice bridge and down the West Coast of America in one violent displacing wave after another, none of which invoke moral angst. Once history is out of the way, the millennial reveals a world of perpetual motion that, if you push it back to Pangea, as Olson does, is as much geological as it is biological—or, say, a determining order of cosmos, a prevailing habit of the Real. Flows slow and seem to stop, but the movement just shifts scale, new centres form, from micro to macro, and around them stable structures. Then migration becomes centralized, hierarchical, and stable until some other wave or expansion, some multitude on the move, crashes into it and the pieces scatter.

Which was not much comfort to the Pequods, or anyone else who found themselves in the path of that juggernaut out of Europe in the 17th and 18th centuries. Olson didn't have much to say in the poetry about that dimension of the English encounter with the existing inhabitants of the place he otherwise writes in such detail. It is a painful absence in some ways. But the issue was not out of mind, although as usual for Olson, his emphasis was on understanding the big picture rather than expressing moral judgments. After the publication of *Call Me Ishmael*, he planned out a companion volume to be called *Operation Red, White, and Black* which fell through when he was unable to find funding. The proposal, included in the *Journal of the Charles Olson Archive #5*, began with the judgment that: "... the reality of our past has been so laid over by the moral assumptions of the writers that we know nothing of our selves. I see in the Indian, white and Negro life here on this continent a series of FACTS which, if properly selected, juxtaposed and coldly told, will together make a FABLE mostly now unknown." Earlier in 1947 he had noted: "or *Open* here 6. CABEZA DE VACA: and turn back to Indians via de Vaca's medicine, so that you catch all three—White, Indian, Negro at once." And then, in a further note: "But the first fact is that the American Indian has made a life out here in North and South America a hell of a lot longer than we whites: 10,000 years ago he came, and from that time to 1500 A.D. (Anno Diaboli in his reckoning) he was boss here."

Olson's recognition of 1500 as Anno Diaboli for the native Americans clarifies his sympathy for their circumstance, but his thinking focusses largely on the wandering de Vaca who briefly crystalized an exceptional American reality, a new world in which the Europeans and Africans took up the mode of life of the Native Americans they encountered in their walk from sea to sea, integrating their knowledge of this place, and living together peacefully. Having become a healer using Native knowledge and techniques, de Vaca and his companions were followed by increasingly large numbers of Indians until they encountered Spanish conquistadors in Northwest Mexico. The new world ended when the Spanish gathered up de Vaca's native followers and sold them as slaves.

Olson's SPACE connects only tenuously with these "historical" issues. It occurs in another register of phenomenological encounter, the event of the open, "free of the forms of centralization and hierarchy typical of Europe," and entangled with the process that Emerson points out goes on day and night. Both spaces exist simultaneously in an irreducible complexity of contradictions without hope of resolution. Olson's SPACE announces the end of the space and time of Euro American modernity and the various dualist apparatuses they enliven through their separation. It embodies sheer physicality entangled in *spacetime* as the projective emergence of the Real.

In that sense, Olson's understanding of "history" opens into a new dimension. Writing about Thoreau in *The Senses of Walden*, Stanley Cavell observed that "… America exists only in its discovery and its discovery is always an accident; and to the obsession with freedom, and with building new structures and forming new human beings with new minds to inhabit them; and to the presentiment that this unparalleled opportunity has been lost forever." Given these terms, the SPACE Olson claims in *Call Me Ishmael* names the encounter with the open as discovery. It is the open as specifically discovery after the closed, well-trodden spaces of Europe. Olson does not propose this "space" within the modern discourse of binaries, and specifically a binary involving *time* and *history* as a series of causally related moments. He moved beyond that Newtonian box of containers that hold the world hostage to their discrete mutually-exclusive measures. Time, then, not as a succession of discrete moments; not even as relative or dilated. Space not as an empty container; not even bent or contracted. At Goddard College, Olson was explicit that it "is rather quantum physics than relativity which will supply a proper evidence here, as against naturalism, of what Melville was grabbing on to when he declared it was *visible* truth he was after. For example, that life, that light is not only a wave, but a corpuscle. Or that the electron is not only a corpuscle, but a wave." Time, then, as an aspect of emergence, a dynamic field of space/time/matter.

Locked in the duality of time and space, imperial culture defines its spatial control in terms of temporal achievement, as the apex of a narrative of history. For Western Europe this has meant an attachment to the achieved form as a confirmation of the cultural perfection of Empire. An Empire of forms dictates the limits of the imagination in compulsory hierarchies of value and excellence, and within that, recapitulates the forms of Empire. Time becomes the time of power within the forms of Empire. They are varied and ubiquitous in every register of life and thrive within the closure of the fantasy of perfection. Olson's SPACE reopens time into the imperfections of liberty's prodigal entanglements. Space doesn't *contain*, it *opens*, it is *opening*. The shifting forms of sovereignty mark the change of Empire's achieved time of consolidated conquest into the restless networks of American hegemony, an entanglement that also yields the times of Charles Mingus and Thelonious Monk, of Louis Zukofsky and Robert Creeley, of Philip K. Dick and Diane Williams. The entanglement of resistance. The entanglement of restless imagination. The entanglements of the prodigality of the opening, the projective.

Taking his lead from the mathematics of Bernhard Riemann and the process philosophy of Whitehead, and locating them in the strangeness of Bohr's quantum physics, Olson wrote the end of a world of discrete objects and temporal progression and in its stead wrote world as a dynamic creative manifold emergence. Olson moves beyond modernity's space/time binary and establishes a continual dynamic of manifold congruencies that express the open where *spacetime* emerges as/in liberty, undetermined. We are returned to discovery as event, our event. In this sense there is no "history" in *The Maximus Poems*. Even with their incessant attention to the minutia of America's past as he located it in often obscure texts, the past does not unfold in a meaningful order. There is only the discovery of this moment in all its richness.

The texts remain, remnants of the multiplicity of *spacetime*'s diverse emergence. And the texts, when deployed within another text, begin to embody *spacetime* in complexities of relation that undo past-present-future—say, on Madam Gross's lawn in *Maximus* III.135: "even as that fox / was seen by me, that what // I offer you as now out of my right eye myrtle / flower and leaf are loud by presence solely // and gone in the thought." Even as Olson is decentred by the fox, objectified, recomposed in that entanglement of forms of being, he is (dis)located by the mass of recorded details of events that are gone but that are here, that are here, as related in the previous three pages of the (not) past that are entangled in the moment on the lawn. The event is discovery, surprise, projective, liberty.

In the 1960s and into the 70s, resistance to the brutality of U.S. violence spread around the globe even as the two superpowers competed for dominance: the armed struggles in Southeast Asia; the anti-Soviet movements in Eastern Europe; the anti-colonial wars in Africa, the anti-imperialist and anti-capitalist student uprisings in Europe and the Americas, black militancy and self-defence in the United States. The disciplinary orders of the ruling powers began to lose their hold.

Various forces in the United States intersected in this event: the spread of the counterculture, the New (and elements of the Old) Left, the women's movement, various identity groups, artists and writers of many stripes, and ordinary people who, confronted by Selma, My Lai, and Kent State, had enough and were energized to fight for justice on multiple fronts. This worldwide mass movement included diverse modes of resistance. Because of its nature as *mass*, no single interest or issue, no single demand or orientation, no single strategy or tactic, dominated. It opened forms of life into the multiplicity of their actual composition in resistance to the law's containment. One of its prods was the continued thinking of liberty and of a lost or undiscovered America.

Among writers and artists living and working in some state of resistance to the imperial apparatus, *The New American Poetry* was a significant provocation, offering a focus for one range of resistance to what Hardt and Negri call "the mass refusal of the disciplinary regime." Barney Rosset's Grove Press, which published *The New American Poetry* in 1960, was active in opposing U.S. Imperial ambitions on multiple fronts, both political and artistic. In addition to *The New American Poetry* and books by Bertolt Brecht, Samuel Beckett, William Burroughs, Alain Robbe-Grillet, LeRoi Jones/Amiri Baraka, Jean Genet, Michael Rumaker, and Octavio Paz, Grove published Regis Debray's *Revolution in the Revolution* (1967), *The Autobiography of Malcolm X* (1967), *Fidel Castro Speaks* (1970), Franz Fanon's *The Wretched of the Earth* (1967), *Che Guevara Speaks* (1968), and numerous other works that were central to the resistance. Because of this, the CIA targeted Rossett and the press in Operation CHAOS, its domestic espionage program.

Part of the conquer-and-control program of the U.S. involved monopolizing information dissemination, maintaining control over the representation of its violence and the resistance to it. *The New American Poetry* was implicated in the push to resist that control. Every word assaulted U.S. expansionist violence and the empire of forms central to its cultural control mechanism. Olson's essay, "Projective Verse," became a celebrated articulation of an opening beyond that constricted real. If the book raised the American flag (or a fragment of it) on its cover, it was to recall the myth of revolutionary intent entangled in the nation's confused thought of itself. To undertake to rewrite America remains an American thought if only because the original claim was textual. The poets in *The New American Poetry* did that repeatedly, leading to a proliferation of radical poetries that quickly spread beyond the book's initial limited (mostly white male) contributors to include a diverse uproar, including, as Ammiel Alcalay has pointed out, Ann Charters, Hettie Jones, D.H. Melhem, Sonia Sanchez, Joanne Kyger, Diane di Prima, Susan Howe, Rosemary Waldrop, Ntozake Shange, Alice Notley, Eileen Myles, Ann Waldman, Daphne Marlatt, Kathleen Fraser, Diane Wakoski, and many others. One of the centres of that uproar, one of its provocations, as Amiri Baraka confirmed, was Olson's projectivist poetics, which in his autobiography, Baraka described as a bible that gave "voice to feelings I had about poetry and about society."

But Olson's sense of politics extended his poetics beyond the poem into the meat of the day with which the poem is entangled. As Baraka went on to note, "What fascinated me about Olson was his sense of having dropped out of the U.S." At the Berkeley poetry conference in 1965 (amid the international political uproar), Olson introduced this politics into the mix, resisting the institutional inertia that threatened the conference itself with becoming integrated, despite its content, into the disciplinary regime, in this particular case, of Literature.

In 1962 at Goddard College, Olson announced that poetry readings had become a bore: "… it's become a performing art, you feel as though you have an audience, and as if you're supposed to do a concert or something." His unease had to do with the loss of poetry's contact with the immediate, the revelation of language's naked entanglement with liberty. The projective, not as an idea, but as exposure, the dynamic of exposure and the refusal of the disciplinary regime that emerges to limit its opening by commodifying and institutionalizing it. In Berkeley, after several days and a series of conventional readings, Olson took to the stage with a bottle of Cutty Sark and famously held it for over three hours. It was a stunning performance—performance is the wrong word—presenting, presencing, a revelation of mind at work in all its flawed but beautiful amplitude as it resists the pull of the "what-you-do-on-stage," an offering of contact, or as Al Glover proposed, a spontaneous recital in Avicenna's sense of ta'wil as the revelation of the soul's ascent.

Olson came to Avicenna through Henry Corbin's work in 1960 in the essay, "Cyclical Time in Mazdaism and Ismailism." Three days before his event in Berkeley, he read from Corbin's *Avicenna and the Visionary Recital* regarding the two groups of terrestrial angels: the ones on the right who know and order, and the ones on the left who act and obey and who are the titular spirits of writers. The Avicennan notion of the ta'wil, according to Corbin, "usually forms with tanzil a pair of terms and notions that are at once complementary and contrasting. Tanzil properly designates positive religion, the letter of the Revelation dictated to the Prophet by the Angel. It causes the descent of the Revelation from the higher world. Ta'wil is, etymologically and inversely, to cause to return, to lead back, to restore to one's origin and to the place where one comes home, consequently, to return to the true and original meaning of a text." Olson's Berkeley ta'wil stunned an audience waiting for a poetry reading (including Olson's friend, Robert Duncan, who famously walked out in the middle of it). It was a marvellous moment in which Olson's politics/poetics came together in a stunning "admission:" "You know—I'm the white man. I'm that famous thing, the white man. The ultimate paleface. The noncorruptible, the good. The thing that runs this country, or that is this country." Olson's revelation comes during an admission of a sense of inadequacy and jealousy: "And I sat in Gloucester, suffering, suffering! That the world had been captured by Allen and Peter and Gregory, and in fact, their own master (like my Pound), Burroughs."

Coming from someone considered by many to be one of the most powerful men in the world of contemporary poetry, a patriarchal figure, albeit perhaps a cult figure at that, this confession was deeply political in its self-exposure of the poet's wounded finitude. It was a public outing of the duplicity of the image of implacable masculine authority. He went on to mention Gregory Corso's reading in Buffalo earlier in 1965, and revealed one source of his sense of inadequacy to be his "protected" existence: "I never read in a coffee house in my life. I never spent an hour in jail." The statement about being a white man follows, which in this context, seems to be a confession of his understanding of the way his "social identity" (big white male) has negatively limited his experience of the world, including access to funky reading venues. He goes on: "And in fact, the only advantage I have is that I didn't [run the country], so I can stand here among men who have done what I couldn't do, can't do." Acknowledging his rejection of a powerful role in the post-war Democratic Party, he also expressed his solidarity with those who not only never had the choice of sharing in that white, patriarchal power, but who were subject to its brutality and violence.

Beyond that, the implications call attention to Olson's growing consciousness and acknowledgement of the emerging democratic diversity of voices rising in America (and around the world), the eruption of contradiction into the body politic, out of the resistance to USAmerican imperial violence (many inspired and provoked by *The New American Poetry*) and his desire to stand among them. It announces his awareness of the inequity at the heart of American life. A few minutes later he responds to Ed Sanders, saying, "I don't like that first Maximus. I never have, because of that goddamn principle which is phallic—I mean, it's like a phallic image. And, you know, that's a lot of bull shit ...."

Around this time Olson was composing the Maximus poem that begins, "I have been an ability—a machine—up to / now. An act of 'history', my own, and my father's, ..." He goes on to identify his own immigrant past: "my father a Swedish / wave of / migration after / Irish? like Negroes / now like Leroy and Malcolm / X the final wave / of wash upon this / desperate / ugly / cruel / Land this Nation / which never / lets anyone / come to / shore ...." If it is a "filthy land," a "foul country" where "human lives are so much trash," (the eternal disappointment) it is also still potential—the United States does not, in other words, control the final determination of *America*, that endless potential of liberty: "And an end to Hell / — end even to Heaven / a life America shall yield / or we will leave her / and ask Gloucester / to sail away ...."

With thanks to Daniel Zimmerman, Douglas Barbour, and Peter Quartermain for the use of their brilliant minds and generous help.

Who put the "x" in *O~~cc~~xident?*: The Empire of Neo-Obscurantism

—for Benjamin Hollander

I was sorting through some books the other day, looking to thin out my bookshelves and make room for new arrivals, when I came across a heavily marked up copy of Heriberto Yépez's *The Empire of Neo-Memory*. Back in 2013/2014, a loud, emotional public exchange of views circulated about the book and its primary subject, the poet Charles Olson. When I say "emotional," I mean really loud. And when I say "heavily marked up," I mean verging on manic. As I paged through the book and read the angry, marginal scrawls, I had to wonder how a book of such little substance managed to arouse such emotion and capture so much attention. It offers, finally, little more than a lightweight caricature, a character assassination really, of Charles Olson, a poet of enormous and significant influence, along with a weird, brief hatchet job on the work of Philip K. Dick—a pioneering, postmodern science fiction writer—thrown in for good measure.

One thing it is *not* is scholarship—Yépez never develops the kind of measured, detailed inquisitory relation to the texts that scholarship requires. Instead, he carefully selects passages and manipulates them to "prove" a point he had already arrived at through animus. He uses text. He does not explore it or ever allow it to speak to him. Nor can what he does reasonably be called critique—there is no reference to Olson's poetry at all, no attempt at analysis. Judgment replaces analysis. He offers only antagonistic gestures that use passages from a few carefully selected prose texts. Nor could it even remotely be considered "theory"—it is all smoke and mirrors, mystification and obscurantism, the insertion of "x"'s in words to mystify them, massive, unsupported generalizations about "history," and a little graduate school Freudism. It is simply a provocation—a poke in the eye, a textual Tar Baby thrown at the poets and scholars who continue to take their lead from and explore Olson's radical re-thinking of the poem and his ground-breaking work.

Yépez's text caused such a clamour because he composed it to ignite maximum outrage in targeted readers, while establishing his immaculate credentials as bull-goose post-Marxit-(wannabe) "Language" poet. It barrages the reader with negative caricatures of Olson, disguised as critical and psychoanalytic insights (Oedipus, anyone?). There is not one significant passage in the book where Yépez provides a careful textual analysis of Olson's work—not even a sloppy one. Instead, he deals out a succession of cheap shots beginning with the drawing on the cover which depicts Olson as an addled simian doing the lip flipping thing with his finger. From there it's all downhill.

Throughout it all, Yépez creates an illusory sense of his own authority by locating himself as part of a Romantic, ill-defined anti-Empire discourse and playing on the guilt of North American intellectuals. Whenever his *ad hominem* attacks become too tedious and obvious, he shifts gears and launches into an anti-Empire rant, wrapping himself up in its moralist aura, though it becomes clear before too long that even his "Empire" is a caricature, no doubt heavily influenced by the *Star Wars* mythos. Empire, in Yépez's meagre conceptual universe, is just a synonym for Evil. The book positively oozes with moralist self-righteousness and indignation.

The target of this provocation is not so much Olson as it is anyone who takes seriously his contribution, not just to writing but to the thinking of a new possibility for poetry beyond the literary definitions and institutions of modernity. Yépez's strategy is to offer caricatures of Olson so violently arbitrary and demeaning that readers becomes entangled in their outrage—much sputtering ensues, mangled curses (and many manic scrawls). This, however, is part of the game, essential to Yépez's plan, perhaps the nastiest part of it. Once you open your mouth to defend Olson in detail against a flurry of inaccuracies or lies, you are done. You have just identified yourself as what Yépez calls "the residue of Olson idolatry," and thus removed yourself from any serious attention. Meanwhile the sniggering legions of morally justified anti-Empire Good Guys turn their collective backs on you and carry on with their (textual) struggle against the Imperial Death Star by writing more lyric poetry.

As I recall, it took me multiple attempts to actually finish the book because I would become so outraged, 1), I simply couldn't read any more without exploding or offending the people around me in the waiting room or on the bus; and 2), I felt compelled to try to write a—not rebuttal, which is pointless, but some kind of response to his manipulative methodology. Responding to details accomplishes nothing in this case. There are so many inaccurate and misleading details you get lost trying to be coherent about them. And he has already pigeonholed and dismissed any resistance to his slanders. On the one hand, I couldn't read any more. It made me sick. On the other, I kept coming back to it because I wanted to understand what he was doing, if indeed he was doing anything beyond just being really mean to Olson and Dick. As everyone noted, his section on the Mayans is lovely. At times, he almost seems to make sense. There are occasional flashes of an inchoate sense of almost-meaning. But it turns out the guy behind the curtain (a reference to a classic American film, all of which, by the way—really, ALL U.S.-American films—Yépez dismisses in an epic one-liner as "training for war") is sitting pat with a busted flush.

The mystery of *history* is the issue. At least I, along with Hegel and a few others, find it to be a mystery. For Yépez, however, history, the immense fact of all that has been, the wind propelling Benjamin's backward-facing angel, is merely "a hegemonic homogenization of neomemories. History is formed to create empires ...." There's a one-liner for you. Apparently Yépez hasn't read Olson's special view of history, which deals with something very much like that question, and might have helped him clean up some of his derivative ideas and realize that whatever "history" is, it's a lot more complex than that.

It is so easy to get lost in the verbal smokescreen Yépez generates to obscure his unrelenting superficiality. After much work, however, I was able to get past the provocations and mystifications and arrive at what seems to be his central idea. It is a kind of syllogism that goes like this:

—*Olson uses history in his poetry* (this is sort of true—though Olson doesn't use history (as narrative) so much as attempt to undo the official narrative of the past by scouring the archives and introducing original records that thicken and complexify our experience of history);

—*history is memory* (this is seriously muddled—it kind of depends, doesn't it?—what does "history" mean here? I think Yépez confuses it with narratives of past events, as if that was the limit of the thinking of history. But even then, is a chronicle from 900 CE technically a "memory"? Only metaphorically.);

—*all memory is neo-memory* (this is pure razzle dazzle bullshit—neo-memories apparently are pleasant false memories—but Yépez can't use false memory because of the Freud scandal—and besides, it's too straightforward—"neo" is more sexy/mystifying than "false"—which begs the question, are all memories "false?" And if that's the case, how would we know?);

—*neo-memory is the foundation of Empire* (now we plunge into nonsense. There are many foundations to Empire. While it's true that fake glory stories are part of the culture of Empire (or of any culture, for that matter), I suspect that foundations, if we really want to get into that metaphysics, are far more material than false narratives about chopping down cherry trees or winning wars);

—therefore, etc.

And that's what he has to offer. That and his pretty section on the Mayans.

In the process of developing this intellectual edifice, Yépez comes up with a razzle dazzle "critique" of Olson's sense of space that culminates in an outburst where he turns time and space into moralist categories that arise out of his anti-Empire moralist hysteria: "Time is the enemy of Empire. | Space is the foundation of totalitarianism." Good Time. Bad Space. It is the world conceived within a Compulsory Paralytic Binary State (CPBS). And more foundations. That is some pretty heavy thinking. Move over Deleuze. Outta the way Baba. Here comes the man who put the "x" in Oxident.

Speaking of which, what's with the bloody "x" in *Oxident*? And why Occident at all? It's an unusual term in the 21st century, more at home in the 14th or 15th when Occidental colonialism was starting to rev its engine. As the etymological dictionary points out, "As a geopolitical term, sometimes with a capital O, [it is] always somewhat imprecise," which is perfect for Yépez. Furthermore, the OED says Occident is wed in all cases to colonialism's old pal, the *Orient*, without which the *Occident* makes no sense. They are the two halves of the world. Given the current status of the word (and concept), ~~*Orient*~~, you'd think *Occident* would have suffered a similar fate. The Medieval vibe, however, suits Yépez's politics, and since he is immune to subtlety, he is down with it. *Occident* was associated with another antique word of the time, *Christendom*, although Christendom was never half of anything the way that Occident is. Whatever else *Oxident* means to Yépez, and he is quite skilled in making sure that is never clear, it locates his thinking in the same CPBS that informs all the thinking in this book. It embodies what William Blake called Generation, a cosmos made up solely of mutually exclusive opposites and moralist codes.

Never one to allow complexity to cloud his moralism, everything must be either Good or Bad in Yépez's universe. If he can moralize Space and Time, nothing can stand in the way of his CPBS. This includes history which, as he will happily tell you, is Bad. In fact, it's really Bad. It creates really Bad things, like Empire, which in Yépez's book is the absolute worst thing of all. Except maybe for amassing stuff, like meaning. Nor will he allow himself to be confused by facts, especially when they contradict his repeated assertion of Olson's "illusions of pantopia," an utterly ridiculous idea that Olson somehow conceived of Gloucester as paradisal, a place of euphoric bliss. Say what? Even the most superficial, undergraduate reading of *The Maximus Poems* would immediately put that nonsense to rest. You have to wonder if Yépez has actually read any of Olson's poetry. It sure doesn't seem so.

The central part of the book is the long section on the Mayans that is meant to buttress his accusation that Olson was a low-down-gringo-dilettante-interloping-Imperialist-cultural-appropriator. Yépez's moody, lyrical soliloquy has been praised even by some of his critics as a moving, impressionistic evocation of Mayan thinking. As he dismisses Olson's reading of the glyphs he encountered in the Yucatán, Yépez claims a kind of—I don't know what else to call it other than "blood knowledge"—based on his genetic and cultural link to the elder civilization. The problem is his evocation of shared blood knowledge (he sounds a lot like D.H. Lawrence), while lovely, yields no useful information on the glyphs that Olson attended to, other than to claim Olson got it all wrong because he lacked that Mayan blood connection that pulses through Heriberto's authentic Mexican veins.

That was 2013. In the meantime, Dennis Tedlock published *The Olson Codex---Projective Verse and the Problem of Mayan Glyphs* in 2017. Tedlock, the anthropologist and scholar who gave us the definitive translation of the sacred Mayan text, the *Popul Vu*, knows his glyphs. He tracks Olson's movements in the Yucatán, tracks his reading, tracks his correspondence, tracks his forays into the Yucatán countryside, mapping Olson's experience as he thought about and translated multiple glyphs, based on his sense that they embodied poetic thinking and could be read as poems. Using scholarship rather than blood knowledge, Tedlock studied the same glyphs that Olson studied in *Mayan Letters*. He found that, although Olson makes errors in some of his translation attempts, his readings of the glyphs are mostly accurate. It's a question of imagination versus blood. The poet's imagination was able to experience the meaning of the glyphs. The blood knowledge, while lyrical and moving, mostly had nothing pertinent to add.

And then there is the *Oxident*. The swapping out of two c's for an x is curious. It stands out. You have to notice it. The gesture seems to want to recast the word in a new register, the way Derrida does with difference/différance. But Yépez is never clear how the new register differs from the old one other than looking a bit sexier (though I did hear someone compare it to a brand of laundry detergent). It tries to suggest a sophistication of meaning it never produces, which may have to do with Yépez's anxiety about *amassing meaning*. It's as if there really is no difference between Occident and Oxident other than the "x," which is nothing but a sign of Yépez's desire for an intellectual originality and subtlety that he is sadly lacking. In fact, on some pages of his book you can find both Occidental and Oxidental. Is that a clue? It seems to suggest that Yépez decided late in the game that the "x" would look really cool and original, and did a search and replace that unfortunately missed a few items. Oops.

One last thing—the constant character assassination that dominates the book at a certain point starts to look more and more like a smoke screen for Yépez's real target: Olson's influential essay on poetics, "Projective Verse." Yépez hates it intensely. It's almost as bad, maybe even more heinous, than Adam Smith's *Wealth of Nations*. Why? Apparently, because it yields meaning and meaning is—you guessed it—Bad. And why is meaning Bad? Because, by an act of sheer chutzpah, Yépez declared it so. According to his declaration, meaning and capital are equivalent. He further declares (you may have noticed there's a whole lot of declaration going on without much demonstration to back it up) that by meaning something in a poem, the poet is no better than a dirty, rotten poetic J.P.

Morgan, a vicious exploiter of the poetic masses, and Bad. Really Bad. He calls it *amassing* and ties it into his post-Marxism:

> Thus, I have said that these are Oxidental [sic] poets because they amass. Their poetics are capitalist poetics which hordes, which monopolizes, which rejoins, which appropriates. Neo-memory = private property. Can poetry be something other than greed? … Or could it be that the most radical poetry was that whose signs managed to trap nothing, that did not desire the permanence of meaning in its material body or syntactic associations? Images that evaporate all content as soon as it is sensed?"

The "permanence of meaning in its material body?" In what world is meaning ever permanent? And what "material body" does this refer to? A text? But a text is just words. He must mean (Bad) words because he opposes it to (Good) images. But what is permanent about words? And since when do images (even evaporating ones—whatever that means) lack meaning? Is he for real? Does this nihilist poetics, jerry-rigged on the ruins of classic post-Marxist moralism, sound at all familiar? Think back a few years before the LangPos stormed the Bastille of Academia armed with meaningless texts and evaporating images, only to find out how sweet it was and turn over their revolutionary credentials in exchange for some big money prizes, academic appointments, and book deals from Harvard (no greed there, eh?). Yépez sure sounds like that earlier nihilist/post-Marxist production, the rhetoric surrounding the poetics formerly known as L=A=N=G=U-A=G=E.

It comes as no surprise then, to find that he is deeply connected to the Players from that old "movement" as they have morphed into the current Board of Directors of Post-Avant American Poetry, Inc. Yépez is the translator into Spanish of the essays by one of LangPo's founders, and in turn was published by said founder in a journal he edited. He is also connected to *Chain* magazine, and Chain Links Press (the publisher of his book), which emerged from the LangPo Poetics Program at SUNY Buffalo. Excuse me, but this sure looks like the same old you-scratch-mine-and-I'll-scratch-yours-grifter-bullshit one has come to expect in the Pobiz market where group allegiance plays a far greater role than poetic imagination in the distribution of art booty. You want to talk capitalism?

In a final historical irony, if you do a little bit of genealogical digging, you'll discover that the Yépez name was granted to the family in 1492.

That was a big year for the O~~cc~~xidant / Christendom. The name was a gift bestowed on them by a grateful King Ferdinand and Queen Isabella on the triumphant Christian return to Spain after 300 years of exile. It came with the village of the same name which was the site where the newly minted Yépez family had defended Christendom and the O~~cc~~xident and drove the Moors out of Iberia and back into the benighted Orient from which they had crawled. Maybe that's why he is so fascinated with Oxident.

Maximus IV V VI— Measuring the Incommensurable

In October or November when discussion about this topic*—which back then was called "Mystics and Spirituality in Post-1945 Poetics"—was coalescing, the first thing the participants did was immediately and universally object to the word *mysticism* as an accurate description of Olson's relation to what we call *the divine,* or, say, *sacred.* People proposed a few alternatives including the phrase *secular divine,* a phrase Olson adapted from Whitehead's proposal in *Process and Reality* that "the secularization of the concept of God's functions in the world is at least as urgent a requisite of thought as is the secularization of other elements in experience." Olson used this creative oxymoron a couple of times, notably in *A Bibliography of America for Ed Dorn*, where he called it something USAmerica had achieved but was in danger of losing. A few other suggestions got thrown into the hat, but nothing seemed quite to fit Olson's work, in spite of the fact that everyone acknowledged a dimension to the work addressed to the sacred that demands recognition. It seems to me that this aversion on our part toward a recognizable vocabulary responds to an aversion inherent in Olson's work, and the question confronting us is what is the basis of that aversion of the work?

My attention here is limited to *Maximus IV V VI,* which I think is as far as Olson was able to take his epic. Keep in mind that *The Maximus Poems* was not a *project.* From the beginning, it was a process, a journey the poet committed himself to, a venture into the unknown. It was *projective.* In the first volume of *The Maximus Poems*, composed in the 1950s and published in 1960, Olson felt his way toward a path forward from his initial foothold, *offshore* as he put it. It was the beginning of a voyage with no destination. And while Olson wrote the poems included in

Volume 3, George Butterick composed the book after Olson's death using the poet's manuscripts. Given Olson's deep engagement with form and morpho-dynamic composition, the absence of his shaping intelligence sidelines *Volume 3* from consideration here. While the poems are endlessly interesting, the book is not an Olson composition.

Olson composed every aspect of *Maximus IV V VI,* as he continued to move ahead after the first book, and worked to unfold the poem and his thinking. It represents his work as far as he was able to take it before he died. Both Jack Clarke and Al Glover expressed to me that sense of the deep significance of *IV V VI.* Glover compared it to the moment at Newport in 1965 when Bob Dylan performed his electrified "Maggie's Farm" to a shocked and hostile folk music crowd who thought it was still 1955. It was an announcement—"I ain't gonna work on Maggie's farm no more," Dylan sang, and clearly that was the case. The music confirmed it.

Like Dylan at Newport, *Maximus IV V VI* announced the end of something and the initiation of something new, a renewal, an instauration, an origin. "Immediately when I began reading *IV, V, VI* I felt the change," Glover said. "Enormous. And that is the change you ask about. And it in many ways performs the change from 'the fifties' to 'the sixties.'" That change was convulsive. I would characterize it as the eruption of an enormous creative energy that transgressed all old, authorized art and political boundaries, all the cultural claptrap that constituted postwar U.S. imperial establishment power. Form was crucial. Creative invention embraced formal convulsions as a way to meet and address the world in its unprecedented revelation. Form is love in Olson's cosmology, a love that embraces the world and is embraced by it in a radical way. The creative outburst/tumult that exploded from that fracture in the U.S. culture machine was fueled by libidinal energy, liberated first by the civil rights movement, and then amplified in outbreaks of active resistance in the form of the Black Power movement, the anti-Vietnam war movement, the feminist movement, and the gay liberation movement, all of which were interconnected and fed into the convulsions disrupting the worlds of art, music, writing, and popular culture. Olson's poem announces a new dispensation for what was formerly known as poetry, a new mode of knowledge, a poetic gnosis.

I'd go so far as to say that to fully enter the event that constitutes *Maximus IV V VI,* you have to read the original 1968 Cape Goliard/

Grossman edition. A large, beautiful book (20 cm. x 28 cm.), each page offering a physical, textured surface for Olson's compositions. The words hang or drift or burst into the space that surrounds them on the page. The first volume of *Maximus* consists of what is clearly a collection of poems. Even at their most formally disruptive and projective, they still announce themselves as poems. But something shifts in *IV V VI.* Rather than the long letter format that dominated the earlier volume, *IV V VI* passes from poetry to .... To my mind, it's the concretization of the rejection of literature and the literary that Olson so insistently announced at Berkeley in 1965. It's the beginning of the Republic of Nothing but Poetry. It's the realization of Lyotard's distinction between the modern aesthetic, which attempts to compensate for the withdrawal of the Real with the solace of good form, and the postmodern that denies the solace of good form, searching "for new presentations, not in order to enjoy them but in order to impart a stronger sense of the unpresentable." "B. Ellery   Cinvat Bridge   aer" and "tesserae / commisure / Jan 19th 1962" make no pretense about being poems in any remotely traditional sense. Absolutely singular, positioned starkly in the centre of the large, empty pages, the words claim your attention even as they frustrate your attempt to penetrate or contain the language. And don't forget the wholly blank pages that periodically introduce—silence, for sure, as well as space—silent spatiotemporal eruptions in the midst of the unfolding language. This is just to say that the book is a unique *event* and should be addressed as such.

But what kind of event? Well, not mystical, for sure. The initial, universal discomfort among panelists with *mysticism* no doubt has to do in part with the current intellectual atmosphere which is dominated by militant sociology and the deep materialism that founds it. *Mysticism,* and the Mystery it is rooted in, removed from the mode of spiritual apprehension which it is native to and subjected to the reductive, unidimensional gaze of the materialist, become identified with a lack of rigour, a kind of fuzzy self-indulgence if not delusion. When Reason presumes to dispel all shadows with universal illumination, mystery is rendered obscurantist, and those addressed to Mystery, the mystics of yore, as foolish or psychologically wounded at best, and hucksters at worst, somehow connected to the even more scandalous *occult.* Even for those of us for whom the Mystery of creation is an ever-present provocation to think beyond the Given, the designations *mystic* and *mysticism* are tainted by an aura, a faint taste, of the disreputable, the intellectually lazy, what some people refer to as *woo-woo.* Definitely not Charles Olson, in any case, as the original panel's dissatisfaction indicates.

Then, *deus ex machina,* Robin Blaser, who always hovers around my reading of Olson, showed up in the form of a letter from 1999 I stumbled upon while sorting an ancient stack of papers on my desk, and literally instructed me to go reread Michel de Certeau's *Heterologies,* specifically the chapter called "Mystic Speech." De Certeau is concerned to reclaim mystical speech as a legitimate mode of thinking, specifically with the ways that 16th and 17th century mysticism "proliferated in proximity to a loss," and is in fact what he calls a "trope for that loss:" "We find," he writes, "on the one hand, in the context of a degenerating tradition darkened by time, an effort to go beyond; and on the other hand, a progression from a cosmos of divine messages (or 'mysteries') to be understood, to itinerant practices which trace in language the indeterminate path of a mode of writing.... They were experiencing in their shattered Christendom another fundamental decline: that of the institutions of meaning. They were experiencing the disintegration of the sacred world." Locating mystical writings (he is dealing with the flowering of mystical works by writers such as Meister Eckhart, Angelus Silesius, Hadewijch of Anvers, and Saint Teresa) at a particular moment of cultural/spiritual radical instability, De Certeau finds in them an attempt to move beyond the crisis in a new mode of writing grounded in the recognition of indeterminacy. That's a sense of mysticism we'd do well to keep in mind as we circle this problem of Olson's—shall we call it, belief?

One option that came up in my conversation with Al Glover about Olson's book was the notion of *esoteric* as opposed to *mystical.* Esoteric has the advantage of being connected to a particular mode of relation to language. Henry Corbin in his several discussions of Avicenna's philosophy draws on the distinction between *zahir* (exoteric) and *batin* (esoteric). In "The Theme of the Voyage and Messenger," he proposes: "... the whole field of symbolic hermeneutics ... is designated by the word *ta'wil.* It is a process of eclipsing the apparent (the *zahir*), in order that what has been hidden may appear (the *batin*)." *Ta'wil,* by the way, as Corbin proposes in *Creative Imagination in the Sufism of Ibn 'Arabi,* is not about allegorical exegesis, but transformation, the transfiguration of the "literal texts" into Persons. Note the shift in the nature of the relationship between reader and text from one of control through interpretation, the attribution of meaning, forcing the text to signify, to one of personal relationship, reading as entering into an active, intimate relation with a Person.

Knowledge is the issue. Arthur Versluis, in *Restoring Paradise*, argues that "esotericism has as its central characteristic gnosis, meaning experiential insight into the nature of the divine as manifested in the individual and in the cosmos." For the sake of brevity and to keep it simple, by *divine* I mean that profound, incommensurability of What Is, as Robert Duncan had it—what leaves us stuttering in the face of the night sky, an infant's gaze, the rising of the Star we daily circle. It is tied up with the experience of Spirit as "openness and expansion of vision," as Karl Kerenyi has it, "a primordial experience of man." Versluis' *gnosis* crucially links his discussion of esotericism to poetry's potential for transformative knowledge (experiential insight), which poetry achieves through the rhythmic manipulation of nested sonic/ideational/image fields—Pound's melopoeia/logopoeia /phanopoeia.

Glover was justifiably reticent about using *esoteric* given the association of any inner truths, any private vocabulary available only to a few, with secret societies, fraternities, and the English Department. None of those would have been attractive to Olson, an immaculate, unconscious outsider—even when he was supposed to be some kind of cult leader—who staged his performance at the 1965 Berkeley Poetry Conference precisely to call out those of his cohort who were signing up for membership in the Fraternal Brotherhood of Literature and entrance into its sacred rituals of largesse bestowal. *Esoteric* can't shake a certain sense of disreputableness, similar to *mystical*. In the case of esoteric, the scandal is tied to anxiety over elitism, knowledge that is available only to a privileged few. This anxiety has to do with the way the prevailing form of democratic culture in the West has developed to demand that everything be available to everyone whenever they want it. If it's not available, it's elitist, the great sin against democracy.

But there is always an inner and an outer when it comes to language. As Versluis points out, any written language opens itself to further—esoteric, inner—reading, whether it's Krazy Kat, *Ulysses*, or the assembly instructions that accompanied your new grill. No matter how hard you try to keep it *transparent*, as they say, it will always open, and then open, and then open again, depending on the reader's commitment and relation to the text. There is always more to be read, something further to be discovered in the text. And when the text is the outcome of creative, open, formal compositional technique, all the more so.

Maximus IV V VI spills out its inner workings in a convulsive, cataclysmic origin, a splitting open of the Earth itself. Like the rest of the words floating around here, the word *origin* currently has a somewhat scandalous, say metaphysical, edge to it. Identifying origin as metaphysical, intellectual fashion holds the thinking of origins to be naïve and—non-materialist. The idea of originality and origins is seen as delusional since everyone is always already under the influence of someone and there is no metaphysical beginning. As with the Christian creation story, it's presumed that if there ever was a beginning, hypothetically speaking, it happened a long time ago and has nothing to do with the current state of sociology.

But what about origin, not as absolute and abstract, but as finite, processual, and plural, origin as a moment of opening, a moment of revelation? Such origins are front and centre in Olson's thinking. Campbell Copland in *Gnomic Verse: a poly-modern morphology of poetic revelation*, argues, "No one's last page has been turned in the Origin Story of the Universe. In fact, if anything, it's something we need *to catch up* to, this Story of Origin, our story of origin, and find a way back into, not around, or past, but right through the thick of it." This is exactly Olson's move at the outset of *IV V VI*. He decentres the opening narrative, constantly qualifies the poet's voice with the testimony of a witness ("she") and opens it into an origin, a renewal, a literal rupture in the surface of the earth, a split in the tectonic plates that gradually results in the planetary formation that we, in our imaginary (delusional) central position, assume is Real, i.e., permanent. No Maximus announces himself from offshore. Instead, the poet relates his awkward leap into a storm, a leap validated and qualified by a woman's commentary, and invokes a world splitting asunder. In so far as Maximus enters the action of the poem, his is a non-central position, and he is just another player in an unfolding, unanticipated revelation of meaning, not as project or experience of completion that a subject can return to, but as *opening* itself, the exposure of the subject to and within the expansive proliferation of finitude.

There is certainly enough material there to justify talk of an *esoteric* meaning. And if you *want* to understand it, you *can*. Commitment is what counts, not immediate availability. Is it any less democratic for that? Versluis argues an esoteric work requires one to "enter into and dwell in the imaginative realm the creator generates (or reveals) through the work, and doing so is an initiatory process through which the reader or audience develops cosmological or metaphysical insights." He posits three kinds of readers:

1. Closed readers, who come to a work with predetermined theses that disallow their imaginative entry;
2. Sympathetic readers, who enter into a work imaginatively;
3. Initiates, who see the work as mirroring a process that they seek to undergo in themselves.

The parallels with readers of poetry are obvious. Readers experience a closed text not because of the text, but because of their attitude and stance toward it.

The word *initiate* (v) is rooted in an active network of temporally conditioned meanings inflected by various senses of beginning, entrance, to enter upon, to go; *movement, process,* in other words, and *origin.* Initiates (n) are simply those who embrace the text and work to enter its imaginative field. That said, the word *initiate,* like *mystic* and *esoteric* raises certain difficulties. If Olson would have balked at the idea of his work as *esoteric,* and I suspect he would have, he would have been even more resistant, I think, to the idea of initiates and initiation—which is ironic given that much of the reaction against Olson and his students after his death used that vocabulary to criticize and dismiss the event and work their relations informed.

To return to the question I have been skirting, possibly even evading, if *Maximus IV V VI* is not mystical or esoteric or an initiation, and yet continues to attract those words even in its aversion to them, what kind of event is it? To figure that out, it remains for us to enter it rather than understand it. I think that's one of the things Olson meant when he said that which exists through itself is what is called meaning. There is no other way to get there than to go through it. Meaning is a unique experience of entrance into an otherness. It is a Whiteheadian event, "a nexus of actual occasions, inter-related in some determinate fashion in an extensive quantum." Elsewhere Whitehead calls an event a spatio-temporal region, as opposed to the Newtonian notion of simple location in space. The universe consists of events rather than objects in space. We are an event always in relation to other events as Creation proceeds.

The event of *IV V VI* originates out of a leap into a storm (on St. Valentine's Day, no less) which introduces a blood sacrifice and a sacred recitation of divine origins. The event invites you to enter a primordial scene, but refuses to be contained. The meaning escapes at the limit of signification. I can point to a number of, for me, significant observations/questions about the text that follow from that, crises of signification woven into the compositional bones of the book, its form, that circulate in my thinking of it and influence my experience of meaning:

—in the ritual sacrifice that opens "Dogtown to Maximus I," the human, Merry, dies, dismembered by the bull. In the primordial, mythic world the ritual arises within and in response to, it is usually the Bull—the Bull of Heaven, the Minotaur, Mithra's Bull, the Taurobolium—that dies at the hand of the hero;

—if you count the poems, Maximus has been demoted to a minor player, displaced by Dogtown (a sacred geographical site) whose letters *to* Maximus make up the backbone of the book. The few letters *by* Maximus are decentred, scattered unpredictably within a larger, unstable field of diverse modes of writing;

—one of the four letters from Dogtown to Maximus (III) is missing;

—the letters from Maximus in the first volume have been largely replaced with fragments and ejaculations—"tesserae / commissure";

—two blank pages separate the penultimate and ultimate poems of *V*;

—another two blank pages follow the last letter from Maximus and precede the ultimate poem of *VI* (before the Fort Point section); the Fort Point section contains no letters and no attributions to or from any identity.

There's much more, but this is enough to think about while approaching the Event, say as one approached Eleusis on the Sacred Road from Athens toward the celebration of the Mysteries, hopefully with the intent of entering its imaginative field and engaging its dynamic energies.

Carl Kerenyi, in a discussion of Minoan culture's embrace of the somatic rather than the abstract, uses the word *gesture*. "Here I am speaking not of cult gestures side by side with other equally characteristic gestures of simple human existence, but of *the* gesture which time and time again, in different forms of movement, represents the identical situation of man; his non-central position which demands an 'opposite' and can be understood only as an 'opposite.'" Referring specifically to Bull leaping, he goes on: "The gesture grows out of the game, but game and body are one, a single, indivisible gesture, free and at the same time, controlled, which can well be said to have been inspired by a transcendent presence." Minoan Bull leaping buzzes insistently around the opening sacrifice in *IV V VI*. Olson was thoroughly familiar with Minoan Crete as an important site, as he saw it, in the early realization of a human potential later lost to the violent incursions of the warrior cult of Zeus-worshipping Achaeans. Bull leaping exemplified a culture that, as Kerenyi has it, "saw the world primarily in its plant and animal aspects," that decentred human vision.

I think of *Maximus IV V VI* as akin to Kerenyi's gesture in the way it constantly locates me in a non-central position which demands recognition—experience—of a transcendent *opposite* where transcendent is understood not as out of the world, but as a further dimension of the world, here as folded and unfolded, opening into the surprise of not human, the non-central, an opening beyond the self-enclosure of signification. As Jean-Luc Nancy puts it, immanence means to remain within oneself and transcendence "is nothing other than the passage to the limit. It is not the crossing over of the limit; rather, it is the being-exposed on the limit, at the limit and as limit."

Some people have proposed that Olson was a poet of "historical geography." I'm not exactly sure what they mean by that, but I can live with it if we acknowledge a couple of things: First of all, that the geography of *IV V VI* is *sacred geography*. Ruth Van Dyke points out that sacred geographies are not just places. They are "alive with meaning, bound up with histories, religious practices, and cosmologies. Axis mundi and memory anchors create connections across spatial and temporal realities.... Special places demarcate cosmologies on current and ancient landscapes. Sacred geographies are marked by shrines, rock art, votive deposits, trails, alignments, and archaeological sites." That last run-in fact could well describe *Maximus IV V VI*: *marked by shrines, rock art, votive deposits, trails, alignments, and archaeological sites.*

Secondly, *history* is a word we use to inure ourselves to the profound mystery of Time. Robin Blaser, referring to Whitehead, points out that Olson's sense of "history" "will not be the history of those powers, as we usually understand them, but 'history as primordial and prospective.'" Henry Corbin argues that whereas we tend to think of humans as being *in* history, history is actually "*in man*." This is sacred history, what he calls *hierohistory.* In fact, after having said there is no word for the Event of Olson's book, I will contradict myself and suggest that one possibility or dimension worth holding in mind is *Time*. I'd argue that every aspect of *IV V VI* works to originate—instaurate—the experience of the complexity of the mystery of Time in a myriad of facets and permutations, from primordial time to sacred time, interrupted time, clock time, calendrical time, heroic time, mundane time, past time, present time, mythic time, chronicle time, horological time, chronometric time .... What we call "history" is just one of those elusive experiences/faces of Time, a name for the sublation of Creation if we understand "Time" to be a way to designate the outpouring, the continual emergence, of the world which is destroyed even as it becomes. In his discussion of Hegel's concept of *Aufheben* (sublation), Jean-Luc Nancy describes it as *the already-past-of-becoming and the becoming-already-past as truth that exposes itself.* It is the Moment as it always already passes, and having passed reconstitutes the Moment passing. Nothing is lost even as everything is lost. It is to come face to face with the Mystery of Creation, the ultimate decentering.

Like his friend, Robin Blaser, and like Jean-Luc Nancy, Olson was raised Catholic and like them, though he rejected the Church and its doctrines, he never lost his deep sense of the sacred heart of the world and the necessity to address it and our current relationship to it, to give it form. Our Lady of Good Voyage is no casual metaphor, but an actual presence that transforms throughout the poems, now the Virgin, now Nut, now Potnia, now our Lady of Wild Things. Olson's stance—his dynamic relation to/within the event that is the world, our world, a world in which as Nancy says, the sacred is *fluttering and exsanguinate*—has no category. It proceeds from a primordial experience that eternally precedes and gives rise to categorical determination without becoming identical to them. Because of this exposure of/to/within Time's uncontainable mystery, *Maximus IV V VI* emerges out of an origin that eternally precedes those determinations of the experience of the divine or sacred which give rise to institutionalized practices and doctrinal discipline. Categories signify conclusively, whereas Olson dances at the edge of signification without signifying. Looking back in this essay at the rejected language of those categories and the resurgent sense that circulates around them, the sense that is that primordial experience, the ground of meaning, you could say, *Maximus IV V VI initiates an experiential knowledge* in *an inner dimension* of *itinerant practices* which *trace in language* the indeterminate path of *a mode of writing* in response to *the disintegration of the sacred world.* It's an ingeniously concocted event, a material tool, that returns us to a primordial experience of the sacred, a transformative gnosis that opens the world toward further articulation, further knowledge, further form.

* This essay was prepared for presentation at the 2022 Louisville Conference on Literature and Culture.

Olson's Buffalo

"When wallflowerism becomes sufficiently established to control history then we have a hell of time believing what is said (of what is said)—the Herodotean Way—over what we suspect (& we are suspicious, no?) & therefore speculate as to, what went on, like REALLY. It's the urge toward the MONO—. . ."
—John Clarke to Tom Clark, 1/20/87

When Charles Olson first came to Buffalo in 1963, it had been some 18 years since he'd turned from politics to writing as the work which would centre and drive his life (although, in another sense, as the Berkeley reading demonstrated, he never left politics). Daniel Belgrad, in *The Culture of Spontaneity*, usefully locates Olson in this regard within a community of writers, artists and musicians, arguing that Olson's poetics are inherently political, having largely been formulated in response to his experience of the liberal/corporate takeover of the Office of War Information and the Office of Facts and Figures (which had been led by Archibald MacLeish) in 1942 and 1943. He came to Buffalo with a significant body of work already accomplished. *Call Me Ishmael*, *Y & X*, *The Mayan Letters*, *In Cold Hell, In Thicket*, *The Maximus Poems*, and *The Distances* had all been published, as well as "As the Dead Prey Upon Us," "The Kingfishers," "The Lordly and Isolate Satyrs," not to mention the important essay, "Projective Verse." *Maximus IV V VI*, though unpublished, was already written. He'd been to Yucatán and led the wild, intellectual free-for-all at Black Mountain. Crucially important for many of those who came to Buffalo to work with Olson, was his tremendous push to rethink the epic as an address to an unfolding world, a world in process. How, that is, to rethink this crucial mode of poetry and move it past the limits it had been taken to by Pound and Williams. He was what Al Glover recalls as "a living connection to an 'old' tradition rather than simply an isolated lyrical voice which was pretty much all there was otherwise." Though Donald Allen's anthology, *The New American Poetry,* had opened people's eyes to a wider range of writing than Glover's comment might suggest, his point about the dominance of the lyric mode still holds true.

All this work was implicated in a move away from the "literary," finally claiming for poetry an altogether other range of importance. What Olson founded in Buffalo, what followed from his arrival there, begins with that. "Literary" in this context, that is in relation to Olson's work and to the work he engendered in Buffalo, refers both to the conventions, modes and procedures of writing that mark, however broadly and ambiguously, what is proposed at any given moment as the institution of "literature," and also with the "life worlds" such practices are implicated with, something loosely called, say, the "literary life," complete with all its competitions, prizes, career paths, disciplinary bodies, and canonical aspirations—the literary, then, as institutionalized practices deeply implicated in upholding the status quo. Crucial to Olson's sense of a move beyond or around the literary, was the understanding that it's possible to reconnect with or recover energies that pre-exist their historical institutionalization into a specific, fixed grammar of social practices. And even more importantly, that to do that, to push oneself toward that connection, is to disrupt or alter that grammar, a profoundly political act.

Such a move involves two crucial linked concepts—the *ordinary* and the *archaic*—and how they might be seen—or revealed—as converging in a new world. The ordinary is just that—where we are, what we do, here, today, this laundry, those dirty dishes, that which is arrayed around us. Olson's crucial move is to understand that the ordinary, as such, is archaic, has always been, so that what we in fact are estranged from, as Heraclitus and Wittgenstein had it, is so familiar because it has always been there. In this sense, Olson's proposal is not so much anti-literary—a move which paradoxically is locked in an economy with the literary (the fate of the oppositional and the non-ordering) as pre-literary, an antithetical decentring in whose prolific and devouring wake the unprecedented is recovered.

Olson's *projective* accompanies this convergence. Like form and content in the famous proposal that emerged from the Olson/Creeley correspondence, they are really a Janus-faced energy. To take up the archaic/ordinary invokes the projective that is its method, the way forward. And to take up the projective invokes the archaic/ordinary, which is its ground.

One more term is crucial to this antithetical practice—*community*, which Olson famously had as *polis*. Of all these terms, this is, in some ways, given our current condition, the most difficult to come to terms with, if only because of the ubiquitous nostalgia for it. Following Jean-Luc Nancy here, I'm proposing to come at this term along the lines of what he says in *The Inoperative Community*, "*happens to us*—question, waiting, even imperative—*in the wake of* society," what appears to us as "neither a work to be produced, nor a lost communion, but rather as space itself, and the spacing of the experience of the outside, of the outside-of-self." I don't think I need to dwell here, on how Olson's sense of America as space foreshadows Nancy's proposal. One of the ways Olson's poetics, as enacted in the Berkeley reading, are antithetical to the literary (in both the senses given here) is their insistence that such a discharge of energies arises from the circulation and generation of those energies within just such a space as Nancy identifies, and that that process is the act in which community reveals itself to itself.

Such a proposal undermines not so much the concept of *genius* (there's still room for the extraordinary within the space of the ordinary) as the promotion of individual production and the specific product, even in its current generic, non-author specific forms. It holds that work to the responsibility of an ordering intervention. Genius, as the Romantics knew it, is an especially intense receptivity to those circulating energies previously mentioned. But the community orders (as in ordinary) itself out of the exchange—the call and response—that arises in the projective practice of the ordinary. Whatever else such a community may be, it's a "place" where hierarchical/anti-hierarchical orderings are dissolved in a synergistic circulation of authorities (authoritative finitudes, Nancy might say) that egg each other on toward their further possibilities—which are the further possibilities of the self-revelation of the community as well.

The critics of the community Olson engendered in Buffalo have from the beginning proposed its defining relation as one of dominance and submission, with Olson positioned as what's been called the "High

Priest." Typically, those around him were identified as "disciples," "acolytes," or some other typically religious term meant to signify a loss of "autonomy" or "individual authority." Within such a community as I'm attempting to define here, however, such traditional vocabularies (mostly derived from Enlightenment polemics against the *ancien régime*) having to do with static hierarchical relations of power—equality, autonomy, derivative, original, subservient—as well as the accompanying package of anti-religious/pro-Reason pejorative labels like *cult*, *church*, *disciple*, etc., are drained of meaning and become inoperative, along with the cosmology that generates them. This is not to say specific persons who still passively identified themselves in that old cosmology didn't enter into such relations. But they weren't part of what I'm calling "the community," which actively proposed itself as further. In any case, as we've known for some time, that old cosmology (the cosmology of critical modernity) is in acute, probably terminal crisis. Writing of the modern critical passion in *Children of the Mire*, Octavio Paz says: "In love with itself and at war with itself, it cannot affirm anything permanent or take any principle as base, its sole principle being the negation of all principles, perpetual change." One of Olson's great contributions here, as Ralph Maud has pointed out, links the resolution of that crisis to the emergence of the archaic/ordinary, to propose that what he called, after Toynbee, "the post-modern," is identical with the archaic/ordinary.

This exercise in clarifying vocabularies does not intend to provide some theory that can include Olson's work, and what it engendered in Buffalo, in a neat package. Rather, it aims to open our sense of relation to the provocation and the challenge of the work before turning to what followed from that, the response to that call, what Olson furthered. Each call elicits a response, but each response in turn becomes a call. That is the circulation of authoritative finitudes. How else understand what happens with Frontier Press or in the *Magazine of Further Studies*, for instance, unless you simply want to give up the game and resort to literary judgments, which in the final case can only say what isn't ("this isn't literature") not what is. Given that, each instance in this circulation remains its own splendid and irreducible finitude.

The earliest appearance of community in this sense was around Harvey Brown's Frontier Press. Harvey Brown came to Buffalo in the fall of 1964. Like many of the others then flocking to the city, he came from Cleveland, Ohio via the Al Cook connection. Cook, who had been teaching at Case Western, was hired as Chair of the English Department at the new State University of New York at Buffalo and given tremendous resources to build the Department. Many of those he had worked with and taught at Case Western were hired to teach at Buffalo or followed others there as students. Unlike most others, however, Brown was a millionaire, a designation of some consequence in 1964. His grandfather had invented a hoist that facilitated the offloading of materials from river barges, and the money he accumulated from his invention propelled his family into the upper echelons of Cleveland society.

By the time Harvey Brown got to Buffalo, he had rejected both his social position, preferring the company of jazz musicians to debutantes, and his financial position. His relation to the money he inherited was based on the understanding that it embodied two contradictory energies or powers: accumulation and circulation. Call them angels. Brown felt that to capitulate to the angel of accumulation was to give power over your life to money, to allow it to rule your spirit. To give that power over to the angel of circulation, on the other hand, was to subjugate money to spirit. That was the path he chose, and Olson became one of the main instruments he used to realize it.

Harvey Brown's connection with Charles Olson was immediate and intense. In so far as they shared a sense of political priorities, Olson fit into Brown's plans to use his money to further certain specific ends. Brown, through his connections with jazz musicians in New York and Cleveland, had started a recording company to further the work of struggling artists such as Don Cherry, Ornette Coleman, Clifford Brown, and Clifford Jordan. Brown understood the work of these artists to make up the ground of a new American republic, the visionary incarnation of Winthrop's City on a Hill. It was an eccentric community whose importance was both in its antithetical message, and in the method it had pioneered: improvisation based on the call and response of traditional African-American music (see Brown's fascicle "Jazz Playing" in *The Curriculum of the Soul*). That method for Brown resonated precisely with Olson's sense of the projective, and that correspondence provided the basis for Brown's ongoing support for both the recording project, and for Frontier Press.

His first act was to fund *Niagara Frontier Review*. After he arrived in Buffalo during the fall semester of 1964, he took over active editorship of the magazine. The *Niagara Frontier Review* eventually ran to three issues between 1964 and 1966 and became one of the centres for the diverse writers represented in Donald Allen's anthology, *The New American Poetry*. In addition to Charles Olson, Edward Dorn, John Weiners, Ray Bremser, Robert Duncan, Gary Snyder, and LeRoi Jones (Amiri Baraka), the magazine also carried work by John Temple, Diane di Prima, Al Glover, Fred Wah, the jazz musician Don Cherry, Stephen Rodefer, Herbert Huncke, Charles Boer, and Andrew Crozier. The third issue also carried Cantos CX and 116 by Ezra Pound.

Olson's interest, however, extended beyond the magazine, and largely through his instigation, Harvey Brown expanded Frontier Press into book publishing. The initial idea was to publish books central to Olson's current thinking but otherwise out of print. The project soon expanded beyond that, however, with the "editorial" participation of Ed and Jenny Dorn, and Ron Caplan, so that the list eventually emerged out of a kind of uncentred collectivity. Deeply interested in the new poetries then emerging, Caplan first met Olson in 1963 when he'd gone to visit the poet in Gloucester. As the book-publishing venture took shape, Olson suggested to Brown that Caplan, who had a small design business in his native Pittsburgh, be involved in designing the books. Given their shared interest, Caplan's involvement soon extended beyond design to participation in the selection of books for the press list. The Dorns had been in Buffalo that summer when Ed Dorn taught in the first Buffalo Summer Program in Modern Literature. The process was so open, that it is almost impossible at this point to know who was responsible for which books. As Ron Caplan writes, it was "eccentric but with a strange unity."

> I know there were books I loved that I wished were in print—the Haniel Long stuff in particular, and Spring and All. I think Mid-American Chants was something we both had in waiting. Lenz is Harvey. I THINK I remember it being something Dorn wanted.... I think Olson was the main person to please in choosing the books. Then Dorn. Then? Perhaps me ....

Between 1967 and 1971, Frontier Press published 25 books and pamphlets. There is no other list quite like it (see Appendix 1 for a Checklist of Publications). For all its eclectic mix, however, certain unifying features leap out.

It is, above all else, a political list, though the definition of politics here needs to be pushed beyond its institutional sense toward a kind of visionary activism (see Charles Olson's 1968 Berkeley lecture). During the time the press was active, the U.S. war against Vietnam was in full swing, and the social discord it bred in the U.S. was reaching crisis proportions. More and more Americans actively opposed a government that, in turn, was trying desperately to repress them, using increasingly violent tactics that culminated in the slaughter of unarmed students at Jackson State University and Kent State University in May of 1970. All those involved in Frontier Press shared a sense of the extremity of the Constitutional crisis and an understanding that it was first and foremost a visionary crisis. To move ahead (to finally discover America) necessitated the nurturing of an eccentric, antithetical community that might provide the ground of an American conversion, as Emerson would have it. Call it a recovery of what had been lost to the usurpation of America by the Angel of Accumulation.

The politics of the Frontier Press list proliferated in unpredictable and often surprising directions. The core books suggested by Charles Olson—Brooks Adams' *The New Empire*, W.E. Woodward's *Years of Madness*—characteristically propose a reading of American history that is antithetical to the authoritative history that founds the current regime of power. Adams proposes a history that explains the advent of an American Empire whose origins he locates in European pre-history. Woodward radically rereads the U.S. Civil War in terms that call into question the assumption that it was waged to end slavery.

Other books supplement that reopening of American history. The Haniel Long books are two of the most beautiful productions on the list. *Interlinear to Cabeza de Vaca* re-presents us with an extraordinary figure from the days of the Conquest, a Spaniard who, rather than colonising America, was possessed and transformed by what he became lost in. It leaves us in another America, one yet to be discovered. *The Paths of the Mound-Building Indians* by Archer Butler Hulbert also moves through that range of experience. Tracking the archaic paths over which the America of today is built, the book re-opens this world to its archaic realities, the hidden realities that found and shape such mundane experiences as a trip to the store. The *Book of Daniel Drew*, with its marvellous introduction by Ed Dorn, gives us a lucid revelation of primitive accumulation in America, one most historians and free marketeers have rushed to hide. Those politics become explicit in Alexander Berkman's *Memoirs of a Prison Anarchist,* as well as in the pamphlet *The Decline and Fall of the 'Spectacular' Commodity Economy*, reprinted from the Situationist International of December, 1965.

The poetry equally reflects that visionary, antithetical politics. One of the great contributions of Frontier Press was to reprint William Carlos Williams' *Spring and All*, which had been out of print for almost 50 years. H.D.'s *Hermetic Definition* had never been in print. It had been copied by hand by poets visiting the Beinecke Library, and circulated around the U.S. Norman Holmes Pearson, H.D.'s literary executor, claimed he was unable to place it with a publisher of sufficient standing and proposed that Brown was trying to make a profit off the pirated edition. Both Brown and Caplan felt that Pearson was holding back the book for reasons of his own, and that the only way to force his hand was to go ahead and get it in print. In any case, there was a great clamour among poets to have the poems made available so they could work with them. From the point of view of many poets, the prestige of the publisher was less important than having the poems to work with, and that was the position Brown took. He illegally published the text, beautifully designed by Ron Caplan, in 1971, and continued to distribute it for free until he died. Within a year of the Frontier publications of *Spring and All* and *Hermetic Definition*, both books had been copyrighted and published by New Directions in trade editions and have been in print ever since.

Frontier Press was also well known for publishing contemporary poetry and fiction in beautiful editions designed by Graham Macintosh, Ron Caplan, and Philip Trussell. The writing was diverse, including work by Ed Dorn, Edward Sanders, Michael McClure, Stan Brakhage, Albert Glover, and Robert Kelly. As different as all these writers are, most of them had been in Buffalo during this period and had participated in the energetic exchanges that took place there. Not that they constituted in that sense a unity or held some common "theory." Only that the energies unleashed arose out of a common provocation, and are, in that very general sense, part of a community, both the more general community that the Allen anthology registers, as well as the community specific to Buffalo at that moment.

Some of the work—Sanders' *Peace Eye*, for instance—is specifically political in its address. But even the work that isn't—Dorn's love poems,

McClure's mammalian cosmological body poem, Kelly's visionary investigations—are radical departures from the then (and largely still) dominant notion of the well-made poem as literary construct. That departure for parts unknown to the "literary" imagination constitutes, even more than any explicit content otherwise would, the nature of the "political" as it in turn constituted this antithetical community.

One of the criticisms of Frontier Press that eventually arose from within that community was that, however valuable the work being done, the high quality of the production standards themselves were interfering with, or slowing down, the circulation of the work. Not that Brown's work wasn't deeply admired. But some people wanted to be able to get things in print faster. "Some of us wanted to move more quickly than Harvey," Fred Wah writes. Wah had come to Buffalo from Vancouver via New Mexico, drawn by Al Cook's active solicitation of poets to join the new program at Buffalo. He became involved on the editorial board of *Niagara Frontier Review* at Olson's suggestion. At the time he was a graduate student in linguistics taking Olson's seminars. Sharing Wah's desire for more speed were John Clarke, a new Assistant Professor in the English Department, and Albert Glover, a graduate student in Olson's seminars.

Clarke had met Olson in the spring of 1964. Al Cook had directed Clarke's dissertation on William Blake and was trying to hire him away from the University of Illinois, Champagne-Urbana. Clarke came to the interview knowing nothing of Olson, and with several reservations about the possible move to Buffalo. After the interview, there was a party at Cook's house. Clarke recalls:

> Later that night Charles came down to the party. I was sitting on a straight chair by the fireplace and he sat down on the couch, like so ____* and the connection was instaneous—maybe that's a new word, I meant instantaneous, but like that one better, it accents the <u>sta</u> etymon .... Olson's report of the meeting, as someone later told me, was that he dug my pants, the material they were made of, and the way I was sitting with my legs crossed. Upshot of course was that all other considerations were blown away: I was coming to Buffalo.

Al Glover had come to Buffalo in the fall of 1964 from McGill University. He was following his teacher, Irving Massey, who Cook had also hired. Knowing nothing of Olson, but being interested in contemporary poetry (he had won a poetry prize at McGill the year after Leonard

Cohen had won the same prize), Glover enrolled in Olson's two graduate seminars (Poetry and Myth and Contemporary Poetry). The fourth person involved in the move toward more speed was George Butterick, later to be Olson's editor and literary executor.

The issue these four addressed with their collective desire for more speed was the "projective" and the community founded on or within it. The projective method relies on speed—speed of production and speed of circulation—to reach a kind of escape velocity needed to break free from the inertial pull of the "literary." Before Olson left Buffalo in the fall of 1965, he had proposed founding an institute along the lines of the Princeton Institute of Advanced Studies, with which he'd been connected through Black Mountain College. When he left, and Al Cook was unsuccessful in getting the new University at Buffalo to support the project, Clarke, Wah, Glover, and Butterick decided to go ahead on their own.

They immediately began publishing *The Magazine of Further Studies*, the first issue of which appeared in the fall of 1965. "I think it was Glover's IBM Selectric we used," Fred Wah writes. "And we got a big roll of corrugated stuff for covers ... and us and our wives wld set up in one of our basements and cut covers and paint chicken blood (George wanted the thing to decay in the readers' hands) and glue fur." Butterick's desire for decay emphasized the projective nature of the magazine, the fact that as you held it, it disintegrated, leaving you with nothing to hold onto but what was further. Butterick was successful in that the various objects and substances applied to the covers of the magazine have by and large either faded over time or fallen off.

Between 1965 and 1969, IFS published six issues (see Appendix B, item 8). Al Glover describes the first issue as "awkward" beside the professionalism of the *Niagara Frontier Review*: "this homemade thing that did put most people off. The lucky part was that Charles (and then Robert Duncan shortly) were interested in finding a means of production outside the establishment, even the 'small press' one." Olson joins the conversation in the second issue, Duncan in the sixth.

The magazine was unique for its time for a couple of reasons, both of which had to do with the rejection of the showcase model of the poetry magazine, already prevalent even then among small press magazines. The showcase magazine typically presents poems completely isolated and decontextualized. They appear as beautiful (or ugly) objects on the page.

This mode of presentation reinforces the culture of the literary by stripping the poem from the intellectual matrix it is part of, and then emphasizing its object status as a pure literary event.

The Magazine of Further Studies refused, first of all, to isolate the poem. It included, in the body of the magazine, letters, prose exchanges, and bibliographies (most from the Poetry/Myth class John Clarke took over when Olson left), so that the poems also presented there were clearly proposed as one kind of event in a larger discourse that included many different kinds of events. They were not products with implicit value in and of themselves. On the contrary, the form emphasized the larger discourse.

As the magazine developed, it increasingly embodied an active conversation, further undermining the product-status of the "poetry" it included. Rather than including poems intended as finished and self-sufficient literary products, the magazine increasingly published fragments, challenges, responses, broken utterances that provoked other broken, incomplete utterances, so that by the final issue, the magazine had become a kind of clamour, a convocation of a conversation, in action. The result was that even within a single issue, there was nothing to hold on to, not even a poem, which could be proposed as "literature." There was an event that constantly pushed beyond itself.

The Institute of Further Studies went on to publish several items that reinforce this sense of an antithetical dynamic. In 1968, there was a burst of small publications, designed as "letters." The goal, according to Al Glover, "was to be fastest, and Charles did, in fact, love the speed." Olson would send poems he'd just written from Gloucester, and they'd be printed and distributed within a week (see Appendix B, items 3,4,5,7). Again, the push here was to move the poem into the realm of discourse, communication, provocation, and conversation, and away from the object-status that turned it into a commodity and founded the culture of the "literary."

Other publications aimed toward the same goal. John Clarke pushed the Institute to publish plate 25 from William Blake's *Milton*. His plan, though it wasn't finally realized, was to mail the "letter" to the delegates at the Democratic Party Convention in Chicago. The Olson note, (item 4), was another provocation printed as a postcard for immediate dissemination.

Perhaps the most lasting accomplishment of the Institute of Further Studies has been the ongoing publication of *The Curriculum of the Soul.* Olson's "poem," "A Plan for the Curriculum of the Soul," first appeared in *The Magazine of Further Studies* #5. After Olson's death, the Institute decided to break up the curriculum into discrete topics and get different writers to take them on. 29 fascicles (including one numbered 0—Charles Olson's "Pleistocene Man"), initially imagined as akin to the Cambridge Ancient History Project, were assigned to various poets with relationships to Olson's work. In his review of Clarke's *In the Analogy*, Al Glover called it both "a collaborative epic," and "a bouquet on the grave:"

> Original "vision" was of a large book written by "Olson"—and I would still, someday, hope to publish it as such. It is that sense of "Homer" and would make only the second one (this one, of course, somewhat different in its concept of "history" and "narrative") in "the tradition." You see it in "The Mushroom" ("as if we were all one voice / of various sounds"—since revised: "we are all one voice / of various sounds".

The reference to "Homer" is to Milman Perry's famous proposal that, rather than an individual, Homer was the name given to a collective of bards who had invented and assembled the *Iliad* and the *Odyssey* over hundreds of years.

The notion of "epic" here, and as it always was used by Olson, is not what is now proposed as a monomaniacal drive toward a singular representation of the world. Olson always saw that development of epic as a late, literary derivation, something he hated. In *Pleistocene Man* he had it as "Classical/Representational:" "WHY I HATE | Greeks & Italians | [The Vatican since | Dante | [Grecian since | the earliest Renaissance | — including in fact Thomas Aquinas at least] | is | the <u>*Classical*</u> — <u>*Representational,*</u> either one | THE STATE———COLORED TELEVISION." The pre-literary "epic," as he proposed it, was a communal invention of culturally shared narrative meanings, the invention of a cohesion of diversities within the otherness of language that revealed the world's incommensurable plenitude. The problem for Olson was how get to a procedure, a method that would make possible a similar mode of knowing/speaking as/for community.

The *Curriculum of the Soul* addresses that issue in its own way. Whether it is an epic is, in a sense, beside the point. Perhaps more important is its conscious invocation of a specific notion of community. The community revealed here in relation to Olson's provocation, and the call and response of the participants, is anything but uniform, anything but a communion with and within, say, a "theory," the unobstructed visibility of what John Clarke called the MONO. It is rather a register of the immensity of the relations of authoritative finitudes circulating within and beyond the space of the thought Olson's work provokes.

Both this sense of community and of epic are central to the work of John Clarke which always moved, as he proposed in his seminal work on poetics, *From Feathers to Iron*, "to [constellate] the epiphany in a communal place." Perhaps more than anyone else to emerge from "Olson's Buffalo," Clarke worked with unwavering dedication to further the understanding of the complex implications of the notions that haunt this essay, and to realize them in his life and work. Never given to the kinds of self-promotion required for literary success, he was largely unknown outside a small group of dedicated readers when he died in 1992. "I personally enjoy the ultimate freedom of being unknown," he wrote to his friend, Al Glover.

Clarke's work culminated in three interrelated efforts: the editing of ***intent.**: letter of talk thinking & document*, *From Feathers to Iron: A Concourse of World Poetics*, and *In the Analogy*, which is made up of six books, each consisting of a sequence of 40 sonnets, and a seventh incomplete book. In many ways, the newsletter, ***intent.***, was a furthering of the work begun in the *Magazine of Further Studies*. By the time of its publication (11 issues between 1989-91), small press magazines had generally opted for the showcase model, though some exceptions existed. *Exquisite Corpse, Sulfur,* and *Rolling Stock*, for instance, embedded poetry in a context of reviews, polemical articles, and letters. By and large, though, even those magazines that thus contextualized poetry, still presented the poems themselves as literary productions.

Clarke's goal in ***intent.*** was to provide an alternative to that situation. In a letter to Tom Clark, he discussed using the poems Clark sent as reviews, situating them in a larger discussion of films that themselves are embedded in the thematic discourse of each specific issue of the newsletter. Clarke's insistence that all submissions, including poems, adhere to the particular theme of a given issue established each issue, not as a showcase, but as a space within which a community was revealed at work in language. Themes included Plants & Animals, For the Sexes, Alphabetics, UFOs, Heaven, Trust, and Embryons.

Each issue embodied that community in conversation by including a wide range of work that was transgenerational and trans-genre-ational. The lead article was always from the ancestors, establishing the continuity of the conversation. Charles Olson, Robert Duncan, Eric Gill, Dora Marsden, Robert McAlmon, Simone Weil, and H.D. were featured in various issues. Art work, poems, reviews, essays, and letters were collected from sources as diverse as *The Fugger Newsletter*, contemporary writers, both known and relatively unknown, musicians, and children of various ages, some as young as 7 or 8. The operative centre of each issue was "The Mail," an encapsulation of the enormous correspondence Clarke carried out with a myriad of writers around the world, as well as what he came to call "The Editor's Quotron." The Quotron was a collection of quotes from diverse sources relevant to the theme at hand. It extended the conversation taking place in the newsletter beyond the bounds of the moment, or perhaps more accurately, situated that moment in its further complexity. This use of quotation as a way of locating the work in a world of thinking and talk became crucial to the practice of the epic that Clarke developed in his own poetry.

The two places where, in his final years, he worked that out were *From Feathers to Iron* and *In the Analogy*. These two books can be seen as embodying the methodology and practice of Clarke's projective art—though such a distinction finally won't hold up. *Feathers,* the book of "poetics," is not only a "poetic" text—a text where language is constantly pushed toward what Roman Jakobson called the "poetic function"—it literally incorporates poetry in its body. Clarke's earlier book of poems, *The End of This Side*, is reprinted within the text as part of an elaborate complicating counter structure of footnotes that amplify, develop, and sometimes overtake the thinking of the text. In the same way, *In the Analogy* develops a complex argument within the structure of the sonnet sequences, while also incorporating chunks of "theoretical" thinking in the numerous quotations which precede each of the sonnets. In this way Clarke confronts and demolishes the still dominant Platonic notion that poetry and thought are distinct, even at odds with one another. He creates an interdependence of texts that enacts a complex passionate thinking.

This work was not meant to demolish or escape genre. Instead, it calls our attention to the inadequacies of our thinking of genre and comes out of Clarke's reading of Romanticism as an unfinished project. Blake, Friedrich Schlegel, Novalis, and Coleridge were all active in his thinking. The title of *From Feathers to Iron* comes from a letter by John Keats. At the heart of the writing is Clarke's ongoing struggle to further Olson's work with the epic. As Clarke thinks the issue through in *Feathers*, it becomes evident that it is not a literary problem. If anything, it might be called a political problem, as long as politics is kept located within the visionary. His push is always toward the reconstitution, or re-cognition, of the *elsewhere* here, something he argues we lost with the collapse of Minoan civilization. This is one of the ways in which he continued to address Olson's proposal about the archaic/ordinary. *From Feathers to Iron*, a complex and difficult book that defies summary, proposes the problem as a loss of order and sees the epic as the form of what it calls the strengthening method of world completion. Within this framework, poetry plays a role that has nothing to do with the literary.

By the late 1980s, Clarke had been writing sonnets for a number of years. More than 1,000 of them remain unpublished in his notebooks. For someone so thoroughly focussed on the importance of the epic, it was always curious to him that he had been given to write so extensively in what was the quintessential lyric form. During the last five years of his life, he came to see how he could push that form beyond its limits toward the scope necessary for the epic. The result was an enormous outpouring of work that he called *In the Analogy*. *In the Analogy* consists of six completed books and a fragmentary seventh. Clarke's plan, as Cass Clarke has transcribed it in the opening pages of *In the Analogy*, was to write twelve books, pushing it toward the classic epic form.

Much of the recent criticism leveled against the epic has focussed on what's proposed as the inherent totalitarianism of the form, as handed down in the literary tradition from Virgil to Pound. As John Thorpe pointed out in the introduction of *From Feathers to Iron*, however, "Clarke doesn't envision the epic as a literary genre so much as an inherent human narrative comprehension, wherever there's an interplay of story with its telling." In *In the Analogy*, Clarke made that archaic comprehension a continuing projective event of community, the voice not of a single person (or even mythical persona), but of a world, itself revealed in a clamour of relations.

To accomplish this he embedded each sonnet, as well as each sequence of sonnets, deeply within a world of thinking. Several quotations precede each poem and each sequence of poems. The quotes are myriad and diverse, and provide a universe within which the poems are actively located in conversation. Some quotes mirror the poem, others contradict it, some seem to be its inspiration, while others raise questions about the issues it addresses, and still others develop thinking tangential to it. The overall result pushes the reader into the world of thought, out of which the poems arise. The very notion, "Clarke's poems," is called actively into question at every moment, even as the poems proceed to address the questions crucial to the epic impulse as it asserts itself here, now. Here is Clarke, for instance, on the issue of the hero:

Devil's Triangle

"How should the hero now speak? Who is after all—a vision?"
—Nietzsche, *The Birth of Tragedy*

"Texas has a lot on its head."
—Edward Dorn, "The Degeneration of the Greeks"

"Power can stage its own murder to rediscover the glimmer of existence and legitimacy."
—Baudrillard, "Precession of the Simulacra"

"Happiness is not based on oneself, it does not consist of a small home, of taking and getting. Happiness is taking part in the struggle, where there is no borderline between one's own personal world, and the world in general."
—Lee Harvey Oswald, Letter to his brother

If we are the seminal fluidity, then we contain already,
as Whitman knew, *everything*, "diddling" (Poe) as well as
the Good, however forced sometimes the dilation as seen
from old heroic organization before the shit rolled like
termite droppings into the load-bearing bridges for everyone
to cross into Dealy Plaza, Dallas "takes us" November
22, 1963, and not only Oswald and Ruby, but Guy Bannister,
Shaw, Ferrie, Bloomfield and Permindex, now Roscoe White
and more aliens up from the South, Watergate's Sturgis,
Union survivors up North, all those insane in Honolulu

> since the birth of the Nation/Hail to the Chief shot
> American Transcendentalism out of the feudal individual
> and delivered into the hands of Walt's "unprecedented
> average," thank you Abe, thanks Jack, now it's up to us.

This is what Clarke calls a non-central position, as opposed to a non-ordering intervention. That Clarke's epic finally is fragmentary is as rich and full of complexity as every other aspect of this extraordinary work.

The influence of Olson's Buffalo—and finally it must be seen, I think, in those collective terms rather than singularly—is not easy to measure, precisely because the resistance to the literary is central to its thought of itself. Movements come and go. Theories are hot one day and cold the next, mirroring the dynamics of the consumer culture that gives rise to them and the controlling conceit of "modernization" that has seized "reality" in this century. But the sense of "work" that this community of circulating, authoritative finitudes consistently embodied, continues to percolate quietly and invisibly in diverse corners of the world. What it will give rise to, what it has already given rise to, is a *remains-to-be-seen.* Donald Byrd has proposed that the work "of Olson and Clarke demands our attention as few others because they occasionally find means to make and to think at once. That is, they bring evidence that there are means of preoccupation with life that is sufficient to life." This is as accurate and concise a sense of the various threads winding through this brief history of Olson's Buffalo as anything said so far. *To make and to think at once.* What's at stake in such a mode will always exceed itself as it pushes to shake off the stupor of the literary and realize poetry's possible vocation.

Special thanks to Al Glover, Ron Caplan, and Fred Wah for their invaluable assistance in putting this history together. All errors and inaccuracies are my own. Also, thanks to B. Cass Clarke for generously allowing me access to John Clarke's papers.

The Legacy of Charles Olson and the Struggle for a New American Poetry

"Learned and leisurely hospitality is the only antidote to the stance of the deadly cleverness that is acquired in the professional pursuit of objectively secured knowledge. I remain certain that the quest for truth cannot thrive outside the nourishment of mutual trust flowering into a commitment to friendship."
—Ivan Illich

Thinking about Charles Olson's legacy always brings me up against the question I see haunting his work: how are we to be here where we now find ourselves? And the more abstract question that one rests on: what am I, or, plural, what are we? From the beginning of Olson's life as a poet, this question centred his thinking. "Projective Verse" puts it front and centre and posits it in terms of *stance,* a word which, while it raises the issue of emotional/intellectual attitude, does so specifically in relation to a physical posture, a way of placing and holding the body in the world. Olson's thinking about how we are to be here always begins with a body oriented in the world. Mind you, Olson's *body* is far more complex than the current medical and sociological models propose. There is no inner and outer, nor is there a separate "self" susceptible to the control of ideology. There is the absolute immanence of *fleshmindheartspirit* which are different resonances of the same deeply somatic event.

Stance begins with *body* which is a complex event. The self implicit in this event is not identifiable as an individual identity or ego in the manner of bourgeois individualism with its essential split between "self" and "world" (society) echoing the split between "mind" and "body" and "subject" and "object." Olson's *bodyself* is an *opening-toward-the-world* in multiple interrelating frequencies or modes that is at once physical, emotional, intellectual, and spiritual. In terms of poetry, this *bodyself* event in its *opening-toward-the-world* articulates or composes a further event in language that is commensurate to, that meets the opening world with an opening to the world. As many have noted, in Olson's thinking there is no individual subject in relation to (and in control of) an object. Instead, nested events open with and toward a further world. In any case, this is how I would explain Olson's famous dismissal of the "lyrical interference of the individual as ego" and his proposal about energy transfer through the poet. Nor was it just a matter of theory. Olson followed through, living this initiating gesture throughout his work, and it led him to new modes of *being-at-work* that resisted the culture of individualism that characterizes art production in modernity. He moved not just to write in a new mode, but to transform the mode of creation that led to writing—you could say to change his stance toward the world.

His move to SUNY Buffalo in 1963 was central to the transformation he had been going through from at least 1959-60 as his vision of the significance of Gloucester, not to mention poetry, expanded beyond the historical geography he is sometimes identified with. Arguably the process had been going on for longer. During this time, he was reading deeply in mythology and the work of Carl Jung, and had immersed himself in what he called "the protogonic weather" of the "other side of heaven." His imagination led him, not so much away from historical geography, as into it, through it, and out the other side into the swirling cosmos it was an aspect of.

Two other factors in 1960 contributed to his metamorphosis: ingesting psychedelic substances with Timothy Leary and Allen Ginsberg, and discovering the work of Islamic scholar, Henry Corbin. Both events were deeply significant. His radical address to the Berkeley Poetry Conference followed. By the time he got to Buffalo in 1963, he had moved far beyond the first volume of Maximus. A "lapsed" Catholic, Olson's poetry always included an address to what is called *the sacred* (what he called the *seculardivine*), but it emerged more and more strongly in his work at this time. This transformation led to *Maximus IV V VI* and beyond.

Chief among the targets of Olson's attack were the institutions of the official literary culture that organized writing based on rules, whether conscious or unconscious. Based on individual production and ownership of art commodities, official literary culture regulates art production through an evaluative procedure that determines and rewards something called "literary excellence" which involves the perception of the mastery of certain arbitrary constraints and procedures by an autonomous, creative individual. What it loses is the truth. In other words, the lyrical interference of the individual as ego is not limited to the writing of this or that poem, but operates at all levels of activity in its determination of form. It is a *stance* and at its most fundamental level, including the mode of reception, it establishes the form of the creative act through its limitation of what's called (acceptable) "content."

That's why Olson publicly rejected the professionalization of poetry at least as early as his residency at Goddard College in April 1962. At that time, he articulated a public resistance to the process of self-commodification implicit in a scene of "poetry readings": "It gets to be kind of a bore, because it's becoming a performing art, you feel as though you have an audience, and as if you're supposed to do a concert or something." Chief among the objects of his negative attention was the increasing institutionalization of many of his New American cohort as they jockeyed to turn their newfound fame into professional Literary success in the prize and appointment Market. Olson's rejection of the "poetry reading" as a staged performance at Goddard presaged the extraordinary Event he created 3 years later at the Berkeley conference in his demand—maybe plea—for a nation of nothing but poetry which leaves no room for the use of poetry as part of an exchange. You're either in or you're out.

I thought of that the other day while I was reading Ivan Illich on conviviality. Illich conceived conviviality as the remedy for the disease of what he called the industrial mind. Much of his thinking focused on the ways tools in industrial culture create and reinforce the industrial mind, working to isolate and enslave people to a world-destroying system that "is organized for indefinite expansion and the concurrent unlimited creation of new needs, which in an industrial environment soon become basic necessities." Convivial tools on the other hand nurture "individual freedom realized in personal interdependence and, as such, an intrinsic ethical value." Interdependence is the key word here. Convivial culture is based on relationships and the different modes and forms of knowledge such a focus allows and promotes. Illich organized his own intellectual life on just such principles, promoting and organizing situations in which knowledge arose out of the dynamic between friends sharing wine and food around a table. In that sense it requires an *out* and an *in* which establishes a space of filial intimacy and an ease of relation that leads to a mingling of minds beyond the compartmentalization of knowledge and limiting etiquette characteristic of authorized thinking in the academy.

In Buffalo Olson found a group of people with whom he could venture forth—both intellectually and actively—into a world of uncharted thinking/acting of being-together-at-work on the mystery of creation (rather than studying Literature or kvetching about history), the antithesis of the lyrically interfering ego. Much like Illich's conviviality, this being-together-at-work Olson found in Buffalo formed an inside based on mutual trust and a common commitment. One manifestation of that new intimacy was the creation of The Institute of Further Studies, a group of Olson's students engaged in expanding and realizing energies unleashed in the excitement of Olson's teaching and companionship. This intimacy would be used against them in years to come.

I don't want to spend a lot of time to debate the nature of the relationship between Olson and the group of students who gathered around him. A much-repeated view echoes Tom Clark's disparagement of it as a "coterie of 'angeloi', graduate disciples" who were mindlessly enraptured and uncritical in their awe of their guru, Olson. He is caricatured as a "high priest" to their slavish adulation. I think the relational dynamic within the group that made up the IFS was radically different than Clark's caricature. Clark represents a mode of being/perceiving, a cosmology, informed by the image of the heroic, individualist author that was central to the old configuration of the Band of Brothers whose passing Clark mourned. The Band of Brothers consisted of those heroic individual (male) poets in the 50's who knew and supported each other in their battles with the Establishment, but were each a giant in his own right. In that world, a world of sharp dichotomies, you are either autonomous or slavish, and all Clark could see was the absence of autonomy. The relational networks that displaced that were invisible to him. Their great sin was to create collectively and anonymously, a fundamental violation of the idea of heroic individualism.

In USAmerican culture, individualism is right up there with mom, apple pie, and guns at the top of the pantheon of defining values. It's a slippery notion, though, with multiple meanings. Most would include some sense of a singular, autonomous, rational human being in charge of their own destiny—at least potentially. That figure haunts the precincts of modernity. From the invention of opera and the virtuoso voice, to the defining subject matter of novels, to the [myth of the] educated voter, to the property-owning capitalist, to the existential hero, the individual is the basic unit modern life. It's fitting in that the concept of individualism arose with and as part of the Enlightenment's critique of the ancien regime, especially the Church's demand for doctrinal unity, and was pitched as part of a humanist revolution. Clark uses religious language to try and diminish Olson's students, referring to them as disciples and acolytes. Jack Clarke's response was to suggest that novice was more accurate, as in Novalis's The Novices of Sais.

What's actually at stake, as Clarke's suggestion implies, is nothing less than a new way of knowing based on intimacy and affection. Illich again: "... things which are finally important must be capable of being shared with others whom I love first and then want to talk to. And this conviction will have considerable impact on the way in which I assess and express my own insights." This brings to mind for me so many nights of my youth spent (or mis-spent) sitting with a bunch of friends at someone's kitchen table talking through the night. It usually also involved a big bottle of cheap wine an endless supply of cigarettes, and a joint, but while they added a certain "je ne sais quoi" to the gathering of minds, they were not necessary for the experience of knowledge as an emotional event.

Illich proposes this relational mind as a "we that is truly a plural I": "In this way one can foster the growth of an open group of people who are moved by fidelity to each other as persons and dare to maintain fidelity even if the other one becomes a heavy burden. But in order to pursue truth within the horizon of "we" that is truly a plural "I", a "we" that is arbitrary, that is unique, that slowly emerges, that cannot be put into any class, then it is first necessary to shed a certain number of extremely sticky and persistent university-derived academic etiquettes, like the organization of knowledge into specialized and exclusive disciplines." Olson forayed into this territory in the first volume of the Maximus poems where the relational—the poems are literally correspondence—fundamentally structures the unfolding process of the poem, establishing its finitude and the multiplicity of its Herodotean authority. But where he finally found his *nation of nothing but poetry* was in the Buffalo formation, at the center of which was The Institute of Further Studies, which included Jack Clarke, Al Glover, Fred Wah, and George Butterick.

What that alembic nurtured is, to my mind, best exemplified in the *Magazine of Further Studies*, a periodical published by the IFS which ran to 6 issues between 1965 and 1969. The first issue appeared in the fall of 1965. "I think it was Glover's IBM Selectric we used," Fred Wah writes. "And we got a big roll of corrugated stuff for covers ... and us and our wives wld set up in one of our basements and cut covers and paint chicken blood (George wanted the thing to decay in the readers' hands) and glue fur." Butterick's desire for decay emphasized the projective nature of the magazine, the fact that as you held it, it disintegrated, leaving you with nothing to hold but what was further. Al Glover describes the first issue as "awkward:" "this homemade thing that did put most people off. The lucky part was that Charles (and then Robert Duncan shortly) were interested in finding a means of production outside the establishment, even the 'small press' one." Olson joins the conversation in the second issue, Duncan in the sixth.

The magazine was unique for a couple of reasons, both of which had to do with the surpassing of the showcase model of the poetry magazine based on recognition of individual literary excellence, already prevalent even then among small press magazines. The showcase magazine typically presents poems isolated and decontextualized. They appear as beautiful (or ugly) objects on the page as created by and attributed to an individual author in pursuit (conscious or unconscious) of literary excellence as it is defined by one authority or another—at least enough excellence to convince some editor to publish them. This mode of presentation reinforces the culture of the literary by stripping the poem from the intellectual matrix it is part of, and emphasizing its object status as a pure literary event attributable to an induvial author and eligible for prizes and inclusion in some pretentious book called The Best [fill in descriptor] Poetry of [fill in year].

The Magazine of Further Studies refused, first of all, to isolate the poem. It included, in the body of the magazine, letters, prose exchanges, and bibliographies (most from the Poetry/Myth class John Clarke took over when Olson left), so that the poems that were also presented were clearly proposed as simply one kind of event in a larger event that included many different kinds of events. They were not proposed as products with implicit value in and of themselves. On the contrary, the larger discourse was emphasized. The effect was an experience like Illich describes, the pursuit of truth "within the horizon of 'we' that is truly a plural 'I', a 'we' that is arbitrary, that is unique, that slowly emerges, that cannot be put into any class …."

As the magazine developed, it increasingly embodied an active conversation among semi-anonymous voices, further asserting the non-product status of the "poetry" it included and the magazine itself. Rather than poems intended as finished and self-sufficient literary products, the magazine increasingly published fragments, challenges, responses, broken utterances that provoked other broken, incomplete utterances, so that by the final issue, the magazine became a [divine] clamor, a convocation of mind(s), in action, always pushing further out of affection (*philo-sophy*). It includes nothing that resembles "literature." Instead, a complex event constantly pushes beyond itself.

The projective, for Olson, was predicated on speed as a way of escaping the gravitational pull of the Given, and speed, in Olson's world, was achieved within the relations of a *being-together-I's-in-work*. Whatever else such a "community" may be, in Olson's practice it was a "place" where hierarchical/anti-hierarchical orderings were dissolved in a synergistic circulation of authoritative finitudes that egged each other on toward their further possibilities—which were the further possibilities of the self-revelation of the *being-together* as well. This, I am suggesting, is an important legacy of Olson's work for what remains of the New American Poetry as it continues to thrive in pockets around the continent.

I like to think of them as what Peter Lamborn Wilson called Temporary Autonomous Zones. They are ways of coming to the work (of resistance) together beyond the Literary's demand for an individual author. It is a stance or orientation that celebrates that which is beyond the "me" and opens into a mutual creativity. The grass-roots creative explosion of the 1960's was the matrix of this thinking. The constrictive energy of the late 70's and 80's (Just Say No) which rose up against this opening took multiple forms from the rise of Creative Writing to the academic institutionalization of formations calling themselves *avant-garde*. Just as emergent neo-liberalism reenergized the thought of creative work as *individual*, massive monetary grants and institutional largesse in the form of jobs, promotions, grants, book deals, and prizes flooded the poetry market from the streets to the classroom, rewarding individual "excellence" while reimposing Literature's disciplinary orders.

The Institute of Further Studies remained a site of resistance to this development. Jack Clarke and Al Glover continued the *being-together-I's-in-work* that was part of the originating energy of the small press insurrection which fed Allen's anthology. *A Curriculum of the Soul* is one result of that, a physical and intellectual homage to *being-together-in-work*, to the "we that is truly a plural I." Proposed as an epic in Millman Perry's sense of the Homeric epic as the result of the work of many anonymous bards, the *Curriculum* presents the individual fascicles that make it up without reference to any authors either in the contents list or at the head of the various "chapters." Only at the very end on the colophon page are the names of individual writers listed, almost an after thought. Like *The Magazine of Further Studies*, it is a "synergistic circulation of (semi-anonymous) authoritative finitudes."

Jack Clarke followed through with that spirit in his magazine, *intent.* Subtitled *a magazine of talk, thinking, and document*, *intent.* broke free of the display case model by gathering together in each issue an embodied community in conversation through multiple modes, including a wide range of work that was transgenerational and trans-genre-ational. Clarke insisted that all submissions to *intent.*, including poems, adhere to the particular theme he assigned each issue as a way to establish the magazine as a space within which a dynamic, complex relational event revealed itself at work in language.

The lead article always came from the ancestors, establishing the continuity of the conversation. Charles Olson, Robert Duncan, Eric Gill, Dora Marsden, Robert McAlmon, Simone Weil, and H.D. were featured in various issues. Art work, poems, reviews, essays, and letters were collected from sources as diverse as the Fugger Newsletter, contemporary writers, both known and relatively unknown, musicians, and children of various ages, some as young as 7 or 8. The operative center of each issue was "The Mail," an encapsulation of the enormous correspondence Clarke carried out with myriad writers around the world (on his typewriter), as well as what he came to call "The Editor's Quotron." The Quotron collected quotations from diverse sources relevant to the particular issue's theme. It extended the conversation taking place in the newsletter beyond the bounds of the particular moment, or perhaps more accurately, situated that moment in its further complexity.

The term *New American Poetry* gets thrown around a lot these days to establish legitimacy of this group or that group, but without much attention to what it specifically designates. Donald Allen was vague at best about what he meant by the name he invented beyond what he called resistance to "all those qualities typical of academic verse." The nature of "academic verse" has changed quite a bit since 1960 when it was synonymous with followers of Eliot. Today it includes Creative Writing manufacturers, as well as formerly self-declared avant-garde formations that have seen the light and been welcomed back into the bosom of Mother Academia. The other defining aspect of the New American Poetry as evident in Allen's organization of his anthology is the importance of identity-within-a-community. Each of the sections in the book is made up of a group of poets who knew each other and worked together within the same geographical community. This arguably is a face or facet of *being-together-I's-in-work*, a 'we' that is truly a plural 'I'. You can find many other examples of this legacy: Ed Dorn's *Rolling Stock,* Ken Warren's *House Organ,* that online disturbance known as *Dispatches from the Poetry Wars.* But the spirit of Olson's legacy is best seen in the countless anonymous local formations—temporary autonomous zones—where the new American poetry continues to thrive animated by the spirit of collective resistance and mutual work.

Appendices

Appendix I
Checklist of the Publications of Frontier Press, 1965-1972

1. Dorn, Edward. *Rites of Passage.*

a. First edition, 1965.
THE RITES OF PASSAGE | a brief history | EDWARD DORN
Perfect binding; pp. [i-vi] 1-155 [156]. 15 x 21.5 cm.
On copyright page: "Cover by Raymond Obermayr".

b. Second edition [retitled], 1971.
By the Sound | [line drawing of a house by the sea] | Edward Dorn | Frontier Press | Mount Vernon, | Washington | 1971
[1-13]^4; pp. [i-vii] 1-199 [200]. 13.8 x 21 cm. Paper wrappers.
On copyright page: "Drawings by Flavia Zortea | Design by Ron Caplan".
Note: Ron Caplan writes: "The cover—an odd green, like a slash of light downward—that's not mine.... They tore off the 'old' ones and pasted the new ones on. Of course, the rest of the book was as I designed it."

2. Adams, Brooks. *The New Empire.*
Second edition, 1967 [1902].
[device] | *BROOKS ADAMS* | *THE NEW EMPIRE* | *Frontier Press* | *Cleveland, Ohio* [dot] *1967* | [to the left of the previous two lines] [publisher's logo]

[1-6]^{16} [7]^{8} [8-9]^{16}; pp. [i-vi] vii-ix [x-xii] xiii-xxxvii [xxxviii-xl] 1-197 [198] 199-228 [229-232]. 13.7 x 20.8 cm.
On p. [iv]: a poem by Charles Olson. On copyright page [vi]: "The book was composed and printed by the Crimson Printing Company, Cambridge, and bound by Stanhope Bindery, Boston."

3. Sanders, Edward. *Peace eye.*
Second (enlarged) edition, 1967.
PEACE EYE | Ed Sanders | [device] | [publisher's logo] | FRONTIER PRESS | Cleveland, Ohio
Loose sheets triple-stapled through the spine and glued into paper wrappers; pp. [1-84]. 20.8 x 26.6 cm.
On p. [5]: introductory poem by Charles Olson. A 6.3 cm. wide strip of very red (C11) paper is folded around the cover, and on it [in black]: "2nd ENLARGED EDITION".

4. Woodward, W.E. *Years of Madness: A Reappraisal of the Civil War.*
First edition, second impression [photo offset], 1967 [1951].
[device] | years of madness | [device] | w.e. woodward | [publisher's logo] | frontier press, inc. | cleveland, ohio | 1967
Perfect binding; pp. i-vi [1-2] 3-311 [312-314]. 14.5 x 23 cm.
On copyright page: "Copyright Helen Woodward 1951 | Copyright Frontier Press 1967"

5. *The Decline & the Fall of the "Spectacular" Commodity-Economy.*
First edition, 1967.
THE DECLINE & THE FALL | of the | "SPECTACULAR" | COMMODITY-ECONOMY | [publisher's logo] | FRONTIER PAMPHLET NUMBER ONE | FRONTIER PRESS
[1]^{10}; pp. [i-vi] [1] 2-10 [11-14]. A single triple-stapled gathering. 15 x 22.7 cm.
On verso of title page: "This essay, 'The Decline and the Fall of the 'Spectacular' Commodity-Economy', originally appeared in the *Situationist International,* December, 1965." At foot of back cover flap: "design: ron caplan".

6. Hulbert, Archer Butler. *Paths of the Mound-Building Indians and Great Game Animals.*
First edition, second impression (photo offset), 1967 [1902].
HISTORIC HIGHWAYS OF AMERICA | VOLUME 1 | [rule] | Paths of the Mound=Building Indians | and Great Game Animals | ARCHER BUTLER HULBERT | *With Maps and Illustrations* | [publisher's logo] | FRONTIER PRESS, Inc. | CLEVELAND, OHIO | 1967
$[1\text{-}9]^{8}$; pp. [i-ii] [1-11] 12-13 [14-17] 18-34 [35-37] 38-42 [43] 44-46 [47-48] 49-50 [51-53] 54 [55-56] 57-67 [68] 69-76 [77-78] 79-93 [94] 95-98 [99-101] 102 [103] 104-109 [110] 111-127 [128] 129-140. 13.2 x 18.8 cm.

7. Long, Haniel. *If He Can Make Her So*
First edition, 1968
[first four lines in yellow green C120] IF | HE CAN | MAKE HER | SO | [black] Haniel Long | Selection and introduction by | Ron Caplan with a painting | from the work of John Kane | [green] [device] | [publisher's logo] | FRONTIER PRESS | PITTSBURGH, PA | U S A
$[1\text{-}5]^{8}$ $[6]^{6}$ $[7]^{8}$; pp [i-viii] ix [x-xx] 1-3 [4] 5-16 [17-18] 19-23 [24] 25-27 [28] 29 [30] 31 [32] 33-35 [36] 37-42 [43-44] 45-49 [50] 51 [52-54] 55-79 [80] 81-83 [84] 85 [86-88]. 16 x 25 cm.
Contents: Introduction, "Haniel Long", by Ronald Caplan, Pittsburgh Memoranda (section title for the following 5 pieces) "Prologue," "Homestead 1892," "Mrs. Soffel 1902," "Henry George 1913," "Two Memoranda 1914," Notes for a New Mythology (section title for the following piece) "How Pittsburgh Returned to the Jungle," A Pittsburgher En Route (section title for the following piece) "New Mexico," Piñon Country (section title for the following piece) "The Bandits," The Grist Mill (section title for the following piece) "If He Can Make Her So," Malinche (Doña Marina) (section title for the following piece) "She who speaks to you ....," Atlantides (section title for the following piece) "The Simplest Way," Bibliography (section title for the following piece) "Selected Books of Haniel Long".

8. Dorn, Edward. *Twenty-Four Love Songs.*
First edition, 1969.
Twenty-four | Love songs by | Edward Dorn | frontier press | 1969 [slightly red C12] [device]
$[1]^{16}$; pp. [1-32]. A single double-stapled gathering. Trim size 13.7 x 19.4 cm. Cream laid paper with vertical chain lines watermarked "LINWEAVE TAROTEXT". Cover size ± 15.2 x 22.6 cm., light olive (C106) stock with deckled fore edge.
On page 31: [slightly red] "Designed & printed in San Francisco by Graham Mackintosh".
Contains 24 numbered poems. The number at the head of each poem is printed in slightly red.

9. Long, Haniel. *Interlinear to Cabeza de Vaca.*
Second edition, 1969 [1936].
INTERLINEAR TO | [deep red (C14)] Cabeza | deVaca | [black] *His Relation of the Journey* | *Florida to the Pacific* | *1528-1536* | [deep red] [cross] | HANIEL LONG | FRONTIER PRESS
$[1\text{-}2]^{8}$ $[3]^{4}$ $[4]^{8}$; pp. [i-vii] ix-xii [xiv-xvi] 1-34 [35-40]. 10.6 x 17.6 cm.
Colophon p. [37]: "INTERLINEAR TO | CABEZA DE VACA | was originally published in 1936 by Writers' Editions, 'a cooperative group of writers | living in the Southwest, who believe that | regional publication will foster growth | of american literature,' and is here pub- | lished by Frontier Press in an edition of 4000 | copies in monotype Bembo and handset | Perpetua on Mohawk Vellum. | Design: Ron Caplan. 1969."

10. [White, Bouck]. *The Book of Daniel Drew.*
Second [?]edition, second impression [photo offset], 1969 [1910, 1911, 1930, 1937, 1965].
THE BOOK OF | [photo of Daniel Drew] | DANIEL DREW | NEW YORK CITY | FRONTIER PRESS
$[1\text{-}5]^{16}$ $[6\text{-}7]^{14}$ $[8\text{-}14]^{16}$; pp. [i-vi] vii-xii [1-2] 3-423 [424-428]. 13.7 x19.7 cm.
Contents include "Introduction" by Edward Dorn.
At the foot of the inside flap of the dust jacket: "COVER DESIGN : RON CAPLAN".

11. McClure, Michael. *The Surge.*
First edition, 1969.
Cover title: on a folio of deep orange [C51] wove paper folded quarto, ± 16.2 x 23.8 cm., with deckled fore-edge, [medium olive C107, upside down from right to left] "THE | SURGE". Inside front cover [medium olive] "MICHAEL | McCLURE | frontier | press | 1969
[1][6]; pp. [1-12]. A single double-stapled gathering. 15.5 x 23.3 cm.
On p. [11]: "*The Surge* was first published in *Foot,* (1962)". On p. [12]: "DESIGNED & PRINTED BY GRAHAM MACKINTOSH".

12. Berkman, Alexander. *Prison Memoirs of an Anarchist.*
Second edition, 1970 [1912].
PRISON MEMOIRS | *of an* | ANARCHIST | ALEXANDER BERKMAN | [publisher's logo] | FRONTIER PRESS | PITTSBURGH
[1-16][16] [17][8] [18][16]; pp. [i-xx] [1-2] 3-98 [99-100] 101-488 [489-490] 491-498 [499-500] 501-533 [534] 535-538 [539-540]. 13.6 x 20.8 cm.
At foot of dust jacket front flap: "COVER DESIGN : RON CAPLAN".
Contents include "Introduction: Alexander Berkman" by Kenneth Rexroth.

13. Büchner, Georg. *Lenz.* Translated by Michael Hamburger.
Second English edition, 1969 [1947].
LENZ | Georg Büchner | TRANSLATION BY MICHAEL HAMBURGER | FRONTIER PRESS | 1969
[1-2][16]; pp. [1-6] 7-52 i-v [vi-vii]. 10.5 x 17.7 cm. Paper wrappers.
On p. [6]: "DESIGN BY RON CAPLAN"; pp. i-iv, "Introduction," by Michael Hamburger; p. v, "Principle dates in the life of Georg Büchner".
The first of a series that includes items number 16 and 19, all with identical binding.

14. Dorn, Edward. *Songs Set Two—A Short Count.*
First edition, 1970.
[slightly red (C12)] SONGS | [medium brown (C58)] SET TWO | [black] A Short Count | [medium brown] This volume | is to honor | the Scald | [slightly red] EDWARD | DORN | [medium brown] frontier press 1970
Perfect binding; pp. [1-32]. 11.3 x 15 cm.
On p. [32]: "designed & printed by Graham Mackintosh"
Contains 19 numbered poems. 13 is blank.

15. Williams, William Carlos. *Spring and All.*
Second edition, 1970 [1923].
Spring | & All | William | Carlos Williams | FRONTIER PRESS | 1970
$[1\text{-}7]^8$; pp. [i-viii] 1-98 [99-104]. 10.6 x 17.7 cm. Paper wrappers.
On p. [vi]: "SPRING AND ALL WAS FIRST PUBLISHED IN 1923 | BY THE CONTACT PUBLISHING COMPANY"

16. Brakhage, Stan. *A Moving Picture Giving and Taking Book.*
First edition, 1971.
A | MOVING | PICTURE | GIVING | AND | TAKING | BOOK | STAN BRAKHAGE | FRONTIER PRESS | West Newbury Mass 1971
$[1\text{-}3]^8$ $[4]^6$ $[5]^8$; pp. [i-viii] 1-65 [66-68]. 10.7 x 15.2 cm. Bound in leather covers with gilt stamped title.
On p. [67]: "DESIGN BY PHILIP TRUSSELL | 1971".

17. Dorn, Edward. *The Cycle.*
First edition, 1971.
The Cycle | by | Edward Dorn | Frontier Press | West Newbury Mass | 1971
$[1]^{16}$; pp. [1-32]. A single double-stapled gathering. 24.2 x 32 cm. Paper wrappers.

18. Dorn, Edward. *Some Business Recently Transacted in the White World.*

First edition, 1971.
SOME BUSINESS | RECENTLY | TRANSACTED IN | THE WHITE WORLD | FRONTIER PRESS 1971
[1-6]^{4}; pp. [i-x] 1-83 [84-86]. 10.5 x 17.5 cm. Paper wrappers.
Contents: "A Narrative with Scattered Nouns," "A Epic," "Of Eastern Newfoundland, Its Inns & Outs," "C. B. & Q.," "The Terrific Refinery in Biafra," "Driving Across the Prairie," "The Garden of Birth," "The Sheriff of McTooth County, Kansas ," "Greene Arrives on the Set," "Some Business Recently Transacted in the White World."

19. Glover, Albert. *Trio in G.*
First edition, 1971.
A TRIO IN G | Al Glover | Frontier Press | West Newbury | Massachusetts | 1971
[1-4]^{8} [5]^{6} [6]^{8}; pp. [1-92]. 15 x 20.8 cm. Paper wrappers.
On p. [6]: "Drawings and design by Philip Trussell".

20. H.D. *Hermetic Definitions.*
First edition, 1971.
[within an ornamental oval frame of roses in deep red (C13) and gray green (C122)] Hermetic Definitions | HD | [below] 1971
[1]^{4} [2-5]^{8}; pp. [1-72]. 22.6 x 15 cm. Covers of heavy white stock glued at spine.
Contents: "Red Rose & A Beggar," "Grove of Academe," "Star of Day."
No imprint, no colophon, no copyright. This edition was printed from an autograph transcription of a manuscript version at the Beinecke Library. The title, "Hermetic Definitions," is printed as it appears on the manuscript. Inserted in the copy at Yale is a note by Norman Holmes Pearson: "Illegally published by Harvey Brown Frontier Press West Newbury, Mass. 1971, in what Brown asserts was an edition of 1600 copies 'none for sale'. If so, most were hidden for later profit. Note that the title is *Hermetic Definitions* rather than *Definition* and that the text differs from the New Directions edition. Text from an earlier version surreptitiously obtained by Brown." Brown continued to

distribute to book free until he died in 1990. Hundreds of copies mildewed in his mother's basement.

21. Kelly, Robert. *Cities.*
First edition, 1971.
[two large dots over the "i"s] CITIES | ROBERT KELLY | FRONTIER PRESS | 1971
[1-5]^4; pp. [i-vii] 1-65 [66-72]. 10.7 x 17.6 cm. Paper wrappers.
On copyright page: "AN EARLIER VERSION OF THIS ACCOUNT APPEARED IN THE IOWA REVIEW." "DESIGN BY RON CAPLAN".

22. Kelly, Robert. *In Time.*
First edition, 1971.
R*obert* K*elly* | IN TIME | FRONTIER PRESS | WEST NEWBURY, MASS *1971*
[1-6]^8; pp. [i-viii] 1-11 [11a] 12 [12a] 13-33 [33a] 34-46 [46a-46c] 47 [47a] 48 [48a] 49 [49a] 50 [50a] 51 [51a] 52 [52a] 53 [53a] 54 [54a] 55 [55a] 56 [56a] 57 [57a] 58 [58a] 59 [59a] 60 [60a] 61[62-66]. 17 x 21.5 cm. Paper wrappers.
On p. [vi]: "DESIGN BY RON CAPLAN".

23. Anderson, Sherwood. *Mid-American Chants.*
Second edition, 1972 [1918].
Sherwood Anderson | Mid-American | Chants | FRONTIER PRESS | 1972
[1-9]^4; pp. [i-viii] 1-62 [63-64]. 21.5 x 26 cm. Paper wrappers.
On p. [iv]: "Book Design by Ron Caplan"

24. Dorn, Edward. *Gunslinger*: Book 111.
First edition, 1972.
Gunslinger | by | Edward Dorn | Frontier Press | West Newbury Mass | 1972
[1]^{20}; pp. [1-40]. A single double-stapled gathering. 19.8 x 30.4 cm. Paper wrappers.
On p. [5]: "BOOK III | THE WINTERBOOK | prologue to the great | Book IIII Kornerstone".

Appendix 2—
Checklist of the Publications of the Institute of Further Studies, 1969-1997

1. Olson, Charles. ["That there was a woman"]. 1968.
1 p., 15.5 x 20.2 cm.
Dated, "March, 1968".
Folded once in an envelope, 16 x 10.5 cm., with the printed return address, "THE INSTITUTE OF FURTHER STUDIES | [device] [to the right of device] Box 25 [dot] Kensington Station "Buffalo, New York [dot] 14215".
Reprinted as *Maximus* III.189 (Butterick 583).

2. Olson, Charles. ["Added to making a Republic in gloom on Watchhouse Point"]. 1968.
1 p., 15.5 x 20.2 cm.
Dated, "March, 1968".
Folded once in an envelope, 16 x 10.5 cm., with the printed return address, "THE INSTITUTE OF FURTHER STUDIES | [device] [to the right of device] Box 25 [dot] Kensington Station "Buffalo, New York [dot] 14215".
Reprinted as *Maximus* III.190 (Butterick 584).

3. Olson, Charles. ["Wholly absorbed"]. 1968
1 p., 15.5 x 20.2 cm.

Dated, "LX VIII".
Folded once in an envelope, 16 x 10.5 cm., with the printed return address, "THE INSTITUTE OF FURTHER STUDIES | [device] [to the right of device] Box 25 [dot] Kensington Station "Buffalo, New York [dot] 14215".
Reprinted as *Maximus* III.191 (Butterick 585).

4. Olson, Charles. ["I like something in the American which does honor a Hotspur of itself"]
Postcard, 17.7 x 12.7 cm. Recto, a photograph of Jacqueline Kennedy Onassis and Alice Roosevelt Longworth. Verso, eight hand written lines in blue signed, "Charles Olson": "I like something in the American which does honor a Hotspur of itself, | and even defines it as in fact close to the | condition of valor. What does, though, always ultimately | show up though, in their skin, or the health of it, some sickness | through their eyes seen almost to have the right | color or '[?]' from the edge of known and admitted | danger—is some poverty (actually they have saved | themselves from the glories of god ism | Charles Olson"
At top left of verso, "SOME OF THE SUBTLEST OF ALL POSSIBLE TRAIL-BACK, Mrs. Aristotle | Onassis, left, attending the christening of Rory Catherine Elizabeth | Kennedy, 11th child of the late Sen. Robert Kennedy, at St. Luke's | Church, McLean, Va., Sunday, Jan. 12, 1969, chats with Mrs. Alice | Roosevelt Longworth."

5. Olson, Charles. "Clear Shining Water." 1968.
Postcard. 41.7 x 19 cm. The card is double folded to 14.2 x 19 cm. On the front of the folded card is a drawing of "The Judgement of Paris" from a Greek vase, reproduced from Jane Ellen Harrison's *Prolegomena to the Study of Greek Religion*, p. 295. On the back is the printed return address, "THE INSTITUTE OF FURTHER STUDIES | [device] [to the right of device] Box 25 [dot] Kensington Station "Buffalo, New York [dot] 14215." Printed across the inside of the unfolded in three panels, "CLEAR, SHINING WATER", De Vries says, Altgermanische". At foot of third panel, "CHARLES OLSON, | Institute of Further Studies, July 1st, | 1968".

Reprinted in *Additional Prose.* Ed. George Butterick (Bolinas, Four Seasons Foundation, 1974). 71.

6. Blake, William. *Milton,* pl. 25 [1968].
1 p., 18.5 x 26.2 cm.
Double folded in an envelope, 19 x 10 cm., with the printed return address, "THE INSTITUTE OF FURTHER STUDIES | [device] [to the right of device] Box 25 [dot] Kensington Station "Buffalo, New York [dot] 14215".

7. Pound Ezra. "The Child's Guide to Knowledge" [1970?].
2 pp., 18.5 x 26.2 cm.
12 line epigraph by William Blake. Double folded in an envelope, 19 x 10 cm., with the return address, "The Institute of Further Studies | BOX 482 | CANTON, NEW YORK 13617".

8. The Magazine of Further Studies. Buffalo, NY. 1965-1969.
All issues 22 x 28 cm. loose sheets wrapped in corrugated paper covers and triple stapled through the spine. The cover of each issue has a different art work.

a. No. 1: "Lament for the Makaris," by William Dunbar; "Berkeley," by Robert Hogg; "Seven," by John Clarke; "from Don Cherry," by Harvey Brown; "Four poems," by Albert Glover; "Mythology / Poetry, Bibliography 1" and "III Pleistocene Mythology, A Bibliographic Beginning," by John Clarke; "Five poems," by George Butterick; "Two poems," by Stephen Rodefer; "Jazz Clarke Poem," by Charles Doria; "You've lost that lovin' feeling," by David Cull; "from Mountain," by Fred Wah; "Three poems," by John Weiners; "Placemats," by John Clarke.

b. No. 2: "crow feather," by Ruth Fox; "Pleistocene Mythology," by John Clarke; "The Blue Garden," by Charles Doria; ""I'd call you sweet but," by Colette Butterick; "For Andrew Crozier—wherever he goes, the same way, always," by John Temple; "Notes on the Possibility of a Phenomenological Poetics—The Body's World," by Charles Sherry; "Two Poems," by Charles Sherry; "ISHMAEL:8:X:sixtyfive," by Daniel John Zimmerman; "Plus X," by Patricia Jamieson; "Notes from Class," by George Butterick;

"Nothing Done," by Jim Braemer; "Three poems," by John Weiners; "2 songs for children," by John Temple; "The Canoe, Too," by Fred Wah; "Notes (for I. Massey 9/28/65 on C. Olson," by Albert Glover; "Poem for Planters," by Albert Glover; "It's no fun anymore," by Jack Clarke; "As to the Exomorphic," by J. Clarke; "The Lamo," by Charles Olson; "traitor poem," by Dave Cull; "Beasts of Burden," by Mac Hammond.

c. No. 3: "Al, | Imagine: simply to be an animal," by Charles Olson; "Furs," by Fred Wah; "Five poems," by John Weiners; "As I walked home last night," by John Temple; "Letter A," by Lewis MacAdams; "The Mountain, the creek, all ends in the lake," by Fred Wah; "from Black Creek," by Ruth Fox; "Sections from Subway," by George Butterick; "Two poems," by Duncan McNaughton; "Poem," by Robert Hogg; "The Lesbian is dead," by Duncan McNaughton; "Enough animus so it all has will," by John Clarke; "I see a whale in the South-sea, drinking my soul away," [review of *Sailing after Knowledge*, by George Dekker, and *The Savage Mind*, by Claude Levi-Strauss] by Albert Glover; [review of *Human Universe and Other Essays*, by Charles Olson] by John Clarke.

d. No. 4: "Hell and Heaven: Psychemimeisis to beyond the rainbow bridge," by David Tirrell; "The qanat spurts the geyser," by Ed Sanders; "By fixes only move," by John Clarke; "3 songs," by Robert Hogg; "for my friend," by Charles Olson; "Fingers of the Sun," by Ed Sanders; "Poem for Turning," by Fred Wah; "that otherwise than how the story goes," by Ron Caplan; "Proem," by George Butterick; "Drugs and the Unconscious" by John Weiners; "the mute," by Ed Billowitz; "by honor," by Ed Sanders; "Blake letter November 4 1967," by John Clarke; "Dear Royal Members my west view in this," by David Tirrell; "Letter, October 18, 1967," by Fred Wah; "Moon morning 6 Nov '67" by John Clarke; "A letter and a drawing for John Clarke 11/7/67," by Albert Glover.

e. No. 5: "Second tale: return," by Robin Blaser; "it is a dark cold hard tin forest," by Ron Caplan; "Letter, May 15, 1968," by Fred Wah; "La Barranca del Cobre," by Drummond Hadley; "Insulted," by John Weiners; "Where the daughter goes the mother must follow," by John Clarke; "The quality of goods, the explicitness," by George Butterick; "[review of *Megalithic Sites in Britain,* by A. Thom], by Peter Riley; "from *Art and Artist"* by Otto Rank; "Prophetic hieroglyphs: world forecasts," by Albert Glover; "Magic rite," by Ed Sanders; "A plan for a curriculum of the soul," by Charles Olson.

f. No. 6: ["letter to John Clarke"], by Charles Olson; "I am very glad and all alone in the world," by Mary Leary; "He said, that when he would step out into the street," by George Butterick; "I point to my own absolute (?) experience of," by Fred Wah; "it was all tainted with myself, I knew it all to start with," by John Clarke; "Three poems," by John Temple; "Thinking along the lines that," by John Clarke; "A lifetime," by Robert Hogg; "I shall never forget the maniacal horror of it all in the end," by Robert Creeley; "Lockd in a fiery Tree," by Duncan McNaughton; "the black dog is third dog," by Albert Glover; "'...we found marginal," by Buri; "But what's wrong with mortality?" by Albert Glover; "SO," by Fred Wah; "Thirty-six years after my birth was the time," by John Clarke; "At this point I would distinguish the following kinds of form," by Robert Duncan; "Dear Diana—Buga Nov. 4, 1968," by Ed Billowitz; "so I put my hand out further, a little further," by Buri; "Dear Jack & Mary," by David [Tirrell]; "Ah no, I cannot tell you what it is," by John Temple; ""Out of the well-heads of the new world," by Fred Wah; " ... so much as there is a steady flow of breath," by Fred Wah; "So like play," by Charles Olson.

9. *A Curriculum of the Soul* (in order of publication):

0 Pleistocene Man	Charles Olson
21 Vision	Drummond Hadley
22 Messages	James Koller
3 Woman	John Wieners
18 Ismaili Muslimism	Michael Bylebyl
19 Alchemy	David Tirrell
16 Dance	Lewis MacAdams, Jr.
13 The Arabs	Edward Kissam
27 Sensation	Anselm Hollo
1 The Mushroom	Albert Glover

14 American Indians	Edgar Billowitz
11 Novalis' Subjects	Robert Dalke
2 Dream	Duncan McNaughton
7 Blake	John Clarke
12 The Norse	George F. Butterick
17 Egyptian Hieroglyphs	Edward Sanders
6 Earth	Fred Wah
24 Organism	Michael McClure
20 Perspective	Daniel Zimmerman
8 Dante	Robert Duncan
25 Matter	John Thorpe
15 Jazz Playing	Harvey Brown
28 Attention	Robert Grenier
23 Analytical Psychology	Gerrit Lansing
26 Phenomenological	Joanne Kyger
9 Homer's Art	Alice Notley
10 Bach's Belief	Robin Blaser
4 Mind	Michael Boughn
5 Language	Lisa Jarnot

Curriculum of the Soul fascicle publication dates in order of appearance: 0:'68 / 21:'72 / 22:'72 / 3:'72 / 18:'72 / 19:'72 / 16:'72 / 13:'72 / 27:'72 / 1:'72 / 14:'72 / 11:'73 / 2:'73 / 7:'73 / 12:'73 17:'73 / 6:'74 / 24:'74 / 20:'74 / 8:'74 / 25:'75 / 15:'77 / 23:'83 / 28;'85 / 26:'89 / 9:'90 / 10:'95 / 4:'99 / 5:'02

10. A CURRICULUM OF THE SOUL

a. First edition, limited, 2010.

[in gray reddish orange C39] A CURRICULUM OF THE SOUL | THE INSTITUTE OF FURTHER STUDIES

[1]^{4} [2-51]^{8} [52]^{4}; [i-vi]^{1}[i-vi]^{2} vii-xxvii [xxviii] [1-2] 3 [4] 5-21 [22] 23-29 [30-32] 33-53 [54-56] 57-61 [62-64] 65-91 [92] 93 [94-96] 97-118 [119-120] 121-147 [148-152] 153-193 [194-196] 197-250 [251-252] 253-270 [271-272] 273-297 [298-300] 301-320 [321-322] 323-360 [361-362] 363-396 [397-398] 399-424 [425-426] 427-460 [461-462] 463-482 [483-484] 485-533 [534-538] 539-561 [562-564] 565-576

[577-578] 579-607 [608-610] 611-620 [21-622] 623-628 [629-630] 631-653 [654-656] 657-693 [694-696] 697-747 [748-750] 751-765 [766-768] 769-835 [836-838] 839-852 [853-856]. White wove paper, 19.5 x 25.4 cm. Gatherings sewn with white thread. Covers grey reddish orange striated silk over boards, 21 x 25.5 cm. At the top of the spine a strip of paper, 7 x 3 cm, has been pasted. On it: [in gray reddish orange within a single line box:] A CURRICULUM | OF THE SOUL
Contents: 29 fascicles of *The Curriculum of the Soul* in numerical order.
Colophon [p. 855]: A CURRICULUM OF THE SOUL | (a multi-genre collaborative text in 28 books) is derived from "A Plan for a | Curriculum of the Soul" written by Charles Olson. John Clarke, who both | selected and assigned the subjects, served as general editor for the project | until his death in 1992. Since then Albert, Glover has continued this work | and is solely responsible for the final editing of the text. | Thanks to Victor Coleman, proofreader. || The authors, in order of appearance, are | Charles Olson; Albert Glover; Duncan McNaughton; John Wieners; | Michael Boughn; Lisa Jarnot; Fred Wah; John Clarke; Robert Duncan; | Alice Notley; Robin Blaser; Robert Dalke (editor and translator); George | F. Butterick; Edward Kissam; Edgar Billowitz; Harvey Brown; Lewis Mac | Adams, Jr; Ed Sanders; Michael Bylebyl; David Tirrell; Danny Zimmer | man; Drummond Hadley; James Koller; Gerrit Lansing; Joanne Kyger; | Robert Grenier; John Thorpe; Anselm Hollo; and Michael McClure. || This book has been set in Giovanni Mardersteig's Dante types and printed | on Mohawk Superfine papers. The printing was carried out by Levellers | Press. The binding is by Sarah Creighton. The design and typography are | by Michael Russem of Cambridge, Massachusetts. || Fifty copies of this book have been numbered o through 49. | This is number
51 copies printed for the Institute of Further Studies by Glover Publishing on the occasion of the Charles Olson Centenary, 2010.

b. First trade edition, 2016 [2 volumes]
A CURRICULUM OF THE SOUL | VOLUME ONE | EDITED BY JOHN CLARKE AND ALBERT GLOVER | [design] | THE INSTITUTE OF FURTHER STUDIES | & | SPUYTEN DUYVIL | NEW YOUR CITY
Perfect bound in paper wrappers. Pagination as in 10.a. through page 424. Cream wove paper, 20.5 x 28 cm.

Includes fascicles by Albert Glover, Duncan McNaughton, John Wieners, Michael Boughn, Lisa Jarnot, Fred Wah, John Clarke, Robert Duncan, Alice Notley, Robin Blaser, Robert Dalke (editor and translator), George F. Butterick, Edward Kissam, and Edgar Billowitz.
Spuyten Duyvil Roots and Branches Series.
A CURRICULUM OF THE SOUL | VOLUME TWO | EDITED BY JOHN CLARKE AND ALBERT GLOVER | [design] | THE INSTITUTE OF FURTHER STUDIES | & | SPUYTEN DUYVIL | NEW YOUR CITY
Perfect bound in paper wrappers. Pagination as in 10.a. pp. 425-856. Cream wove paper, 20.5 x 28 cm.
Includes fascicles by Harvey Brown, Lewis MacAdams, Jr, Ed Sanders, Michael Bylebyl, David Tirrell, Danny Zimmerman, Drummond Hadley, James Koller, Gerrit Lansing, Joanne Kyger, Robert Grenier, John Thorpe, Anselm Hollo, and Michael McClure.
Spuyten Duyvil Roots and Branches Series.

Bibliography

Adams, Brooks. *The New Empire.* Cleveland: Frontier Press, 1967.

Agamben, Giorgio. *Nymphs.* Tr. Amanda Minervini. London: Seagull Books, 2013.

Alcalay, Ammiel. *A Little History.* Ed. Fred Dewey. LA and NY: re:public / UpSet Press, 2013.

Alcalay, Ammiel. "Republics of poetry." Electronic Poetry Center. University at Buffalo. October 2005. Web. 4 January 2014.

Allen, Donald. "Introduction." *The New American Poetry 1945-1960.* NY: Grove Press, 1961.

Anania, Michael. "When Buffalo Became Buffalo." *Plume Poetry.* Web. https://plumepoetry.com/essays-and-comment-michael-anania/#. Viewed 17 April 2022.

Archambeau, Robert. "Hating the Other Kind of Poetry." *Coppernickle* Fall (2015): web, http://copper-nickel.org/hating-the-other-kind-of-poetry/. Viewed 9 November 2015.

—. "Poetry Warrior: Robert Creeley in His Letters." Rev. of *The Selected Letters of Robert Creeley*, ed. Rod Smith, Peter Baker, and Kaplan Harris. *Notre Dame Review* Summer/Fall 2015: p. 251-255. Online at https://ndreview.nd.edu/assets/166954/archambeau_review.pdf. Viewed 16 October 2022.

Baraka, Amiri. *The Autobiography of LeRoi Jones/Amiri Baraka.* 2nd ed. Chicago: Lawrence Hill Books, 1967.

Baudrillard, Jean. *America.* Tr. Chris Turner. London and NY: Verso, 1988 [1986].

Bey, Hakim [Peter Lamborne Wilson]. *T.A.Z. The Temporary Autonomous Zone, Ontological Anarchy, Poetic Terrorism.* 2nd edition. NY: Autonomedia, 2003 [1985].

Belgrad, Daniel. *The Culture of Spontaneity: Improvisation and the Arts in Postwar America.* Chicago: U of Chicago P, 1998.

Berkovitch, Sacvan. "A Model of Cultural Transvaluation: Puritanism, Modernity, and New World Rhetoric." Diss. City University of New York, 1997. Trans-Atlantic Conference. Harvard University. Web. <http://web.gc.cuny.edu/dept/renai/conf/Papers/Keynote/Bercovit.htm>. Viewed 23 Feb. 2011.

The Big Lebowski. Dir. Joel and Ethan Coen. Polygram, 1988. DVD.

Blake, William. "America: A Prophecy." In *The Complete Poetry and Prose of William Blake.* Ed. David Erdman. Garden City NY: Anchor/Doubleday, 1982.

Blaser, Robin. *The Holy Forest.* Revised and Expanded Edition. Ed. Miriam Nichols. Berkeley: U of California P, 2006

—. "The Violets: Charles Olson and Alfred North Whitehead." In *The Fire: Collected Essays of Robin Blaser.* Ed Miriam Nichols. Berkeley: U of California P, 2006. Pp. 196-228.

Boughn, Michael. *Cosmographia – a post-Lucretian faux micro-epic.* Toronto: Book Thug, 2011.

Brito, Manuel. "The impact of the poet-editor: some questions." *Revista Canaria de Estudios Ingleses,* 62. April 2011, pp. 81-96. (Rpt. Servicio de publicationes. Universidad de Laguna. Nd. Web. 3 January 2014.).

Cavell, Stanley, *Pursuits of Happiness.* Cambridge: Harvard UP, 1981.

—. "Recounting Gains, Showing Losses: Reading *The Winter's Tale.*" In *Disowning Knowledge in Six Plays of Shakespeare.* Cambridge: Cambridge UP, 1986.

—. *Philosophical Passages. Wittgenstein, Emerson, Austin, Derrida.* Oxford: Blackwell, 1995.

—. *The Senses of Walden.* Chicago: U of Chicago P, 1992.

Certeau, Michel de. *Heterologies: Discourse on the Other.* Tr. Brian Massumi. Theory and History of Literature Vol. 17. Minneapolis: U of Minnesota P, 1986

Clark, Tom. *Charles Olson: The Allegory of a Poet's Life*. NY: W.W. Norton, 1991.

—. *Robert Creeley and the Genius of the American Common Place*. New Directions, 1993.

Clarke, John. *Blake*. In *A Curriculum of the Soul.* Canton, NY: Institute of Further Studies, 2010.——In the Analogy. Buffalo: ***shuffaloff***, 1997.

—"Letter to Tom Clark, 28 June 1991." *Dispatches from the Poetry Wars.* Web. https://wayback.archive- it.org/12142/20201105010759/ https://www.dispatchespoetrywars.com/documents/john-clarke-to-tom-clark-28-june-1991/. Viewed 16 Octobrer, 2022.

Copland, Campbell. G*nomic Verse: a poly-modern morphology of poetic revelation*. Canton NY: Glover Publishing, 2021.

Corbin, Henry. *Avicenna and the Visionary Recital.* London: Routledge and Paul, 1961.

—. *The Concept of Comparative Philosophy.* Tr. Peter Russell. Ipswich MA: Golgonooza Press, 198.1

—. *Creative Imagination in the Sufism of Ibn 'Arabi.* Tr. Ralph Manheim. Bollingen Series XCI. Princeton: Princeton UP, 1969.

—. "Cyclical Time in Mazdaism and Ismailism." In *Man and Time: Papers from the Eranos Yearbook.* Bollingen Series XXX. Princeton: Princeton UP, 1983 [1957].

—. *Spiritual Body and Celestial Earth.* Tr. Nancy Pearson. Bollingen Series XCI: 2. Princeton: Princeton UP, 1977.

—. *The Voyage and the Messenger: Iran and Philosophy*. Berkeley: North Atlantic Books, 1998.

Creeley, Robert. "Introduction." In *Charles Olson: The Allegory of a Poet's Life* by Tom Clark. 2nd ed. NY: W.W. Norton, [1991] 2000.

—. "The Kind of Act of." In *Collected Poems (1945-1975)*. Berkley: U of California P, 1982.

—. *Pieces.* NY: Scribners, 1969.

—. "Reflections on Whitman in Age." In *On earth: Last poems and an essay.* Berkeley: U of California P., 2006.

Crevecoeur, J. Hector St. John de. *Letters from an American Farmer and other essays.* Cambridge, MA: Belknap Press of Harvard UP, 2013.

Curti, Merle. "The Reputation of America Overseas (1776-1860)." *American Quarterly* 1.1 (Spring, 1949): pp. 58-82.

Cusimano, Oliver. "Written in the company of the memory of the conversation following the seminar dedicated to Giorgio Agamben's *Remnants of Auschwitz: The Witness and the Archive.*" Unpublished essay.

Deleuze, Gilles, *The Fold: Leibniz and the Baroque.* Minneapolis: U of Minnesota P, 1993.

Derrida, Jacques. "The Law of Genre" (1979, trans. 1980). *Acts of Literature*, edited by Derek Attridge. NY: Routledge, 1992.

Dorn, Edward. "An interview with Barry Alpert." In *Interviews.* Ed. Donald Allen. Writing 38. Bolinas: Four Seasons Foundation, 1980. Pp. 7-35.

—. *Road Testing the Language: an interview with Edward Dorn.* {By Stephen Fredman]. Documents for New Poetry 1. San Diego: Archive for the New Poetry, University of California at San Diego, 1978.

Duncan, Robert. *The H.D. Book.* Berkeley: UC Press, 2011.

—. "Man's Fulfillment in Order and Strife." In *Collected Essays and Other Prose.* Ed. James Maynard. Berkeley: U of Calfornia P, 2014.

DuPlessis, Rachel. "Considering the long poem: genre problems." *Readings: response and reactions to poetries.* Issue 4. Birkbeck, University of London. Nd. Web. 14 January 2014.

Emerson, Ralph Waldo. "The American Scholar." In *Essays and Lectures.* NY: Library of America, 1983. Pp. 51-72.

—. "Circles." In *The Essays of Ralph Waldo Emerson.* Cambridge, Mass.: The Belknap Press of Harvard UP, 1987.

—. "Self-Reliance." In *Essay and Lectures.* NY: Library of America, 1983. Pp. 257-82.

—. "The Divinity School Address." In *Essays and Lectures.* NY: Library of America, 1983.

Frey, Hans-Jost. *Interruptions.* Trans. Georgia Albert. Albany: State U of NY Press, 1996.

Gilbert, Alan. "Charles Olson and Empire, or Charles Olson flips the wartime script." Paper presented to the National Poetry Foundation Conference on American Poetry in the 1960s, University of Maine, Orono, July 2000. Text available on the Olson Now documents page, Electronic Poetry Center, http://epc.buffalo.edu/authors/olson/blog/Olson_and_Empire.pdf. Viewed 15 July 2015.

Goldstein, Robert Justin. *Political Repression in Modern America from 1870 to 1976.* Cambridge, MA: Schenkman Publishing, 1978.

H.D. "Ear-Ring." In *Three Stories by H.D.* Ed. Michael Boughn. Toronto: Book Thug

—. *The Sword Went out to Sea (Synthesis of a Dream), by Delia Alton.* Ed. Cynthia Hogue and Julie Vandivere. Gainesville: UP of Florida, 2007.

H.D. and Robert Duncan. *A Great Admiration: Correspondence 1950-1961.* Ed. Robert J. Bertholf. Venice CA: Lapis Press, 1992.

Hacking, Ian. *Rewriting the Soul: Multiple Personality and the Science of Memory.* Princeton: Princeton UP, 1995.

Hanegraaff, Wouter. *Esotericism and the Academy: Rejected Knowledge in Western Culture.* Cambridge: Cambridge UP, 2012.

Harding, D. W. *Words into Rhythm.* Cambridge: Cambridge UP, 1976.

Hardt, Michael and Antonio Negri. *Empire.* Cambridge, MA: Harvard UP, 2000.

Hegel, G.W.F. *Aesthetics: Lectures on Fine Arts.* Tr. T.M. Knox. Oxford: Clarendon Press, 1975.

Howe, Susan. *The Birthmark.* Middleton, CT: Wesleyan, 1993.

—. "Interview." Poet.org. Posted 6 September 2011. https://poets.org/text/open-field-susan-howe-conversation.

Illich, Ivan. *The Rivers North of the Future.* As told to David Cayley. Toronto: House of Anansi, 2005.

—. *Tools for Comviviality.* London: Marion Boyars Publishing, 2021 [1973].

Jakobson, Roman. "Linguistics and Poetics." In *Style and Language.* Ed. Thomas Sebeok. NY: Technology Press of MIT, 1960.

Jennings, Francis. *The Invasion of America: Indians, Colonialism, and the Cant of Conquest.* Chapel Hill: U of North Carolina P, 1975.

Johnston, Devin. *Precipitations: Contemporary American Poetry as Occult Practice.* Middleton, CT: Weslyan UP, 2002.

Kambourli, Smaro. *On the edge of genre: the contemporary Canadian long poem.* Toronto: U of Toronto P, 1991.

Kerenyi. Karl. *Dionysus: Archetypal Image of Indestructible Life.* Tr. Ralph Manheim. Bollingen Series LVX – 2. Princeton: Princeton UP, 1976.

Literary Modernism and the Occult Tradition. Ed. Leon Surette and Demetres P. Tryphonopolous. Oronto, ME: National Poetry Foundation, 1996.

The Long Poem Anthology. Ed. Michael Ondaatje. Toronto: Coach House, 1979.

Lydon, Michael. *Ray Charles: Man and Music.* NY: Riverhead Books, 1998.

Martin, Meredith. *The Rise and Fall of Meter: Poetry and English National Culture, 1860—1930.* Princeton: Princeton UP, 2012.

Materer, Timothy. *Modernist Alchemy: Poetry and the Occult.* Ithaca NY: Cornell UP, 1995.

Melville, Herman. *The Confidence Man: His Masquerade.* Ed. Parker, Herschel. NY: Norton, 1971.

—. *Moby-Dick, or The Whale.* Ed. Parker, Hershel, and Harrison Hayford. NY: WW Norton, 2002.

Middleton, Peter, "The Longing of the Long Poem." *Jacket* 40. 2010. Web. http://jacketmagazine.com/40/middleton-long-poem.shtml. Viewed 9 January 2014.

Mingus, Charles. "Better Git Hit in Your Soul." *Mingus Ah Um* (Columbia CS 8171), 1959.

—. "Eat that Chicken." *Oh Yeah!* Atlantic (SD 1377), 1962, CD.

Nancy, Jean-Luc. *Hegel—The Restlessness of the Negative.* Tr. Jason Smith and Steven Miller. Minneapolis: U of Minnesota P, 2002.

—. *The Sense of the World.* Tr. Jeffrey S. Librett. Minneapolis: U of Minnesota P, 1997.

—. *The Truth of Democracy*. Tr. Pascale-Anne Brault and Michael Naas. NY: Fordham UP, 2010.

The New American Poetry. Ed. Donald Allen. NY: Grove Press, 1960.

The New Long Poem Anthology. Ed. Sharon Thesen. 2nd ed. Vancouver: Talon Books, 2001.

O'Hara, Frank. "Personism." *Yugen* #7 (September 1959). Rpt. in *The Poetics of the New American Poetry.* Ed. Donald Allen and Warren Tallman. NY: Grove Press, 1973.

Olson, Charles. *Call Me Ishmael.* [1947]. London: Jonathan Cape, 1967.

—. "Captain John Smith." In *Collected Prose*. Ed. Donald Allen and Benjamin Friedlander. Berkeley: U of California P, 1997.

—. Charles Olson at Goddard College April 12-14, 1962. Ed Kyle Schlesinger. Austin: Cuniform, 2011.

—. *Charles Olson Reading at Berkeley.* Transcribed by Zoe Brown. San Francisco: Coyote, 1966.

—. *The Maximus Poems*. Ed. George Butterick. Berkeley : U of California P, 1983.

—. *Mayan Letters*. Ed. Robert Creeley. Cape Editions 17. London: Jonathan Cape, 1968.

—. "Operation Red, White & Black." *OLSON, The journal of the Charles Olson archives* 5 (Spring 1976): 27.

—. "Paterson Book 5." *Evergreen Review* 3 (Summer 1959).

—. "A plan for a curriculum of the Soul." *Magazine of Further Studies* #5 (1968?).

—. "Projective Verse." In *Human Universe and other essays.* Ed. Donald Allen. NY: Grove Press, 1967. Pp. 51-62.

—.*Proprioception.* Writing 6. SF: Four Seasons Foundation, 1965.

—. "Under the Mushroom." In *Muthologos. Vol.* 1. 1963. Bolinas, CA: Four Seasons Foundation, 1978.

—. "The Vineland Map Review," In *Collected Prose.* Ed. Donald Allen and Benjamin Friedlander. Berkeley: U of California P, 1997.

Olson, Charles, and Robert Creeley. *The Complete Correspondence.* Ed. George Butterick. Vol. 2. Santa Barbara, CA: Black Sparrow Press, 1980.

—. *The Complete Correspondence.* Vol. 8. Santa Rosa, CA: Black Sparrow Press, 1987.

Pascal, Blaise. *Pensées.* Tr. A.J. Krailsheimer. NY: Penguin, 1966.

Paz, Octavio. *The Labyrinth of Solitude: Life and Thought in Mexico.* NY: Grove Press, 1962.

Perloff, Marjorie. "Charles Olson and the "Inferior Predecessors": "Projective Verse" Revisited." *ELH* 1973.

—. "A reply to Ralph Maud's 'A Challenge to Marjorie G. Perloff.' *Minutes of the Charles Olson Society* 8 (June 1995): pp. 34-36.

—. "'To Give a Design': Williams and the Visualization of Poetry." In *William Carlos Williams: Man and Poet.* Ed. Carroll F. Terrell. Orono, Maine: National Poetry Foundation, 1983.

Pound, Ezra. "A few don'ts by an Imagiste." *Poetry Chicago* 1.6 (March 1913).

—. "Psychology and Troubadours." In *The Spirit of Romance.* NY: New Directions, 1968.

Quasha, George. *Axial Stones—An Art of Precarious Balance.* Berkeley: North Atlantic Books, 2006.

Rasula, Jed. *The American Poetry Wax Museum: Reality Effects, 1940-1990.* Urbana, IL: National Council of Teachers of English, 1996.

Riddel, Joseph. *The Inverted Bell.* Baton Rouge: Louisiana State UP, 1974.

—. *Purloined Letters.* Baton Rouge: Louisiana State UP, 1995.

Rowe, John Carlos. *The Cultural Politics of the New American Studies.* Ann Arbor: Open Humanities Press, 2012.

Sainstbury, George. *Historical Manual of English Prosody.* London: Macmillan and Co., 1910.

Saroyan, Aram. "The Hero and the Gunslinger: Did Robert Creeley and Ed Dorn lose their way in middle age?" Poetry Foundation, April 28, 2009. http://www.poetryfoundation.org/journal/article.html?id=236554.

Sauer, Carl O. "Environment and Culture during the Last Deglaciation." *Proceedings of the American Philosophical Society,* Vol. 92, No. 1 (Mar. 8, 1948), pp. 65- 77.

Scheidel, Walter. "Republics between hegemony and empire: How ancient city-states built empires and the USA doesn't (anymore)." *Princeton/Stanford Working Papers in Classics.* http://www.princeton.edu/~pswpc/pdfs/scheidel/020601.pdf. February 2006. Viewed July 2015.

Shakespeare, William. *The Winter's Tale.* In William Shakespeare, *The Complete Works.* NY: The Viking Press, 1969.

Simon, Myron. *The Georgian Poetic.* Berkeley: University of California P, 1975.

Smith, Wilfred Cantwell. *Belief and History.* Charlottesville: UP of Virginia, 1977,

Surette, Leon. *The Birth of Modernism: Ezra Pound, T.S. Eliot, W.B. Yeats, and the Occult.* Montreal & Kingston: McGill-Queen's UP, 1993.

—. "Ondaatje's Long Poem Anthology." *Canadian Poetry Journal – Studies, Documents, Reviews* 6. University of Western Ontario. 1980. Web. 3 January 2014.

Sword, Helen. *Ghostwriting Modernism.* Ithaca NY: Cornell UP, 2002.

Takase, Aki. "In a Sentimental Mood." *My Ellington.* Intakt (CD 213), 2013, CD.

Taylor, Charles. *A Secular Age.* Cambridge, MA: Harvard UP, 2007.

Thelma and Louise. Dir. Ridley Scott. MGM, 1991. DVD.

Thoreau, Henry David. *Walden, or Life in the Woods.* NY: Signet Classics, 1999.

Tillinghast, Richard. "Yesterday's Avant-garde." *The Nation*, 19 November 1983: 501.

Todorov, Tzvetan. "Poetry and Morality." *Salmagundi* 111 (Summer 1996).

Turner, Victor. "Liminality and Communitas." In *The Ritual Process: Structure and Anti-Structure* (Chicago: Aldine Publishing, 1969.

Upward, Allen. *The New World.* Boston : Houghton Mifflin, 1915.

Van Dyke, Ruth. "Sacred Geographies." In *Oxford Handbook of the Archaeology of the American Southwest.* Ed Barbara Mills and Severin Fowles. Oxford: Oxford UP, 2017.

Versluis, Arthur. *Restoring Paradise: Western Esotericism, Literature, Art, and Consciousness.* SUNY Series in Western Esoteric Traditions. Albany: State University of NYP, 2004.

Watten, Barrett. "The Impact of The Poet-Editor: Some Questions." Interview by Manuel Brito. *Revista Canaria de Estudios Ingleses*, 62; April 2011, pp. 81-96. https://riull.ull.es/xmlui/bitstream/handle/915/12563/RCEI_62_%28%202011%29_07.pdf?sequence=1&isAllowed=y

Wellman, Donald. "Creeley's Ear." *Jacket 2,* No. 31 (Oct. 2006). Web. http://jacketmagazine.com/31/rc-wellman.html. Viewed November 11, 2015.

Williams, William Carlos. *Collected Poems, 1909-1939.* Vol. I. Ed. by A. Walton Litz and Christopher MacGowan. New York: New Directions, 1988.

—. *Collected Poems, 1939-1962.* Vol. II. New York: New Directions, 1988.

—. "Measure". *Spectrum* 3.3 (Fall 1959): 133-58.

Winthrop, John. "A Model of Christian Charity." In *Sermons that Shaped America.* Ed. Barker, William S. and Samuel T. Logan, Jr. Phillipsburg NJ: P&R Publishing, 2003.

—. "On Liberty (The Little Speech)." The Constitution Society. http://www.constitution.org/bcp/winthlib.htm. Viewed July 2015.

Wittgenstein, Ludwig. *Philosophical Investigations.* 3rd Ed. London: Blackwell. 2008 [1953].

Acknowledgments

"Measure's Measures" first appeared in *West Coast Line* 28:3 (Winter 1994/95): 93 105.

"Beyond "Projective Verse"—the Poetics of Proprioception," "Picking up the Injuns: Poetics as Transformation," and "What Is a Soul and Why Might It Need a Curriculum? Charles Olson's 'A Curriculum of the Soul' for Skeptics" first appeared in *O—Three Lectures and a Postscript.* Toronto: shuffaloff / Eternal Network, 2010.

"H.D.'s Recitals" first appeared in *Narthex and Other Stories* by H.D. Toronto: Book Thug, 2011.

"Exody and Some Mechanics of Splendor" first appeared in *Talisman* 15 (Winter 1995/96): 158 61. Reprinted in *The Recovery of the Public World: Essays on Poetics in Honour of Robin Blaser.* Ed. Charles Watts and Edward Byrne. Talon Books: Vancouver, 1999. 356-360.

"The New American Poetry Revisited—Yet Again" first appeared in *Dooney's Café,* 20 August 2013.

"The H.D. Book" first appeared in a slightly different form as the Introduction to *The H.D. Book* Berkeley: U of California P, 2011.

"Olson's Buffalo" first appeared in *Minutes of the Charles Olson Society* 38 (November 2000): 5-22. Reprinted in *The World in Time and Space: Toward a History of Innovative American Poetry, 1970-2000.* Jersey City, NJ: Talisman House, 2002.

ABOUT THE AUTHOR

MICHAEL BOUGHN worked in the Teamsters for 10 years before returning to university to earn a PhD in 1986 after studying with poets John Clarke and Robert Creeley. He is the author of ten books of poetry, including *Iterations of the Diagonal, Dislocations in Crystal, 22 Skidoo / Sub-Tractions, Great Canadian Poems for the Aged Vol. 1 Illus. Ed.* and *Hermetic Divagations—after H.D. Cosmographia – a post-Lucretian faux micro-epic* was short listed for the Canadian Governor General's Award for Poetry in 2011, prompting a reviewer in Toronto's *Globe and Mail* to describe him as "an obscure veteran poet with a history of being overlooked." He published a descriptive bibliography of H.D., and co-edited Robert Duncan's *The H.D. Book.* His most recent book of poetry is *The Book of Uncertain—A Hyperbiographical User's Manual.* From 2014-2018 he edited the online poetry disturbance known as *Dispatches from the Poetry Wars* with co-conspirator, Kent Johnson.